THE ORDER OF THE OWED
BOOK ONE

CARIN HART

For those who dream of their white wedding, but who get turned on by the idea that your partner loves you so much, the day is drenched in red...

PLEASE NOTE

Thank you for checking out *Bloody Wedding*!

This is the first book in a new series that has ties to some of my other works. For those who have read *Dragonfly, Really Should Stay,* and *Ride with the Devil*, you'll see/hear about some familiar names. Especially since Adrian hired Kylie at the end of *Ride with the Devil*, and when that doesn't work out, he decides to take matters into his own hands...

Like most of my books, this is a dark romance due to elements that involve the FMC and MMC and their world. Relying on the bully and secret society romance tropes, as well as forced marriage, *Bloody Wedding* tells the story of Adrian and Loni, and brings readers to the world of the Owed in the small town of Harmony Heights.

Bloody Wedding includes: a secret society that has its own laws and plays outside of any rules; childhood/teenage bullying; explicit sex scenes (including a scene of foreplay between the 17-year-old FMC and the

18-year-old MMC); on-page murder; off-page murder (including a staged suicide); domestic violence (the dead groom definitely deserved it for slapping the FMC); blackmail/forced marriage; dubcon; orgasm denial; praise kink; religious imagery; guns; knives; smoking; drinking; previous cheating (the FMC was in a relationship with another character years ago while having a year-long affair with the MMC); a dead parent; anxiety; betrayal; allusions to sex work (approved mistresses for the Order's members); sex trafficking; and mentions of past stalking by the hero.

Happy reading!

xoxo,
Carin

SAVE
THE
DATE

will wed

avalon
dougherty

on

JUNE
24

TUESDAY   AT 7 PM

2025

at

The Church
of
St. Catherine

PROLOGUE, PART I

LONI

"Just the tip," pants Desmond against my lips, fingers tugging my hair, his body pinning me down on the bed. "You can trust me, baby. Just the tip... just to feel what it's like."

My lashes flutter. "Don't ask me that."

"If you loved me, you would—"

Then it's a good thing that I don't. That letting him guide me into one of the bedrooms in the Reynolds family's massive house has nothing to do with this farce of a relationship of ours, and is only because I couldn't refuse a future Owed when he asked me out two months ago. Somehow we've become the most gossiped-about couple at Harmony Heights High ever since. I just have to hold out a little longer. With graduation only a week away—

and the Claiming ceremony coming in August—this can't be anything more than a fling.

Unless Desmond Claims me. Unless I'm his Offering, and the idea of that turns my guts cold even as he does everything he can think of to get me hot.

Hot enough to forget the last seventeen years of training. I've been taught from the cradle that, one day, I would be meant for a member of the secret society that rules our town. That comes with expectations that we both know, and I'm more than happy to remind him.

Anything to jerk away from his sloppy kisses and wandering hands...

One of them thumbs the button on my jeans. I slap at it. "You know I can't."

His free hand lands on the side of my jaw, turning my head so that I can't miss the lust in his deep blue eyes. His dark hair is slicked back, unruffled, mainly because he might be desperate to touch me, but I'm only clutching the comforter underneath us.

He blows out a breath once he sees the determination written on my face. This isn't the first time he tried to push me to go past just making out with him, and I'm guessing the taste of beer on his tongue and the high of the graduation party that Sebastien Reynolds is hosting for the entire senior class has convinced Desmond that I might give in tonight.

Until I thin my lips, and he scowls, flopping onto his back next to me.

Sebastien's parents are out of town. So is his older brother, Alexandre. The party started three hours ago, but has probably been raging for about two. I know we're not the only ones making use of the countless guest rooms, even if I wince a little to see how much we've rumpled the bedding.

Desmond told me he just wanted to talk somewhere that it was quiet. *Talk*... right. When all he ever does is brag about the position waiting for him at his father's firm, how he'll be inducted into the Order once school's done, and how he wants to enjoy the rest of his time before then. *Talk* when, the second he had me behind closed doors, his hands were on my ass, mouth finding mine, backing me up until I had nowhere to go but flat on my back on some expensive-looking, rarely-used bed.

But Desmond... he stood up for me. In a town where my last name should mean I'm part of the inner circle, one of the founders' boys made it so that I've forever been an outcast. Until Desmond decided he'd had enough of the bullying and teasing and the sly comments coming from the Heirs' table—my name for the five boys in my class who think they're better than the rest of us—and sat with me.

He stood up for me, and I thought I finally made my second friend other than Haven. Only he didn't want to be friends. He wanted to be *more*, and for weeks now, I've let him for reasons I only wish I understood.

That Loni Dougherty. Easy pickings, huh? She should be grateful for any attention, but if he knew the truth—

Desmond takes a lock of my hair between his fingers, giving it a gentle tug. "That shit is so outdated. Do you really think the Owed stay virgins until their wedding night?"

I know better. "No, but that's different."

His brow furrows. "How?"

Can he really be that clueless? Considering he's convinced himself that I'm not using him the same way he targeted me, good chance.

"You're a guy, Des. They'll expect you to have experience. But if I do..."

I won't be an Offering. I won't be a wife.

I'll be a mistress. A toy.

One of the Used.

"Who would know?"

"The man they make me marry might have an idea."

I really, really hope he won't. Then again, by the time I've been married off, I'm just hoping the new generation of the Owed are like Desmond here and don't give a shit about the old traditions.

He has no problem trying to fuck me now. If my father's hinting around the subject has any merit to it, I might be looking at my future husband at this very moment.

I pale.

Desmond frowns. "Loni? You okay? You don't look so good all of a sudden."

That's because, with barely two months to go until someone Claims me, I know I'm only kidding myself that my future is mine. That any choices I make can change the life's plan set for me the moment I was born into a family with connections to the Order of the Owed.

I won't be one of the Used. A glorified mistress that is fucked and, well, used, then discarded. No protections. No prospects for any children. No hope of escape because if there's one thing I'd learned from eavesdropping on my mother and her society friends when I was a kid, it's that the men in the Order might tolerate their wives, but they will never loosen their hold on a whore their charter says they can keep on the side.

I'll be a wife if I must, and like my mother, and her mother before her, I'll overlook my husband's indiscretions if I have to, but I won't be little more than a pussy to a man who thinks he can rule with his dick.

A man like Desmond St. James is quickly becoming.

He's eighteen now. I'll be eighteen next month. According to the society, I can be engaged—be *Claimed*—during the first Claiming ceremony after I'm of age. By August, I'll know exactly who I'll be Offered to whenever he's ready to make me his bride.

The men in the Order have until they're thirty to be married, with an heir on the way. The heir part is negotiable, depending on the wedded pair; the married part is not. So, on the one hand, I'll be engaged in August. I could be married by Christmas, or waiting until I'm on my way out of my twenties if my groom is the same age as me.

Or I could be left waiting, one of the rare few who are raised to be an Offering with no takers—

Knock. Knock. The doorknob twists. *Bang.*

"Desmond? You in here? Open the door."

My breath catches in my throat as the familiar and undeniably demanding voice finds its way past the locked bedroom door. Desmond stiffens before letting my strawberry-blonde strands slip free from his hold.

With an aggrieved sigh, he runs his fingers through his hair with one hand. The other gives a sorry pat to his blue balls as he awkwardly rises up from the bed. Taking the opportunity to make sure I'm decent, that my jeans are still buttoned and my shirt covers the rest of me, I slide to the edge of the bed and sit up, heart thudding inside my chest.

Adrian Heller.

The kingmaker among the Heirs. His uncle is Jack Collins, the current head of the Order; the current *King*, the title that the first rule accepted hundreds of years ago, as a middle-finger to Great Britain after the Revolutionary War. His cousin, best friend, and enforcer is Dallas Collins. Though Dallas is tapped to take over the Order when his father inevitably retires—passing the reins, as it were—everyone at Harmony Heights High School knows that Adrian is the one pulling the strings.

Desmond is both terrified and jealous of him. Adrian is the only one who can get Sebastien to even pretend like he gives a shit about the Order that rules all of us. He's taken his future role as kingmaker seriously, lording over our age group for as long as I can remember.

He's been my biggest bully for even longer.

My biggest tormentor.

My biggest secret...

Swallowing his annoyance, Desmond schools his features into an expression of nonchalance. At least, he tries to. As he approaches the door, it's better to say that he has a look of constipation on his face. He's still handsome in that slick, moneyed way of the St. Jameses, but then he pulls in the door, and I'm suddenly captivated by Adrian's beauty.

When I've seen how cruel he can be, it's not fair that,

on the outside, he looks like an angel. From the tousled sandy brown curls to his tanned complexion, and the way his coloring makes his pale green eyes pop... lush, pink lips, sculpted cheekbones, how they hollow whether he's puffing on one of his cigarettes or not...

Even at eighteen, his lean body is made for a suit. Adrian in a polo shirt with a popped collar and a pair of pressed jeans just isn't right, but hell if he doesn't look good.

He glances at me, dismissing me just as quickly as though I'm not worth his time or effort. I should be used to the sting by now. In a way, I am.

He jerks his chin. "There you are. Bas said he thought he saw you coming up here."

So what did Adrian do? Knock on every door to see who had snuck away with who?

If I didn't know better, I'd say no. But since I do know...

Desmond peers over his shoulder at me before facing Adrian again. "Just looking for a little quiet time with my girl."

Adrian's upper lip curls, gaze drawn back to me.

I give my head a royal shake, refusing to quail under his stare.

His attention returns to Desmond. "Connor was looking for you."

Connor Heyward, another one of the Heirs. It wouldn't be out of the realm of possibility that Connor would need Desmond for something, and as the lowest-ranked member in their circle, Desmond has no choice but to go.

But why is Adrian playing messenger? He's second, beneath Dallas, and no messenger boy... unless he has his own ulterior motives.

His gaze flickers my way once more, as though he can't help himself. My heart rate speeds up.

Oh, yeah. He has an ulterior motive, all right.

Desmond blinks, back gone straight. "Is it important? Can it wait?"

"It's Order business," Adrian says flatly.

So, no. Whether you're a longtime member or just about to get branded in, the Order comes first.

Desmond waggles his fingers at me. "Come on. Let's go."

"No," cuts in Adrian. "Just you. But don't worry about Loni, Des. I'll make sure she gets back to the party in one piece."

Desmond chews his tongue. It's obvious he's prepared to argue, that leaving me with another boy—especially *this* boy—is the last thing he wants to do, but it's Adrian Heller, so Des just looks at me again.

"That okay with you?"

I'm an Offering. Before my mom died, my parents put me through etiquette school—that didn't really take— and ingrained in me that, in Harmony Heights, we must always obey one of the Owed. Even if he isn't quite Owed yet...

"Of course," I say, trying to sound as meek as possible.

Over Desmond's shoulder, Adrian smirks. It's gone by the time the other boy turns to face him, but I know what I saw.

Shivers of excitement go up and down my spine.

Meek, remember? Stay meek—

Desmond scratches the back of his neck. "Well, if Loni's cool with it, I guess I can't complain. I'll find you when I'm done, babe. Yeah?"

I nod, and though I'm sure he wants to stay, he slips past Adrian, heading out of the room and down the hall.

Adrian watches him go out of the corner of his eye. Seconds later, he chuckles under his breath before he nudges the door shut with his shoe. A quick *click*, and I'm locked in this room again. Only now? It's with the boy who pulled my pigtails on the playground when I was five. Who teased me when I first developed at eleven. Who told everyone freshman year that I use a cucumber to play with because no man would ever want me, Offering or not.

The boy I should hate, that I do every shower after he's finished, and who crooks his finger now, waiting expectantly for me to go to him.

I take slow steps toward him. His gaze roves over me, taking me in from head to toe. I think he likes what he sees... until a muscle tics in his jaw.

"Do you have any idea what it does to me, knowing you're up here with him?"

Not this again. "He's my boyfriend, Adrian."

His soft green eyes darken at the b-word. "It's a phase."

I huff. "I know that it isn't going to last. That Desmond is just fucking around—"

But Adrian shakes his head. "Not Desmond, Loni. *You.* Point taken. You wanted to see if you'd make me jealous. It worked. Now I'm here."

"I didn't ask you to come up after us," I remind him. In fact, I'd done the exact opposite. With Desmond squirreling me away in the corner of the living room, keeping me to himself—or hiding the fact that we were together, I'm not sure—it was easy to avoid Adrian. He could live it up with the rest of the Heirs, and I could pretend that my heart didn't ache to have him be the one shielding me from the rest of our classmates instead of Adrian being the fucking bully leading the charge.

He does so now. Closing the gap between us, suddenly I'm under his complete control, and a thrill runs through me as I have every last iota of his attention.

"No, but you must've known that I wouldn't be able to stop myself." Adrian fists my hair, wrapping it tightly but careful not to pull too hard even if he yanks my head back just enough to have my lips parting with a gasp. "Not when you look like that."

I'm wearing one of my favorite soft yellow blouses and a pair of jeans. Nothing special, though my jeans highlight the curve of my ass—and they're *Adrian's* favorites. Mainly because he's such a goddamn pro when it comes to flicking the button open, pulling on my zipper, and getting his fingers inside my panties without any resistance.

Not from the jeans, and not from me.

He does so now, running two fingers on his left hand through my damp curls while keeping hold of my hair. His mouth drops to the side of my throat, sucking on it, tonguing it, all while his middle finger searches for the entrance to my pussy.

He finds it, and I groan even as I manage to grit out, "We can't keep doing this."

He chuckles against my neck. "Says fucking who?"

The entire Order of the Owed might have something to say about one of the golden boys of the next generation defiling an Offering ever since the beginning of senior year…

A year. A whole fucking year. Whenever we can sneak away, whenever I can convince myself that—like he's eight instead of eighteen—he only picks on me because he likes me, I'm helpless to surrender to Adrian Heller.

I can't let Desmond fuck me, not when I allowed Adrian to do it first. And he didn't even have to start with any of that 'just the tip' shit. He wanted me to let him in, and I… I did.

Two months left, I think, as he fingerfucks me now, getting me ready for what I know is going to happen next. Just two more months to pretend that I own a tiny sliver of the riddle that is Adrian.

Because in two months? He'll Claim his Offering, and it won't be me.

The rank-and-file society members have their choice of the available Offerings. But the inner circle, Jack and his lackeys… Adrian, Dallas, and theirs… have to have the best. The pick of the litter, basically, and though these are all arranged marriages to keep the Order in power, Adrian's Offering was told at the beginning of the year that he would be Claiming her at the end of it.

And since Adrian's Offering is my best friend, Haven, of course I know. Just like how I know that she'd rather cut out her own tongue than ever use it to say 'I do' to a man who spent our entire teenage years fucking with me.

Before he started just *fucking* me.

She wouldn't care that I stupidly, ridiculously fell for my bully. Haven would be happy, and then maybe she could find an Owed that would suit her better. But Adrian... he's the kingmaker, remember? Without a position close to the king, what is he? I know him. He'll never go against the Order.

He'll marry Haven. If not this year, then sometime in the next few. These trysts will be nothing but a memory... which is why I give myself over to him now as he takes his hand out of my pants long enough to start working my jeans down past my ass.

I can't help it, though. As if I need to hear the truth more than he does, I tell Adrian, "Haven is your Offering."

Especially when he's touching me, when he's inside of me, I know we can't escape our fates. That doesn't stop me from letting him do whatever he wants to me.

I'm still putty in his hands even as I remind him, "My best friend will be your wife. And I'll belong to—"

He tilts my head further back, nipping my bottom lip. "You belong to me, Loni."

I don't. I *can't.*

That's not how our world works. I've accepted that for all of my seventeen years. One day, I'll be a powerful man's wife, whether I love him or not. I'll watch as Adrian's cruelty only deepens without our secret trysts to tie us together. He'll marry Haven. *Fuck* Haven. It won't matter that he was mine first, or that—deep down—I have to admit that I've been fooling myself all of senior year.

He's *never* been mine.

A leopard can't change its spots. An asshole is an asshole, and his irrational desire to consider me his possession doesn't change the fact that he's bullied me since grade school. He's made my life hell since middle school. In high school, only my future as an Offering keeps me from being a complete outcast... no thanks to Adrian Heller.

The same Adrian Heller who goes back to sucking on my neck, leaving another hickey I'll have to hurry to hide...

And yet, I don't tell him to stop. In fact, I arch my neck, giving him better access to my throat.

He rumbles in approval, his fingers sliding up my shirt, under my bra, kneading my boob now that he has my pants down. It's a possessive gesture, one of undeniable ownership, and I try to forget the latest rumor I heard this afternoon before I arrived at the party.

The rumor that Desmond plans on Claiming me.

He didn't tell me so. Part of me wonders if earlier was just a test. A way for Desmond to see if I was worthy of being his Offering.

Maybe I passed, but as Adrian switches his focus from my neck to my mouth, kissing me as if he can swallow any of my denials, I have to admit that there's only one boy that I'd Offer myself to.

But why do that when he already has me?

Don't think, Loni. Enjoy the moment. Enjoy the feel of his hands on you, the way he's guiding you to the wall, knowing that he will pin you against it and fuck you fast. Furiously. As if he can't get enough...

Desmond tasted like beer. Adrian has his own vices. There's always a hint of smoke about him, the suggestion of fire and ash. Devilish side for this angel, I guess, especially when he's too smart to let the booze make his decisions for him.

Oh, no. We both own this insanity.

I'm gasping into his mouth now. My hands scrabble for his belt. I can't change the future, but let me enjoy the present as long as I can.

"Please, Adrian. I need you."

"God, I fucking love it when you beg," he smirks, throwing his head back as I cup him through his jeans, his belt dangling open.

It's okay. In these stolen moments, Avalon Dougherty can have the kingmaker on his knees before long, too.

I'm not his Offering. I can never be.

But right now? I'm his, and if that's all I can have of this capricious, beautiful riddle of a boy? Who treats me tenderly, telling me everything I've always wanted to hear, then pretends I don't exist other than to knock me down?

I hate him, but I love him, and I only hope that this time... *this* time, I might actually fuck him out of my system.

spoiler alert:

I DIDN'T.

PROLOGUE, PART II

LONI

"You go out first. Got it?"

Adrian is leaning lazily against the head-board, a satisfied smile tugging on his lips as he folds his hands behind him to cradle his neck.

He's stretched out, his lean, toned body enough to have my mouth watering. All of the Heirs play on Harmony Heights High's lacrosse team, and I can see evidence of all of those afternoons of practice in the limber muscles and the defined lines.

I was already scooting around the room, gathering up my clothes, but when he calls out to me, I can't help but look at him.

Look at him—and *stare*.

His smile widens.

For a second, I think that it wouldn't be so terrible to wait for round two... but then I remember where we are and I force down the lust working its way through my heavy body.

Clothes, I tell myself. Get dressed.

Go.

I return to searching for my panties and sandals. What was supposed to be a quick fuck up against the nearest wall turned into more than that once Adrian had me in position. Somehow, we ended up naked in bed, Adrian on top of me until we both finally came in a rush of sweaty limbs and *I love you* gasped at each other, our clothes left in a whirlwind all over the floor.

I think about that as I gather up my underwear. Mere minutes ago, I had Adrian Heller panting for little ol' me. Now?

He's booting me out the door.

Now, I know Adrian is only doing that to make me feel like shit for shoving him off of me once he finished. It's like he *wanted* to keep me up here longer than he should've, and he's repaying my eagerness to return to the party by reminding me how—despite his pretty words when he's actually screwing me—that all I am is a hole to him.

I'm too frustrated to be hurt. Damn it. Why don't I ever remember that about him when he's touching me?

Luckily, I've built up a decent shield against Adrian when I'm not letting my libido rule my brain. In answer to his order, I nod, then use my toe to move my panties closer.

Now that I have all my clothes, I give him my back so that I can quickly get dressed.

He lets out a sound of approval at the sight of my ass.

I shiver, then get mad at myself for being so damn easy. Because I'm not. Not really. I'm just the idiot who fell in love with a boy who will never be able to truly love her back...

"I know," I say, and if the words come out clipped, I doubt he gives a shit. "I gotta hurry, too. Desmond's probably wondering what the hell happened to me."

He might not pick up on my tone, but he clicks his tongue when he hears Desmond's name.

"Don't worry about Des. I never do."

I shimmy on my panties. God, I need a shower—or even a quick splash at the bathroom sink—but it's been too long already. While I was in Adrian's arms, it was easy to forget the suspicious look on Desmond's face when the boy who has been my biggest tormentor all through high school suddenly decided to become Mr. Chivalrous. If it was any other Offering, it would be expected of him... but everyone in Harmony Heights knows that Loni Dougherty is Adrian Heller's target.

Desmond isn't stupid. He thinks with his dick most of the time, but when he gets the job at his father's firm, it's not *completely* due to nepotism. Like most of the Owed, he's smart and charming and manipulative.

So is the boy in front of me, and I hate that I only ever remember that when I'm pulling on my clothes after another encounter with Adrian in the shadows.

"I have to. Whatever this is... whatever we've been doing... I agreed to go out with him. Until I get *Claimed*—"

It happens so quickly. Focusing on getting dressed so that I'm not second-guessing climbing back into bed with

Adrian, I never saw him move. But he must've. Before I know it, he's standing in front of me, cupping the back of my neck, lowering his mouth so that he can shut me up with another kiss.

And fool that I am, I *let* him.

He pushes me closer so that there's no escaping him. I *breathe* Adrian, groaning into his mouth on an exhale.

When he finally releases me, his green eyes spark in a mixture of dare and defiance. I know exactly what he's thinking, too. I might be living in the real word instead of some fantasy realm where we could actually have a future, but Adrian? At least for this moment in time, he's the only one Claiming me.

And, damn it, I let him do that, too.

Taking the rumpled yellow sweater from my hand, he waits for me to finish clasping my bra in the front, then twisting it around so that I can stick my boobs in the cups. As soon as I've got the straps up over my shoulders, he gently eases the sweater over my head.

As I guide my arms into the sleeves, he reaches out, brushing his thumb over the latest hickey he gave me. I'll have to hide it with my hair until I can get home to cover it up. Here in this room with Adrian, though? I lean into his caress.

"Don't worry about Des," he says again. "Connor will keep him busy, and when we're done, I'll call my boy twice and he'll let Des go. You go down there... he never knows. Okay, Loni? No one has to know."

I nod, because what else can I do?

"Look, I've got plans with the family tomorrow. Some pre-induction bullshit. We still have one week in school, though." With another hand, he tucks a strand of messy hair behind my ear. "Maybe we meet in the band room while they're rehearsing for the end of year concert in the auditorium."

His jizz is pooling inside of my panties. My lips are bruised from the force of his possessive kisses. I have at least one new hickey that he won't stop playing with, and my foundation might not be enough to hide it from Desmond, my dad, and the rest of Harmony Heights.

And yet...

"Okay," I whisper breathlessly.

"That's my girl."

I don't miss the way that Adrian puts emphasis on the 'my' part of his statement. Hearing Desmond refer to me as that... that really pissed him off, didn't it?

Another facet to the enigmatic Adrian Heller. He sneered at Desmond when he left the Heirs' table, choosing to sit down with me, and only told me a week later that I wasn't allowed to date his friend while we were fucking on the side.

I called his bluff. A future Owed, he might expect every designated Offering to be as meek as we're brainwashed into becoming, but he made me like this. Whether he realizes it or not... by using the weight of his power as one of the most popular kids in school *and* from a high-ranking legacy family, he kept me on the outskirts of the society. I never fell for it hook, link, and sinker, and I'm probably the worst Offering in all of Harmony Heights... and that's exactly why I know that, for all of his claiming me in private, Jack Collins's nephew will never be able to Claim me as his.

If he wanted to? He wouldn't hang back, telling me to leave first, to leave on my own. He'd walk proudly beside me, hand-in-hand, letting the whole town know that we're together.

But we're not. Like always, I'm just his dirty little secret, and nothing will ever change that.

The regret is slipping in. Without the rush of his hands on me, his mouth on me, his dick stretching me until I don't know where I end and he begins... I look at him, my beautiful Adrian, and I see more devil than angel in that smirk.

God, I need a shower.

Going up on my toes, I press a quick to his mouth.

Adrian rumbles in satisfaction. "Be a good girl. Don't let anyone see you go."

My stomach drops down to my sandals.

Right.

Dirty little secret.

Got it.

ONE
INVITATION

LONI

Ever since I was a little girl, I knew I was meant to be an Offering to one of the Owed. I just never expected they'd go so far as to send me an invitation to my own wedding.

But that's what I'm looking at. Stuffed in an envelope bearing the full name that I haven't used in a decade, the cardstock thick, the foil design both elegant and ostentatious, is an invitation that requests my presence at the wedding of Avalon Dougherty to Desmond St. James two weeks from today.

The wedding is supposed to take place at the Church of St. Catherine in Harmony Heights. The same church where I was baptized, had my first Communion, got confirmed, and now I'm slated to be wed to... to...

Desmond fucking St. James.

Hell, no.

With one decisive motion, I tear the invitation in two. Both halves of the cardstock flutter to the floor, but I'm already reaching for the envelope again as if this can't be real. As if this has to be a mistake, or a sick joke, or a goddamn nightmare.

Nope. Despite going by my middle name—*Marie*—and my mother's maiden name—*Howard*—ever since I fled Harmony Heights as a scared, angry, heartbroken eighteen-year-old kid, the front of the envelope has *Avalon Dougherty* scrawled in golden ink. Beneath it, the address to the apartment in Bridgewater where I've lived for the last seven months after my job moved me again.

I'm an auditor. Numbers make sense to me in a way that people never have, and as I stare at the envelope, I'm thinking of one in particular: *thirty*. I only have two years until I hit the big three-oh, and to me? That means freedom. No one in the Order's two hundred-year-plus history has ever Claimed an Offering who was older than that. Probably because the men all have to have locked down their trophy brides before then, and why would any of the budding leaders of our town—my hometown —choose a woman older than him?

Misogyny and ageism have always been as much a part of the Order's charter as the bylaws that have ruled my family's life for, well, *ever*. When I was still an Offering, I looked past them like I was supposed to, but then I escaped Harmony Heights, and I finally started to see through the bullshit.

The men are all born into wealth and legacy. Trained from the cradle in control, tradition, and utmost dominance, the Owed have been passing down the power and influence necessary to rule Harmony Heights through the generations with blood pacts, oaths, and strict rules to follow.

Then there are the women. Most aspire to be an Offering. After being chosen from prestigious families with ties to the Order, they're destined to become wives for a new generation of the Owed. We're groomed for beauty, obedience, and virginity, and if we fail in any way, we end up as one of the Used.

Mistresses. Whores. Side pieces... the discarded women who are only accepted when they're pleasuring a member of the Order, I would've done anything to avoid that fate.

And I did. At least, I *thought* I did. I got out. I went to college. I had a couple of boyfriends who wanted me for *me*, not because of my pedigree and the last name I shed. I almost adopted a cat. I got two promotions in four years, and have moved three times since then.

I cut contact with my old life. My mom passed when I was sixteen, but with Dad being a member of the Order, he knew that I could never break free of the Owed if we had a relationship. And maybe I do blame him in a way for my leaving in the first place, but he did arrange for me to get out. He paid for my college.

He's the only Owed that I honestly feel like I still *owe*.

I haven't spoken to Desmond St. James since he publicly ended things between us, sneering that I would never be worthy of becoming his Offering. But even though the invitation is torn in two, facedown on my living room floor, I know what name I read next to my old one.

Desmond St. James... why the hell would *anyone* think that I'd accept his Claim to me now?

I never attended the Claiming ceremony. I was gone the first week of August, and when no one followed me out of Harmony Heights, ready to drag me back to a future I no longer had any interest in, I thought they'd been happy to see the back of me.

Maybe they were. Or maybe they were just biding their time until they could arrange a wedding that I've been unceremoniously summoned to attend.

My wedding.

Oh, *fuck,* no.

There has to be a mistake. The last thing 'King' Jack Collins pronounced before I escaped was my demotion. After everything that happened, I wasn't allowed to be an Offering anymore. I'd be shunted aside, left for the men in the Order to use as they wanted, a glorified hooker.

So why am I being promised to one of the Owed? Especially *Desmond*?

My first instinct is to call Dad. Still holding the envelope, the rest of my untouched mail a scattered pile on the back of my couch, I search for my phone. When I'm not doing an on-site audit for my latest clients, I work from home. I'd taken a break from my spreadsheets and my laptop to go down to the lobby to get my mail, leaving my phone on my desk.

I grab it now. It might've been ages since I made my

obligatory Christmas call—one of three times of year I allow myself to reach out to my Dad, along with Father's Day and his birthday in October—but he's one of my top contacts. I select his with a shaky thumb, nibbling on my bottom lip as it rings.

And rings.

And *rings*—

"Hello. You've reached Peter Dougherty. I'm sorry, but I can't come to the phone right now. If you leave your name, number, and a short message after the beep, I'll get back to you as soon as I can. Great. Thanks. Go."

Beep.

"Dad. It's Loni." Because, to him, I will always be Loni. "Hi. I..." Shit. Do I just tell him? What if he knows? What if he's in on it, and now he's screening his calls so that I don't freak out before the Order gets its way? I shudder out a breath. "Look. Call me when you get this message, okay? I... yeah. I need to talk to you."

I disconnect the call, tapping my fingers against the back of my phone case.

The envelope is still in my other hand. I flap it, growing more and more agitated as I begin to worry that this might *not* be a mistake, and I glare at the address.

As far as Dad knows, I'm still living in Maplewood. I had only recently moved to this apartment last Thanksgiving, and it slipped my mind to mention it when I spoke to Dad at Christmas.

But someone knows. Joke or not, someone in the Order knows enough about me and my history to put my recent address on the outside of the envelope, plus Desmond's name on the invitation on the inside...

Hang on.

My jaw goes tight. My fingers crumple the edge of the envelope.

My gaze darts to the left corner, then the right. Just in case, I flip it to the back, but there's nothing written along the flap.

So, no return address. I have no idea who sent it because they refused to add that to the envelope. And, considering I just noticed that there isn't a stamp on it or a postmark, it's clear that my invitation didn't come through the mail.

Oh, no. Someone hand-delivered it.

You can't blame me for being so oblivious. I've been Marie Howard for so long that seeing Avalon Dougherty on the front threw me for a loop. It only got worse when I read the invite, but none of that matters now as realization hits me.

Someone brought this here. Got into my building, figured out a way to get this envelope inside of my mailbox, picking that one in particular out of the rows of others alongside it.

I don't know when. I usually let my mail pile up for a few days before making the trip downstairs unless I have a reason to head out that way. It could've been this morning. Yesterday. Monday, even, since I'm pretty sure I cleaned out the small cubby after buying groceries Saturday morning.

But they were here, whoever *they* are. They could come back.

A part of me has always expected that the Order wouldn't really let me get away from them that easily. I've been holding my breath, counting down the days until I hit thirty. I'm twenty-seven now, turning twenty-eight next month. I was so fucking close.

But they were here, and that means that the next time they return?

I can't be.

A COUPLE OF HOURS LATER, MY DAD STILL HASN'T CALLED me back yet.

Like always, my phone is on vibrate, but I've tucked it into the back pocket of my jeans so that I have it with me as I dash around the apartment. Just in case I don't notice the pulse against my ass, I pause every couple of minutes to check the screen, huffing when it's empty.

It's even worse when I get a buzz, only for it to be a spam text or a reminder from my boss about a company deadline. Not Dad, though I do call him twice more so he knows it's important.

I learned my lesson as a kid. Never put anything in writing if it can be used against you. So, messaging about the invitation? Not a good idea, especially when Dad's never left Harmony Heights before. He's as involved with the Order as ever, even if he's just another of the rank-and-file members who attends monthly meetings, nods at other Oweds, and rubs absently at the brand on his palm while watching the evening news instead of secretly running the entire town.

I was only considered a high-pedigree Offering because there's been a Dougherty in the Order ever since its inception, and the women in my line have all been in the same position I was before I snapped it.

I'm not going back. I'll give my dad a heads up so that he can handle the inevitable fallout the same way he did when I left for college, but other than that, Desmond can wrangle a brand new bride for his late June wedding.

Because part of me knows that I've long been outrunning the Order, I always jumped at the chance to skip around so long as the moving expenses were covered by my company. You know what the best thing about doing that is? I don't bother unpacking. Not completely. I always have my essentials together, and with a little bit of time, I can gather everything I need and be out in hours.

It takes three for me to pack up my SUV, leaving the furniture and appliances that came with the apartment behind, but taking the key with me in case I decide it's safe to return.

Where am I going? No clue. Just out of Bridgewater right now since the only thing on my mind is getting away from the apartment that the Order tracked me to.

Can they find me again before the wedding in two weeks? I really hope not, and I get to cling to that hope for a little over a half an hour before I pull into the parking lot of a small convenience store to grab an energy drink, a matte black coupe following in right behind me.

I'm not paying attention to the other driver. Grabbing my debit card and my keys, I lock my car, then hurry inside. Four bucks later, I tap my nails anxiously against the aluminum can as I return to my car.

"Looking good, Loni."

Loni.

My head jerks up. I'm Marie now. I ditched my first name years ago, but I know that name.

I know that voice.

And there he is. Dallas Collins, a decade older than I last saw him. His face is more rugged. His dark green eyes harder. His body broader, with muscles bulging against the tight black tee he has on. His short-ish sandy brown hair—similar to his cousin's—is tousled and falling forward in his face. As a small smile tugs on his lips, he runs his fingers through his hair, leaving track marks in the wild curls.

A black spade is tattooed along the side of his throat. Leaning up against the driver's side of my SUV, one arm is crossed over his middle. He salutes me with the other hand, making sure to flash the Order's brand on his palm.

A lump lodges in my throat. The slippery condensation on the side of the ice-cold can combined with my suddenly shaky fingers means that my four dollars go down the sewer once it drops out of my hand. The can pops open, the carbonated drink spraying everywhere, but while I gape at Dallas, he just raises his eyebrows at the mess I've made.

I shake my head, stepping away from the puddle and the spray. Forcing the lump down with a rough swallow, I find my voice: "What are you doing here?"

A small laugh. "Making sure you RSVP."

Fuck.

"The invitation. You sent it."

Of course he did. Dallas might be Jack Collins's only son and the future head of the Order, but even when we were kids, Dallas was his father's top enforcer. He knows everything about everything when it comes to the Owed, and makes sure it all goes according to his father's plan.

He nods. "That I did. And when you left, I was waiting to make sure you started for home. The wedding is all set to go, so you don't have to worry about anything but showing up for your dress fitting, sweetheart. But you... you headed north instead of west." He clicks his tongue. "If you can't remember the way to Harmony Heights, you can follow me."

A gesture toward the black car I barely noticed before.

The same car that's parked behind mine, blocking me in.

Apart from us and a truck that might belong to the bored clerk inside of the convenience store, no one else is in the lot. Cars whizzing past on the main road are too preoccupied with their own journeys to notice that Dallas has put a stop to mine.

What the hell am I supposed to do?

And that's when, before my panicking brain can come up with any idea, Dallas's voice turns uncharacteristically conversational as he asks, "How's your dad been? Talk to him lately?"

Bastard.

"No," is my hesitant answer. "I haven't."

Dallas reaches behind him, pulling his phone out of his pocket. "Let's call him."

Dad didn't answer his phone any of the times that I did, but when Dallas dials the number?

He picks up on the second ring.

"Mr. Dougherty. It's Dallas. I have someone who wants to talk to you." Pulling the phone away from his ear, he jerks his chin at me. "Come on. Daddy wants to say 'hi'."

My stomach twists. The invitation was bad enough. But this? I don't like this.

Still, I know better than to refuse. As defiantly as I can at the moment, I stalk over to him, snatching the phone before holding it up to my head. "Dad? Is that you?"

"Loni."

It's just my name. The nickname I stubbornly clung to after Mom died because she thought Avalon was too prissy and I was her Loni. The only one who's called me that in years... until Dallas Collins followed me to this rundown Quick Stop.

It's just my name, but I can hear the resignation in it.

My eyes shutter closed. "You knew about this."

There's a long pause on Dad's end before he sighs. "I didn't have a choice."

I squeeze the phone, a rush of anger flashing through me. "Bullshit."

"Loni—"

"No, Dad. You knew. You knew that they were after me and you didn't tell me."

The father of the bride who gives her away to her groom... even if he isn't there to walk me down the aisle, no member of the Order could Claim me without getting both my father's approval, and the head of the society's.

Yeah. He knew.

Fuck.

Another sigh. "The Order protects me. I owe everything to the Owed. You know that."

I bite down on the corner of my mouth. "You mean they own you. That it?"

"They'll protect you, too, if you let them. If you don't fight them." Dad pauses, then adds, "You had your fun. Now it's time to come home and do what you were born to do."

My eyes snap open. "I'm not marrying Desmond St. James."

"You don't have to. But, Loni... if you refuse to be an Offering, Jack has threatened to end the Dougherty's affiliation with the Order. As the head of our family, I'll be cut off. I need you to understand what that would mean."

Damn it.

I do. God, I wish I didn't, but I *do*. If Jack Collins has decided to let me be an Offering after all, if I don't marry Desmond, I'm basically signing my father's death warrant.

You don't leave the Order of the Owed without repercussions. As an Offering, Jack could look the other way when I left. But Dad? He's been a member since his induction forty years ago. He knows things that Jack wouldn't allow a non-member to know, so, when he says cut off, he means executed.

So that's it. That's why Dallas is here, and why Dad's obviously been waiting for this call. I needed to know my options: either I give up my life, or I doom my dad to losing his.

Fuck!

Without saying goodbye, I end the call. Shoving his phone back into Dallas's waiting hand, hoping like hell that his old scar twinges, I glare up at him.

He arches an eyebrow.

I just resist the urge to gouge him in the eye with the keys I'm still holding.

Instead, I shudder out a breath. "Don't worry. I know my way back to Harmony Heights."

His lips twitch. "I thought you might."

TWO
I DON'T

LONI

I t takes nine days before Desmond comes to see me.

I don't know what takes him so long other than the fact that I'm a sure thing. When Dallas gave me the choice of continuing to run and letting my dad pay for my absence or sucking it up, returning to Harmony Heights, and agreeing to marry a man I haven't spoken to in a decade, there wasn't really a choice at all. Dad's the only family I have left. Mom got sick when I was fourteen, dying when I was sixteen, and I never had any siblings. My parents were only children, too, so no aunts. No uncles. No cousins. Even my grandparents are gone, leaving just me and Dad.

I can't let anything happen to him.

So, with Dallas and his nondescript matte black coupe following behind me, I drove all the way back to my childhood home. It was a relief to see Dad, a little fatter, a little grayer, and with the weight of the world on his shoulders. He was alive, though, and as Dallas parked out front, even getting out to help me lug my suitcases inside, I knew I would be spending the next two weeks with my father.

After that? I'm not really sure. After an Offering marries her Owed, she goes to live with him. I figured that would be the same for me and Desmond. I'll have my own room if I request it, but in the eyes of Harmony Heights, I'll be his wife.

His property.

His.

I don't go to him. That's not how it's done. Once an Owed Claims their Offering, he's in control. It's up to him to do whatever he can to convince his Offering to accept him in return. I guess, since King Collins has decided that I'm being shackled to Desmond for the rest of my life, he figured he didn't have to. By returning to Harmony Heights, I've already agreed to marry him.

When the alternative is allowing my father to die instead, what else could I do?

But then, nine days later, I'm sitting on my childhood twin bed, tapping at my computer, when Dad's careful knock breaks up my concentration.

To pretend like this isn't happening to me, I've thrown myself into my work. It's the perfect distraction, and I hold up my finger as though Dad can see me before realizing how ridiculous that is.

Closing the lid on my laptop, I set it aside. "Yes?"

"Loni, honey? You have a visitor."

My heart lodges in my throat. Dad's been avoiding me just like how I've been choosing to stay in my old room, sneaking down to the kitchen for food whenever I'm sure he won't be there. I'm basically a prisoner because his position is clear: the Order wants me to get married, and he listens to the Order.

My whole damn life, the Order has come first for everyone I know. Mom. Dad. Haven. Desmond.

Adrian…

Huffing slightly, I move toward the door, wishing that for once… just once… someone chose Loni Dougherty over the secret society that governs every moment of our lives.

By the time I open the door, Dad is gone. I don't have any illusions that he's gone down to entertain our guest. This is the first one I've had since I returned home. Part of me wondered if I might hear from Haven before I quickly accepted that that wouldn't happen. The last time I spoke to her, we were both seventeen, butting heads, and she told me to call her when I stopped fucking up my life.

I left home a week later, too much of a chickenshit to tell her. I made it impossible for her to reach me, too, and if she ever tried, I have no idea. She probably was the first one to say 'good riddance' when I ran.

Well, no. That was probably Adrian, and if it wasn't? That's only because he'd have to find someone else to torment the way he did me.

Did he? I don't know. If I'm being honest, one of the reasons why I've stayed inside the house is because I'm afraid I might run into Adrian. And I… I can't. I even went so far as to ask Dad to see the guest list for this farce of a wedding to make sure that he wasn't on it.

To my surprise, he wasn't. Not because he'd be there for me, but because Desmond and Adrian were tight when we were growing up. They were part of the same clique, the handsome, rich, powerful boys who would be the men who ruled Harmony Heights after high school was done. Dallas is coming, of course, but that's the only familiar name from the old days on the list.

I don't know how I feel about that, but as I trudge toward the living room, I tell myself it's for the best.

I buried my positive feelings for Adrian so deep, leaving only hurt and hate on the surface. Him showing up at my wedding to the boy who dumped me when he found out I wasn't a virgin would be like rubbing salt into an open wound.

No, thanks.

It's bad enough I have to confront Desmond, let alone become his bride. I don't know what made him change his mind all these years later. It's not like I could go back to being a virginal Offering even before I moved on and had my fun with some of the guys I met outside of Harmony Heights. True, he was the boyfriend who tried everything to get me to sleep with him before the Claiming, but, oh, did he fucking lose it when rumors spread that I slept with *someone*—and he knew damn well it wasn't him.

I haven't seen him since the Monday after the graduation party at Sebastien Reynolds' house. I didn't know that someone heard me and Adrian fucking in the guest room, or that they watched me and my wild hair walk out on my own. So excited to spread the word that a future

Offering was giving it away already, they didn't stick around to see who was in the room with me.

Everyone thought it had to be my boyfriend. Only Desmond knew he left me behind with Adrian, so after he called me a whore and dumped me in front of the entire lunchroom the following Monday, he accused Adrian of being the mystery guy I fucked.

Only he was Adrian Heller, the head of the Heirs, and the boy who bullied me so consistently over the years that not a single kid in our school believed I would ever sleep with him.

The damage was done anyway. I was branded the school slut, Desmond wanted nothing to do with me, neither did Haven, and after I went to confront Adrian about the both of us coming clean...

Yeah. I was gone the second I hit eighteen and, technically, my father couldn't stop me. Now, ten years later, I'm back in his house, walking into the living room to meet—

"Desmond."

My body goes cold the same way it used to when he had his lips on me. Just seeing him standing in the middle of the room, head tilted just enough to show his contempt for our much smaller home, eyes immediately undressing me as he looks me over, head to toe... being face-to-face with Desmond St. James for the first time in a decade has me thrown back to the last time we met.

Ew.

His grin turns to one of approval as he stalks toward me, arms outstretched, waiting for a hug that I know better than to deny him.

His arms close around me. A hint of whiskey mingled with a dark cologne fills my nostrils. It's dangerous in a way that only adds to my uneasiness, though I force a smile to my face as he reluctantly releases me.

Desmond fucking St. James. His face is sharper than it was, his dark hair shorter. It's still slicked back, like how I remember, and his suit fits him very well, damn it. There's still a miasma of ooze coming off of him, making him oily—or maybe that's just the expression on his narrow face as he reaches out his hand.

I take it, and he guides me toward the couch where we both sit down.

He speaks for the next ten minutes, telling me all about his life. I learn where he went to school—the same local, private college that all of the Owed attend—and how he did follow in his father's footsteps, getting that ol' nepo push right to a top-floor office once he had his degree.

He doesn't ask me about myself. Of course not. He never seemed to give a shit about me when we were dating, always filling the silence with his thoughts, his hobbies, his future. Even now, when I try to add something to the conversation, his jaw goes tight, his eyes flat, as though I'm offending him by just speaking up at all.

He hasn't even used my name, I notice. Does he know that I'm Loni? That I'm the woman he's set to marry in less than a week? He must, but I could be a robot for all the attention he shows me.

And, like a robot, he decides he can order me around.

"Gilda told my father that you had your final dress

fitting yesterday afternoon." He flicks his fingers at me. "Go on. Get dressed. I want to see it."

He waits expectantly for me to do just that.

I tuck a lock of hair behind my ear, staying seated. "Oh, um. I thought it was bad luck to see a bride in her gown before the wedding."

"And? Go do what I said. I want to see what I paid for."

That's weird. "My dad is the one who bought the dress."

I know because he wrote a check to Gilda for the final alterations. He paid for a stock dress that looked like something I might wear, then hired the Owed-affiliated seamstress to tailor it to fit my body.

"Of course he did. I'm taking his dirty daughter off his hands. The least he can do is pay for the wedding. But, Loni, baby... that's not what I meant, and we both know it."

I want to see what I paid for...

I tremble. Holy shit. He means *me*, doesn't he?

Considering he reaches out, trailing a finger suggestively from my knee up toward my crotch, I'm pretty sure I'm right.

His lips curl. "Know what? Where's the dress? Your room? Perfect. We'll both go there, and I'll watch you put it on. And when you change out of it again, I'll see how good the rest of my Offering performs for her fiancé."

I slap his wandering fingers, the same way I once did when I was seventeen. "Desmond, I don't think that we're supposed to—"

"Supposed to? Who gives a fuck about 'supposed to'?"

He scoffs, fisting his hand angrily. "You'd let Heller fuck you, but not me? Is that it?"

Heller.

The derisive way he spits out Adrian's surname has me jumping up, stepping away, eager to escape the same old accusations.

"Desmond, I—"

"He might've had everyone else fooled. You, too. But maybe that's just how you get your kicks. You need a man to treat you like shit to get you ready? Fine with me, Loni. Trust me. When your future bride is a worthless slut, it's easy to put her in her place."

You'll never be worthy of being my Offering...

I gasp. I can't help it.

And then I lie.

"There was never anything between Adrian and me—"

I don't even get to finish my denial. Not really. I'm just beginning my thought when fury flashes across his features and Desmond is lunging up from the couch, hand snatching my wrist so that he can shake my whole damn body.

"Don't treat me like I'm stupid," he sneers, my brain rattling around inside of my skull. "I'm not stupid. I won. You get that, you dumb bitch? I got the King to let me have you. And after we get married on Tuesday, I'll make sure to rub it in Heller's face every fucking chance I get. And you... I'll be fucking you until you forget you ever let some other guy have that pussy before I did."

He wrenches my arm again, shoving me away this time. I know that's exactly what he planned on doing in my bedroom if I'd gone along with his commands, but hearing him promise to fuck me... knowing that, as his wife, I'll eventually have to...

"Don't touch me," I gasp, rubbing my wrist. "You stay away from me."

I just wanted the few feet between us to stay there. I should've known better because he stalks toward me.

"Do you know how lucky you are that I'm willing to *marry* you? You should be one of the Used, but I'm letting you be my wife. You should be grateful."

Grateful? *Grateful*?

I'm scared. I'm angry. I'm stuck between a rock and a hard place, and no matter what choice I make, it seems like the wrong one. And now this pompous dickhead thinks I should let him fuck me because he's forcing me to marry him?

Hell, no.

Going up on my tiptoes, nose to nose with Desmond, I snap, "If I had any choice in this, asshole, you wouldn't even be the last one!"

Screaming at him felt pretty good. For a couple of seconds, I'm glad that I shot back, but my satisfaction disappears the instant he rears his hand and swings, slapping me full-strength across the face.

The force of his hit has me landing on the floor of the living room in a crumpled heap. My cheek screams in agony, but I clamp my teeth together, holding back the scream from my throat.

His expensive shoes land inches away from the hand I use to pull myself into a seated position.

Desmond crouches down so that we're on the same

level. "Remember that, Loni. You *don't* have a choice. You *will* marry me on Tuesday. Unless you want the King to get involved."

If I never see Jack Collins again, that would be too soon.

I shake my head, my other hand clapped to my cheek, trying desperately to quell the throbbing. My ear is ringing. My heart pounding.

And yet, when I meet the certainty in his stare, I refuse to give him what he wants. I refuse to fight back again.

Instead, I nod. "And you'll see me in that damn dress then. Not a minute sooner."

It's not a victory. Lying on the floor, praying my Dad doesn't walk in on Desmond hovering over me... when he nods, letting the matter of seeing the wedding dress drop, it's not a victory.

But I take it as one anyway.

Something tells me that, as his wife, there will be plenty of battles to fight and (hopefully) win.

I DON'T WANT TO DO THIS.

I don't want to do this.

I really, *really* don't want to do this...

But it's happening.

The last few days have been a blur. I'm still staying at my father's house—the back of my skull pulses in a headache whenever I think I'll be passed off, given away, and living with my *husband* after the wedding—but whether he has his regrets or he's waiting for a temper tantrum, he's kept his distance. I think the man has left his study maybe five times total in the last fourteen days, and one of them was to ride in the limo with me to St. Catherine's so he could *literally* give me away.

I tried to tell him about my meeting with Desmond, but his last sneers—the reminder that I lost any credibility I had when I was seventeen—have me staying quiet. Instead, I piled on the makeup, hiding the red mark on my pale skin until it had faded some. Luckily, the marks of his fingers on my wrist didn't bruise. No one knows that he attacked me, and I'm going to keep it that way.

He thinks I'll go meekly. I don't want to do this, but I will, and I already have a plan in mind.

I'm an Offering. Even though Jack Collins revoked that title a decade ago, he obviously gave it back if I'm going through with this today. As an Offering, I have protections that other women in the Order don't.

Simply put, if he lays his hands on me again once we're married, I can petition the King for an end to our marriage. And since we don't do divorce, there's only one way to save an Offering from an abuser who hurts his wife instead of taking care of her: excommunication from the order.

All it will take is Desmond hitting me one more time, leaving a visible mark, and he'll be dead. I'll be free.

Does that mean there aren't abusers in the Order? Of course not. Many of the men just know how to hit without leaving proof. Others keep their abuse emotional or financial rather than physical. And then there are the women who tolerate it because they don't want to be the reason their husbands die.

I won't let my Dad be excommunicated or executed. But Desmond?

I'll turn on him with a smile.

Thinking of my short marriage is the only reason I can find to smile at all today.

I'm wearing a six thousand-dollar wedding dress, all lace and ruffles and the hand-sewn beading Gilda added to the bodice, but it feels like a prison-orange jumpsuit. Desmond is standing in front of the altar, unable to hide his smirk that I just walked down the aisle to him. Father Francis is prepared to start the ceremony as the echoes of the final chords to the wedding march die out.

This is it. It's happening. I'm about to get married to Desmond St. James—

—or am I?

Out of the corner of my eye, the doors at the back of the church push open. A man in a suit stalks in, a last-minute guest I'm assuming, but instead of grabbing a seat in one of the last pews, he starts down the same path I took with Dad mere moments ago.

He clears his throat, wordlessly calling for attention.

I swivel my head, looking at him, and nearly faint on the spot.

It's him.

It's Adrian.

And he's holding a gun.

THREE
RIGHT ON TIME

ADRIAN

He doesn't know it yet, but Desmond St. James is going to die.

Not right away. That would be sloppy. And I pride myself on not being sloppy.

Besides, I have every right to take matters into my own hands, and I plan on it. For the Order's sake, though, I figured I ought to be discreet. Isn't that what's expected of the Owed? Hide in the shadows, play puppet master, watch the rest of Harmony Heights dance when we pull their strings.

So, I hired an assassin. The Hummingbird came highly recommended, and I reached out to her almost immediately after Dallas let me know that there were rumblings that Desmond had decided that, after all this time, he would attempt to Claim Loni.

But he can't. She's mine, and the fact that he didn't

have the balls to tell me himself only reinforces my belief that he knows that she belongs to me. So they had a public fling that lasted a couple of months when we were kids. That prick still took the one thing in this world I wanted more than anything, then he threw it away as if it were meaningless.

And he thinks that he can just swoop back in all these years later, after all the time I spent waiting to be able to go after her at last, and I'm going to *let* him?

No. The moment Desmond tried to Claim her as his Offering, I started to plot. And when the Hummingbird wasn't free to take on such a short contract, she passed my details onto another hired killer.

Nicholas Reed—along with his twin—in turn came even more highly recommended by the Hummingbird. For half down now, half after I received proof of his death, I could get rid of my rival without ever getting my own hands dirty. Not that I mind; I don't. But I'm so used to doing back door deals and consulting in the shadows, making sure the Order's reputation is untarnished, I moved forward with the hit.

Everything was done on a burner phone. It could only be traced back to me by the details I texted, plus my initials serving as a signature on an informal contract. Before June 24th, the Reed twins would eliminate Desmond. Loni wouldn't be forced to marry him, and considering I've tracked her over the years and know that she hasn't been close to settling down with anyone else since she escaped Harmony Heights, I'd be free to make her mine once I passed my thirtieth birthday.

Until then, Jack still thinks I'll fall in line. Until then,

Loni is in danger of falling prey to the Order's bylaws. I'd burn down all of Harmony Heights before I see her as one of the Used, and if someone else tries to marry her?

I'll see them dead, simple as that.

Only it's less than two weeks away from the scheduled wedding date and I haven't heard a peep from Nicholas Reed, or anyone in the Order, either, other than Dallas. If he hadn't tipped me off, I might not even have known it *was* happening until it would be too late. Desmond sure as hell is keeping his trap shut. Jack knows better than to tell me; my mom is his sister, and I've inherited my sense of determination from her side of the family. I'd stop this wedding if I knew—which is exactly what's going to happen, hired help or not.

But, hell. Where's the honor among murderers? The Hummingbird stopped responding to my messages, and she was the one who was in contact with Nicholas Reed, arranging the hit. I haven't heard anything since, and I don't like that at all.

I need confirmation. I need to know that Desmond will be out of the picture before he gets anywhere near Loni. On the plus side, Dallas assured me that my Loni has no intention or desire to marry Desmond, and that she's basically been barricaded in her family home with her old man until the 24th. She's as safe as she can be for the moment, and if I have it my way? It'll stay just like that until I can finally make her mine again without having to involve the Order.

I tried once, and I lost her.

This time, I refuse to—no matter what.

Loni thought she could escape me. That because I let her hide for a decade, she was safe from me.

No. She's always been mine, and I'll make sure that she... and everyone else in Harmony Heights... knows it.

Huh. I guess my invitation got lost in the mail.

At least, how else can you explain why the parking lot for the Church of St. Catherine is full nearly two weeks later, but I still don't *technically* know about today's affair?

A Tuesday evening wedding... only in Harmony Heights, and only because Father Francis is the Order's personal priest. As corrupt as anyone in town, there isn't anything he won't do for the right amount dropped into the offertory basket.

The sanctity of confession? It doesn't exist in this church.

Marrying a woman against her will, who is only agreeing because she's determined to save her father's life? *That* does.

And that's exactly what's about to happen inside of the church. Or, I should say, is *supposed* to happen—but, invitation or not, I'm here, and I'm ready to crash this wedding.

In the Order, there is no divorce. Once a marriage is done, the only way out is cashing in on the 'til death do you part' clause. If there's domestic violence? The Order executes the abuser after a quick inquiry. Cheating? The Order executes the cheater after a quick inquiry; fucking one of the Used being an obvious exception. Any marriage-ending offense usually leads to a funeral.

In this case, Loni's marriage to Desmond will begin with one.

Nicholas Reed is on my shit list. The Hummingbird finally replied to my latest message, informing me that she passed along the details to the Reed twins, then moved on to her next contract. She did offer to come after Desmond when she was done with her most recent kill, but it was too late.

I can't risk him marrying Loni. If he does, she'll always be his wife. Even if I arranged his death after, she'd be his widow. Blood oath or not, she'd be untouchable. Unless I gave up everything I've worked for my entire life, exiling the both of us from Harmony Heights, hiding out from the Order and its enforcers... she would never be mine the way she was meant to be.

But because there *is* a blood oath, I can stop this if I want to.

And, fuck me, do I want to.

There is a Beretta Tomcat sitting on the passenger seat of my car. A pocket pistol with a .32 caliber six-round magazine, it's my concealed carry weapon. Everyone in the upper ranks of the Order has their preferred piece, and this one is mine. A little larger than my phone, it's simple to tuck it inside the waistband of my pants so that it's easily within reach.

Once I'm ready, I get out of my car. I adjust my suit jacket so that it covers the stainless steel barrel of the gun, then stride purposely across the parking lot.

The wedding is scheduled to start at seven. That's ten

minutes from now. I waited until the last possible moment for Reed to come through, and now it's come to this.

If you want a job done right, you have to do it yourself.

Apart from me, there's only one other person in the lot; everyone else must be inside, waiting for the opening chords to 'Here Comes the Bride'. He's an Order member, too, but like me, he's not the type who attends weddings for shits and giggles.

Honestly? If it wasn't for the brand on his palm marking him as one of us, it would be easy to forget that Sebastien Reynolds is even a member. He wants nothing to do with the Order, leaving his family's legacy in the hands of his older brother, Alexandre.

But he's not here because of Order business. He's here for me because his loyalty is to his friends and not the society that he rebels against at any given moment.

Bas is sitting on his parked bike, boots planted on the asphalt as the sleeves of his leather jacket rest on his handlebars. It's the end of June, warmer than it has been lately, but he wears the jacket whether it's winter or summer. At least, this afternoon, the jacket is protecting his skin against the scorching metal.

From a distance, he seems too pretty to pull off his biker schtick. Most of his facial features are delicate, his eyelashes long as fuck, with a pair of cheekbones so sharp, they could cut paper. Closer, you see the battle scars. A divot missing from his right cheek. An inch-long slash over his eye that never healed right. A slight bend to his nose after it was broken twice in the same year.

Bas is pretty, but he's wise to that fact. Sensitive, too. When we were younger, he would jump into any fight to prove that he was more than his beauty. Nowadays, punching first, asking questions later is another way for him to rebel.

The Owed accept the world as its due. Scrappy Bas is proof that some of us will fight for what we want.

Feeling the weight of the gun on my hip, I'm in agreement. If I want Loni, I have to take her.

And I will.

Bas extends his hand, clasping mine in the same handshake our crew has used since middle school. As I go through the motions, I remember how Desmond used to be one of the five of us.

Do I regret that he has to die now? Not even a little.

Our friendship died the moment he went to Jack and requested Loni as his Offering. Our friendship, and Desmond himself. He was a dead man walking, even if he didn't know it.

He should've, though. Just like that pathetic prick shouldn't have ever tried to come between Loni and me. Not then, and especially not now.

My obsession with Avalon Dougherty has been the biggest open secret in Harmony Heights for more than a decade. It seems as though the only one who didn't know how desperate I was for her was Loni herself, so I call bullshit on Desmond's weak explanation that he thought I hated her.

Why? Because I bullied her? Because I made it so that everyone stayed away from her?

I made *her* untouchable. I claimed her as mine before

I was old enough to Claim her, and what did Desmond do? He tried to fucking *date* her.

And she *let* him.

Rage bubbles up inside of me. I tamp it down like I always do, nodding at Bas as he releases my hand.

The past can fucking stay there. I've spent years working toward my future, one plan at a time.

Good thing I'm a master planner.

The most important part of being one is knowing when to pivot. The Hummingbird was booked? Nicholas Reed flaked? It's fine.

Adrian's got this.

"Who's inside?" I ask Bas.

I got him to agree to keep an eye on the church for me while I waited to hear something, anything from Reed. Since that meant he didn't have to sit inside, a witness to another arranged marriage, Bas wasn't hard to convince.

He knows exactly who I mean.

"Jack didn't come. Neither did Stephen." Stephen, my 'mentor' and Jack's second, the man who is tapped to guide Dallas into taking over the Order when Jack finally steps down if Stephen ever gets sober enough to do his job... so, well, *never* on both counts. "Oliver is here, but that's it for the old guard. A bunch of seat-fillers. Loni, of course. Her dad. And Desmond... he showed up fifteen minutes ago, the cocky bastard acting like he's on top of the world."

Desmond broke the bro code. He knew that I wanted Loni. That I've *always* wanted Loni. Not only did he make a move on her in high school, but he thinks he can marry her now?

No fucking way.

"Dallas?" I ask.

Bas jerks a thumb over his shoulder. "Guarding the door, making sure the bride doesn't flee." He scoffs. "Loni really doesn't want to get married today, but Jack's given the order. If she doesn't, Peter Dougherty is done."

In his own way, Dallas is as much of a rebel as Sebastien. We might be cousins, but we're as close as brothers. He called me as soon as Jack gave him the orders to deliver a wedding invitation to Loni, and he filled me in on what happened after that every step of the way. With an encyclopedic knowledge of the Order's rules long beaten into him, he's the one who reminded me that a blood oath trumps everything in our world.

When it comes to Dallas, he'll do anything to stick up his middle finger at his father.

Me? I couldn't care less what Jack thinks. Dallas knows the laws. Me? I know where the bodies are buried, what kind of skeletons are in the closets of prominent Owed, and how to make the numbers speak to me.

In Harmony Heights, *I* am untouchable, and today? I'll prove it.

More importantly, planners pivot.

Loni needs to walk out of here a married woman. I can't let her marry Desmond, but look at me. I'm in a suit. I planned on convincing her to give me a second chance in two years… why not move up the timeline?

Suddenly, the church bells ring out. The muffled sounds of familiar organ music reaching us outside the closed doors.

I check my watch.

"They're early," I muse. "Someone must be antsy in there."

Someone who wants to have this wedding over and done with before anyone can stop them.

Bas chuckles under his breath. "Desmond always was a bit premature. Ask any of the girls down at the Court. I've heard some shit about that little weasel."

I'm not surprised about that. The Court—better known as The King's Court, an Order of the Owed's gentleman's club—is where members go to pick out one of the Used to enjoy. Not me. It didn't seem right, fucking one of the club girls when, one day, I'd have Loni as my wife. I stuck to town girls, anyone who didn't have any ties to the Order, during my early twenties. Now? I'm too busy with work, the Order, and plotting my future to worry about getting laid.

Bas, though? He's never been shy about his relation-ships with the Used. Like me, like Dallas, he refused to Claim any of the Offerings during the last nine Claiming ceremonies. Unlike me and Dallas, as the second-born son of one of the founding families, he doesn't *have* to. That's Alexandre's job, and I always thought his wedding would be the first of our inner circle.

Nope. Looks like that honor will belong to me.

Just like Loni will.

I remove the Tomcat, check the magazine, then clap Bas on his shoulder. "You coming to watch the show?"

He shakes his head. "Nah. But I'll be right out here to see what happens after."

Fair enough. I have a level of protection; both my lineage, and my Claim. Bas? He's started enough shit over the years that Jack is just itching for a reason to kick him out of the Order. And while Dallas and I would never allow that to happen, that's one fight that Bas does studiously avoid.

"Wish me luck."

"As if you'll need it." Bas's lips split into a grin. "Make those hours at the shooting range count, buddy."

"Hey. Anything worth doing is worth doing right."

Especially when forever is on the line.

With the pistol in my hand, I flash Bas a grin of my own, then start for the stairs that lead up to the church's doors. I've spent far too many mindlessly boring hours inside of St. Catherine's. The big wooden doors open right up to the back of the church, with confessionals and the holy water stand on one side, the votive candle rack on the other. Pews stretch out in front, lined up against a single aisle that leads to the altar.

A sculpture of Jesus Christ on a cross is posted on the wall, watching over the pulpit. The organist is hidden away somewhere, leaving the ghostly music to filter around the entire church.

As I approach the doors, the music gets louder. Instead of the hymns I'd grown up on, the wedding march comes to a close. Somewhere inside of St. Catherine's, my Loni has just walked down the aisle to Desmond St. James.

That realization has me moving on autopilot. I don't even think about it. I just *go*.

Throwing open the door, stalking right through with the Tomcat in my hand, my gaze goes straight to the altar. There's Father Francis, wearing his white vestments and embroidered stole. Desmond is in a suit, bored, looking like he's simply attending just another business meeting instead of gazing raptly at the stunning vision across from him.

Like I do now.

Shit.

My heart skips a beat.

My fingers tighten on the handle of the gun.

My jaw flexes.

Loni...

I've seen her in photographs. I've seen her in surveillance camera footage. I've watched her live a life from states away, so I know what she looks like. I haven't been rubbing one out to the memory of a seventeen-year-old girl all these years. I've become more and more addicted to the woman that she's grown into.

And all of that pales in comparison to seeing Loni Dougherty like this. Her face expertly made up to hide her adorable freckles, soft hazel eyes gleaming in barely masked distress, her lithe body meticulously tailored inside of a satin dress with lace embellishments and a sheer bit of fabric covering one shoulder. Her strawberry-blonde hair is twisted up and out of her face, pinned back by a diamond piece, showing off the column of her slender throat as she swallows nervously.

Standing there, in a wedding dress meant for another man, she looks like a princess.

A motherfucking princess.

My princess.

Desmond St. James's fate was sealed the moment he tried to Claim Loni. As soon as I knew that she was walking out of St. Catherine's a married woman, so was hers.

I clear my throat as I stalk down the aisle, heading right for them.

Her head snaps over at me. A moment later, so does Desmond's.

His expression becomes terrified. I swear to God, I see a flash of relief on Loni's before she shuts that down.

It doesn't matter. I saw it, and knowing that I did, I smile.

"I hope I'm not too late," I announce to everyone gathered inside of the church.

Mumbles, whispers, and a general confusion passes over those assembled—but the instant I lift the gun, a hush falls.

And my smile becomes a determined thinning of my lips as I stalk toward the bride. It takes everything in me to rip my gaze from Loni's loveliness, but I want to see Desmond's fear. I want him to see the gun and know that, if he'd stayed away from her, this wouldn't have had to happen.

More than anything, he needs to understand that he brought this all on himself.

So maybe my lips curve a little at the ends, a satisfied smirk, as he holds up his hands, begging, pleading, calling my name the instant before my finger tugs the trigger. It's too late. Besides, I'm not the one he should've been apologizing to—

Bang.

Bang.

Bang.

—oh, no. That's the stunning beauty whose pristine wedding dress gets dotted with red as the three bullets slam into him in quick succession, spraying his blood all over her before he drops to the aisle—and all hell fucking breaks loose.

Ah, well. I've always known how to make an entrance when necessary.

FOUR
I DO

LONI

I don't scream.

Someone else does. Probably half the church does. The shouts rattle around my stunned brain, echoing in my ears, but they sound so far away at the same time.

Maybe because the gunshots ringing out deafened me in their wake. Or maybe because a part of me is floating above the scene, taking it in like a stunned spectator, separate but here at the same time...

Shock, I think, my body trembling, my breath coming too, too fast, Desmond's warm blood rapidly cooling on my skin. Most of it is pooled beneath him where he fell, a pretty crimson pond, with my bouquet lapping at the edge of it.

Oh. I must've dropped the flowers. I flex my fingers, noticing that my hands are empty, and swallow the hysterical laugh bubbling up my throat.

He's dead.

Dead.

Dead. Dead. Deaddead*dead*.

And the man who killed my groom? Is stalking toward me as though the people screaming, running, escaping the pews aren't anywhere near enough of a distraction to keep him from getting to me.

He's definitely a distraction on *my* end.

I haven't seen Adrian Heller in almost a decade. He's as fiercely beautiful now as he was then, though the gun held lazily in his grip makes him dangerously so.

I hope I'm not too late.

To kill Desmond? To make me some kind of *pre-widow*, killing my groom before we could even get to the 'I do's?

Oh, no. He's right on fucking time.

I notice small differences as the world falls away, leaving just the two of us standing here. His hair is a little darker than it used to be, making his eyes seem even lighter in comparison. He wears his suit like a second skin, only he doesn't have on a tie like the other wedding guests. His dress shirt is slightly unbuttoned, a sliver of his bare chest on display. A pair of small golden hoops wink in his left ear. His lazy expression hides the heat in his gaze.

Me. He's looking at *me*.

And I'm looking back.

Because it's Adrian. *Adrian*.

That does it. It might've taken me longer than it should to realize what was happening, but as reality zooms back in, I look around, seeing that there aren't any wedding guests left. Everyone has fled from the man with the gun until only me, Adrian, and the dead Desmond are arranged near the front of the church.

Run, I think. *Run.*

Grabbing my ruined dress, cursing my unwieldy heels, I turn from Adrian and start toward the empty first pew.

In my mind, I know I'm not getting away from an unrepentant murderer. I'm getting away from Adrian Heller.

From my past.

From *him*—

"Not so fast, Loni," murmurs Adrian. The gun is gone, tucked away or tossed aside, but his hand is empty enough that he can grasp my upper bicep. The touch of his skin on mine short-circuits my brain, the sound of my long-ago nickname in his suave voice only adding to it, and I stop.

I just... stop.

He's not squeezing my arm. He's not grabbing me, yanking me, pulling me the same way that Desmond did the other night at my dad's place. He just has a firm, possessive hold on me as he easily guides me back to the altar.

And it hits me: I'm not getting away from anyone, am I?

I walk around Desmond, grateful that he fell face-down so that I don't have to see the last expression on his face before Adrian killed him. He leads me, kicking Desmond's shoe as he tucks me into his side, careful that I don't come too close to the corpse.

I don't have any idea what he's doing. Killing Desmond... desecrating the church... showing up here when I haven't seen him in so damn long... none of this makes sense. Moving me toward the altar of an empty church? That makes even *less*.

Only it's not empty. Not entirely. The rest of the wedding guests have all rushed for the doors—including Dad—but there are still two others waiting to meet Adrian and me at the altar: Father Francis and Dallas Collins.

Dallas has a weapon of his own out. Holding a gun in his grip, standing right behind the priest, he nods at Adrian. Like he's in on it. Like this was all some kind of plan...

In front of me, Father Francis is trembling. Speechless.

Terrified.

Adrian grins. "This is the part where you make Loni my wife."

A squeak escapes me as I turn my head sharply, looking him dead in the face.

He winks at me.

My mouth falls open, but I still don't scream.

He didn't—

He can't—

He *is*.

I jerk my arm. Without any other reaction, he releases me.

I shake my head, too stunned to find the words just yet.

Adrian shrugs. "You know what Jack said." Jack. The

King is Adrian's uncle, but for as far back as I can remember, he's never referred to the man by either title. Not the King, not Uncle Jack, but simply Jack as if he has nothing but contempt for the relative who controls the Order of the Owed. "You need to be a married woman. Your other groom is sadly indisposed at the moment. Luckily, I'm more than happy to take his place."

I work my jaw, struggling to understand. Finally, I whisper, "You want me to marry you."

A ghost of his old familiar smirk. "I insist on it."

Can he do that? I admit, I forgot a lot of the Order's ridiculous laws, bylaws, and loopholes. As an Offering, I only needed to know about the ones that affected me. The others were left to the men in the Order, and I foolishly believed that my husband could deal with all of that. Then I was stripped of being an Offering and forgetting it all... that was my own tiny act of rebellion.

I was Claimed. Both Dallas and Desmond made that clear. Desmond Claimed me, and Jack Collins granted his Claim. He's supposed to be the one marrying me, but he's dead, and Adrian *killed* him.

Is this why? To get to me?

It can't be.

Can it?

No. It's not possible. This is just a decade's worth of his animosity building up. Instead of simply being my bully, he's here to fucking ruin my life in the most public way he could. Marrying Desmond wasn't my first plan, but my family would be set for life as inducted, protected members of the Order if I did. But what does Adrian do?

Takes away the one benefit to me giving up my new life in favor of returning to my old one.

Murdering Desmond might be taking it a step too far, granted. Too bad there's never been a line he wouldn't cross when it came to getting a rise out of me. For so many years, I was his favorite target. Not even falling for him and giving him my heart, body, and soul saved me from the dark side of Adrian Heller.

And now he's here, showing it off. Shooting a man in cold blood, executing him in the middle of the church... that hint of danger I was always drawn to has me unsure if I want to see if he'll really go through with it... really *marry* me... or if I should take my chances on whether he'll shoot me next or not.

Would he? The boy I knew wouldn't, but the man he's become in my absence?

I... I don't know.

He's obviously capable of murder. That doesn't shock me. To ascend the ranks of the Order, an Owed needs to be. To prove your loyalty to the society, plenty of its members have to kill in its name. Then there are enforcers who are charged with eliminating threats to the Order, from within it or outside of it. Dallas is one of them. Maybe Adrian is, too.

What do I know about him? Nothing... except that, ten years later, one possessive look from this man has my entire body suddenly on fire.

What does that say about me that, instead of freaking the fuck out, I want to get closer to him?

No.

He knows it. I can tell from his expression. He's daring

me to step into him, and when I don't, he hikes up his pants, squatting down so that he can grab the bloody bouquet from the floor.

Adrian gives the bouquet a casual flick, knocking loose a few stray droplets of blood still clinging to the flowers. Then, satisfied, he offers it out to me. "Come here, my bride."

Here comes the bride… all dressed in white…

I glance down.

Red.

I'm covered in red.

Seeing Desmond's blood staining the white petals, dotting the white fabric… that snaps me out of my daze at last.

"You can't do this, Adrian." Even as he settles into his place in front of Father Francis, waiting for me, still holding the bouquet in his gun-free hand, I struggle to resist the urge to touch him, to make sure it's him, to make sure he's *real*.

I haven't quite given up on running yet. To, from, away… but that's impossible. With Dallas and his lazy grin watching both the priest and me with a predator's gaze, I'm not leaving this church a single woman—and we *all* know it.

Still, I need to put some space between us, and even if it's only a few feet, I stumble in my heels away from Adrian.

His eyes sparkle, one part mischief, one part dare. "Be careful of the corpse under your feet, princess. You don't want to get any more blood on that dress of yours."

Then, with the slightest movement, he transfers the

bouquet from his right hand to his left. He twists the wrist on his right hand, drawing my attention to the brand on his palm. The ruined skin.

The mark of the Owed.

It's a flash of a reminder that, in Harmony Heights, a man like Adrian Heller can do any fucking thing he wants.

Including marrying me, it seems.

He jerks his chin at Father Francis. "The longer you take, the more that blood will seep into your carpet, Father. Might want to get a move on."

Father Francis's eyes dart to Adrian's hand. I can just about see the gears spinning in his mind, wondering whether he should force me to marry Adrian or find a way out of this for the both of us.

He doesn't know that I didn't want to marry the dead man on the floor. Or maybe he does, but that wasn't going to stop him.

It's not going to stop him now, either, because Father Francis... he saw the mark, too. He knows that Adrian is a member of the Order, and that it'll be up to the Order to deal with the fallout from Desmond's death inside of St. Catherine's. For all he *does* know, this was arranged. Maybe Adrian's uncle gave him permission to do this.

Just like with Desmond, though, I don't know why he would want to be my new groom—but he's standing there, with Dallas as his witness, as he waits for me to do my part.

As if I've forgotten, Adrian holds out the bouquet to me once more. "Princess."

Okay. I can't help myself. This is insanity, all of it is,

but that's the second time he's used a name for me that no one ever has before. I thought I was hearing things before, but that time... there's no denying it.

Jack is the King. Dallas is his only child, and the first fistfight I ever saw in person was in second grade when an older kid called Dallas 'Prince'. Dallas blackened Stu Marone's eye and knocked out his two front teeth. Afterward, Sebastien Reynolds took a pair of safety scissors out of his backpack and hacked off half of the older boy's hair while Connor Heyward pinned Stu down. Desmond took the cheap shot, kicking Stu in the nuts while he was already on the ground.

Adrian, of course, was the one who told Dallas about the unfortunate nickname before coming up with a way to distract the schoolyard monitors so that the other boys could get revenge on Stu for upsetting one of them.

From then on, I always thought of the quintet as a solid group. No one referred to them as anything other than the Boys, though I gave them my own secret nick-name in middle school: the Heirs. Everyone knew that, one day, those five would rule the Order—and Harmony Heights.

Ten years later, Jack Collins is still in charge. Dallas is obviously a top enforcer, and Adrian must be right up there with him. Do I know what happened to Connor? Or Sebastien? No. Not yet.

And Desmond... being in the Order didn't save him. In fact, I'm pretty sure it condemned him.

Or maybe that was just me.

But 'Princess'? I have my legacy in the Order, my family going all the way back to the beginning, but I'm no princess. I was a sullied Offering who rejected becoming a Used until some way, somehow I ended up in this bloody wedding dress.

I swallow, and ask, "Princess?"

Adrian waits for me to accept the bouquet from him.

Knowing that he'll only answer me if I do, I clutch it with trembling fingers.

He nods. "'Princess' because that's what you look like to me right now, Loni." He lifts his hand, dappled with blood, warm and alive, and he caresses my chin. "You look like *mine*."

I swallow roughly. He shifts his hand, trailing it down the column of my throat, nestling his fingers in the curve of my shoulder before cupping the back of my neck.

He turns us both so that we're facing Father Francis.

"Let's get on with it, Father. And hurry, if you would." His gaze slides my way. "I'd like to reach the part where I get to kiss my bride."

My pulse jumps at the thought. With his gentle hold on me, he feels it.

And he laughs. "You seem a little eager, too, princess. Good. Because I fucking *do*."

He does.

But what about me?

FIVE

HOME

ADRIAN

She tastes just the way I remember.

I lingered on our kiss after Father Francis finally gave me his blessing, allowing me to kiss my bride. I tipped Loni back in my arms, holding her tight so that she didn't fall and couldn't escape my lips, and I kissed her with all the unsaid promises that come along with the stock-standard wedding vows.

There wasn't time for us to write our own. I made a mental note that we would have to have a vow renewal before our wedding reception, but once Father Francis announced to the assembled crowd—to Dallas, just Dallas—that he pronounced Loni and me as man and wife, I kissed her, then whisked her right to the car waiting for us in the parking lot.

It was full when I parked. Now? It's empty, and if she seems surprised that there isn't an array of squad cars waiting to arrest me for first-degree murder, she's smart enough not to remark on it.

Ten years away from Harmony Heights has made her forget who owns this town. So long as it happens within the town's borders, I could walk up to anyone affiliated with the Order, take them out, then flash my palm and it would be like it never happened. We police our own, and even if I wasn't Jack's nephew, I had every right to gun down Desmond the way I did.

I swore an oath in blood, and he paid for trying to break it with his.

The way I see it, it's just another figure to add or subtract. A longtime friend subtracted from my life in order to add the woman I've always considered mine. His death was Desmond's fault. He never should have gone after Loni, and now all of Harmony Heights knows she is abso-fucking-lutely off-limits.

It'll spread like wildfire through the town. I know that much. Everyone at the wedding was affiliated with the Order, one way or another. While half of the crowd left because they didn't want to get involved in personal business within the society, the other half must have run straight to the Fortress to tell everyone what they saw.

I'm expecting a call from Jack sooner or later. Dallas stuck around St. Catherine's, offering to do the clean-up for me, but that's not all. As a wedding gift to me and Loni, he promised to keep his father off my back until at least tomorrow. That way, we have a wedding night before I have to explain myself to the King.

Not that I'm worried. I'm not. I was in the right, and he knows it.

Oh, no. The only thing I'm worried about is Loni. Loni, and her reaction to becoming my new wife.

The only comment she had after we left the church was, "I guess Dad decided to go home." She said it quietly as she took in the empty lot, and when her body seemed to sag under the weight of her bloody wedding dress, I eased an arm around her and helped lead her to my car.

She didn't say another word until I pulled into the circular drive of my three-story home. A softly whispered, "Yours?" that I answered with a very firm, "*Ours.*"

I helped her out of the car, looping my arm through hers so that we could walk up the steps together. Then, because I consider us married now, I hefted her up in my arms so that I could carry my bride over the threshold.

That was about fifteen minutes ago. Since then, she's drifted from room to room, taking in the first floor with a strange expression on her pretty, pretty face. She's in shock, I know she is, and—if she's anything like the Loni I remember—there will be hell to pay when she finally comes out of it, but for now, I follow behind like a lovesick puppy dog as she meanders in wobbly heels through the front room, the kitchen, the dining room, the living room, and, finally, the hall outside of the first-floor bathroom.

I watch her take it all in, marveling over our place. And it's *our* place. The moment I walked out of my parents' home for the final time as a resident, I took the money in my account and found a house that would be the starting point for my future; the future I would one day have with this woman. Deep down, I always planned on making it work out between us. If I couldn't go after her right away, I would when I had to, and I'd bring her back here.

Just like I did tonight.

If it wasn't Desmond who I had to eliminate for trying to Claim her, there would've been someone else. For Loni's sake, I kept my interference to strict blackmail and threats of extortion to erase any of her other lovers. With Desmond, I could've bought him off if necessary, but because it *was* Desmond... he paid with his life instead of cash, just like any other Owed would who crossed me.

In the hall, there's a large oval antique mirror that I bought because the gilded frame reminded me of Loni's delicate beauty. Sometimes, I would walk by it, and I'd see myself reflecting back, wishing I could catch a flash of her wavy strawberry-blonde hair, her striking hazel eyes, and those adorable freckles dotting the bridge of her nose.

It's there now. She's staring at her face in my mirror, prodding some stray blood spatter that managed to decorate her cheek.

She hasn't changed yet. A stray lock of hair has fallen free of her elaborate updo. The diamond piece has shifted a little. The dress, of course, is ruined.

Luckily, I called in a few favors among the Owed. I say favors... I reached out to those in my books, those in my ledgers, those who wouldn't want their secrets getting out, and I asked for one of my own. I didn't want anyone interfering with my wedding to Loni tonight, but if it all went off without a hitch like I planned, I would be bringing her home with me.

She would already be out of sorts, planning on

marrying one groom, going home with a different one. At the very least, I wanted her to have some sense of famil-iarity. While Peter Dougherty was at the wedding—a visible prop to remind Loni why she was going through with it—I had eight men remove every trace of the woman who had been staying with him.

I left her SUV parked in his driveway for the moment, but everything else? It's in a spare bedroom because, well, let's just say that I'm not necessarily the optimistic sort. More pragmatic than anything, and I'm not playing for just one night.

I'm playing for keeps.

Forever.

And if that means our marriage starts like so many of the Order's arranged marriages, so be it. I expect it, though that doesn't mean I won't at least *try* to put her at ease. After all, she did just watch me kill a man. I don't blame her at all for being wary.

Especially since she's Loni, and as much as I'm addicted to this woman, I know I've fucked this all up since the beginning. Hopefully, this is a new one, and we can start over.

Huh. Maybe I have a bit of a silly optimistic streak after all…

I wait until she glances away from the mirror to break the silence. "If you want to take a shower before we go to bed, I can help you out of that dress."

I was going for gentle. Fuck. Do I even know how to be gentle? Probably not since, the moment I make the genuine offer, clarity finds its way to her eyes. I hear the words again, and I can only guess how she interpreted them.

I basically just said I'd help her strip so that she could freshen up before we go to bed together.

And that's exactly how she understood it.

Her eyes go wide as she steps away from me, moving toward the living room. "Bed? Oh, no, no. I'm not sleeping with you, Adrian. Not again. Never again."

I make a non-committal sound to that. Oh, I have every intention of getting this woman under me as soon as possible. Is that tonight? Probably not. Not even I am that big of a dick to try and convince her to fuck me after the day she's had.

At least, that was my plan... until she nibbles on her bottom lip, and, as always, she has my cock's complete attention.

Then she sighs before saying, "I have to be honest with you. I have a boyfriend," and that's all I'm thinking about right now.

I grit my teeth, giving nothing away.

Boyfriend.

She's full of shit. I would know if she was seeing someone, and if it got serious, I'd end it. I always have. She's only throwing this in my face because she thinks that might get me to release her from being my bride, but if so? She's dead wrong.

Besides, Loni dating someone didn't stop me from fucking her before. Why would she think it would stop me now when her boyfriend is fictional?

Still, the reminder stings. I know damn well she only agreed to date Desmond to make me jealous, and if it worked... if that's part of the reason I looked forward to having to pull the trigger myself when Nicholas Reed flaked on me... well, us Hellers do tend to hold a grudge.

I pause a moment, then flick a curl from out of my eyes. "Not anymore, you don't," I tell her, letting her have her fantasy. "You're my wife now. I'm your husband. There won't be anyone else for either of us anymore."

She frowns. "No Used?"

"No Used," is my firm response.

That surprises her, but she recovers quickly. "What about you? To marry me today the way you did... you were still available? No Offering in ten years?"

I know what she's really asking me. Unfortunately for Loni, she hasn't been stalking me over the years. She doesn't know the history of my love life like the way that I obsess over hers. I don't fault her for wondering, though I am irrationally pleased that she cares enough to ask.

"None," I assure her.

"What about Haven?"

I should've known that was coming. One of the last times we were together, she made it a point to remind me that Haven Smith was meant to be my Offering. I let her believe that because I was too worried that I'd scare Loni off by making it clear that I would have her or I would have no one.

Loni left. For ten years, it had been no one, but even if I did what Jack wanted me to do, even if I decided to Claim Haven, I wouldn't have. I'm not Desmond. I won't break the bro code, and Haven? Even before what happened to the poor girl, she belonged to Connor.

For Loni to mention her childhood friend so easily,

I'd bet she has no idea what Haven went through last year. All of my research tells me that their friendship ended when Loni ran so it wouldn't surprise me if she didn't know.

Should I tell her?

No, I decide. Let her get comfortable with me first. Then, if she chooses to be part of the Order again for good, I'll call up Connor and call in a favor. For now, though, I twist the truth so that I'm stilling be honest with my wife.

After all, the best marriages start off with a tenet of honesty. That's why one like my parents have, or Jack and Aunt Reese had, are always doomed to fail…

"I never wanted Haven, Loni. No other Offering, either, and definitely not any of the Used." A hint of doubt creeps into her tired, guarded expression. Suddenly, there isn't anything I won't do to see that doubt erased. "I will make this as clear as I can: today was no accident. I only ever wanted you."

And now I have her.

Her distrustful eyes go even wider than before. "Don't tell me that the last time you got laid was—"

"Of course not. And I know the same is true for you. But that was just sex, princess. What we had… what we *have*… is so much more than that."

I'll make sure of it.

My wife doesn't seem to agree.

"You made my life hell, Adrian. I thought I got away… that I *escaped*. But, look at you now… you're doing it again."

"Oh, Loni. Call it that if you must, but I never

stopped." And she'll figure that out sooner or later. "But that's the past. Put it where it belongs: behind us." I step closer to her, getting rid of the gap existing between us. "We have the rest of our lives to look forward to."

I'm ready to forget the past. To forget the mistakes I made, and the long, lonely years in between.

I am.

I don't think she is.

Wrapping her hands around her middle, ignoring the darkish brown blood stains, she says to me, "You really want me to believe that you waited all this time for me?"

She's not letting this go. Fair enough.

I think back.

"Four years," I finally answer.

Her pretty forehead furrows. "What?" She nibbles her bottom lip again, a temptation if I ever saw one. Her taste lingers in my mouth, but I'm dying for another hit. "Four years? Is that how long we have to stay married before I can go?"

She can't honestly believe that.

Sure, there are some arranged marriages between Owed and their Offerings that end amicably. No divorce, of course. They'll still be married in the eyes of the Order, but they can live separate lives on their own.

That won't be us, and I make sure she knows it.

"Oh, I'm never letting you go," I tell her, my tone light though my words are a fucking promise. "I was just telling you exactly how long I've been specifically waiting for you. Four years."

Almost to the day.

I was twenty-five. Loni had just turned the same age.

It was her birthday, and I was feeling melancholy, missing her. In between clients, I was obsessively stalking her social media pages when I noticed that she posted a picture with a guy.

There was a caption: "Our hard launch as a couple", followed by a comment he added beneath it that said, *happy birthday, babe.*

I almost smashed my phone to bits, throwing it against the nearest wall of my office.

I knew that face. That smarmy face belonged to a gym bro with dark blond hair who worked with my Loni. I was assured theirs was just a co-worker relationship, that there wasn't anything between Loni and Bradley.

Maxwell and Dimitty's has a very firm "no fraternization" policy; I know because, when Stephen approached them on my behalf to form a partnership with the Owed, I had them add it. So, once I cooled down, I made a few phone calls.

A week later, I had him transferred to an office across the ocean. Their relationship didn't last the rest of the month.

That was the last man she ever posted on her socials. As for me, the jealousy that I experienced when I realized that Loni entered into a semi-serious relationship made me lose the last of my interest in any woman that wasn't her. I haven't been with anyone since, and though I've been dealing with one hell of an erection since St. Catherine's, I focus on what's important.

Like getting Loni out of that fucking dress.

SIX

ASHTRAY

ADRIAN

oni opens her mouth, ready to comment on my confession, but before she can, I gesture for her to follow me through the living room. The stairs to the second floor are on the other side of it, and I tell her so.

She pauses in the middle of the space. "I get my own room."

I glance over at her. She's wearing a look of pure determination.

Damn it. I knew this would happen.

I arch an eyebrow at her. "You know the Order's laws."

"The ones that affect the Offering, yeah." She gives her head a defiant shake. Another stray strand of her elaborate hairstyle falls into her face. With a rough brush of the back of her hand, she knocks it away. "Of course I do."

My fingers fucking itch to see if her hair is as soft as I remember.

I flex them, then move until I'm standing in front of her. I reach out to my wife. She isn't expecting it, and when she jerks her head out of my reach, the only thing that happens is that that same strand falls forward again, giving me perfect access to it.

I suck in a breath through my nose, forcing back the shudder that threatens to run through me.

God, that's fucking *soft*.

Loni was always soft wherever she let me lay my hands on her. The underside of the swell of her tit. Along the side of her waist. The curve of her ass. The hollow of her throat.

The inside of her pussy.

I twist my hand, ready to trace the back of my fingers along the edge of her jaw.

She steps away. "Don't touch me, Adrian."

Her eyes glare at me in sudden hatred, the tendons in her neck standing out a sure sign of her restrained fury.

With a small nod, I lower my hand, a hint of an amused smirk tugging on my lips.

I can do hatred. She's looked at me like that most of our lives, but that didn't stop me from owning her once. Her heart... her body... she was mine when we were little more than kids.

As far as I'm concerned, she's never stopped being mine, and now that we're married, she'll just have to get used to it. I won't let her go, and the Order says I don't have to. The wedding license will be signed and filed in the morning. The Church will be ready for Wednesday mass; I'll see to that myself. I'll replace the stock golden band used at every arranged wedding because *my* bride deserves the best. *Loni* deserves it, and whether she hates me now or not, I made my vow to her.

I'll be the best husband she could ever dream of, and not even she'll be able to stop me. Before long, I doubt she'll want to. I won her over once. I look forward to doing it again.

Now, if she was afraid? I'd have more work to do. Indifferent? I'd be rolling up my shirtsleeves. But hatred?

I've missed hate sex with Loni Dougherty almost as much as I've missed *her*.

So, no, I won't push her tonight. I want her in my bed, but I accept that that won't be happening so soon.

After all, we have forever now.

'Til death do us part.

Does that mean I'm going to let her tell me that I can't touch her? I'm a cruel bastard, but I don't ever want her to be afraid of me. So, instead of reminding her that she is my wife, I decide to play this little game of Order politics with her.

"So you know about the Offerings' responsibilities to their Owed. Great. Then you'll know that you get your own room if you want it, but you have to spend one night a week in my bed with me."

There are no rules about what happens in the marriage bed; at least, not in the Order's charter. I'd be naive if I said there aren't husbands who simply take what they want from their wives. It happens, and like murder, it's not necessarily a crime in the Order's eyes as long as the Offering is unharmed. *Forcing* your wife, leaving her in pain… that *can* be grounds for an intervention by Jack and his council.

Not that I would do that. When I have Loni again, it'll be because she invited me in. Still, I understand the rule about making it so that an Offering must spend at least one night a week in her husband's bed. The whole purpose of pairing up an Offering and an Owed is because the Order insists on matching bloodlines and creating future members.

They want us to fuck so that we have kids. Me? I just want Loni where she belongs.

She can't fight me on this. Just like how a wife can claim her husband isn't worthy of her, an Owed can give up his Offering if she doesn't do her part. She signed her life away to save her father's. Something tells me she'll do the same thing if it's threatened again.

If there's one thing the Order of the Owed knows, it's how to hit you where it hurts. Jack won't threaten Loni to get her to fall in line. He'll threaten her father.

And he definitely knows how to get me to do what's expected of me…

When she doesn't argue, I say, "Pick a day."

Loni doesn't hesitate. "Monday."

Smart. Today is Tuesday, and while I'd put money down that Desmond purposely arranged for an unusual Tuesday wedding, believing that he could take *my* princess and make her his wife without me ever finding out, it makes sense that Loni would choose Monday as our night. It's the furthest from Tuesday, and she probably thinks she can figure a way out of this before then.

Not gonna happen. I let her get away from me once. I

had every intention of waiting out the clock, going after her again once Jack couldn't use his position to stop me—or punish Loni for *my* insolence—but once I knew that Desmond was trying to steal her out from under my nose?

All bets were off.

She is mine.

My bride.

My wife.

My princess...

Mine.

"Monday it is," I agree. "Now, another rule. We have to have at least four meals together throughout the week. You can choose two, and I'll choose two. Fair?"

"Breakfast counts."

"I'm not really a morning person. I don't do breakfast."

A hint of triumph flashes across her face. "If you miss it, that's not my problem."

A hint of triumph that's there and gone again, all while I try to hide mine.

She remembers. She doesn't like that she does, but she remembers enough about me that I was shit until I had my morning coffee and cigarette, even back during my high school days.

She wants to have breakfast with me, though?

Oh, I'll be there.

That thought makes me realize that I haven't had a celebratory smoke yet. I didn't want to do so in the car in case the smoke bothered Loni, but inside of the house, with the air purifiers running, it should be fine.

Reaching into my suit jacket pocket, I pull out my cigarette case. I pop it open, take out one of my smokes, then swap the case for the lighter engraved with my initials: AJH.

Loni watches me closely. Her pretty hazel eyes flicker from the unlit cigarette in my hand to the ashtray on my coffee table. It's empty. Clean. Still, there's no denying what the heavy crystal ornament with the dip in the middle for ash is.

Her nose wrinkles. "You still smoke?"

I shrug, thumb poised on the spark wheel of my lighter. "Why?"

"I thought you would've given it up by now."

I cock my head, waiting for her to explain.

"What? Hasn't anyone told you it's not attractive to kiss an ashtray? I won't do it. And, okay, maybe it looked cool when I was seventeen so I got over it, but lung cancer's a thing, Adrian. So is secondhand smoke."

Well. She's not wrong, is she?

Most people my age vape. I got hooked at sixteen by Maggie, my father's former Used. Mom would be in the kitchen, directing our cook on what to make even though she refused to ever dirty her hands with household work. It was a convenient excuse to leave the bedroom to Dad and Maggie since my father didn't even have the decency to fuck his whore at the Court like the rest of the higher-ranked members of the Order. Probably because Mom is Jack's sister, and it would look bad on him if his own blood wasn't enough to satisfy her husband's lecherous gaze, wandering hands, and insatiable need to get off every couple of hours.

I couldn't relate to my ice-cold mother. Even when I started sleeping with Loni, it was more about having a part of her that no one else could than the pleasure it gave me; though, not going to lie, her pussy was like Heaven to me. So Dad's being a hound dog? Hell, I just went four years without sex. I was prepared to wait another two because, fuck it, I've had my taste, and it's all sour compared to the woman glaring at me in a bloody wedding dress.

But Maggie...

Some Used are chosen to be a companion. A second wife, as it were, without any of the perks. The social status. The power. The protection. However, since they *are* chosen, they have their own benefits, which is why, two hundred years later, this glorified prostitution continues in Harmony Heights.

But others? Others are basically that. They're whores who get summonsed, get fucked, then shown the door.

My father's and Maggie's arrangement lasted until I was nineteen, getting ready to move, and I found her waiting for me in my bed, naked as the day she was born. Telling me she wanted to see if I could fuck her as thoroughly as my dad, she offered herself to me—and I looked down my nose and told her I don't do Dad's sloppy seconds. She had the nerve to be scandalized while I was fuming that she wanted me to stick my dick somewhere that my father's had been for *years*.

He found out because that's what we Hellers do. He made a phone call to Jamie, the woman who runs the Court, and Cecilia was being dropped off at our house within an hour.

But Maggie... if I remember anything other than those perky tits and the come-hither look on her face, it was how she left every rendezvous with my father with a cigarette on her lip.

She gave me my first smoke. I choked, and she patted my back, and I remember shaking her off. But the first time I took a puff in front of Loni and she bit down on her bottom lip like it did something to her... I've never stopped. I've never had a reason to.

Until now.

I glance down at the one in my hand. Without a word, I slip my lighter back into my jacket pocket. The unlit cigarette gets tucked behind my ear.

Her expression turns puzzled, but I don't acknowledge it. Instead, I say, "One question for you, Loni, then I'll show you your room." I'd already offered her dinner in the car ride over, not too surprised when she shook her head, refusing it. I'll get some food into her tomorrow, but for now, she needs to unwind—and get the fuck out of that dress. "What do you say, princess? Deal?"

It's obvious that she thinks I'm leading her right into a trap. The tacked-on *princess* doesn't help. And, fuck, of course I am, but why not?

She nods.

"When it comes down to it, who would you have rather met at the altar this evening? Desmond? Or me?" I want nothing more than to stroke that slight furrow in her brow, but I behave myself, keeping some distance between us even as I add, "And don't say neither because that's not what I asked. Given the choice between only the two of us, who would treat you better? Be a better husband to you?"

I can see the sudden anger she can't quite hide as she mulls over my question.

Because I'm not being fair, and we both know it.

Desmond rejected her in front of the entire school. By doing so, he rejected her in front of the entire Order. So he decided a decade later to attempt to Claim her. He hurt her, and I'm well aware of it.

But the way I betrayed her was even crueler. When I could have been honest and open about my love for her —about my *addiction*—I sided with the Order with the belief that, come the Claiming ceremony, I could make her mine, and then she'd understand that everything I did, everything I *will* do, is because I've considered Avalon Dougherty mine from the time a freckle-faced kindergartner shared her cookie with me during snack.

At five, it was a crush.

At ten, it was an annoyance.

At fifteen, my feelings for her got me through the worst of my hormones.

At eighteen, she was mine until she wasn't.

I'm twenty-eight now. A quarter of a century that I've longed for her, *needed* her, and she's mine again.

My ring is on her finger. She's in my home, and even if she's sleeping in another room tonight, on Monday, I'll have her right where I want her.

Right where she's always belonged.

And I will do anything I have to, eliminate any threat in my way, do whatever it takes to keep her there.

Desmond's blood still stains her wedding dress. I'll

have to get my hands on it to preserve it just the way it is before one of the Order's cleaners decides to try to restore it to its pristine condition. Fifty years from now, when the red blood is deep brown, the lace yellowed with age, I'll look at the blood and recognize it as just another price I paid, a sacrifice I made, a promise I kept... and I'll smile.

Just like I do now when Loni spits out, "Desmond."

Oh, *princess*.

"You were a terrible liar when we were kids," I tell her. My grin widens. "It's nice to see that that hasn't changed."

Her lips part, another lie ready to spill, or maybe a denial. I don't know. It doesn't matter. I know the truth, and I'm going to take advantage of the way she's suddenly flustered.

My hand goes to her hair again—soft, it's so fucking *soft*—before slipping through the strands, palming the back of her head. Holding her in place, I lower my mouth until it's brushed up against hers. She gasps, and I kiss her with everything I have in me. Only when I'm growing light-headed from the lack of air do I release her.

That same dazed expression from before turns her beautiful face into one that dazzles me.

"What... what was that?"

"You said you won't kiss someone who tastes like an ashtray," I remind her. "I'm going to give up smoking for you. This is what I want in exchange."

"I... *what*?"

I've knocked her off-kilter. This is the only way I'm going to get her to agree, and maybe I'm a bastard, but that's exactly what I'm going to do.

"To kiss my wife *as* my wife whenever the fuck I want

to." I press my lips to the corner of her mouth, a whisper of the kiss I just gave her. "Even if it's just my tongue right now, I'm going to get inside of you whatever way I can."

She sucks in a breath.

I press my finger to her lips.

"Come upstairs with me, Loni," I murmur. "Let me show you to your room."

I don't give her the chance to refuse. With my hand on her upper back, I help her heft up her gown so that she doesn't stumble on the stairs. I want so desperately to lead her into my bedroom—*our* bedroom—but I keep going until we're in front of the room that I designated as hers... for now.

Dropping a kiss to the top of her head, I murmur, "Sleep well tonight, princess. Your first full day as Mrs. Heller begins tomorrow."

SEVEN

EXPLOSION

TEN YEARS EARLIER

LONI

"Loni, sweetheart? Can you come down? We have company."

My bedroom door is open just enough that Dad's shout catches my attention over the tapping of my fingers on my computer's keyboard. School's done in a week, but I've always been a bit of an overachiever. Math's my subject, and while I'm going to get a good grade in English, Mrs. Rollo offered us an opportunity to write an essay about what we hope to accomplish in the years following graduation for extra credit.

I'm an Offering. My fate was sealed when I was born to parents involved with the Order. Still, while marriage is almost one hundred percent going to happen and *soon*, I have other aspirations. Attending the local Order-run college to further my education, joining some of the charities that the other Owed wives take part in... maybe getting a cat since Dad would never let me.

I'm just describing the kind of cat I've always wanted —an orange one without a single brain cell would be perfect—when Dad's voice calls upstairs.

Company? It's Sunday night. Who would be here?

I check to make sure that I look decent enough in case it's Order company, and when I flounce into the cozy den where Dad entertains his guests, I'm glad I did.

Holy shit. It's the *King*.

Jack Collins has been the head of the Order for as far back as I can remember. I know he only took over for the previous King around the time I was born, but Order politics didn't interest me when I was younger. I only really know who he is because he's Adrian's uncle.

And now he's sitting on our couch, holding a glass of some brown liquor, while Dad paces nervously behind him.

I stop short, viscerally aware that his green eyes—just like his nephew's—are on me.

Dad clears his throat. "This is my daughter, Avalon."

Jack's lips curve in a practiced, charming smile, but his eyes narrow just enough that I get the vibe that he's taking my measure—and that he doesn't like what he sees.

I gulp, but I've been trained. My own smile never waves. "Hello."

Avalon...

My dad is the one who named me 'Avalon'. Growing up in Harmony Heights, his father already a member of the Owed, he was fascinated by the idea of the head of the society being known as the 'King', surrounded by an inner circle that are referred to as the 'old guard'. I'm not really sure why, but it led to him developing this fixation with King Arthur, Camelot, and the Knights of the Round Table.

Mom let him do it, but gave me the nickname 'Loni' that they both used religiously—unless I was in trouble.

Uh-oh.

This can't be good.

See, Dad's always wanted to climb the ranks of the Order. It was his way of becoming a knight himself, but while he was at the right level to be given an Offering— and theirs was a rare love match where Mom actually wanted to be Claimed by Dad—nothing he did could break him into the old guard.

And then I was born. Well aware that I was destined to be classified as an Offering to a future member of the Owed, he saw me as his chance to social climb. If my husband was one of the most powerful Owed—or the son of one—then that would help Dad's status.

Unfortunately for him, I *did* catch the attention of one of the sons of a founding family. Adrian Heller. From those very first days of kindergarten, he'd teased me, bullied me, and made me cry. Everyone said it was because he liked me, but when all I'd ever done was say 'hi' the first day of school and share one of Mom's fresh-baked chocolate chip cookies with him, it didn't make sense to five-year-old Loni why he was so mean.

He got meaner over the years. *Crueler.* Up until senior year, I was convinced that I must've done something to him in another life for him to focus so intently on keeping me apart from the rest of the kids in town. I was an outcast, and Dad gave up on the hope that I'd be his ticket to a better job, more prospects, and an invitation to hang out with some of the most powerful men in Harmony Heights down at the Order's club, the King's Court.

"I hate that I have to disturb you so late on a school night," he begins, resting his ankle on his thigh as he leans back into our couch like it's his very own throne, "but once the accusations made their way to the Fortress... it's my duty to come and make sure they're founded."

I get a sinking pit in my stomach. "Oh. Um. What accusations?"

"I'm sure you're aware that there was a get-together at Guy Reynolds' home last night. That ne'er-do-well son of his hosted it, but I'm assured most of the senior class was there." The King pauses pointedly for a few seconds. "One of the future Oweds saw you there."

I can't deny it. "Yes. I went with my boyfriend. Desmond."

"Yes... but it wasn't Desmond St. James who you went upstairs with. No. Apologies. You *did* go upstairs with him... but I believe he was downstairs with the Heyward boy when someone heard your name being called through the door. It was obviously in the middle of... sexual activity. The other Owed saw you leave the room, hair mussed, fresh hickey on your neck... but he doesn't know who was in there with you. *Was* it Desmond?"

As I stand there, under their scrutinizing stare, it

takes everything I have not to slap my hand over my makeup-covered hickey. It's not like I can deny that, either, when someone obviously snitched on me, but all I can say is, "Desmond didn't do anything."

"Then who was in that room with you, Avalon?"

An Offering keeps her Owed's secrets. Even if Adrian can never Claim me—and, technically, he won't be inducted into the Order until the end of August when the Claiming ceremony is scheduled—I Claim him.

He doesn't want anyone to know about me. I can't tell his uncle that it was Adrian.

My father moves toward me, puppy dog look on his face.

"Did you sleep with someone last night? I know that many of the Owed can be... persuasive, honey. I was, too, once. Just like I know there are plenty of things two young people can do that wouldn't jeopardize your standing as an Offering... is that what happened?"

Poor Dad. It must be so embarrassing, having to ask his seventeen-year-old daughter whether or not she's sexually active, but when the Order rules our lives... it's not just about making sure I'm being safe, or that I know what I'm doing.

My virginity was what I was supposed to bring into my marriage, and without that... there won't be a marriage at all.

I'm not a good liar. I never have been. While Adrian's always said he's the type of guy to act first, ask for permission later, my mom taught me that I'll never get in trouble for telling the truth.

She's not here. It's only been a year since she got sick

and died, and while the grief is more a dull ache than a constant stabbing sensation, there are moments when I miss her so much, it's hard to breathe.

Having Dad's palpable disappointment choking me while Jack Collins taps his fingers against the glass that Dad must have offered him when he showed up to shatter our worlds again (and all because it's *my* fault)... this is one of them.

But he's waiting for an answer, and it's Dad I'm talking to when I whisper, "I know. Dad, I'm so sorry... but I did it."

He shudders out a breath. "But it was just the one time?" he asks hopefully.

No, Dad. It's been going on since September, and I've lost track of how often I told myself I wouldn't do it again, only to forget the moment Adrian turned his devilish grin on me...

Before I can bring myself to say a much more discreet version of my answer, Jack says, "It doesn't matter. The damage is done, Peter. All that matters now is who thought they could ruin an Offering before the Claiming ceremony?"

Oh, shit.

I shake my head. "I... can't tell you that."

"Loni..."

Jack holds up his glass, cutting Dad off. "Can't or won't?"

See? That's why he's the King. He must understand loyalty, even when I know I'm taking the fall for it.

But that doesn't stop me from boldly—with a touch of terror I hope I'm hiding well—telling him: "Won't."

He lets out a theatrical sigh that sends a warning shiver up and down my spine. "I was afraid of that."

And that's when I realize that this discussion?

It's only just beginning...

I THOUGHT THAT SITTING THROUGH A HALF AN HOUR OF Dad and Jack Collins grilling me on my sex life was the worst thing that could've happened to me after being caught with Adrian. Silly Loni. Sunday night, while I laid in bed much later, holding my phone open, waiting to see if Adrian might call... I had no idea how much worse it was going to get.

He never called. To me, that meant three things: the rampant misogyny in the Order meant that I was the only one being blamed for fucking someone before the Claiming ceremony so Adrian got off scot-free; his uncle gave him a pass because he's Adrian fucking Heller; or, the most likely one, he denied it, and since no one in Harmony Heights would ever believe that he'd stoop so low as to stick his dick inside Loni Dougherty, they figured the boy who took my virginity had to be someone else.

Took my virginity... that's exactly how the two men saw it. Like something precious had been stolen from me, and now that I wasn't pristine enough to be an Offering, I'd be demoted. To what? The King wasn't sure yet, and I think he was waiting to break me down enough to see who I gave it up to in order to decide my fate. There are some women who are married to Owed who have no ties to the society at all. I could be one of them.

Then again, there are the Used. Women who are good for one thing, and one thing only... and I just proved that I'll get on my back and spread my legs without the burden of a wedding ring and a marriage license.

To go from being a treasured Offering to one of the degraded Used? That was my biggest fear, but I guess I wasn't scared enough to keep Adrian at a distance once he showed an interest in me. He told me that, all along, he's thought of me as his. That, when we were younger, it came out like teasing, but now that we were grown, he realized it was because the thought of anyone else being able to have me fucked with his head. That there's a thin line between love and hate, and that he loved me.

No. He *fooled* me.

Because while I didn't expect him to call me after Dad sent me to my room so he could walk the King out himself, still trying to plead my case so we could stay members of the Order without him having to turn his only daughter over to work at the Court as one of the Used... while I knew better than to wait for a call that would never come, I at least thought he would say *something* when Desmond confronted me during school on Monday.

It was at lunch. I'd hoped that the rumors had only spread as far as the head of the Order, but I should've known better. If Jack Collins learned that one of the latest classes of Offerings was acting like a slut in an Order home, someone had to have told him. Someone who was at the party, who saw me leave the bedroom and either guessed or had their ear to the door so they could hear the way Adrian couldn't keep quiet when he called out my name.

Someone who must've spread it all over Harmony Heights because, in the middle of lunch, Desmond didn't come to sit with me. Instead, leaving me to sit at the table alone—*mortified*—as he announced to the entire sixth-period lunch gathered in the cafeteria that I was a whore and a slut and not worthy of being his Offering before he dumped me with a flourish, then, to my horror, accused Adrian of fucking me.

You could've heard a pin drop. Even people who pretended they weren't listening when Desmond yelled at me couldn't hide their interest when Adrian leaned back in his chair at the Heirs' table and laughed so derisively, I nearly crawled under the table and died on the spot.

Nope. Though I did shove my chair back and run from the room when he finished laughing before calling out to Desmond: "You don't honestly think that I would fuck *her*, do you?"

It wasn't a denial, but the amused laughter, as though it was *funny* to him, the idea that he would ever debase himself by choosing someone so useless, so worthless as to bestow his magical dick on? He didn't have to admit that he was fucking at all; that was just expected. A gorgeous future Owed with money, charm, and the respect of the entire school behind him... the bigger shock to me was that—if I can believe him—he'd never had sex before that first time we did.

And all because we had a senior project assigned

together during the first marking period, back in September. He insisted I go to his house to do the work, and on the third time over, he brought our computers up to his bedroom instead of his family's dining room. And while we ended up getting an A on the project, we didn't get any work done that day... or the next few while we focused on figuring out how to fuck better than that awkward first bounce.

I was his first, he was mine, but I expected him to pretend that wasn't so. Just like I knew Desmond wouldn't take it well if he ever discovered that, though he thought he was my boyfriend, he was really the cover for my relationship—whatever you call it—with Adrian.

All of that I could deal with... but when the rumors reached Haven and she met me at my car in the parking lot after a torturous day of school, her reaction hurt the worst.

Like Dad, she was disappointed. More, she was *angry*. And not because she found out that I'd been caught fucking some mysterious guy in Sebastien Reynolds's house. Oh, no. It was because she was supposed to be my best friend, and the second she knew it was me in there, it was obvious to her who the guy was.

For a heartbeat, I thought she'd be upset that I'd gone behind her back to fuck the Owed she would be Offered to in two months. And that just goes to show how I'd let my twisted fling with Adrian screw up the rest of my life that I believed that for even a single second.

Haven didn't want Adrian. Like me, she was going along with being an Offering because that's what we were both raised to believe was our duty. But despite her pedigree, she wouldn't marry Adrian Heller because he was so cruel to me. Hearing that I sacrificed my future for a boy who seemed to *hate* me...

That's why she was so angry. That's why she was so hurt. I didn't even *trust* her to tell her, and I don't think she'll ever forgive me for it.

Stupidly, I thought everything might blow over by Tuesday. Yeah, right. The gossips had only gone into over-drive after Desmond's theatrics on Monday afternoon. Everywhere I went on Tuesday, people pointed and whispered, all while Adrian was fucking *untouchable*.

No one knew it was him. No one but me. I kept his secrets, and he let me *suffer*. Dad locked himself in his office while Jack made up his mind about what to do with me. Haven refused to talk to me. Desmond called me names when our paths crossed, and Adrian acted like he was above it all.

Is it any wonder why I snapped?

That's why, instead of driving straight home after school, I got in my car and floored it to the outskirts of Harmony Heights, to the richest parts of a rich town, parking in Adrian's driveway and hoping like hell he'd come down to talk to me.

His Mustang was in the drive, so I knew he was home. Banging on the door, not even caring right now if his sweet housekeeper answered, I shouted his name.

Within minutes, the door swings in. Adrian lifts his eyebrows at me, though instead of slamming the door in my face, he steps out onto the wraparound front porch, closing the door behind him.

That's new.

Normally, he spirits me away inside before anyone can see me. I have to park a street over when I visit, then go around back. The fact that my car is in front and I'm not sneaking around... he can tell I'm serious.

Too bad *I* can't tell from the flat expression with the whisper of a smirk if he cares or not.

"Loni. I'm so glad to see you. You want to come inside?"

It's a casual invite, but I don't buy it. "No. Trust me. I think it's better if we meet out here."

He purses his lips.

That does it. "Yes, Adrian. In public. Where anyone might see me. Sorry, but after the last couple of days... we have to talk."

He reaches into his pants pocket, pulling out a crumpled pack of cigarettes. He flips the top, choosing one. He settles it on the edge of his lip, leaving it there while he trades the pack for his lighter.

Adrian sparks it, lights the tip, and breathes in deep. The tip of the cigarette catches, turning cherry-red as it burns. Exhaling, plumes of smoke filtering from his nose, he removes the cigarette.

"No one gives a shit what Desmond St. James says," he announces because, yeah, he knows exactly what this is about. "He's just jealous because he can tell you're not into him. He must've made it all up—"

I let out a hollow laugh. "Make it up? Did you forget what we did in that room? Because whoever knows... they know what went on between us."

"Us?" Another drag. Another puff. "He threw out an

accusation because I was with you when he went downstairs. It was a lucky guess. He has no fucking clue. Besides, don't worry about it. School's done in a week. You won't have to talk to half those people again. And now Des isn't your boyfriend, so, the way I see it, it's a win-win."

My mouth falls open. "How can you be so blasé about this?"

"Because it doesn't matter. The Claiming ceremony is in August—"

"There isn't going to be a Claiming ceremony, Adrian!" I explode. "At least, not for me. Not when the King decides to make me one of the Used because someone saw us and *told* him."

Adrian removes his cigarette again, leaving it between his middle and pointer fingers. "Jack knows?"

I nod.

"And... you told him you were with me?"

Would it have been so terrible if I had shared Adrian's secrets with his uncle?

"No," I tell him, my voice so ice-cold, it could be December instead of June. "And I'm fucking glad I didn't. That way, I can end this clean."

He surges toward me. "Loni—"

I dance away. "You think it's me you're ashamed of. Well, Adrian Heller, did you ever think that it's *you* that *I* should regret?"

His eyes flash. "Don't you dare."

"Why not?" That tiny sliver of emotion is enough to spur me on. "Be honest. Is that what this whole last year was? Some kind of... of... what? A long con? Is that it? You fuck me, make me fall in love with you, then ruin my life?"

The mask cracks just a little more. "What? Avalon, no—"

The explosion inside of me burns even brighter than his forgotten cigarette, smoldering between two shaky fingers.

And the fallout? It's massive.

Avalon. He called me Avalon.

No.

"I hate you." It's such a simple statement, but I mean it, and it's so damn freeing. I point at him, edging back to my car, tears swimming in my eyes... but at least I feel a small weight lifted from my shoulders as I begin to make my escape. "I hate you so damn much!"

And I never want to see Adrian Heller again.

How could I have ever thought that I loved him?

I *hate* him.

EIGHT

WHO DID THIS

LONI

hate him.

I hate him.

I haaate him.

Hm. Why isn't that working?

I'm lying in an oversized bed, the AC cranked so high, I've snuggled beneath the heavy comforter that—annoyingly—smells like vanilla and chamomile. Two of my favorite scents, and I could pretend that was a coincidence... I could be pissed that the bedding is refreshed as though Adrian often has female company... if it wasn't for the fact that nearly everything I own is in this room.

The luggage I brought with me from Bridgewater, stuffed full of the clothes I unpacked back at Dad's. My makeup bag. My laptop tote. My headphones. Some of the knick-knacks that decorated my childhood bedroom all relocated to this room in Adrian Heller's house.

In my *husband*'s house.

Of course. If I can believe Adrian, he spent the last two weeks prepping this room for me since he knew that —despite Desmond's name on the invitation—I would end up marrying *him*. That's what he told me before he finally left me alone in this room... but not before he insisted on unzipping me so that I could finally climb out of the monstrous wedding dress I've been trapped in for hours.

The first thing I did was pee. There was a bathroom one room over from mine, and he pointed it out since he seemed pretty set on the whole 'Loni needs a shower' thing. Being spiteful, I changed into a pair of sleep shorts and a t-shirt, did my business, then locked myself in the bedroom.

It seemed like an eternity since I watched Desmond's body buck as each one of Adrian's three bullets found their home in his torso. There's an old-fashioned clock on the wall. To my shock, it was barely after nine when I climbed into the bed. I was exhausted enough that I hoped I would fall right to sleep, but the clock is ticking, it's past midnight now, and I'm wide fucking awake.

The ring on my finger just about burns. Knowing that Adrian is the man who slipped it on there... I twist it, and even as I try to dig down and remember how much he hurt me, how much I've hated him over the years, I don't take it off.

I married him. I married Adrian Heller.

More importantly, *he* married *me*.

It was no accident. That's what he said. He waited years for me... *Four* years.

And I'm having a hard time believing that.

Adrian Heller isn't a liar; at least, not when it comes to me. Unless he's changed that drastically over the last decade, I know that much about him. He's honest to the point of cruelty, telling me his truth whether it'll hurt or not. I don't count the rumors he spread because, whenever I confronted him, he admitted to them, and that part was true.

The only thing I could never understand? Was why he would spread them in the first place. Why he *cared*.

Oh, he told me he loved me. Always in the heat of the moment, when his fingers were running through my hair, his dick inside of me, his lips marking me in the only way he could (or would). He admitted it like he was ashamed to feel such strong emotions for the girl he couldn't stop himself from terrorizing, just like I echoed the sentiment, knowing he would only see it as my weakness.

Who fell for their bully? I tried not to, but there were times when he was so kind... so sweet... so *consumed* with me, I found it easy to look past how mean he could be when we weren't alone. He was protecting himself, I believed. His status in the Order, his future as one of its leaders, and the Offering who would one day be his bride.

It was supposed to be Haven.

It was never Haven.

But it wasn't anyone else, either, not really—and I can't help but cling to that in the silence of this dark bedroom.

Because it's me. Adrian Heller refused to take an Offering at every ceremony he participated in over the years, but then Desmond tried to Claim me, and Adrian *shot* him.

He *killed* him.

And I've never been more turned on in my whole fucking life.

That's *my* truth.

I loved him once. Even when he pushed me away, I was drawn to him like a moth to a flame. I knew he would singe my dusty wings. I accepted I would only burn... but for as long as it lasted—for that whole year when he was *mine*—I allowed myself to love him.

And then, when he could've stood up for me for once... when he could've told the world that we had something between us... he stayed quiet. He kept me his dirty little secret even when the King himself called him to the Fortress.

Adrian didn't lie, but he didn't tell Jack Collins the truth, either. He let his uncle form his own opinions, and when it was all said and done, I knew there could never be any hope for Adrian and me. The most I could be was his mistress. He'd marry Haven because it was expected of them, and I'd be thrown to the rabid dogs of horny Owed who'd use me, wreck me, and forget me if I was lucky.

They'd chain me if I wasn't.

So I escaped. I ran. I applied to the first community college that popped up on my Google search, and I left Harmony Heights far behind me.

Only I thought I did, but I clearly didn't. And now, ten

years later, the life I once dreamed of... the life I fought so desperately to forget... has caught up to me. Like he said, I am Mrs. Adrian Heller. I'm married to the man who broke me once, but who killed to take my groom's place before I could become Mrs. Desmond St. James instead.

I should be losing it. Earlier tonight, when he was guiding me to this room, his hip bumped into my side. The heavy, hard bulge of his gun reached me through the lace and bulk of my dress. He's armed with the same weapon that took out Desmond. I should be afraid that he could turn it on me.

I should be—but I'm not.

He won't hurt me. Physically, at least; not the way Desmond did. But emotionally? I was always fragile around Adrian. Seeing him now for the first time in ten years, the guard I built up shattered the moment our eyes met in St. Catherine's.

The longer I lie here, the worse it gets.

Desmond made it perfectly clear that he expected to consummate our marriage as soon as he left the church. That that was how it was done in the Order. If that's the case, why did Adrian walk away from me so easily? I don't understand his motives at all, and hours after he slipped down the hall, I can't stop thinking that he went off to do something else.

To do some*one* else...

He said he wouldn't go after any of the Used. I want to believe him, but... shit. Look at him. The angelic boy he once was has turned into a man made of sin. I nearly swallowed my tongue when I saw him. He's so fucking *beautiful*, and I'm supposed to believe he's mine?

No. I shove the blankets away from me. Not mine.

I'm *his*.

That's the distinction. That's the way Adrian sees it, and when I think that? I might just understand him a little more.

Maybe.

Or maybe I'm just fooling myself.

Ugh!

I can't sleep. And maybe I'm just as crazy as he must be because I don't think I'll be able to until I make sure that he's somewhere in the house. That he didn't have Father Francis marry us in the religious ceremony before slipping out to do whatever it is he does. The only marriage certificate I signed had Desmond's name on it so, unless that can be changed, we're not *legally* married, though something warns me against ever mentioning that to Adrian.

It's a quarter after twelve. Padding out of the well-decorated bedroom in my bare feet, I tiptoe down the hall. Before, I caught him glancing at the first doorway on the right and assumed that must be his. The door was shut then.

It's open now.

Grabbing the doorjamb, I peek inside.

It's too dark to make out his features. Luckily, I grabbed my phone. Not because I had anyone to call—because, um, I *don't*—but because I used the flashlight to guide my way down the quiet, empty hall. It's still on. I lift it quickly, hoping that the sudden flash doesn't disturb him.

Adrian is definitely in bed. Even more importantly,

he's alone. Wearing a pair of low-slung pajama pants and nothing else, my gaze is drawn to his bare chest, watching its slow rise and fall as he snores softly.

I've never seen him so vulnerable. There never was a chance for us to actually sleep side-by-side together. Knowing that, in less than a week, I'll be curled up in that bed with him...

I shake my head. No. *No*. This can't work. Adrian and me? There's no way this can be my happily-ever-after.

I had a plan to get rid of Desmond. That turned out to be way easier than I ever thought it would be, and while Adrian is definitely a wrench I wasn't expecting, that doesn't change things too much. There has got to be a way to get rid of him before I'm in too deep.

I don't know what that is just yet, but I'll figure it out. That's what I do.

The girl that Adrian knew grew up. If he thinks he can just call the shots and I'll do what I'm told... well, he might just regret taking Desmond's place after all.

***

Knock. Knock.

"Loni, you up? Breakfast is ready."

Fuck.

I'm awake. To be honest, I barely slept at all. I crawled back into bed a little before one, got maybe five or six hours of fitful sleep, then gave up on it shortly after the sun rose. I slipped out to the bathroom again, freshening up before Adrian was moving about, and locked myself in my new room once more.

Two hours later, here he is. That's his voice calling through the door. The rap of his knuckles against the wood... I know that knock. If I don't answer him, it'll become more of a bang any minute now.

Breakfast. It was my bright idea to suggest that that be two of the meals I'm forced to share with him. If I thought that I could get this marriage annulled by not following the Order's archaic rules when it comes to marriage, I'd pretend to be asleep. But since I know that it would only piss off the King if I didn't play my part—and, even if I'm pissed at Dad for leaving me alone at the altar yesterday, I know that he'd be on the chopping block again if I test Jack Collins's patience—I take a deep breath, then call out, "I'll meet you downstairs."

"In the kitchen, princess. And don't be late."

I pick up the pillow behind me, launching it at the door. It hits with a muffled *thud* that doesn't do a thing, but at least I feel better.

I allow myself five minutes before I leave the sanctity of my private bedroom. I changed into a cozy t-shirt and a pair of leggings. Instead of those torturous heels from the wedding, I have on a pair of flat white sneakers in case I need to bolt. Without my car, that's basically all I can do. It's probably overkill, but I prefer to be prepared.

Which is why I also have my phone tucked in my bra, and my wavy hair pulled back into a low ponytail...

I walk into the kitchen, head up, hoping like hell he can't tell how nervous I am.

Inside of the kitchen, there's a small table. It seats four; compared to the massive table in the dining room, I get the feeling that this is where Adrian usually eats, leaving the twelve-seater for either dinner parties or, honestly, just showing off his obvious wealth.

The table is set. A pair of coffee mugs are placed opposite each other. Same with a water glass, plus a pitcher positioned between the two seats. A pile of pancakes is on top of one serving plate. Crispy bacon on another. A bottle of expensive maple syrup is next to the pancakes. Fluffy scrambled eggs fill a bowl behind the bacon.

Empty plates tell me where I'm supposed to sit: right next to Adrian, of course.

He's sitting in his seat, a scowl on his face, fingers tapping anxiously against the tabletop. He's coiled tightly, eyes narrowed a little as though he's in some kind of discomfort. A headache, maybe?

Either way, the charming bastard from last night has been replaced by an Adrian I'd hoped to never see again: a pissy, angry bully who was ready to say anything to remind me that I'm just not good enough for him.

I almost turn around. The Loni I once was would have. But now?

I step into the kitchen, the sole of my sneaker slapping just enough to catch his attention.

To my surprise, his scowl fades into an expression of... relief, maybe? Pleasure? I don't know, but he doesn't look as pissed once he realizes that I came down to join him for breakfast after all.

He beckons me toward him. "Come here."

Um. Okay.

I head toward the table. At the same time, Adrian rises to his feet. It's a shame that his bare chest is covered.

Just like how I changed, he's wearing a new suit, the buttons regretfully done up to the top. His tie is a forest green that sets off his eyes—though that could be the look of lust that flashes in their depths as he watches my approach.

He holds out his hand. "Give your husband a kiss."

I blanch, stepping back. "I haven't brushed my teeth yet."

He moves forward, laying his hand on my bicep. "And I haven't had a cigarette in twelve hours. So I don't give a fuck what you taste like right now. I haven't smoked. You owe me a kiss. I want it."

This is some kind of game he's playing. It has to be. There is absolutely no way that he's fiending this bad for his nicotine, but instead of telling me to fuck off and lighting up, he wants me to kiss him.

Only that's exactly what he wants.

Before I can shake him off, he shifts his hand again, finding the pulse point in my neck. I melt against him, bracing my arms on his hard chest, parting my lips to let him find out just how wicked my morning breath can be.

If I thought it would bother him, I'm way wrong. In fact, the kiss seems to last even longer than the one from last night, to the point that I find myself returning to his mouth once he pulls back.

He kisses me again, and when sense slams into me so that I pull away this time, he tightens his grip on my neck.

Adrian rests his forehead against mine. "Ah. Much better."

I shouldn't care.

I shouldn't ask.

I shouldn't—

"Hey. You okay?"

"Internet says it can take a couple of weeks for the nicotine withdrawals to end. First few days are the worst, though, so if I can make it past tomorrow, the rest will be a breeze." He strokes his thumb over my cheek. "I'll be fine."

He might be.

I'm not.

A pulse of pain shoots through me. I wince, trying to cover up the discomfort before he notices it.

Too late.

His gaze narrows on me. "Loni? What's the matter?"

I shake my head. It doesn't matter. He's always been a perceptive bastard.

Never looking away from me, he grabs the nearest napkin and dips it into the pitcher of water to his right. With an expression of pure concentration, he wipes away the thin layer of foundation I put on this morning. Last night, when I took off the heavy wedding makeup, I was disappointed to see that the remnants of the bruise Desmond gave me were still standing out on my face. Instead of purply-red, it was greenish-yellow. A healing bruise, sure, but obviously a mark that I still needed to hide.

So, instead of brushing my teeth this morning, I went to work with the makeup that made its way from Dad's house to Adrian's fucking *mansion*. Too much, and that would catch his attention. Too little, and the bruise would stand out.

I didn't want him to see it. I wish I could understand

why. If he saw it and didn't care, that would break me. But if he saw it and *did* care? That would be worse somehow, I think.

I can tell when he wipes away enough to see the bruise because he sucks in a breath, his cheeks hollowing as he lowers the napkin so that he isn't rubbing the tender skin more than he has to.

Tossing the napkin onto the table, he lays his hand flat, gripping it instead of reaching for me again. "Who did it, Loni?"

I shake my head. "It's nothing—"

A soft rumble deep in his chest, a warning that I'm wrong. That it isn't 'nothing'. "Don't make me ask again. Who hurt you?"

There's no point in lying. "Desmond, okay? So don't think me a heartless bitch because I didn't shed a tear after you killed him. If you ask me, he deserved it."

Adrian's eyes flash angrily. "He deserves far more than a mercy killing. Three shots, and he might've felt one. Fuck. If I knew... he would've felt the whole damn magazine before I let him die."

My stomach twists. It's not hunger. It's not fear at seeing the return of his murderous side.

It's arousal.

Shit.

NINE

RULES

LONI

Seeing Adrian Heller ready to kill for me again does something to me that I'm almost too ashamed to admit—even to myself. I hate him. At least, I'm pretty sure I do. He made my life hell for so long, then betrayed me. I lost everything because of him... and I'd forget all of that because he hates Desmond more than me?

I step away from him. When he lets me go easily, I know I made the right choice. Grabbing my chair, I tug it out, then plop down into it before gesturing toward the spread on the table.

"You cooked breakfast for us?"

Adrian is quiet for a moment. And then, with a hint of a smile, he asks, "Are you trying to change the subject, princess?"

Is it that obvious?

"I don't want to talk about Desmond," I say firmly. "If you do, I'm going back to my room."

"Without breakfast? You refused dinner last night. And Dallas told me you barely touched your lunch yesterday before the wedding."

How does he know that? Well, Dallas told him. Duh. Of course he did. Only... why does he give a shit?

I shrug. "If I get hungry, I'll eat."

Adrian purses his lips, finally releasing his iron grip on the edge of the table. He grabs both of the coffee mugs instead, giving me his back as he walks over to the counter. There's this big stainless steel contraption there. He fiddles with it, and after a couple of tense minutes full of awkward silence, he comes back with two steaming cups of coffee.

He gives me one, putting the other down next to his plate. Sitting down again, leaning lazily into his seat, he nods over at me. "You said one of the meals had to be breakfast. Count this as one of them. Now eat."

I figured that was his idea when he knocked on my door. And, to be honest, it looks pretty good.

Using my spoon, I scoop some of the eggs onto my plate. I swap the spoon for a fork, spearing two pancakes and adding them beside the eggs. Once I pour some of the syrup on top of the pancakes, I grab the tiny carafe of milk I just noticed. A splash added to my coffee, and I'm ready to eat.

Adrian, though, simply watches in approval as I make my plate. His own stays empty. He does pick up his coffee, blowing away the steam before taking a tentative sip. He nods, then sets it down again.

My fork hangs from between two fingers, hovering in the air. I waggle it at him. "You're not going to eat?"

He's not a morning person. Never has been in my experience, and I guess that's something else that hasn't changed about him—and he confirms it with his response.

"Normally, I get something on the way to the office. But this is special... our first meal as husband and wife. I got up and cooked."

He nods at the pile of dishes in the kitchen sink.

I scoff. "I hope you don't expect me to wash those."

I had a roommate once. We had a pact: if we share a meal, whoever cooks doesn't have to clean. I'd do the same with my real husband, but as far as I'm concerned, Adrian is just my business partner.

That's the conclusion I came to last night before I finally fell asleep. Most arranged marriages are really glorified business mergers, only instead of between businesses, they're between families. I'll do what's expected of me, but emotions? Feelings? *Love?* They have no place here.

I might not hate him the way I wish I could, but that doesn't mean I have to love him. At most, there can be a common interest in surviving the Order. That's it.

And kisses, I guess. I'm still not quite sure how I got roped into having to kiss him whenever he wants, but if that will keep smoke out of the house... I guess I can tolerate it.

The way he answers me makes me think we might be on the same page; at least, when it comes to me being his servant.

"I have a cleaning woman who comes in every other day. If I don't get to them before I leave, she will."

Oh. I mean, I guess I didn't really expect him to take care of this huge ass house on his own. Plus, the Hellers have always been mega-loaded. He grew up on nannies and governesses and a private chauffeur until he got his license. A cleaning woman would be standard, huh?

Still, I can't help but choke a little on my swallow of pancake at the thought of another woman walking around this house with Adrian in it...

Don't be jealous, Loni. You have no right to be jealous—

I swallow the lump of pancake. Then, in as casual a tone as I can manage, I ask, "A woman?"

"Yes. Mrs. Gammond. You remember her, don't you?"

Actually, I do.

The entire year of our affair, we had to find ways to be together without anyone seeing us. Sneaking away to my house was a no-go. My father's house is positioned in a cul-de-sac full of Owed families. We would've been spotted almost immediately if I brought him home.

But the Hellers had a secluded house on the outskirts of town. His parents were rarely home, either, so it was easy to use his bedroom when an empty classroom at school or the bleachers behind it weren't available.

I can count the number of times I ran into his parents on no hands because, yup, I never saw them any of the times Adrian let me into his home. But Mrs. Gammond? A kind woman in her early fifties back then, she was the Hellers' housekeeper.

"Yes."

"I poached her from my parents when I moved out. I doubled her pay, and she works half the time. It was a beneficial arrangement for the both of us. She'll do your laundry if you leave it in the hamper, and tidy up your room. Other than that, she'll give you your space while you get used to your home."

Home.

This is my home.

I'm not going back to Bridgewater. I mean, I already knew that. I mailed my key back to the landlord two days after I arrived in Harmony Heights and paid the rest of my lease out of Dad's account to apologize for breaking it so soon. Technically, I had a stipend from work because I moved there to be close to a couple of our clients, but since I also contacted my boss about a family emergency that drew me back home, I didn't want to use the firm's money anymore.

I'm just lucky that they let me return to full-time remote work while I 'take care of my dying dad'.

Hey. It's not a lie. That's exactly what would've happened if I stayed in Bridgewater against the Order's wishes. Now that I'm here and doing what's expected of me, he'll make a miraculous recovery, but for now... my Dad's health very much depends on this marriage with Adrian.

Partnership, I remind myself. And if I'm going to make this work until I can find a way out of it—especially since 'til death do you part' gives me a little wiggle room, and the life of an Owed is a lot more dangerous than I once thought it was—there need to be some rules.

We set some last night. Mainly because we discussed

some of the Order's laws, but I'm ready to set some of my own.

So, in between bites of a breakfast that tastes better than it has any right to, I tell Adrian, "I want to keep my job."

"If it's about money—"

It's not.

There is money in belonging to the Order. The Hellers, being one of the founding families, are loaded with a capital L. My dad is more than comfortable. I don't have to work, but I like the idea of having some independence while I'm playing the part of Adrian's wife.

I don't tell him that. That would make him fight against me just because I want it so badly.

Instead, I say, "I'm not going to just sit upstairs, waiting for you to remember that you married me. You have a job... you do have a job, don't you?"

"I'm a financial manager." A sly smile tugs on his lush lips. "All of the money in Harmony Heights goes through me."

Figures. Our fondness for numbers was one thing we had in common. It annoyed me to no end that, despite the two of us being in the same advanced math class, Adrian made it seem like I was a numbers nerd. The teasing got worse when I beat him on midterms senior year, even though he bought me ice cream to celebrate my high grade—then fucked me in the alley behind the ice cream shoppe.

I shake my head, knocking out one of my few positive memories of my time with Adrian. "That's what I mean. You have a job. I like mine, and it keeps me busy." It allows me to be independent. "If I can work from here, I want to keep it."

"Done," announces Adrian. "I have a study on the third floor that's my workspace from home. I can give you one of the spare rooms next to it to set up your own office. I'll stay out of yours if you stay out of mine."

I can do that. He told me during his tour yesterday that there were a few spots in the house that he preferred I didn't go to unless he was with me. The gym in the basement was one; the study on the third floor was the other. Considering my imagination still had blood on the mind and I conjured up some Bluebeardesque room full of Offerings he sacrificed to the Order, it's a relief to know that they were as mundane as his private work area and his testosterone-fueled playground.

"Great. And I was also thinking—"

"Hang on there. I know what's going on here." He leans back further into his seat, arms crossed over his chest. "You want to establish some more rules."

Took him long enough.

I nod. "I think it'll help this... arrangement between us."

"The word is marriage, princess. Say it with me. Marriage."

Dick. "Arranged marriage," I add, enjoying the fleeting annoyance that flashes across his face. "And I still think we need to set rules if we have any chance of making it work."

"I distinctly remember you trying to do that once before," Adrian reminds me. "Something about telling me I needed to wear a condom when we were both virgins in the beginning and not fucking anyone else. And when I got you to see my point, you changed it so that I couldn't come in you." He chuckles softly. "As if I'd waste a drop of what I had when it belonged to you."

I remember, too. That's how he convinced me that it wasn't such a bad idea if he didn't pull out. That he chose *me* to fuck that first time, and I was so stunned that Adrian Heller was still a virgin—because, even if he lied to get me on my back, it *worked*—that I let him do whatever he wanted. The two minutes he lasted after the most uncomfortable sex I've ever had made me sure he was telling the truth, but the more we spent time together, the better we both got.

And he came in me almost every single damn time.

I snort. "I was such a stupid kid back then. It's a miracle we didn't have a pregnancy scare."

"You wouldn't have been able to get away from me if I knocked you up." His eyes spark. "Maybe that's my plan now."

My stomach turns. Setting my fork down on my plate, I push it all away from me. "You want kids?"

Oh, God. I knew we'd have to have this conversation sooner or later almost immediately after I was forced to say 'I do'. To keep his position in the Order's upper ranks, he needed to be married by thirty. Check. The old guard prefers to see the young guys popping out 'heirs' so that the founding families don't die out. It's not a non-negotiable—it depends on the couple, their fertility, and whether they want to be parents or not—but I saw the spark in Adrian's eyes when I mentioned the word 'pregnancy' just now.

His shrug could possibly be perceived as casual, even if I'm not buying it as he asks, "Do you?"

Ah, fuck.

"I've never really thought about it before," I admit. "Not that it matters right now. I'm on birth control."

A muscle tics in his jaw. "What's the matter, Loni? Didn't want your boyfriend leaving a little something behind?"

Look at that. The return of asshole Adrian.

Okay. So I tried to fabricate a boyfriend so he'd see how insane it was to kill Desmond and think that he could easily take his place. When he called me out for lying later, it became clear that he didn't buy my 'boyfriend' story for a second.

So him bringing up my imaginary boyfriend now? He's fucking with me.

If that's how he wants to play, fine. "More like I wanted to fuck whoever I wanted without worrying about getting pregnant." I grin at him, enjoying the dark shadow that falls over his face at the reminder that he's not my only lover anymore. "I grew up, Adrian. Condoms are a must, but even they're not a hundred percent effective."

He takes a sip of his coffee, composing himself. When he finally does, his tone is still casual, though his body language is anything *but*. "What kind?"

"What?"

"Birth control. What kind are you on?"

He seems really fixated on this, doesn't he?

"An IUD. The one I'm on is a five-year device. This is my third year."

"Good. That'll work just fine."

What? "Excuse me?"

"I waited ten years to make you mine. We're young, Loni. We can have kids later. For now, I want my wife to myself. And maybe that makes me a selfish bastard, but fuck it. Unless you're ready to start trying now?"

Trying... of course. Like always with Adrian, it comes down to sex. He can 'try' all he wants, but my birth control will keep his swimmers from knocking me up... but the look of lust he can't quite hide tells me that he'll enjoy the process.

Mimicking his pose from before, I cross my arms over my chest. "I have to sleep in your bed. I don't have to fuck you."

Adrian shifts his position. Leaning forward, he perches his elbow on one hand, resting his chin on his other palm. "You think you can sleep next to me and you won't be begging me to climb on top of you?"

My cheeks flame, but I refuse to look away from the dare written all over his face. Jutting my chin at him, I tell Adrian, "I know it."

"Like I said. It's been ten years, princess. Don't you want to know if we were as good together as you remember?"

Yes.

"Pass."

He raises his eyebrows.

Remember... I think back, latching onto a memory that doesn't involve Adrian's body pressing against mine, making my toes curl as he pinned me in place, fucking me the same time as he kissed me until I was breathless...

Got one.

"Do you remember the history class we had together? Senior year? How you turned the entire class against me after Mr. Banks sprung that pop quiz on us and you blamed me? How I had to get switched out to Mrs. Andersen's class instead, screwing up my whole schedule so that I didn't get early release for half the year?"

It's one of a hundred little ways that Adrian messed with me when we were younger. Back then, he apologized during one of our stolen moments a couple of days later, but the damage was done. One flippant, off-handed comment from the most popular kid in class had Loni Dougherty an outcast again.

Just like always.

"I remember that perv was looking down your shirt every time he came by your desk to 'help' you," is Adrian's response. His voice is easy. The sudden hard look twisting his features is anything but. "I remember his casual offers to help you after school... you, Loni, no one else... and how he got caught fucking a junior the year after we graduated."

What? I... *what*?

"I needed you out of that class. And if it didn't happen the way it did, I would've had to involve the Order. He wasn't a member. He paid the price anyway when he targeted a different girl, but at least he didn't get his hands on you first."

I blink. "You did that for me?"

"You don't know half the things I did for you."

"But... you bullied me."

"I did," Adrian agrees. "Because I didn't understand

what to make of my feelings for you back then. I tried to protect you. I tried to make you untouchable."

"You tried to make it so that no one else wanted me... because you did?"

"Teenage boys aren't known for thinking with the head on top of their shoulders." Straightening up again, he leans toward the table. Adrian picks up his cold cup of coffee, taking another swig though his eyes never leave my face as he does. "Same for little boys who throw rocks at the girls they like."

I swallow. My own breakfast has gone untouched ever since my stomach went queasy. "You like me."

Adrian lowers his cup. "I don't like you, Loni."

"Then why the fuck did you marry me?"

His lips curve. "Good question."

I didn't expect him to say he loves me. If he did, I might've picked up my half-eaten pancake, slapping him in the face with the sticky, syrupy side of my breakfast. And yet... it's worse that he goes all enigmatic like that right after dropping the bomb on me about Mr. Banks.

I'm done. Yeah... I'm done. I ate most of my eggs. Some of my pancakes. As far as I'm concerned, I fulfilled my obligation. We had breakfast, and now that I have his word that I could keep my job for as long as I can, I have work to do.

However, right as I'm about to get up, his phone buzzes. For the first time since I sat at the table, he takes his eyes off of me momentarily so that he can pick it up. He had it facedown on the table, lost among all of the food, glasses, and utensils, and I never even saw it until he grabbed it.

There's a slight furrow to his brow as he reads the screen before he shakes his head, setting it back down.

I don't expect him to tell me what that was about, either. Even when we had some semblance of a relationship between us, Adrian was always so secretive. Especially when it involved the Order, and now that he's fully inducted into it, there's no doubt in my mind that that buzz has everything to do with the society.

I don't expect him to tell me anything at all—and that's why I'm so stunned when he looks at me again and says, "That was a text from Dallas."

Dallas. Not my favorite person on the planet at the moment. "What did he want?"

"Just to pass along a message. Seems like my uncle wants to meet with me."

Oh.

Wonderful.

TEN
BLOOD OATH

TEN YEARS AGO

ADRIAN

've already gone through four cigarettes.

I'm not a big chain smoker. I have a smoke when I'm feeling stressed; apart from sinking into Loni Dougherty, it's the only thing in this rotten world that calms me. But ever since she got into her car, tears in her eyes, driving away from me... not even the nicotine is doing its fucking job.

It would help if Jack stopped dicking around. He knows I'm out here. I told his secretary that it was important, and Alice simply smiled and said my uncle was a busy man, and he'd get to me as soon as he could.

I mean, fuck. Why not pat me on the head and tell me what a good doggy I am while you're at it?

Instead, I decided to park my ass in one of the chairs

outside of Jack's office. The Fortress is a no-smoking building, but Alice didn't say shit when I pulled a cigarette out of my pack and lit it up.

Her prissy face did pinch a little when I finished the smoke, stamping it out on the fancy carpeted floor. I didn't care. When Jack still wasn't available, I lit up another. And another.

I'm about to light up my fifth when, finally, the heavy door swings outward.

My cousin comes stalking out of the office, head held high, a red blemish on his cheek. I've seen that before. Dallas must've said something that his father didn't like. Because of that, he was backhanded, and the mark hasn't gone down yet.

He nods at me, and I see the fury in eyes just like mine. I return the nod, a silent promise that I'm here to cause Jack even more trouble.

I'll say one thing. My uncle knows better than to lift his hand up to me. Dallas takes it because he has a mental tally of every time his old man ever hit him, with the idea that he'll get his lick back tenfold when the day comes.

Me? If Jack even tried to discipline me the way he does Dallas, I'll burn the whole damn Order down. If my cousin gave me the sign, I'd do it for his sake.

I have the tools to do it, too.

That was Jack's mistake. Using my head for numbers against me, he tossed me at Stephen last summer. The moron was shit when it came to keeping the Order in the black. Within three months, I'd increased our portfolio by three hundred percent, and my 'mentor' became my subordinate as a seventeen-year-old kid became the head of the Order's accounting department.

Jack slapped a fancy title on me: intern to the financial manager, knowing full well that I ran that shit while Stephen went down to the Court to get his cock sucked. And while he seemed pleased to be keeping it all in the family—me increasing our wealth, while Dallas will have to succeed him one day—my uncle should've known better than to get me riled up when I've got the key to the Order's dough.

And that's only the beginning of the shit I know about the society. When I learned from an early age that knowledge is power, I've racked up enough that I've got dirt on nearly every powerful player in Harmony Heights.

I don't play fair. I never have, and I don't see any reason to start now that I'm eighteen. So my tactics aren't nice. So I've been called a bully and worse. I don't give a shit.

I have a plan.

I know what I want in life, and nothing will stop me from achieving it.

Not my uncle. Not my parents. Not Desmond, who fucked up in the first place, thinking he could turn Loni into his girl after all the years I've spent isolating her, making it so that when I did finally let her in on the secret of my obsession, she was so grateful for the attention, she didn't doubt that I had ulterior motives.

Of course I did. All I've ever wanted was her, and right when I thought that I'd done it... right when I thought that I'd Claim her at last in August... she showed up at my house, pretty hazel eyes glittering with tears, and told me that she would never be mine.

No. *No.* For a year, she was. I owned her, making her as addicted to me as I am to her. I got her to the point where she told me she loved me, and I only hoped that she'd get past the way I treated her—the way I *treat* her—in favor of our future together.

Fuck it, I had a *plan*.

The plan derailed when Desmond got involved. I thought I fixed that when not even 'dating' that prick kept Loni from sleeping with me. I owned her, body and soul, and I had every intention of making it official during the Claiming ceremony.

Jack thinks I'm going to accept his hand-picked Offering as my future bride. That was never going to happen. It was Avalon Dougherty or no one, and I decided that not even choosing to be a bachelor for the rest of my life was an option when I could have Loni as mine forever.

But then it got out that she wasn't as virginal as she was supposed to be. Of course not. I was greedy. I couldn't wait until the Claiming ceremony to deflower her. I convinced her to sleep with me a whole year earlier, just another step in a plan that meant she couldn't accept anybody else's Claim.

That, and I just couldn't wait to fuck her any longer.

She was my first. If I have it my way, she'll be my only, just like I'll be the only one for her. That's all I've been working toward... and Desmond ruined *all* of it by getting pissed off at being a fucking cuck.

He found out about us; if not him, someone else who

was at Bas's party. They know what Loni did in that bedroom with me, and because the Order is so fucking hypocritical when it comes to the women in the society, nobody gave a shit who the guy she fucked was. Oh, no. It only mattered that she did what no Offering should do.

And now she was being demoted to one of the Used.

At least, that's the rumor that sent me speeding right over to the Fortress, lighting up cig after cig until Jack called out that I could come into his office. Loni wouldn't be promised to one of the Owed. Nope. She would be given to whichever members wanted her... and there's no fucking way I'll ever let that happen.

Kicking the door closed behind me, I march into Jack's office. I've been in here countless times over my life. The expensive decorations are meant to impress his visitors. I barely notice them.

Why should I when my complete attention is on the surprised expression that seems way too damn false on my uncle's perfect face?

He'd deny it, but he's had more work done than my mom—and that's saying something. He's in his early forties, but you'd be hard-pressed to think he was any older than thirty. His deep brown hair doesn't have a single strand of grey in it (thank you, hair dye). His tanned complexion is the sort of waxy flawless you get from going under the knife. His lips are curved in a practiced smile, while his pale green eyes... his Collins eyes... tell me that I'm the last person he wants approaching his desk right now.

Too fucking bad.

"Adrian, my boy. What a surprise! I thought you'd be

getting ready for the big day. Only a couple of weeks until the Claiming ceremony, you know."

Oh, believe me. I *know*.

I swallow my rage, knowing that if I start this confrontation out with a temper, Jack will dismiss me as a silly little boy who can come back again after he's been inducted into the Order and he wears the brand of the Owed on his palm.

Then, when I'm sure I won't spit in his face, I tell him, "I heard a funny rumor at school this morning. Something about Loni Dougherty being changed from an Offering to one of the Used."

The whole class was buzzing about it. After the way that Desmond called her a whore during lunch on Monday, and then her confrontation with me on Tuesday, by Wednesday, she didn't bother going to school. Technically she doesn't need to. With grades like hers, she could miss the rest of the semester and still graduate easily.

But I want her there. I like knowing where she is, and keeping her where she belongs: within my reach. It bothered me that his obnoxious display hurt Loni, especially since—as far as I'm concerned—her 'relationship' was just Order PR. They wanted her and Desmond to end up together, all while Loni was sneaking off to be with me.

That prick is lucky that I kept my mouth shut when he insulted her at school. Sure, I got back at him by using my pocket knife to slash three of four of his Mercedes's tires, and I would've explained to Loni why I had to sit back as he degraded her... but she blocked me.

She *blocked* me.

I'll fix it. I'll fix everything. That's what I do, after all.

And it starts with making sure that Loni stays an Offering instead of a Used.

Jack gives me a small frown that's only a frown because his lips twitch downward. The rest of his face sure as hell doesn't go anywhere. "Yes. That's unfortunate. She was a very promising Offering for one of our new inductees, but rules are rules. Laws are laws. She knew better, but she's ruined now. I had no choice but to change her status."

"Ruined?" I echo. That's what he calls it? I knew how much stock the old guard put in having virginal Offerings, but come on. It shouldn't matter. It *doesn't* matter. And I'm not just saying that because I'm the one she gave her virginity to. As much as I treasure that, I want everything she has to offer.

And Adrian Heller doesn't share.

Jack doesn't seem to care that I'm fisting my hands at my side. "Yes. I have my suspicions about which one of you scamps had a taste. She's a pretty girl, but she should've made you wait."

Shit. "Me?"

"What? Oh, no. Not you, Adrian. To be honest, I believe it's the St. James boy. They were dating, after all. He must've realized she lost her worth after, and that's why he came to me, pointing out she didn't qualify as an Offering any longer."

That prick.

"It wasn't Desmond," I say.

I can't help myself. Hearing he's the one who was petty enough to try to get revenge on Loni by going to the King himself... I absolutely refuse to let Jack think that

Loni would ever let Desmond's dick get anywhere near her.

Jack purses his lips. "You seem very invested in the Dougherty girl. Huh. Are you sure it *wasn't* you, Adrian?"

I refuse to answer. If I say 'yes', my uncle would only use that as another reason to get rid of Loni. If I say 'no', I'm doing exactly what she accused me of: being happy to fuck her while keeping her my dirty little secret, like she means nothing to me.

So I don't say anything definite at all, choosing instead to tell Jack: "They're just rumors. You can't believe any of them."

Jack shrugs. "Maybe. Maybe not. I will say, though, that the girl didn't deny it."

She didn't? "Okay. Then who was it? Did she tell you it was Desmond in that room with her the other night?"

"She wouldn't say. Between the two of us, that just tells me that the little slut didn't know how to keep her legs closed. She probably doesn't even know who she was entertaining when she finally got caught."

That's bullshit. We were both virgins when I finally made my move. Since then, I haven't wanted to try out anyone else. And Loni... even though I knew she was technically Desmond's girlfriend these last two months, that was just a cover for our secret relationship. While I was sliding home every chance I got, Desmond was lucky if he reached second base out of Loni's sense of duty to the Order.

She honestly believed that, at the end of the summer, I would finish our fling and take Haven Smith as my future bride. And maybe I didn't do much to dissuade her of that belief, too worried that I'd scare her off with the intensity of my feelings... it doesn't matter. I'm formally Claiming Loni mine as soon as I can—

—even sooner if I have to.

Like, oh, *now*.

"I want her, Jack."

"What was that?"

Fuck. "Uncle Jack. I want to Claim her."

He seems slightly mollified at my concession. It irks the poor bastard to no end that I award his wife the proper respect—because Aunt Reese is a sweetheart who deserved better for her Owed—but he's only Uncle Jack when I want something, and even that is like pulling teeth for me.

"Her who? Haven. Of course. That pairing is already in our ledger. No one else will have the chance to Claim her until you do."

My buddy Connor might have something to say about that...

Luckily for him, I won't be standing in his way. "No. I don't want Haven. I want Loni."

Jack sighs. "Adrian. We've talked about this. You are a pureblood Owed. Your line goes all the way back to the first King in Harmony Heights. You can't just have any Offering—"

The hell I can't.

"Dallas is your heir, Uncle Jack. Not me. If I can't Claim the bride I want, then I won't marry anyone at all."

"You don't mean that. If you're not married by the time you're thirty—"

"I lose my future standing in the Order. Yeah. I know."

And I don't care one bit. "So think about it, Uncle Jack." I'll 'Uncle Jack' him to death if I have to. "Do you want me in the upper ranks with Dallas? Do you want me to keep working on the Order's books? Then you let me have this. I want Loni."

A flash of fury darkens his eyes, but Jack pretends like he's not currently fantasizing about throttling me. "She would have to accept your Claim. Will she?"

Good question. After the fallout from the graduation party, I can't say with a hundred percent certainty that she will. I've never seen her so hurt, and I've done fucked-up things. I've pushed her away, kept her alone, did everything I could so that I would be the one she eventually relied on.

Did I go too far? I might've, but that's nothing compared to how far I'll go to get what I want.

Nothing is safe. No one is safe.

Except for Loni.

"Give me a piece of paper."

"Think about what you're doing, boy," he says, even as he pulls open his desk, taking out a heavy piece of card-stock that he uses for moments just like this.

"Don't worry. I am."

Then, before he can stop me, I dip my fingers into my front pocket. I usually keep my phone in the back right pocket, but the front one? That's where my pocket knife lives.

With a quick flick, it's open. And while I told Jack that I'm thinking about it, that's a bald-faced lie because I'm not thinking at all as I slash down the center of my palm like a fucking idiot.

Recovery will be a bitch. Add that to how I'll be formally inducted into the Order next month right before the annual Claiming ceremony, the heated iron branding the center of my right palm. If my left hand isn't healed enough by then, I'll have two wounded palms, but it'll be worth it to be able to do this.

I press my bloody hand to the cardstock until a streaky red print is left behind on the page. I fist my hand, trying my best to stem the blood flow as I trade my knife for one of the expensive fountain pens Jack keeps on his desk.

I scribble my name and date at the bottom, then shove both the pen and the page toward Jack. "Seal it," I tell him. "By my blood, I Claim Avalon Dougherty."

There. A blood oath. It's rare, but not unheard of. One of the bylaws in the Order's charter, a future Owed can Claim their Offering before the Claiming ceremony if they swear it in blood. That way, if someone else tries to Claim her instead, my promise in blood is enough to overrule their Claim.

In the eyes of the Order, I'm swearing to take this woman, honor this woman, and protect her with everything in me. If she's in danger, I will save her. If I have to die for her, I will. If I have to kill for her, that's on the table, and the blood oath will mean I was justified.

I'd do it without the blood oath, but now that I have it... I'm one step closer to making Loni Dougherty mine for good.

Let Jack think I'm only doing that to spare her from the fate of being one of the Used. Loni didn't tell him that I was the one in the room that night. She saved me, and from this moment on, I'll dedicate my life to doing the same for her.

Jack sneers at the bloody print, but that doesn't stop him from grabbing the Order's notary seal and stamping it against his better judgment. "Remember, Adrian. She has to accept you. If not…"

I resent the implication that she won't. So I made her life hell. I admit it, and I only hope I don't end up regretting it. I did what I had to, and someday soon, she'll understand that.

"I'll make sure of it."

ELEVEN
THE FORTRESS

NOW

ADRIAN

I knew this was coming.

I guess I should be grateful that Dallas managed to keep Jack off my ass for as long as he did. I'd hoped for a little more time before he summoned me to the Fortress, but at least it's better than having to leave Loni at home on our wedding night in order to deal with my uncle's bullshit.

Not that it was much of a wedding night. The moment I decided that she would be forced to marry me at (basically) gunpoint, I accepted that it would be a rockier start to our marriage than I had planned for. It took me two years of slowly manipulating her behind the scenes before I switched up, flattering her in private, playing mind games with her until the first time I kissed her, letting her know that I considered her mine.

From our first kiss to our first fuck... I only had to wait about a week before I snuck Loni into my empty house, taking her virginity—giving her mine—in my bed because that's where she fucking belonged.

I have a King-sized bed instead of the Queen I grew up with, but even though it's wider now, I went to bed alone. It was a fitful sleep, every part of me fully aware that she was sleeping only a few doors down. And when I heard her tiptoe down the hallway, standing in my doorway, watching me 'sleep'... I had to grip the sheets beneath me to keep from opening my eyes, climbing out of the bed, and tossing her on top of it.

I had to do this right. Funnily enough, premeditated murder was the easy part. No one can blame me for it—at least, no one in the Order, and that's all that counts—but if I want to keep Loni, I have to follow the same tenets in the society's charter that allowed me to take her in the first place.

So that meant giving my Offering—my *wife*—her own room in the house. That meant not pushing her to spend every waking minute with me, and her sleeping ones, too, no matter how much I desired to. This is a waiting game, and if I have to take my time, convince her to love me again... that's what I'm going to do.

Besides, I thought I had two more years in my timeline. That fucker Desmond screwed up my plan—*again*—by deciding to Claim Loni at the worst possible moment. Tax season is busy for a financial manager, but heading into Q3 is just as hectic in my line of work. Add that to how I've spent the last two weeks waiting to hear from Nicholas Reed about the hit, having the decorator come to get Loni's room ready, and arranging to have her entire life relocated to Harmony Heights... I'm bordering on exhausted with a hint of exhilaration that everything went sufficiently according to plan.

And don't get me started about the goddamn nicotine headache that's pulsing inside of my skull.

Fuck. I knew quitting cold turkey would be a bitch. It's why I've never tried before. But I'm an opportunist. The idea of never kissing my wife just wasn't going to work for me, and if all she wanted was for me to give up my smokes, I'd do it... but only if she satisfied my cravings for a cigarette with her own mouth.

I don't know how I got her to agree. Just like the old days, I said it and she did it, and that gives me hope that I still hold sway over my new bride. I'll gauge the situation, take only what I think I can get away with, and eventually I'll have everything I've ever wanted.

But first, I have to make it out of the Fortress.

We live in Harmony Heights. It's a small town on the East Coast of the United States. We're one of the thirteen original colonies, but somehow, the Order of the Owed has revolved itself around this ridiculous idea of a monarchy. Our leader is nicknamed the 'King', our infamous bar and gentleman's club is known as the King's Court, and the thirty-floor skyscraper that stands out like a sore thumb in our downtown area is called the Fortress.

To the townies who don't have any ties to the Order, it's the Samuel E. Reynolds building, and I know that pisses my uncle off to no end. Even though his ancestor was as much a part of founding both the town and the Order more than two centuries ago, it's not the John B. Collins building. Nope. It's named after the first King of the Order—and mayor of Harmony Heights. That's Bas's relative, a fact my old friend hates almost as much as the Order itself.

Me? I just love how Jack did everything he could to be King, but he can't change the name on the most well-known office building in town.

Like always, I smirk up at the brass letters in front of it as I walk inside the building. We've been in the middle of a late June heatwave the last few days. I'm stubborn enough that I'm in a suit and tie, pointedly ignoring the dribble of sweat as it slithers down my spine. The blast of AC as I walk in is a welcome relief. I ruffle my slightly sweaty curls, shoot a meaningless wink at the concierge at the desk, then head for the elevator.

As King, Jack claims the top two floors of the Fortress. The Penthouse is his elaborate apartment, complete with a balcony on the top that overlooks a view of the nearby park, plus access to the rooftop. Right below it, he has his office. With a secretary/guard dog that blocks access to him, and more shitty art than you can imagine, half of the space is a waiting room, while the other is an office he spends most of his time in.

Richard is his latest secretary. Jack goes through them faster than I used to go through lighters, and when I take in the smarmy twink's smug expression, I decide he'll be gone by the Claiming ceremony. My uncle prefers his secretaries to be competent and smart, and if Richard thinks he can mug at me like that, he's a fucking idiot.

I salute him. "Afternoon, Dick. My uncle's expecting me."

His face falls just enough that I can tell he'd been hoping that this was another one of my unplanned visits. Since my personal office is on the twentieth floor, I get my shits and giggles bothering Jack whenever I have the chance. I know damn well, if I didn't hold the keys to my cabinets and the knowledge locked inside my brain to make sense of my ledgers, I'd be having an accident of my own one of these days.

I'm trouble. I always have been. I'd sooner see the crown knocked off the old blowhard's head, but since Dallas is stalling when it comes to stepping into his father's shoes, I continue to plot, continue to plan, and I make it clear that Jack Collins doesn't fucking scare me.

Some Order members live in fear of being excommunicated or, worse, tossed in the basement. What goes on down there... that's one rumor I haven't been able to substantiate lately. Only the highest-ranked members can get in since you need a passcode and a fingerprint to get past the level of security for the lowest floor of the Fortress. Years ago, there used to be auctions down there. Drugs, guns, girls... everything was sold to the highest bidder, but it was so hush-hush that only the old guard were involved. That got shut down around the time Aunt Reese... died. Since then, I joke that the perverted Owed have wrinkled orgies, plus bloody torture sessions where they kill any of our enemies in the shadows.

I'm not sure which is worse, and since I don't want anything to do with it—and I'm not in any danger of being locked down there—I ignore it. Without a wife, I'm not at that level to participate regardless. Dallas never wants to be. It's his father's business, and the less he has to do with Jack, the better.

Dick over there isn't the only one in the waiting room. Standing by the closed door that leads to Jack's office is a brawny, sour-faced man with bristly, short dark hair, and a perpetual scowl. He's shorter than me by about two inches—a fact that visibly frustrates Luke Wall—but he's almost twice as wide, the suit he's wearing so tight, it resembles a sausage casing on a beefy man my age.

Luke... Jack has plenty of enforcers. Order members who do his bidding for a brand on their palm, access to the Used, and living the high life in Harmony Heights. Dallas is one; training to be the King, his father says. But Jack would never use Dallas to intimidate me.

That's Luke's job.

He scowls. "Took you long enough, Heller. Mr. Collins wanted you here an hour ago."

And? He might have, but I only get four official meals with my wife a week. Fuck if I was going to miss breakfast because my uncle has his panties in a twist.

"Wish in one hand, shit in the other... let's see which one he gets first."

Luke's brow furrows, but before he can respond, I grab the door handle, pull it open, and let myself into Jack's office.

My uncle is on his phone, tapping away at the screen, a focused expression on his wrinkle-free face. He looks good. The newest surgeon touched up some of his work. If you saw him on the street, you'd mistake him for an A-list actor, which is only more annoying because, on the outside, Jack Collins has it all.

Power. Money. Looks.

But he couldn't keep a good woman as a wife, so I don't give a fuck.

"You wanted to see me, Uncle Jack?"

It burns. Every time I call him by that name... I might be twenty-eight now, but he insists on the title whenever we speak. Half the time, I refuse. But when I want something from him? Damn it, he's Uncle Jack again.

He finishes what he's doing on his phone before setting it down. "Take a seat, Adrian."

I'd rather not, but it's also not worth the argument.

I sink down in the thick leather of the office chair opposite of his desk.

He takes a lighter out of his desk drawer. "Need a light?"

My fingers reach up, touching the familiar rolled paper of my cigarette. I leave it tucked behind my ear. "Nah. I'm good."

It's a safety crutch and a temptation at the same time. I *could* smoke if I get desperate enough to light it, but just having it so close is a reminder of what will happen if I relapse.

I want Loni more than I do the relief from this awful headache. Besides, it won't last long. I've tried quitting before, but never really had a reason to. She *is* my reason. There isn't anything I won't do for her.

Except let her go.

"Very well. In that case, I guess congratulations are in order. I hear you're a married man now."

As good as. I did the whole church thing, and I've got the wedding license ready to be dropped off with the registrar down at the municipal building. I asked Loni her ring size over breakfast before I left. I'll have the custom ring started this afternoon, plus a belated engagement ring to go along with it.

So, yeah. I'm fucking married.

"I wish you could've been at the ceremony. It was a last-minute thing, though. Didn't even know it was happening until yesterday."

Come on, Jack. You had a hand in planning Desmond and Loni's wedding. You knew about it and never told me. Admit it.

He doesn't.

"From my understanding, no one was at the ceremony except for my son and the priest of St. Catherine's." He *tsks* his tongue. "Okay. I heard from Father Francis, and I heard from Oliver. Dallas, too. What's your story?"

What's my story? The goddamn truth, and I tell him exactly that. From the moment I arrived at the church, prepared to do anything to stop that wedding from playing out, and how I walked in, figured that just showing up wasn't enough, that I needed to *kill* Desmond so I could take his place, and after the panicked guests in the church cleared out, that that was exactly what I did.

Jack can't fault me. I had the right to do it, and between Dallas and me, it was cleaned up. The body was brought to an Order-run funeral home for a speedy burial; more than Desmond deserves, if you ask me. The church is pristine again, and a large donation from Mr.

and Mrs. Heller will go a long way to ease the priest's traumatic experience.

"Yes, Dallas told me the same." Jack taps his fingers on the desktop. "I know he was involved in this, and I'm not surprised one bit that my troublesome boy decided to interfere. But what about Sebastien?"

Fuck. Of course he's going to zero in on Bas.

I shake my head. "I don't recall seeing him around town lately."

"Mm."

Shit. He's suspicious. Connor has his hands full with Haven right now, so it makes sense he was staying out of it. But Bas? If I needed his help, he'd be there—and he was. No way in hell I admitted that to my uncle, though. Not when he's looking for any reason to get rid of him after what happened three summers ago.

Bas has never wanted to be one of the Owed. Coming from a family whose name is synonymous with the Order has been hard on the younger son, and I get it. Just like I'll protect him from his own sense of self-destruction if I have to.

So I wait Jack out. I'm an excellent liar because I only lie when I need to instead of with every breath. He might think I'm full of shit, but the only way he'll know is if I own up to it, and I'm not about to do that.

Finally, he sighs. "I've been on the phone with the St. Jameses all morning. They want someone to pay. An eye for eye, blood for blood. You understand."

I had been sitting easily in the chair, my body language projecting calm and casual. Suddenly, I lean forward. "Bullshit."

"Adrian—"

"No. That's bullshit. I settled with the priest because he got dragged into something that didn't involve him. Fine. But if Desmond's folks want to be compensated for the loss of their son, that's on you."

"How so?"

God, the way he can pretend like he's blameless… "I Claimed her, Uncle Jack. I made a blood oath to Avalon Dougherty, and *you* sealed it. Ten damn years before that idiot tried to make her his bride, you already promised her to *me*."

Jack's new surgeon is really excellent. He can even move his eyebrows now.

"But she didn't accept your Claim then."

"Because she *left*," I snap, losing my composure. "If she'd been at the Claiming ceremony, she would've." I would've made sure of it. "And yesterday… she married me yesterday. Isn't that accepting my Claim?"

"From how I understand it, she married you for the same reason she would've married the St. James boy: because her father's life was on the line. Would she Offer herself to you otherwise?"

I can't fucking believe this. This… coming from the man who tried to downgrade her from an Offering to a Used only to change her back. I know why he did it, too. For the same reason he did it then: because my uncle will do anything he can to keep Loni from me.

Hell, no.

"For ten years, I've been the perfect Order member. I do everything you ask of me. I've been loyal. You can't deny that."

I'm that good. He has no idea that I've been plotting against him just as long because, on the outside, it appears as if I've been falling in line all along. I didn't chase after Loni. I've thrown myself into fattening up the Order. We're damn near *untouchable* because of me.

I *deserve* this.

"I can't."

Good. "Then give me Loni. That's all I want." All I've ever wanted. "Let me keep her as my wife."

Jack thinks it over for a moment. I know he remembers the blood oath. He can't say that I'm not right. I won't go down for murdering Desmond, but he could easily decide to void my marriage because it's fucking Wednesday or something.

He's the King. What he says goes.

And that's why, when he tells me, "Until the next Claiming ceremony," I have to grip the chair's arms to keep me from launching out of the seat and grabbing Jack by the collar.

"What?"

"I'll let you have your fun, Adrian. But at the next Claiming ceremony, if she doesn't stand there and let you Claim her, you will accept the Offering I choose for you."

I won't. I can say that much. But if he thinks I'll take Haven after all this time when Connor finally has her...

"You see, there's a fresh eighteen-year-old who would be a perfect and willing wife for a Collins."

I blink. Set aside the fact that I'm proudly a Heller, Jack didn't just try to tempt me with an eighteen-year-old *kid*, did he?

"Not necessary," I retort. "I already have one. Remember? We don't do divorce in the Order."

"It wouldn't be a divorce. It would be an annulment."

No.

"Uncle Jack—"

His eyes flash in annoyance, a signal that I'm pushing my luck. "She was never meant to be an Offering. She was damaged. Used. Don't you understand that? I was saving you, Adrian."

No.

He was keeping me in line, and I *allowed* it.

Not anymore.

"If that's so, why did you let Desmond Claim her? Why did you make her an Offering again after all these years?"

Jack shrugs. "Because he doesn't have Collins blood."

"No," I agree, "but a Collins spilled it."

Just like when I refer to him as 'uncle', he enjoys it when I debase myself enough to acknowledge my mother's side. And it's not that I have a problem with Mom. Oh, no. It's her dick of a brother I can't stand.

"You're right," Jack says, a hint of a familiar smile tugging on his lips. "And that was my mistake. I didn't realize how serious you were about Pete's girl, but, in spite of all of this, you did sign a blood oath. I'll explain to Anthony"—Anthony St. James, Desmond's father—"that, in the eyes of the Order, you were right to do what you did. But remember what I said. One way or another, she's become an Offering again. She accepted Desmond's Claim, but blood oath or not, you didn't give her the choice before you married her covered in the blood of an Owed. She has to Claim you."

She will. She has to.

When I don't say anything in response to his pronouncement, he adds, "When she does, we'll host a reception for you both. And if she doesn't... Lily Ann is waiting for you."

She can wait forever. *Loni* is mine.

Jack stands up. Taking his cue, I do the same.

I know when I'm being dismissed.

However, before I go, I look across the desk at him.

"Will you tell her? That she's going to have to attend the ceremony?"

I need to know how to do damage control. As far as I'm concerned, this is just a stupid detail that I'm going to have to pivot around. Loni is my wife. Not even Jack will change that. But if she thinks she might have an out... it'll be a lot harder for me to convince her she wants to stay with me, wants to be my bride—

"No, Adrian." My uncle gives me a thin-lipped smile I know all too well. His lips part just enough to add: "You will."

Damn it.

TWELVE

MONDAY

LONI

Monday came way quicker than it had any right to.

I've now officially been Mrs. Loni Heller for a week. Officially... okay, it's not *official* official. We haven't received a copy of our marriage license yet, though Adrian made me sign that last week, so my license still lists my real name as Avalon Dougherty.

The fake that I've been using is gone. In the trash most likely, along with the hopes that I could go back to being plain, old, boring Marie Howard again.

I'm not. I'm Loni. According to my husband, *his* Loni. I'm wearing his ring, though he promises I'll have a bigger diamond and a better band once the jeweler he hired finishes the job.

Because, like me, Adrian had no idea that he would be a married man come June 24th. He figured it out right around the time I got that invitation to my own wedding, and because Dallas kept him in the loop all along, he made a plan.

He wasn't lying when he said it wasn't an accident. Over dinner last night, he even casually mentioned that he tried to hire an outsider assassin so that I wouldn't have to watch it as Desmond died in front of me at Adrian's hand the way I did.

How do I tell him that, once I got over the shock of it, I was kind of a little flattered that, after all these years, he still considered me 'his' enough that he killed my groom so he could take his place?

I don't, that's how. Because if I did? I'd be stuck. His vow that he'll never let me go... I have no doubt in my mind that he'll stand firm, even if I still don't understand *why* this is so important to him.

He could have anyone in Harmony Heights, but he wants me to believe that he waited for me? That, four years ago, he decided he would come after me once we were both thirty, and then I'd be his for good? That, with that decision, he's been celibate just as long?

I can't see how he's lying, but at the same time... how can that be the truth?

I don't know. I don't ask, and I definitely change the subject when he reminds me that I'll be spending the night in our room—because Adrian insists that his bedroom will eventually be *ours* the same way that this house is according to him—because, whether he thinks I've forgotten or not, I *haven't*.

For the last week, I've buried myself in work. I refused to speak to my dad when he finally got the nerve to make sure I was okay, though I did listen to his message and know that he is. I've eaten most of my meals with Adrian if only because he's a surprisingly good cook, Mrs. Gammond is amazing, and he has excellent taste in take-out when neither one is available to man the stove since he's assured me that, as his husband, it's his responsibility to feed his wife.

I think he's worried about me. I'm usually of an average size, but after I was forced back to Harmony Heights, I dropped ten pounds in two weeks from a combination of stress, nerves, a loss of appetite, and pure stubbornness that kept me going days at a time without eating so that I could avoid Dad's sorry expression whenever he looked at me. Most of that ten pounds came from my face and my ass, and it was almost as noticeable as the bruise that finally faded.

I couldn't hide the gaunt look to my cheeks with foundation, though I tried. And I might've been too nervous to eat that much my first few days, but once I got a little used to the idea of being stuck here, I ate if only to get him to shut up about feeding me.

Plus, I've been lonely for so long, I actually started to hunger for company almost as much as my next meal.

Even if that company is Adrian Heller.

I haven't left the house yet. For one reason, my car is still at Dad's. For another, I'm waiting for the whispers around my bloody wedding to die down a little. I remember what it's like to be the main character of the Harmony Heights gossip mill. It's not fun. I'd rather hide out until someone else steals the show.

I'm not a prisoner. I could leave, but I just don't want to. Eventually, I'll have to. Whether I agree with it or not, being an Offering—and the wife of an Owed—comes with duties and expectations that I'll have to fulfill if I want to keep this position.

And I have to. I have to be the one who wins. For Dad's sake… for mine… when it comes to this marriage, it's unfortunately 'til death do we part', but that death? It won't be mine.

Adrian married me. I'll make him regret it if I have to, but until I see which way the wind will blow, I have to follow the Order's bylaws to a tee.

And that includes spending one night in Adrian's bed every week.

Now, I don't have to fuck him in it. I just have to sleep by his side, but for me? That's worse. It's something I always longed for, cuddling up next to him after sex was done, but that was impossible. We were in the middle of a hidden affair. Pillow talk and snuggles were out of the question.

No. The most I got was a deep kiss, a pat on the ass, and a reminder that he'd be looking for me soon because, damn it, he was so fucking addicted, he couldn't stay away for long.

Silly Loni. I fell for it, too. I believed him. And while I was at least pretty confident that I wasn't one of plenty that he sought out when his dick was hard, I always felt so… so… *used* after. Before long, I ended every encounter with Adrian in the shower, as though I could wash myself clean.

I took one right before dinner, a reminder to myself that I can't forget the past no matter how much he thinks I should. There have been moments over this last week where, for a few seconds, I remember the boy I once loved.

The boy who broke my heart.

It hurts, even now all these years later, but if a casual phrase or a heated stare from my husband propels me into the past, what will his warmth, his scent, the feel of his body close to mine... what will that do to me tonight?

I'm not planning on fucking him, but I hadn't planned on doing it the first time he seduced me when I was seventeen.

Or the second.

Or the third...

I'm going into tonight with my eyes open and my legs closed. At least, that's what I tell myself as I climb into Adrian's bed wearing a t-shirt, sleep pants, and a full set of underwear. It's no chastity belt, but hopefully it's close.

Part of me hoped that I could knock right out before Adrian finished up whatever he was doing in his third-floor study. He had to do some work after dinner, and—with one final reminder—told me that I should wait for him in our room.

It's after ten, but I'm way too keyed-up to sleep. Any sound, from the AC to the settling of the large house, seems like Adrian walking down the hall toward me. I chided myself when he still never showed, but as much as I wanted to say 'screw it' and go back to the bed I've made mine over the last week, I refuse to move.

If I break the Order's laws, how will Adrian react? Will he tell Jack he made a mistake? I doubt it, but he's been so... nice this week, I'm afraid I'll see a return of the bastard who made my school years a living hell.

He's plotting something. Do I know what? Not even a little. That makes me more determined to find a way out without jeopardizing my dad's safety, and if I mentioned that it looks like the Order condones murder these days... who knows? Maybe Adrian will think twice about being a dick to me again.

Oh, no. I think he just wants to use his dick *in* me...

He doesn't hide his attraction to me. If there's one thing I can admit, it's that Adrian has never made fun of my appearance. He's drawn to it for reasons I've never quite fathomed, and it's obvious that he has every intention of sleeping with me the moment I give him any sign that I'll welcome him.

Well, he can wait forever, as far as I'm concerned. He used sex to control me once. I... I just can't let him do it again.

But, I tell you, it would be so much easier if I wasn't so damn attracted to *him*.

There's a lamp on the nightstand that I've kept on so that I'm not just lying here in the dark. When a shadow appears in the doorway, I realize that that was my mistake. If I wanted to pretend I was sleeping, sitting up, watching the door with the light on was a big ol' goof.

"You waited up. I'm so glad."

"Couldn't sleep," I say off-handedly.

"Mm."

He leans against the doorjamb, watching me from across the room. The light in the hall silhouettes him. This new pose draws my attention right to his chest. He must've started to undress on his way over because his jacket is gone. His dress shirt is unbuttoned, the flaps open, giving me sneak peeks of a delectable-looking chest.

His shoes are gone. So are his socks. He's in his bare feet as he crosses his legs at the ankle.

My mouth is suddenly way too dry.

My husband smirks at me. "See something you like, princess?"

Shit. He caught me staring.

I shrug anyway. "Just looking for the best place to stick the knife."

Adrian's smirk deepens. The prick is amused that I haven't given up on cashing in on that 'til death do we part' clause that I pointed out the night after we married. "You'd have to get close to me to do that first."

"I think I can stomach it."

He caresses his upper belly, highlighting his notable abs. "There was a time you couldn't keep your hands off of me."

"There was a time when I thought you were my Prince Charming," I shoot back. "Now I know better."

"Oh? Is that so?"

I snort. "Yeah. I'm married to the villain of this tale."

He chuckles darkly. "You're not wrong. If you had any idea how far I'd go to keep you, Loni... stab me if it makes you feel better. Just know that I'll make you lap up the blood." His eyes spark with undeniable lust. "I told you. I'll get inside of my bride again any way I can."

Except force me, and the longer I pretend that this marriage won't—*can't*—last, the more I wonder why he doesn't just bend the Order's rules in his favor to at least use the body I Offered to him by agreeing to become his wife. He could make me do that. He could make me do *anything*—and there isn't a damn thing I can do to stop him.

But this isn't between us and the Order. This is between Adrian and me, and he won't be satisfied until I've surrendered to him completely.

That's not today. Even if he wants to undress in front of me, showing off that mouthwatering body of his... not today, Adrian.

He knows, too. So, while he probably considers my gawking a tiny victory in this battle between us, he lowers his hands, reaching for his belt buckle as though simply getting ready for bed while having a chat with his wife.

In fact, his tone goes from sinfully wicked and promising to casually conversational as he says, "Do you know who Damien Libellula is?"

THIRTEEN
ONE WAY

amien who?

"No," I answer. "Am I supposed to?"

"Considering you were last in Bridgewater, and that's this little sweet town instead of a big, grimy city, probably not."

Hang on—

"How did you know—"

"So, Damien Libellula... he's this head of a mafia family in Springfield. It's a couple of hours away from Harmony Heights. A real criminal hotspot."

"So nothing like here, huh?" I say wryly, more than a little peeved that he ignored my question.

"Sure. But anyway, I have some... clients who are based in that city. I've heard about some of the stuff that goes down there. And this guy, Damien? He got married a year or two ago. It was a shock to his boys because they didn't even know he was dating anyone, but the kicker is that he wasn't. This gorgeous woman was stalking him, trying to kill him for some reason or another... he's a mob leader, remember, so that happens... and she ended up stabbing him in the side with his own knife. He didn't die, though, and he didn't retaliate."

"He didn't?"

I would've.

"Nope. In fact, he married her. She's the Dragonfly's wife now." Adrian rises up from his lean, slowly removing his shirt, all while adding, "I bet you're wondering why I'm bringing him up at the moment."

I'm too distracted by the ripple of his muscles as he takes off his shirt before dropping it to the floor to do little more than shrug again myself.

His hands drop to the waistband of his pants. "Just a reminder, Loni. Find a knife. Stab me if you want, but don't screw up like Damien's wife. Because if I survive it, a little blood won't be enough to make me stop wanting you. You'll be my wife forever, no matter what."

Forever.

Forever.

Forever—

"What are you doing?"

Sue me. I'm looking for a reason to stop the repeated refrain of the word 'forever' in my brain, and, oh... I found one when Adrian makes quick work of his pants. While he was talking, he unbuttoned them, unzipped them, and now he's stepping out of them.

When he reached for his boxer briefs next, the material doing absolutely nothing to hide the erection behind it, I panic.

He grins. "What do you think? I'm getting undressed."

"*Don't.*"

"Sorry, princess, but no can do. I sleep naked."

It's out before I can stop myself: "No, you don't."

He lifts his eyebrows at me. "And why exactly do you think that?"

Shit. I'm caught. There's nothing else to do but confess... kinda. "I was looking for a bathroom my first night here. I... I must've made a wrong turn. I passed your room—"

A slow, seductive chuckle. "And you peeked in, watching me sleep?"

"No," I lie. "But I might've seen you in bed because, I'm telling you, you weren't naked."

I would've remembered *that*.

"It was your first night here. In case you changed your mind, came looking for me, I didn't want you to feel any pressure. So I wore pants to bed that night."

And now?

"What made you change *your* mind tonight?"

"I've just about rubbed my cock raw since you returned to Harmony Heights. I let you get used to the idea that you're mine. I didn't push you because I know better. But you *are* my wife, Loni. And if you don't want me to fuck you yet, I won't. That doesn't mean I'm not going to hide how much I want you to let me."

With that, Adrian yanks down his briefs. His erection springs out, even more magnificent than I remember. He kicks the underwear away, stalking toward the bed, a daring look on his sinfully wicked face.

"Remember our first time? I do. Sometimes, when

nothing else gets me hot, I remember pushing you back on my bed, kissing my way down your middle, and fumbling to make my cock fit in your tight, little body."

"Adrian," I breathe out.

Crap. I wanted to sound firm.

I did *not* sound firm.

I try again. "Adrian—"

In response, he takes his cock in hand, stroking it slowly.

"I could seduce you." He twists his hand, and I'm helpless to do anything but watch the practiced motion. "I did once before. Come on, princess. I know you remember."

I do, but I won't admit it. Not now. Not while I'm crossing my legs under his comforter to hide how arousing his little display is...

Still, he's waiting for an answer, and for some reason, I feel like I want to engage with him. Almost as though we're having a simple conversation instead of just me gawking at him while he plays with himself.

"I was so worried that it wouldn't fit," I tell him.

He chuckles. "I didn't think I would last."

My turn.

"I thought someone would see us."

His eyes gleam in the lamplight. "I *wanted* someone to see us. Maybe not the first time because we were at my house and my parents walking in... fuck, no. But at school? God, there were times that I got such a thrill, thinking someone could walk in at any moment."

Really?

"You weren't ashamed of being with me?" I ask. Old

insecurities die hard, I guess, and I know I should drop it, but I don't. "I thought I was your dirty little secret."

Another chuckle, darker this time. "That's because you *wanted* to be."

No. I didn't.

Did I?

Adrian lets go of his cock just long enough to climb on top of the comforter, lying on his side so that he can look me dead in the face as he goes back to stroking himself provocatively.

I lick the corner of my mouth.

He rumbles out a groan.

And then, his voice low, his hand quick, he asks, "If I had asked you out like Desmond did, would you have said yes? After the shitty way I treated you? Or did you only crawl into my bed because you liked me being *your* dirty little secret?"

I shudder. I don't know if it's the rough way he sounds or how I just watched him crawl into his bed, naked and sexy and so goddamn irresistible, but instead of telling him to get lost, I whimper.

He releases his cock. "Oh, princess... that's a needy sound you just made. I think that answers my question for me." Reaching out, he slowly peels the comforter away from me.

I let him. I even do the unthinkable and uncross my clenched thighs as I shimmy down a little, letting him see the way my breath is rising, falling, faster and faster as his hand lands on my lower belly.

"I never got to be your boyfriend, Loni, but that's okay. I'm more than satisfied with being your husband."

I shake my head, the hair spilled on the pillow beneath me rustling softly.

"But I am your husband. And you're my wife. Aren't you, Loni? I Claimed you. Won't you Claim me in return?"

Through gritted teeth, I answer his sultry question with a snap. "I married you, didn't I?"

"Yes. You did. And you've spent an entire week as my wife. But this is the first time I have you in our bed, and while I planned on sleeping... how can I do that when my wife makes needy sounds like that for her husband?"

Sleep... how the fuck am I supposed to sleep like this?

Adrian thumbs the waistband of my sleep pants. When I lift my hips, wordlessly giving him permission because I must've fucking lost my mind, he slides his hand beneath them, patting the top of my aroused pussy.

It's all I can do not to squeal.

He rubs my mound, a curious look on his features. It's made all the more devilish by the way his lips quirk upward, his fingers playing along the edge of lace on my underwear.

"Tell me... if I slipped my hand inside your panties right now, would you be wet? *Soaked*? Your body getting ready for the one man... the *only* man... who ever knew how to make it scream for him?"

Two minutes ago, I would've slapped his hand, turned my back, and tried desperately to fall asleep with the pulse of my need running through my super-sensitized body. But that was two minutes ago.

Now?

I suck in a breath, let it out, then glance up at Adrian. "There's only one way to find out."

It's a dare. I know it. He knows it.

He doesn't care one bit.

It's permission, and I think that's all Adrian was waiting for.

Next thing I know, his hand is inside my panties, my back arched, and my body coming completely to life for him.

"God, you're so fucking hot. And *slick*. This... your body made this for me." He swirls his finger in the moisture before shifting his hand, bumping against my clit. "You want me, Loni. Don't deny it."

How can I? I've never been able to. My attraction to Adrian Heller's never been in doubt. Even though I shouldn't, I want him, and I guess that hasn't changed one bit.

When I don't, he eases a finger inside of me. It's been so long since I've had a lover—a year, maybe, or longer, I didn't keep track—and my pussy immediately clenches around the intrusion. I want it. I need it.

I crave it.

"Yes..."

"Told you," he says, the sound so smug, it erases some of my lust-fueled desire. "You were made for me."

I start to squirm, ready to get up and shove his hand out of my pants. I just manage to pull myself into a semi-seated position when Adrian follows me, pushing up from his lean.

He's still stroking me, playing with me, but now he

has one hand in my panties, slowly fingerfucking me, while his other goes to my hair.

Before I can say anything else, he blows a minty, cool breath of fresh air in front of my nostrils.

"I made it a whole week without a cigarette," he says, a hint of pride in his throaty voice. "Sure, I went through fifteen packs of gum to stave off the cravings, and I still get a slight headache every now and then, but it's one week down, princess. That means you owe me a kiss."

I open my mouth to remind him that I never agreed to that, but it's useless. I've kissed Adrian so many times this last week, all because he's working so hard to quit smoking cold turkey, that I've come to crave the way he conquers my mouth like this.

Only this time... it's a little different. Having his tongue plundering mine as he continues to pump his finger in and out of me, developing a rhythm... it's a complete onslaught, and I'm not naive enough to *not* realize that.

I might have given in tonight, but I don't want Adrian to think that he's won the war between us. If anything, it's just a single battle. A setback.

A mistake.

One I'm sure I'll make again before this... whatever Adrian and I have now... is over. But because I know it can't last, despite his certainty otherwise, I need to remember that there's a very good chance that he's fucking with me by, well, *fucking* me.

"I hate you," I say, groaning into his mouth.

In response, he inserts a second finger inside of me

while scraping his canine against my bottom lip. "No, princess. You only wish you did."

I do. Fuck it, I *do*. It would be so much easier to keep my distance if I hated Adrian. If the way he's panting softly, breath warm against my skin, fingers twisting, probing, stretching me... if I hated him, this would just stoke the fire of that hatred instead of having me seconds away from coming all over his hand.

Seconds... Instead of answering Adrian with words, he flicks my clit with his thumb, and that's just what I needed to *explode*. Clutching his arm, digging my fingernails into his muscle as I see stars behind my eyelids, I climax.

It was so fucking beautiful, I almost want to take back the way I told him I hated him. But then, as the blood stops pounding in my ears, all I hear is his voice telling me, "That's my girl. I knew you couldn't resist me."

Oh.

Oh.

Is that what that was about? He needed to prove something to himself? He wanted to see if he could still make me lose complete control with just one touch?

Ugh!

My hands are wrapped around his arm. Feeling a sense of spiteful pride when I see the divots my nails dug out of his arm, I tug and I yank, and Adrian slides his sticky fingers out of my pants.

Once he has, I shimmy to the edge of the bed, climbing right out of it.

Adrian props himself on his elbow, completely ignoring the straining erection lying against his hip. He has a lazy look of satisfaction on his face, almost as though making me come was all he needed.

It fades a little as he realizes that I'm adjusting my pajama pants as I head for the door.

"Where are you going, Loni? You're supposed to be sleeping in this bed tonight."

I know. Damn it, I *know*. But after the way I just let him fingerfuck me to an orgasm without once trying to resist him... and the way that, after all these years, he still has so much power over me...

Damn it!

Where am I going?

Where I always go.

"I'm taking a shower."

FOURTEEN
THE SHOWER

ADRIAN

Oh, fuck, no.

I usually pride myself on self-control, but when it comes to Loni, I don't have any at all.

I don't know where I went wrong. The whole time I was touching her, she seemed into it. She was as receptive as she used to be, and for a moment there, I felt like I was eighteen again, touching my first pussy and hoping like hell not to embarrass myself by coming all over my lower belly.

I wasn't full of shit when I told her I sleep naked. Now, could I have made an exception like I did her first night here? Of course. But with Jack's words from last Wednesday still ringing in my ears, there was no time to ease her into wanting to be my wife. The Claiming ceremony is in six weeks. I need Loni to be so addicted to me by then, the idea that she could choose another Owed won't even cross her mind.

Manipulating her body's response to me worked before. I know how to make her feel good, and even if her heart takes a little longer to get in line, if I have her pussy, I can have Loni.

So I seduced her. It made it even better that the more experienced Loni knew exactly what I was doing because that meant she made a conscious decision to *let* me. In the moment, I wanted to touch her so deeply, fuck her any way I could, just to get her to forget anyone else she ever had while we were apart.

But I screwed up somehow. I thought that giving her an orgasm and forsaking any pleasure of my own would soften Loni toward me. No, damn it. That couldn't be further from the truth. With the evidence of her arousal still on my fingers, she slipped out of my bed.

Shower.

She's going to take a shower.

Like she needs to rinse me off of her. As if she wants to forget the feel of my touch on her skin.

As if pleasure between a husband and his wife is somehow *dirty*.

Yeah.

Fuck, no.

I scoot my ass across the bed, ignoring the ache in my balls as my erection bobs, bumping into my hip. I know exactly which of the four bathrooms in the house is Loni's preferred one, and I all but jog right to it.

If she'd locked the door, I would've kicked the damn thing down. That she didn't bother tells me that she either expected as much from me, or she didn't care that I might follow after her.

Hoping it's the second, I throw open the door.

The shower spray is already on. I see her outline on the frosted glass door, furiously scrubbing her body.

Later, I'll blame that sight on everything that happens next.

Sliding open the door, I join Loni in the shower. She squeals, spinning around to face me. The soap bar drops from her hand. Her arms go up, covering her bare tits and the curls of her pussy.

Please. As if I haven't seen her naked before…

"Adrian? What are you doing here?"

My voice thrums with dark possession. "Turn around, Loni. Face the wall."

"Adrian—"

It's guttural now. "I said, turn around." When she does, *slowly*, I wait until her ass is in front of me before I drop my hands to her hips. "Place your palms against the wall. I've got you, but I don't want you to slip."

This time, she obeys me a lot faster. She slaps her palms against the tile, the position forcing her to either bend over or arch her ass out. As though she knows what's coming, she chooses the latter.

She swivels her head, damp hair falling over her shoulder as she glares up at me. "What's the matter, Adrian?" she says, the taunt in her angry voice evident. "Did you realize that I forgot to get you off and now you're here because I'm easy and available?"

Easy… when Desmond wasn't calling Loni a whore, he was telling everyone she was the easiest girl in Harmony Heights. It didn't matter that she never slept with *him*. That she slept with anyone at all made her worthless in his eyes.

If I hadn't killed him, he could be enjoying Loni's lithe body right now.

That image suddenly seared in my mind, more than anything else, is the reason why I grab my cock, place the tip at the entrance to Loni's cunt, and wait.

She doesn't try to get away. She doesn't shriek or do anything other than scoff.

"Yeah. That's what I thought."

But she's wrong.

"Not even close, princess," I grate out, resisting the urge to just slam into her. "I could give a fuck if I get off tonight. Me and my hand are old pals. I can take care of myself. But you... you let me get you off, then headed for the shower. I wasn't done with you. I figured, maybe this was your way of inviting me in."

Another scoff. "You can't honestly believe that."

I wish I could. When the alternative is that she needed to wash me off of her...

I push a little, seating myself inside of her. Loni goes up on her tiptoes, adjusting just enough to *take* it.

"If you want me to stop, tell me 'stop'. Tell me to get the fuck out. But if you don't, I'm going to fuck you until you remember every goddamn time I had you under me. I'm taking you up on that invitation that's only in my head. So if you don't want to fuck your husband, tell me."

She shudders. "I thought you were going to wait."

Another inch goes in. "A week is long enough in my opinion. Especially with you as my wife."

Loni pushes back, taking even more. "You're not supposed to force your wife to fuck you."

"I'm not. I'll withdraw at any time, but maybe you could stop sucking me in." I lower my head, allowing the shower spray to hit my back as I nip at her throat. "God, I fucking missed this. It's like a vice. You take me so well, and I'm only halfway in. Keep going, Loni. That's a good girl."

"What? *Why*? So you can tell everyone I wanted it?"

I pause. "Don't you?"

Her arms tremble. Her body shivers.

And she snaps, "*Yes.*"

That's all I need.

One thrust and I'm fully seated inside of her. She moans, the music a symphony accompanied by the shower hitting the stall beneath our feet. The rhythm of my heart chimes in, pounding, frantic, *fast*, just like the rhythm of my dick fucking Loni again and again.

I wait for her to say 'stop', but she doesn't. She clutches the tiles, fingers slipping off of the wall, but my grip on her hips keeps her in place. Honestly, she could let go and just hang there, and not a goddamn thing in this world could stop me.

Except for one little word that she never utters.

I knew I wouldn't last. It's been too long, and I needed this too much. Luckily for me, the orgasm I gave Loni in the bedroom has her primed like a rocket. In minutes, she's panting, moaning, squealing as I give her a second one.

I follow right behind her. Changing my hold from her

hips to her shoulders, slamming her down on my cock so that there's no escape from me as I come, I squeeze her to me until the aftershocks stop shuddering down my spine.

The second I release my iron-tight grip on Loni, a change comes over her. She stiffens, then straightens, and turns so that she's facing the shower spray. Without even looking up at me, she gathers some of the water in her cupped palm, then splashes it at her pussy.

And the same sensation that came over me when she said she was going to take a shower has kicked aside my post-nut clarity.

Again. She's washing me off of her *again*.

I let her finish, and when she turns off the shower, I wait until she's left the stall before I do.

Then I point behind me at it, doing my best not to let the rejection color my words any more than it already will.

"Let me make this perfectly clear: anytime you wash me off of you like this, like you're regretting being inti-mate with your husband, I'll mark you again. There won't ever be a time that your body doesn't know that it's *mine*. You understand me? I'll fuck you until you're begging me to let you come, and when you do, you'll plead for more until I'm dripping out of you."

She swallows roughly. "Even if I say no?"

I lift an eyebrow at her. "If I have you under me again, do you really think you will?"

Her expression is scandalized a split second before she turns around, giving me her back. A soft sob escapes her, but when I grab her arm, whirling her around to face me, all I see is hatred and defiance returned to her pretty, pretty face.

Damn it.

"You got what you wanted. Now let me go."

See, that's where she's wrong. I didn't get what I wanted at all. If I did? She would be falling into my arms right now instead of looking like she'd slash me with a razor if I gave her the chance.

I messed up. Not even because I fucked her, though I'd bet she'd say I'm wrong if I told her that. Loni... she was more than willing to fuck me. She could've told me to stop, but she didn't, and I know damn well that's because she both knew it would happen eventually, and she was *waiting* for it.

I wasn't wrong about that. If I got her under me with the intent to fuck, we're going to fuck. She would always accept me in the throes. I know her body too well. I can manipulate it to have her mewling beneath me until the word 'no' never crosses her lips. Look at just now. The only words I heard during our fast and frantic fucking were my name and 'please'.

She knows it, too, and *that* is why she's furious with me.

And while I don't point out any of that to her, I do say, "Don't try to fool either of us, Loni. We were meant to be together. So there were others. I bet you thought of me when they were fucking you."

"Adrian—"

My voice becomes darker. Deeper. "I think that every lover that came after me was a disappointment because you... your body... it's always craved *mine*."

Her eyes flash angrily. "You're being a dick."

"And you didn't disagree."

"Fuck you, Adrian." She grabs a towel, covering herself up with it. "I'm going to bed. And if you try to touch me? You won't see me in your room again until next Monday."

I guess I should be relieved that she's not using my momentary insanity to escape to her private room. Instead, she gathers up her pajamas and, without a look back, marches down the hall toward the room we had both just left.

I let her go, cursing myself as she leaves.

She didn't want to sleep with me. Or, rather, she had no intentions of letting me inside of her so soon. But once I was touching her, she started touching me, and then she tried to act like she couldn't wash me off of her fast enough... and the same Adrian I was as a kid, the cocky prick who thought I could do a piss-poor job of hiding just how much Loni Dougherty meant to me with a cool smirk and a cruel comment couldn't handle the rejection coming from the only person in this world I actually care about.

But I'm fucked up. I always have been. I show love in the worst ways, and while I tried to fix myself over the years, become the man Loni deserves... what just happened in the shower tells me that I have a long fucking way to go.

God, I need a cigarette.

The need for nicotine beats inside of me like a drum. But then I think about how I've used my willingness to give up my smokes to kiss her whenever I had the chance *and that she's been letting me...* and fuck the cigarette.

Luckily, I have other ways to work out my aggression. A round in the basement's gym, beating the shit out of the punching bag, might do me wonders.

Even if it only makes me more pissed off that, when I stalk past *our* bedroom, she doesn't stop me to ask me where I'm going.

FIFTEEN
VISITORS

ADRIAN

On the plus side, Loni was sound asleep in our bed when I finished with my second shower of the night. It was well past one in the morning when I took it, but there was no way in hell that I was going to return to my wife a sweaty, smelly mess after my gym session.

That's the plus side.

I wish I could say that she woke up the next morning, happy and sated and full of love for her husband. Nope. Rising with the sun, she got up to leave while I was still sleeping. I sensed her leaving and instinctively reached out for her.

Her response was to slap my hand, tell me not to touch her, and that she was tender from last night.

Ouch.

I wanted to apologize. I wanted to see for myself whether or not she was okay, but considering she escaped before I'd even pulled myself up, I have to hope that the rough way I fucked her in the shower didn't screw up my chances with Loni *that* bad.

She didn't join me for breakfast, but I honestly didn't expect her to. I left a message for Mrs. Gammond to bring a muffin and coffee to Loni's room when she showed up for work today, then had to head out to the Fortress so I could start mine.

And all that's a lie.

A coward. I'm a fucking coward.

I blame Jack. He put doubts in my head, making me think that Loni would leave me as soon as she got the chance. She won't Claim me, right? I didn't realize how much I was afraid of that until she headed for the shower and the rejection was like a blaring siren in my skull.

Now I'm going to have to figure out a way to make it up to her. Even if she was, she won't admit it if I had scared her, but the way I chased her into the shower... that was pure desperation on my part, plain and simple.

The Adrian she knew wasn't desperate.

The Adrian she knew wouldn't apologize... so maybe I should start there.

You can tell how unusual it is for me to admit any fault by the amount of time it takes me to compose my text to Loni. After closing the door to my office door, telling the communal secretaries on the twentieth floor that I don't want to be disturbed, I ignored the pile of work next to my computer in favor of figuring out the right words to send to my wife.

> Morning, princess. I had to head to the office early, and I think you were still sleeping when I left. Get your rest. Last night… I had a wonderful time, but I just wanted to tell you that, if I came on too strong, I'm sorry. I love you. I'm not perfect. I'll fuck up from time to time, and I want you to tell me when I do. So if I hurt you… I'm sorry about that, too.

There. Like me, they're not perfect, but they're a start.

I hesitated when I added the fact that I loved her before ultimately deciding it had to stay. No doubt she'll think I'm fibbing, that I'm only adding that to manipulate her like the way she accused me of doing when we were kids, but those words are my truth.

Whether she believes them or not.

I don't expect her to answer me. In her shoes, I might leave me on read. Does that keep me from holding the phone in my hand for a few minutes, willing her to respond?

Not even a little.

Eventually, I give up. I set the phone done, telling myself that it's my fault for fucking everything up, then reach for my mouse.

My phone buzzes repeatedly, multiple messages coming in quick succession.

I grab the damn thing so quickly, it nearly slips out of my hand. I swear to God, if it's Dallas or Connor or even Jack fucking Collins texting me right now—

> MY WIFE 🤍🤍
>
> You have nothing to be sorry for.

Whatever happened, I want you to know
I did enjoy myself.

But if you try that shit again next
Monday?

I'll bite your dick off :)

I laugh. From the threat, from the relief that she's not already hitching a ride back to Bridgewater, from the adorable little smiley face at the end... I laugh, and feeling a whole lot lighter, I set my phone down again and finally get to work.

I WORK THROUGH LUNCH, EAGER TO FINISH TODAY'S schedule so that I can get home to Loni earlier.

Mark dropped off a sandwich for me that I nibbled at before wrapping it up and storing it in my office fridge. Some people get super hungry when they're going off cigarettes, but it's been the opposite for me.

Unless you consider how much I'm craving Loni's taste, that is.

My body comes alive when I remember last night. I'm just grateful my office has a personal bathroom because I've been in there three times already, desperate to get the edge off. I'm already warning my poor cock that it's going to be a while until Loni lets us in again, but I'm glad that she didn't revoke permission for the rest of our marriage. Next Monday's going to suck, but there's always the one after that...

Still, I'm fighting another erection when someone

knocks at my office door. Sexually frustrated and annoyed that my orders to be left alone after Mark gave me the sandwich have been ignored, I snap, "Go the fuck away."

The secretaries are used to my volatile personality. Outside of the Order, I have to keep up the charming facade that made me one of the most popular kids in school. Inside? My job is too fucking important to be interrupted by bullshit.

But when the door eases open, a slightly familiar face appearing in the doorway... I don't think it's bullshit after all.

Huh.

"May I come in?"

The man in the thousand-dollar suit is thirty, maybe thirty-one. He has the kind of cultured, moneyed look that Jack's paid out of the ass for. His cheekbones are sharp, his dark blue eyes shrewd, and there's a closely cropped beard shadowing his chiseled jaw.

I don't even get the chance to invite him in or kick him out. As though taking my agreement as inevitable, he steps in, closes the door behind him, then stalks across the room.

I have one seat in my office. Half the time, Dallas is sitting in it, hiding from his father. The other half, I pile up my laptop bag and whatever shit I brought into the office from home to discourage anyone from sitting down and lingering.

Today, it's just my laptop bag. The man eyes it closely, lifts it, sets in on the carpet. Nodding at me, he takes a seat, totally owning it within an instant.

Interesting, I think.

Very interesting.

He leans forward just far enough to extend his hand. "Adrian Heller? I'm so glad we finally have the chance to meet."

Okay. He looks familiar, but... "I'm sorry. Do I know you?"

"We've spoken through a mutual friend, I think." His hand is still extended. "My name is Nicholas Reed."

Oh.

I take his hand and shake it. No wonder he looked familiar. I went on a deep dive, researching the Reed twins, and found a picture of Nicholas, in particular, on the website for Shadowvale Sanitation. Despite being a contract killer on the side, his day job was owning the sanitation company and lumber mill in his hometown.

"Nice to meet you," I tell him, lying through my teeth. He couldn't complete the job for me on time, but he can stop by for a visit? "What brings you to Harmony Heights?"

Sighing, Nicholas leans back into the chair. "I pride myself on my reputation. Mine and my brother's. I've come to apologize in person about a... miscommunication."

I tilt my head, listening. "Go on."

"What do you know about the Hummingbird?"

So we're not going to pretend that he isn't a hired hitman, then? Good. I hate beating around the bush.

"Enough that I tried to hire her first."

"And you know that she's a woman," Nicholas points

out. "It's widely believed that one of the most successful contract killers in my line of business is a man."

"What can I say?" I shrug. "I did my research."

About him, too, and if my unsaid threat is a little obvious... tough shit. I'm still annoyed at the lack of professionalism on his part, and I want him to know it.

"Yes, well, she's made an alliance with the organized crime syndicates in Springfield."

"I heard she married one of them."

Nicholas nods. "Looks like you really did do your research. Yes. She married someone high up in the Sinners Syndicate. You've heard of them?"

I wouldn't have if it wasn't for Johnny Winter trying to force Uncle Jack into letting him move his criminal enterprise into Harmony Heights by snatching a highly prized Offering... "Yeah. I've heard of them."

"And the Libellula Family, too."

Damien Libellula. The mafia leader who I mentioned to Loni the other night.

"Yup."

Nicholas nods. "Did you know she was hired to kill the head of the Sinners Syndicate? She ended up taking out Johnny Winter instead, but she never forgave me for telling Devil everything I knew about the elusive Hummingbird when he asked me my opinion on another hired killer."

Now that? I didn't know that. Though I'm glad to hear that Winter is dead—and I'll have to pass that along to Connor—I'm not sure why this has anything to do with me.

"Interesting."

"You'll see why in a moment," Nicholas assures me. Folding his leg over, poising his ankle on his knees, he steeples his fingers over his lap. "You see, when you tried to hire her, she was just getting married. So she passed your information along to me. I accepted the hit, but I had you down for July 24th, not June. My wife and I brought our little girl to Disney in June. I didn't ignore your contract. I had inaccurate information."

There's an underlying danger to the clipped way he speaks, a sense of darkness in his eyes. I pity the woman who goes home to a man like this, especially when I hear he has a young daughter. Disney? Nicholas Reed doesn't belong in Disney.

Then again, I don't look like I'd easily pull a trigger, and I did, didn't I? I killed because I had to, but I don't think that makes me a murderer. I've learned that Nicholas Reed and his brother, Hunter, only take hits out on people they deem worthy of death. Looks like Desmond fit the bill, and it was only a fluke that had Nicholas flaking on me.

"I'm glad you told me."

He nods. "I've cleared things up with the Hummingbird. Now I'm here to set things straight with you."

Nicholas reaches inside of his jacket pocket, pulling out a rectangular white card. Leaning forward, he hands it to me.

"What's this?" I ask.

"My business card. This number goes straight to my personal line. Like I said, my brother and I pride ourselves on our reputation. I owe you a body in a grave. You need someone taken care of, you call me."

That done, Nicholas rises up from his seat. Palming his business card, I shake his hand again, then watch him walk out of my office without another word.

Weird. He came all this way to talk to me in person when he could've just called me on the phone. Shadowvale is three hours from here; I know because I checked. He must have been *really* pissed off to discover that the Hummingbird got the date wrong.

Ah, well. It can't hurt to have a hired hitman in my pocket.

Reaching into my suit jacket, I pull out my cigarette case. It's empty because, while I refuse to get rid of the cigarette tucked behind my ear, I'm not a glutton for punishment. I can resist one. Twelve? That'll be a little harder.

Still, I've carried the same cigarette case around since my induction. Jack gave it to me, saying that I was a man now, and only boys kept their cigarettes in the pack they came in. I kept it because it's made of gold, and because I know my uncle. If I ever lit up and he didn't see it? I'd never hear the end of it.

Now? I slip the business card into the empty holder. Right as I'm tucking it into my pocket, someone else walks through my door.

From the leather jacket to the way he jangles as he walks, I know who it is even before I glance up at his face. Besides, there are only four people in this world who will just walk into my office, even if Nicholas Reed neglected to close the door behind him when he left.

Bas jerks his thumb over his shoulder. "Who was that?"

"No one important," I tell him. If I decide to use the Reed twins, I'll let my brothers know. Until then? "What are you doing here? I thought you were taking a ride out to the mountains for the week."

"I was, but Alexandre has to choose his Offering in a couple of weeks. Poor guy is flipping out. I told him I'd stick around for moral support, but he got so wasted last night, I left him home with our folks. Now I'm lying low in case he wants to go back to the Court again tonight."

I'm not surprised to hear any of that. Bas, Connor, Dallas, and I all had our reasons for missing the Claiming ceremony, year after year. Alexandre? He's a commitment-phobe, simple as that. He can't fathom the idea of having one woman as his wife, even knowing he can still visit the Used.

It's the *wife* part that Alex has a problem with. He just doesn't want to have one at all, but he'll be thirty in September. This is his last chance before Jack will be able to get an iota of revenge against one of the Reynolds.

Bas throws himself into the chair that Nicholas only recently vacated. "You're married now, Adrian. Any advice for my big bro?"

I can't help it. I think of what married life has been like so far, and my lips quirk upward of their own accord. "Let's just say, marriage has its perks."

Bas laughs. "Holy shit. You already fucked her."

Guilty as charged. "She is my wife."

He shakes his head. "Yeah, but if you need to get laid, all you have to do is join me and Alex at the Court. You didn't need to get hitched, buddy."

Someday, Bas might understand. Probably not today,

but that doesn't stop me from saying, "You're missing out... Fucking someone you love instead of a woman who sleeps with you because the Order says she has to... I'll just say this, Bas: you're really missing out."

His laugh dies, a strange look flashing across his boyishly pretty face. "Shit. You still love her. You still love Loni."

I give him a dry look. "Obviously."

Bas holds up his hands. "No, no. I knew you were obsessed with her. You *killed* for her." An echo of his earlier chuckle, only much more hollow this time. "Everyone knows you pissed Jack the hell off with the church stunt... and, yeah. Duh. You love her."

Yeah.

I do.

And if Bas knows it, I bet the rest of the Order will figure it out before long if they haven't already. And that should make my wife untouchable.

Should.

Too bad I know better.

SIXTEEN

HEATWAVE

LONI

have never, ever known Adrian to apologize. That, more than anything, makes me wonder if the last ten years changed him as much as it has me.

I'd hoped so. I didn't want to think that he was the same bully he once was, and considering my first impression of twenty-eight-year-old Adrian was as an angel with a handgun, murdering one of his oldest friends in cold blood, I was terrified that he changed for the *worse*.

But an apology? When that came through my phone, I was so stunned, I figured it had to be AI or something. Like he asked a computer to spit out someone else's words before passing them off on his own.

So I checked. I ran it through an AI checker, a plagiarism checker, and even Google. Nope. Unless he handed his phone off to someone else—and I've seen how possessive of it he is, so I doubt it—those were Adrian's own words.

I want to believe he meant them. At least then that would justify the second chance I gave him.

I figured the next Monday would be the real test. Sure, he brought me home a bouquet of flowers as a more visible apology, and we've still sat down to every meal together when he's home... and the kisses... whenever the craving hit for a cigarette, he was right there, demanding his due.

But that's as far as he's gone. As though he really understood the power his body wields over mine, he's been careful not to use it again. I was hesitant to trust him the next time I was duty-bound to join him in his bed, but apart from spooning me after I fell asleep, he was the perfect gentleman.

He even wore pajama pants again, a wordless peace offering for me that I accepted with a hesitant smile.

We've been falling into an easy rhythm since then. There are moments when I remember that this wasn't my choice, that in a world without the Order, I wouldn't have been forced into marrying my childhood bully... and there are moments when I struggle to separate this Adrian from the boy he once was.

Tonight is Monday again. We've had a good few days. Dad came over for dinner on Thursday. That was... interesting. In a way, I think he wanted to make sure that I was doing just fine. That, or he finally realized I'd been ducking his calls, and he that was being a pretty shitty dad, leaving me to Adrian Heller's mercy after he, you know, killed a guy.

I didn't realize how lonely I was until Dad came by. I've had a few conversations with Mrs. Gammond when our paths cross on the days she's here, but other than that, the only other person I've seen is my husband. If Adrian's not spending long days at the office, he's finishing his work in his third-floor study. I thought I was a workaholic, but long after I closed the lid on my laptop, he's still at it.

I will say, he does find a couple of hours for me every day. I've learned he has a fondness for watching the same sort of cooking shows I do; that's how he taught himself to cook, he tells me, and I'm only a little jealous that I can still barely hold a knife. A couple of funny sitcoms snag his attention, too, and we catch a couple after dinner before we head to our respective bedrooms.

He invites me to join him in the gym, but I pass. He likes to work out, I like to read, and as long as he knows that I'm safely inside of the house, he doesn't have to be up my ass every minute he's home.

However, the time we are together just reiterates how lonely I am otherwise. Being back in Harmony Heights doesn't help. I used to have friends here, a closer family, neighbors that I grew up around. These days? I just have Adrian.

Is it any wonder that I regard my positive feelings for him as some kind of Stockholm Syndrome? I mean, seri-ously... I should not be as giddy as I was that the bastard had the decency to send an apology text after pushing past my boundaries the night before.

And now it's Monday again. I was in a good mood, but after Adrian disappears after dinner, forgoing our TV time to take care of something for Jack Collins, I'm back on the 'Adrian Heller can jump off a bridge and I wouldn't even be sad' train. Especially when he presses a kiss to the top of my head, reminds me that he'll join me in bed when he's done, then leaves the house while I'm still fucking stuck here.

I could leave. I have a phone. My own cash. A debit card. Nothing is stopping me from grabbing a ride—taxi or otherwise—across town to get my car. I *could*... and yet I don't, and I try not to look too closely at that.

Instead of heading to his room, I stay in the living room, watching the big screen television while keeping an ear cocked for Adrian's return. Even after I start nodding off a little, the show I put on doing nothing to keep my attention, I stubbornly stay put. Only when I feel like I've been stood up do I finally curse under my breath and head upstairs.

ONCE AGAIN, MY STUPID BRAIN FORGETS TO TURN OFF. Even though I did everything I could think of short of taking a sleeping pill, I'm still wide fucking awake when Adrian slips into the room.

When he sees that I'm up, he flips the switch that turns on the dimmer light. It's enough that he can see me without searing my retinas with the stronger one, but when he gets a good look at me, he slaps the wall, triggering the brighter light.

"What's this?"

"Leave me alone, Adrian. It's too hot for me to put up with your shit tonight."

It is, and if I want to blame the fact that heat rises for

my crappy mood instead of him returning back to the house when it's almost eleven o'clock, that's fine.

Because I don't feel abandoned, why do you ask?

And I didn't decide to go to bed naked because I wanted him to regret leaving me alone this long, either...

Two weeks ago, there was a heatwave in Harmony Heights. We hit mid-nineties, and I was glad that Adrian kept the air conditioning cranking as high as he did. It would be humid and soupy and *hot* if I went outside. I used the nasty temperatures as another excuse why I didn't leave, knowing full well that I was avoiding the gossips in town more than anything.

It only lasted a couple of days. I should've remembered that the end of June is really only the beginning of summer in Harmony Heights because now that we just celebrated the Fourth of July a couple of days ago—when I joined Adrian in the back of the house, watching the fireworks from the park only a few streets down from where he... *we*... live—summer decided to make a vicious comeback.

Thermometers outside reached a hundred degrees. The heat index? We're talking one-ten, minimum, and even Adrian's power and money meant shit when the AC got overloaded.

It's hot. It's brutal outside, but even inside... I'm hot. I didn't even try to climb under the heavy comforter. I grabbed a sheet from the linen closet down the hall instead, using that as a covering. Beneath it? I'm butt-ass naked, and from the way his gaze has zeroed in on the length of leg poking out from under the thin sheet, he knows it.

And, yet, even though it's so much hotter in here than it has been, he looks like a sinful devil in his tailored suit.

Seeing that I've already stripped, Adrian starts to do the same. He kicks off his shoes first. The jacket goes next. As he starts to unbutton his dress shirt, he offers, "I could crank up the AC."

"I already tried. This is as cool as it's going to get."

He pauses. "A fan? Would a fan help?"

Probably not. "Don't listen to me. It's not that bad. I just got used to your house being like an igloo, so now that it's a little warmer, I'm bitching. Sex would be a bad idea right now," I add, just in case he starts thinking that a naked Loni means a horny Loni... and he'd be right, but I'm still pissed about being left alone so, yeah, that's going to be a no from me. "But if we're just lying here, it's alright."

"So you're not overheated already?"

I should've known that there was a reason he's asking, but the way he immediately showed concern for me made me more uncomfortable than I want to admit. "Not really."

"Good."

Adrian finishes getting undressed. Since I'm naked— and, whoa, and I'm regretting that boldness a bit now that he's here—it's a bit hypocritical to tell him to keep his clothes on so I don't argue with him as he strips.

I do, however, wish my stupid libido to heel once he slides into bed next to me, so close that I'm instantly flushing.

"My body heat too much for you?"

Prick. "I'll be fine."

"I might not be." He strokes my shoulder with the tip of his pointer finger. "Do you have any idea what you're doing to me, princess?"

Kind of, and it might even be on purpose. Not like I'm going to tell Adrian that... though odds are he definitely knows. "I'm just trying to go to sleep."

"You got to sleep last Monday."

Uh-oh. Danger, danger, Loni. "And now I want to sleep *this* Monday."

"You could... or..."

"Or what?"

His grin is full of wicked promise. "Just remember what I said two Mondays ago. Okay?"

Huh?

"Adrian. You're confusing me."

"So? You're tempting me."

Yeah... this was a mistake. Even so, I play dumb. "To do what?"

"This."

He throws his leg over me, the head of his cock nudging me in the thigh. He nips the edge of my jaw. The heat of his mouth sears me down to my core; his weight, coupled with his dick sliding upward so that it's nestled in the fold of my groin, has me desperate to shift my position so that the head would accidentally slip inside.

Just the tip...

Suddenly, I'm seventeen again. He could fuck me so easily, but Adrian Heller never needed to work to convince me to open my legs to him then. Now? He forced me to marry him. He made me his prisoner, whether that was his intent or not. I'm at his mercy, just like I always used to be, only I don't *have* to be.

Stop.

It hits me a second after I froze beneath him. If I tell him to 'stop', he will—but I don't. Instead, I start to wiggle out from under him.

A possessive hand lands on my hip. "Where do you think you're going?"

"My side of the bed," I snap, not sure if I'm more annoyed with Adrian—or *me*.

His face turns stricken for all of two seconds before he smirks. "Sorry." He's so not sorry. "You said you were hot. I was just outside. The temp in here isn't that bad, but I got it wrong, didn't I? It's not the heatwave getting you hot. It's the way you react to me, isn't it?"

Is he fucking kidding me?

"You're an ass. You know that, right?"

"All's fair in love and war, princess."

I glare at him.

His smirk widens into a flat-out dare.

I take a deep breath.

It's that smirk.

That fucking smirk.

Part of me is willing to do anything to erase that smirk off of his handsome face. The other part? It wants to touch him. Kiss him. *Fuck* him. It's the same part I was unable to resist when we were in high school, and I hate that all it takes is his naked body and that goddamn smirk to get a reaction out of me.

And, oh, does he get one.

Reaching low, never once looking away from him, I grab his dick.

Well, I got rid of the smirk. Then again, the way my palm wraps around his erection... the way his body jolts and his pale green eyes deepen... the sharp breath and the sudden need and desire he can't quite hide... I release him, but it's too late.

I'm suddenly Pandora and, oh, did I just open up a box.

"What was that? Here." He shifts his hips toward me. "Do it again."

I shake my head.

"Go on." He grips his dick, wagging it at me. "You want to. I know you do. Take it, Loni."

He's not wrong.

I fist my fingers. "That was a mistake."

Adrian's jaw goes tight. "It wasn't."

"Forget it—"

His hand lashes out. He circles my wrist, tugging me closer. "I won't."

I gulp. "Let go of my hand."

He hesitates for a moment before flexing his fingers, taking his hand back so that mine lands easily on the mattress.

I sit up, hurriedly putting some space between him and me.

A muscle tics in his cheek. "Get back here."

I shake my head. "We can't do this."

"Why the fuck not?"

I... I don't know. Like, I know there's a reason why I need

to resist him when I've never been able to before, but with his enticing dick right there, and the persuasive lilt to his voice, and my body wanting nothing more than to be close to his...

"I told you. It's hot."

His eyes spark. "That's right. You did. You also said if you just laid down, you'd be fine. So, come on, princess. Why don't you lie down?"

It's a trap. I'm not sure why I'm so certain of that fact, but it's a trap.

Even so, I slowly ease myself backward until my head is on the pillow, my back on the bed, the sheet adjusted so that my tits and ass aren't on display for Adrian to look his fill. I completely forgot just how naked I was before, but after that exchange... I'm intimately aware of that fact.

I frown.

He sees.

"What are you thinking, Loni? Tell your husband. I want to know." And then, to my shock, he shifts closer to me, brushing aside the sheet covering my body. Boldly, swiftly, he thumbs my nipple, sending a jolt of pleasure throughout me before I can even duck his touch. "Fuck it. I *need* to know."

Trust me, he doesn't.

What am I thinking?

I'm thinking about how I thought I could resist him, but I can't. I'm thinking about how I would've given anything to be right where I am now, but that was ten years ago. Today? I know it's Monday. I know the Order has all these ridiculous rules. But if I stay in this bed and he decides he wants to fuck me?

I'm going to fuck him.

I don't know why I'm depriving myself. I failed when I was seventeen, but I've since learned to separate the physical act of sex from love and affection for the person I'm sleeping with. True, I usually feel *something* for a guy if I'm willing to go to bed with him, and there's no denying that the chemistry between Adrian and me is as electric as it once was, but it's not like I'm declaring my undying love for him if I let him fuck me.

Right?

Besides, I *am* his wife. For better or for worse, I'm stuck. Adrian told me he won't go to one of the Used. He's not going to keep his hands to himself forever, and if he won't, why should I?

But I have to. Because while I can divorce sex from love, in the two weeks that I've been Adrian's wife, I've begun to think that *he* can't.

So what am I thinking?

Maybe it's my turn to tell him the truth.

"I hate how much I want to touch you," I spit out at last.

SEVENTEEN

TELL ME

LONI

"So don't," counters Adrian. He trails a finger along the curve of my bare tit. "But that won't stop me from touching you." Pulling away suddenly, gaze darkening as he props himself up on his elbow, he adds, "Unless my wife decides she hates that, too."

I wish I did. Just like I wish I hated *him*.

Instead, I mourn the loss of his possessive touch on my skin, and the unexpected grief has me pushing him, even though I know—we *both* know—how this will end.

"You'd stop?" I ask, disbelief dripping from my tone. "Just like that?"

"No." Satisfied that I was right, I arch my back, and Adrian? He takes my entire tit in his palm, squeezing it while I bite down to keep my moan from escaping. "But I would make you beg for it... make you *crave* the feeling of my hands on you... and then you'd stop this bullshit that you weren't always meant to be mine. Wouldn't you, princess?"

Damn it. Look at me. Like a cat in heat, I'm purring all because Adrian is touching me, making me preen. What the hell is wrong with me?

"I'm tired, Adrian."

"No, but you are trying to avoid your feelings."

I huff.

He lays his hand on my side, undeterred regardless. "What is it, Loni? You gonna be a good girl and let your husband pleasure you the way you deserve? Or will you just wait until I'm asleep to touch your pussy while thinking of me? Either way, I'll be the only name on your lips when you come. "

The way he says that... it's like he knows what helps me fall asleep some of the nights when he's down the hall and I'm nearly willing to swallow my pride and slip into bed with him.

Then again, this is Adrian Heller. He probably does.

He's trying to shock me, isn't he? To say things that will only rev me up so that I inevitably give in.

Well, two can play that game...

"Hey, don't worry about me. My fingers still work fine."

He takes my nearest hand, stroking the underside of my fingers. "Do you know how fucking jealous I am of them right now? When all I want to do is touch my wife... that's all. You can lie there like a motherfucking princess, and I'll be your willing servant. Whatever you want? I'll give it to you. Just let me touch you."

God, he sounds so damn *earnest*.

I *hate* it.

This game of his, that I've got any power... that *I* rule *him*... is laughable. He's one of the Owed. An Offering is nothing *but* that. I was given to him. To use. To fuck. To breed.

But he wants to pretend that he worships me?

Fine.

"I don't want your hands on me, asshole." He quirks an eyebrow, a slow smile spreading on his irritatingly handsome face as I snap, "I want your *mouth*."

"Anything for you, princess." He makes sure I'm flat on my back, then scoots me just enough so that I'm propped up on a pile of pillows at my back. Then, right when I'm about to tell him to forget it, that I didn't mean it, he smirks at me.

That fucking *smirk* again.

"Grab the headboard."

I flatten my palm against the fancy wooden head-board behind me. Suddenly understanding what he expects from me—that, if he can't use his hands, I can't either—I keep my other hand at my side, fisting the sheets in anticipation.

Adrian dives right in. The curls on my pussy don't bother him. The fact that I probably should've shaved a couple of days ago but didn't... he couldn't care less. Within seconds, he's already screwed up the unsaid 'no hand's mandate since he's using his fingers to open my pussy wide as he devours it, but as the pleasure washes over me, I can't find it in me to care.

Adrian was my first in this, too. It wasn't often that we had enough time where he could spread me out and lazily feast on my pussy, but I remember the few times he did even now. But this... I try not to think about how many other women he ate out over the years to make him this impressive at the act, but, God, does he know what he's doing.

Within minutes, I've given up on keeping my hands away from him, too. I have one hand in his hair, guiding him to go where it feels the best, while my other hand plays with my nipple, enjoying the sensation of having Adrian Heller's body between my thighs.

And then he stops.

Just stops.

I could fucking *kill* him for stopping.

"What are you doing? I was just about to come!"

"I know," he answers simply. His smirk has transformed into a wicked grin. "Tell me you love me."

What?

"Tell me, Loni."

He flicks my clit.

I shake my head, refusing him. That's not enough to help me finish, but I just... I *can't*.

He dips his finger inside of me, pulling it out just as quickly. "Tell me you love me."

"No."

A quick slap to my mound. The jolt has me gasping, but I. Need. More.

"All you have to do is say three little words, princess. I know you can do it." He dips his head, lapping at my pussy leisurely while I'm plotting murder in my feverish brain. "You used to tell me that you loved me all the time."

"I *lied*."

He chuckles and, damn it, that's still not enough. "Please. Don't you remember? I know when you're lying. You weren't then. You are now."

"Fuck you!"

"Loni, Loni, Loni... I'm trying. But you said no sex—"

I grit my teeth. "Then what the hell is this?"

"I call this teasing my wife until she admits what we both know: she loves me now. She loved me then. She'll love me forever."

He punctuates each of those statements with another devastating lick.

Damn it.

He's won.

Okay?

He *won*.

All I need is a little stimulation. And if he'll give it to me?

"I love you," I snap, grabbing the back of his head, shoving it against my pussy. I writhe against his face, searching for that little something I need to go off, hoping that I can before he makes me repeat myself. "Okay?"

His answer is a muffled, "Good enough," before he sucks my clit into his mouth, and the orgasm is so fucking great, I almost forgive him for the way he manipulated me this time.

Almost.

As soon as I begin to recover from my climax, a desire to show him that turnabout is fair play has me reaching for him.

Before he can even guess that I'm going to, I grab his

cock. Then, to both of our surprises, I drop my head to his lap, kissing his dick.

"Loni?"

"Mm?"

"You... unh... you don't have to do this." Maybe, but he's leaning closer to me. "I gave you head because I wanted to."

No. He gave me head because he wanted to deny me my orgasm until he made me say words I'm not sure I'll ever easily tell him on my own.

"I didn't expect you to return the favor," he continues, shifting again, thrusting into my hand.

Is that what he thinks? That this is tit for tat?

Ha.

"Just evening the score, Adrian." I lick the head, a leisurely stroke around the crown as his cheeks hollow, tendons standing out in his neck. He's gone still, waiting expectantly for me to suck him into my mouth.

I don't. Instead, I pull just enough away to peek up at him through the fringe of my lashes. I'm still holding him, though, and I *squeeze*. "Now tell me you love me."

I expect anger. If not that, then annoyance. A demand, even.

All I get is a soft chuckle.

"Oh, princess. You don't have to work this hard to get me to tell you what anyone with eyes can see. I fucking *worship* you."

Oh. Well. In *that* case... Letting go of him, I sit up, leaving his erection straining toward me as I rest on my heels.

His eyes suddenly go panicked. Ah, there's the Adrian

I know. "What the hell are you doing? Get back over her." He angles his dick at me, all humor gone. "Suck me."

"No, thanks."

Adrian growls. He fucking *growls*. "Suck your husband, Avalon."

Avalon.

I quirk an eyebrow, dare written all over my face. "And if I don't?"

"You said you wanted my mouth on you. I'll fuck your pretty pussy with my tongue. I'll lap at your tits. I'll suck your nipples until you're climbing on top of me, fucking yourself with my cock, looking for any relief. And then, when you head for the shower again... because I know you, princess... and I know how much it turns you on to have me at your mercy... I'll do it all over again. But while I'll be a selfless lover for you, my wife, sometimes I'll beg to have your mouth on me. This? This is one of those times. So get over here, take my cock in your pretty mouth and *suck* me."

Well. When he puts it like that...

"You're right, Adrian," I admit. "I really do love having you at my mercy."

And, to prove it, I grab his cock again.

He throws back his head, shuddering as a bead of pre-come appears at the tip.

I squeeze him at the base.

He's panting now.

"Please," he whispers, and I'd be a heartless bitch if I ignored the need in his tone. He's not commanding like before. He's *begging.*

I bow my head, swirling my tongue around the tip of

his cock again, gathering up the salty pre-come. I swallow while running my fingers up and down the length of his shaft.

He jerks in my hold, and I squeeze one more time.

Getting the hint, he settles down on the bed again, and I... fuck it. I start sucking his dick for real.

"That's it. Oh, Loni... my good girl. My good fucking girl. Yes. Just like that... *yes*— no. What are you doing?"

I've taken him out of the heat of my mouth, that's what I did.

I bat my lashes at him. "Quick question, baby." It just slips out, but at the moment... the pet name I gave him in the quiet of empty classrooms after school *fits*. "What will you give me if I let you come?"

"Anything," he pants. He jerks his hip. "Whatever the fuck you want, Loni, it's *yours*."

I'll remember that.

He thinks he can control me because he wears the Order's brand? Well, then, I guess I'll just have to control him by his cock.

It's the only leverage I have.

So I use it. Alternating between lapping at the head of his cock, sucking him deep, playing with his balls, and stroking him with as tight a grip as I can manage, I worship his cock, enjoying the way he pants my name like it's his favorite prayer.

"Fuck me," he hisses, propping himself up on his elbow. "Holy shit. You got a mouth like a fucking vacuum cleaner, you know that?"

I smile around his dick.

He palms the back of my head, guiding me to take him deeper. Since his touch is gentle rather than demanding, I let him. The groan that escapes him when I hollow my cheeks, sucking a good three, four inches of him?

It's music to my ears.

I keep going until Adrian starts bucking his hips a little, fucking my mouth. I know him. I know the signs that he's about to come, and though he untangles his fingers from my hair, I surprise the both of us by letting him explode right into my mouth.

After I swallow, I rise up on my knees, thumbing some stray come away from the corner of my mouth.

The daze in his soft green eyes disappears instantly. Almost warily, he asks, "For that little display... what is it you want from me, Loni?"

"Nothing," I tell him, and I mean it.

Honestly? I just wanted to have him at my mercy for once like he said—and, boy, did I.

Adrian isn't an idiot. He accepts that answer readily, a single caress down my sweat-slicked side a silent 'thank you'.

I curl up, my back to him, hiding my satisfied smile.

Panting softly, still lying on his back beside me, Adrian has only one last comment for me tonight: "Heading to the shower?"

Nah. Not tonight. "No need," I tell him.

I'm not sure how he interprets that. Am I avoiding the same thing that happened two weeks ago when he followed me into the shower, losing all control, and fucking me under the shower spray? Or have I—for tonight at least—gotten over my irrational urge to wash him off after we've been intimate?

It doesn't matter. Either way, he squeezes my hip. "Ready to sleep?"

With the endorphins rushing through me? "Yeah."

It takes a little effort since his legs are probably weak as hell, but Adrian eventually gets up, turning off all of the lights. Climbing back into the bed, he drapes his arm over me, snuggling close. It's still undeniably warmer in here than normal, the heat of his skin on mine burning me up... but I don't push him away even as he mumbles softly, "Love you, my wife."

I don't answer him.

But I don't tell him that I hate him again, either.

Why bother? He'll only tell me in that smug tone of his that I'm lying.

And, damn it, he'd be *right*.

EIGHTEEN

HAPPY BIRTHDAY

LONI

t's July 24th. I'm alone, and I'm *furious.*

I don't know what's worse: that Adrian doesn't think it's worth it to come home at a reasonable hour on our one-month wedding anniversary—or that it's my birthday and he has no idea.

You know what? That's a lie. I know which is worse. I know which one hurts more.

Happy fucking birthday, Loni.

Adrian...

He forgot my birthday. Even though I haven't been shy about it coming up—it was kind of nice to have something to look forward to—he didn't mention it at all. Not at breakfast, and not when he sent me a text mid-day that he got roped into an Order meeting after he was getting ready to head out. It was scheduled for six, and he was hoping to be done by seven.

He offered to pick up Italian for dinner; a lucky guess

since I used to go to this one restaurant with my parents every year up until Mom got sick. That mollified me a little... only it's now nine o'clock, and there's no sign of my *husband.*

I shouldn't be pissed. This last month, sometimes it feels like he's really trying to treat this marriage as legitimate. Others, it's clear to me that this setup is like nearly every other Owed-Offering arranged marriage I know of. He gets sex, I get a room, and we basically just exist in this oversized house, living two separate lives except for during meals and on Monday nights.

Funnily enough, I mentioned just last Monday that I was thinking about maybe spending an extra night with Adrian. I mean, it's inevitable. In my experience, the strongest pairings sleep in the same bed every night regardless—unless the husband decides to go to one of the Used. Since that's one thing I definitely don't want... and I've come to accept that I'm not going anywhere... why not slowly start integrating my way into his room while keeping mine, just in case?

And, no, the fact that I came up with the idea after Adrian laid me out on my stomach, propping my chest up on a pillow before climbing behind me and fucking me lazily for a good half an hour until a flip switched and he pounded me so hard that I had to brace myself against the headboard so I didn't go through it all while squealing his name wildly... nope. Not at all.

Today is Thursday. Monday was three days ago, and while I enjoyed the sex with Adrian then, the angrier I get tonight, the more I want to grab a Brillo pad and slough off my skin anywhere he touched me.

It's an unhealthy response. I know that. Finding pleasure in a man who worships my body the way Adrian does... it's just sex, Loni. It's just fucking. I've always suspected that Adrian used the act to control me when I was seventeen. I'm pretty sure that's what he's doing now.

Be a good girl, princess, and you can have your husband's cock... don't you want it? I know you want it—

Ugh!

I thought I was stronger than that. How did this happen? How did I let Adrian Heller worm his way under my skin like an infection I can't get rid of? I *knew* better. What happened to my plan of stabbing his gorgeous, sculpted, delicious chest the first chance I got and claiming self-defense? Anything to escape him before I did what I always do and let him in while forgetting all the reasons I shouldn't...

What happened? I know what happened. He smirked when he relayed the story about Damien Libellula and his murderous wife, making it clear that if I ever tried anything like that, it wouldn't change a thing about our situation.

More importantly, he'd *like* it.

What else should I expect from a man who decided the best way to get a wife was to *kill* the man she was promised to marry?

Desmond. Fucking Desmond.

Why didn't he leave me alone? I was content in Bridgewater. I liked my job, I spoke to my co-workers online and through text, and I had good relationships with most of my clients. Sure, I was a homebody, and the loneliness I've been experiencing in Harmony Heights didn't begin here... but if he hadn't decided to Claim me the way he had, none of this would've happened. I never would've been (basically) dragged back to Harmony Heights by Dallas Collins, and Adrian Heller would just be the ghost that continued to torment me long after I walked away from him, crying.

And who the hell am I fooling? Not me.

I blame Desmond—and it's easy to, dead or not—because I know the truth now. I was never safe from this fate. Adrian told me about his plan. Once I was thirty, once we both aged out of the Order's ridiculous mandate, he had every intention of finding me and making me his wife, with the Order backing him or not. And since he was purposely aging out of the Order's laws... it would definitely be *not*.

I was so stunned when he casually mentioned that over dinner one night that, despite having a mouth that tasted like garlic chicken, I reached over the table and kissed him. It was the first—and only—kiss I've initiated with Adrian, and it was like something shifted between us at that moment.

If he did that, it would've led to his demotion within the Order. Because he's blood, Jack wouldn't get rid of him, but his days as the kingmaker, pulling strings behind the scenes like he's always done... they would be over.

Because of me. Because, for once, he planned on choosing *me* over the secret society that owns us all.

At least, that's what he led me to believe. I know better now.

For a man who seems insistent that I'm his... that I've

always been his… things like *forgetting my fucking birthday* seem to suggest otherwise.

I can't believe it.

Am I being ridiculous, holding this against him? Probably. About two months ago, I had every intention of putting in a little PTO, booking myself a facial at one of the spas I'd been researching, and getting day drunk on a bottle of rosé. It's positively selfish, and I'd been looking forward to it.

Over the last few days, feeling like we were getting closer and closer, I foolishly started to really look forward to spending my birthday with Adrian. Though, considering he's ruined so many of them when I was younger, that might've been a huge mistake…

The year I turned ten, Adrian threw a pool party for no other reason than he suggested it would be fun. Everybody in our class went to his house. The only exception was Haven, and we had a slumber party where we played with an Ouija board and tried to curse Adrian's hair to fall out.

When I was thirteen, I tried hosting my first boy-girl party. This time, he let me have it, and I was having so much fun… until Adrian and the other Heirs showed up uninvited, and I became an outcast at my own party.

I didn't have a sweet sixteen because my mom was sick. That didn't stop him from sending me a bouquet of flowers, signed with a heart and his initials, as though mocking me for turning sixteen without any fanfare.

At least, that's how I interpreted the gesture back then. Now… I was just starting to see a different side of Adrian Heller only to realize that, no, I pinned him down perfectly, and I was an idiot to think he could ever change.

That's the worst part of sitting here, stewing over the last month. I didn't want to think that our relationship was—like it was back then—purely about sex. That Adrian Heller was attracted to my body in a way that didn't quite make sense to me, but when it comes to the person inside, he couldn't care less about Loni.

This proves it.

I grab my phone, making a decision.

If he doesn't want to celebrate my birthday, that's fine.

I'll celebrate it on my own.

IT'S BEEN A LONG TIME SINCE I'VE GIVEN IN TO MY PETTY side, but hell if I'm not enjoying it.

Living on my own at eighteen wasn't as easy as I thought it would be. Having money and Dad's silent support was definitely a privilege that most people don't have, but it was rough. I went from knowing everyone in town and being wary of all of them to being a new face without any baggage.

Once I realized that, it was super fucking freeing. The Order didn't chase me out of Harmony Heights... *yet*... and without my past following behind me like a big, black cloud, I could be anyone that I wanted without my real name weighing me down.

And Marie Howard could be a petty bitch once she was allowed to be.

Back home, once again Loni Dougherty—or, as my

husband insists, Loni *Heller*—I struggled; my forced marriage and my magnetic pull toward my former bully definitely didn't help. Tonight, though? I'm hurt enough that I let the petty take over.

Which is precisely why I decided to leave the house.

Except for a couple of walks when it cooled down a little, I haven't really gone outside. It's not that big a deal for me. In Bridgewater, heading downstairs to get my mail was a notable event. Hiding behind the front door of Adrian's home was no real adjustment at all.

Could I leave? That's something that Adrian answered shortly after he moved me in. Of course I could. I wasn't a captive. I wasn't a prisoner. I was his wife... just a wife whose SUV is conveniently still parked at my dad's house.

If he thought that would trap me, he has his head so far up the Order's ass that he forgets how the real world works. I mean, it's pretty damn obvious he doesn't want me going anywhere, but to think that I can't... hey. When there's a will, there's a way, and I was super fucking willing to stick my middle finger up at Adrian however I could.

Well, no. That's being a little *too* petty. I respect his position in the Order, even if I don't like it. Cheating on him wouldn't just embarrass him; it could be a death sentence for me if he petitions Jack Collins and uses my infidelity against me. There aren't any Used for the Offering. Oh, no. Once we're married to an Owed, that's it—or else.

But ordering a ride and paying for the driver to bring me to the King's Court, that's *perfect*.

Technically, anyone affiliated with the Order is allowed entry. One of the Owed flashes their brand, and since the Used work out of the club, security recognizes them. I was a little worried that I'd have to namedrop Adrian to get in, but when I held up my head and walked into the club, no one stopped me.

Is it because I look like one of the Used? I purposely kept my wavy hair down, brushing against my shoulders, covering my neck. I traded my comfy house clothes for a black dress that would've had Adrian drooling if he got to see me in it. I'd planned on changing into it earlier for our dinner—a tiny celebration at the house—but when he never came home, I didn't bother.

While I waited for the car to arrive, I did. I put on a little makeup, too, and slipped my feet into a pair of heels that I only wore when I had to go into the office to speak with Mr. Dimmity. I look pretty good, if I do say so myself, even if I start freaking out a little that the other clubbers might think I'm for sale.

It isn't until after I stepped into the loud, smokey nightclub that it hits me: my wedding ring. While some Owed buy their Offering a ring suited to them—like Adrian said he was doing for me even though I told him it's fine, I'm not too pressed what it looks like when I'm not the type of girl who bothers with jewelry—most Order wives have the same gaudy gold band on their finger that I do.

If the crowd around me dancing, drinking, smoking, and slinking away to the backroom where the Used are kept, waiting for their visitors... if everyone at the King's Court is a vampire, the ring on my finger is like a wooden cross or a vial of holy water. The universal sign that says 'I'm taken', I'm given a wide berth.

I'm used to it. In the old days, it was because I was Loni Dougherty and, for some inexplicable reason, Adrian Heller hated Loni Dougherty. I know now that there's a thin line between love and hate, and while the world believed he hated me, Adrian himself would say it was the opposite.

Do I believe him? Silly Loni, I think I was beginning to—but after tonight? I'm not so sure anymore.

That's okay. I didn't come here for company. As lonely as I've been, being in the middle of a crowd, even if they're ignoring me… it's better than spending the night alone, pathetically waiting for my husband to grace me with his presence. The gin and tonic that I ordered from the bartender doesn't hurt, either.

I'm not a huge drinker. I have a two-drink limit so, for the first twenty minutes, I nurse this one. Then, because I don't have anything better to do, I cross my legs at the ankle, swivel on my barstool, and peoplewatch.

A few familiar faces come in and out of my line of sight. When I do make eye contact and feel that flash of recognition deep in my gut, I'd drop my head, letting my hair fall forward into my face. They disappear into the crowd, and I let out a sigh of relief.

Rinse.

Repeat.

Halfway through my first drink on an empty stomach, I start to think that this might've been a bad idea. In hindsight, I let my petty side take over, putting me in a situation that, honestly? I'm not the biggest fan of.

I should've just stayed in. I didn't have to confront Adrian when he finally came home, and if I let my unsaid suspicion that there was no meeting... that, secretly, a part of me wanted to visit the King's Court because I was terrified that I might find my husband here with a mistress... lead me into doing something I'm not comfortable with, then that's my problem.

If he goes to the Used, he was never really mine. I need to accept that.

I need to understand that in the Order... that's what happens.

I never wanted to come back to this life, but I had to, and it's time I put on my big girl panties, temper my expectations, and get the fuck over it.

Deciding that I would finish my drink and then hire another car, I turn back around, ignoring the music, the lights, the drugs in one corner, the smoking in another... I forget for a moment that I'm one in a crowd of too, too many.

At least, I do—until someone slides onto the empty stool next to me and prods me on my bare shoulder.

"Loni Dougherty? Funny seeing you here."

My head jerks up.

The man sitting next to me is good-looking in that 'boy next door' kind of way. He has a round face, honest features, shaggy blond hair, and dark brown eyes. There's friendliness in their depths, and a vague interest, plus a charming smile that takes me a second to place.

Max Roberts. My lab partner senior year, and a member of Harmony Heights High School's football team when we both attended the same school.

"Holy shit, Max. Wow! It's... it's so great to see you."

He leans in, about to give me a hug. I freeze, not sure how to go about rejecting him, but I don't have to. Lowering one arm to his side, a sheepish grin touches his handsome face as he runs his fingers through his shaggy blond hair.

When he's done, he settles that same hand casually on the bartop.

Crisis averted.

"You, too. I thought I recognized you when I was crossing to the bar, going for my drink, but as soon as I sat down... I was like, yo, that *is* Loni."

I nod. "Yup. I'm back in town."

Unfortunately.

"I know. I heard you and Heller got hitched." Max whistles, the sound sharp enough that I can hear him over the raucous crowd and the thumping bass. "Never saw that coming."

Yeah. Me, neither.

Damn it. It would be so much easier to simply tap my ear, pretend I can't hear him, then end this conversation. It's a shame that I already responded to him, and when he mentioned Adrian and me getting married, I definitely flinch.

His forehead furrows. "You two doing okay? I mean... I remember how he always used to be so possessive of you when we were kids. All any of us had to do was bring up your name, and he was either having Dallas Collins beat the shit out of us or, you know, being Adrian Heller."

Max doesn't elaborate. He doesn't have to. When it comes to Adrian being Adrian, I had a front-row seat to seeing how sneaky and underhanded he could be. But possessive? That's a new one. I mean, killing Desmond to take his place last month can definitely be considered possessive *now*... but all those years ago?

Interesting.

I'm not sure if I like it, but it's certainly interesting.

Max leans in closer, lowering his voice a little. "I mean it. I might not be in the inner circle like Heller and Collins, but I've got my brand." He flashes his palm, showing the mark on his skin. "If you need help... if you want to get away, I can help you. I can let Jack know and, family or not, he has to follow the charter. You don't have to stay with him if he's hurting you."

Oh.

Oh.

Do I want to get away? I mean, in the beginning, that's all I was thinking about. Plotting my escape occupied my thoughts the first few days I was hiding out in my room. But somehow, along the way, I've just accepted that this is it.

Actually, up until today, I was thinking it wouldn't be so bad to spend the rest of my life with Adrian Heller. I mean, if I *had* to be Claimed, it could have always been worse.

It could've been *Desmond*.

He hurt me. It took more than a week for that bruise to fade, and we weren't even married yet. Adrian... he wanted to resurrect a dead man and kill him again for daring to lay his hands on me.

No. When Adrian puts his hands on me, there's no

pain, only pleasure... and there's no way in hell that I'm admitting that to a boy I haven't spoken to in a decade.

Instead, I give him a small, closed-lipped smile. "You're sweet, Max, but don't worry about me. I can handle Adrian."

At least, I *think* I can.

The look on Max's face tells me he has his doubts, too. Not surprising. I did let Adrian walk all over me for years, and I'm not so sure it's different now that I'm his wife.

But then he says, "If that changes, let me know. After what happened to Haven last year... an Offering is precious. I wouldn't want to see you go through anything like that."

A shiver runs down my spine at the mention of Haven's name.

"Haven?" I echo. "What happened to Haven?"

He hesitates. "You didn't hear?"

"I've only been back in town since the middle of June. With the wedding and everything... I haven't had the chance to talk to Haven yet."

"You're not the only one. These days, if you're not Connor Heyward, you're not getting a word out of Haven Smith."

Connor? "What are you talking about?"

"You don't know? I... Heller didn't tell you?"

Um. No.

Leaning toward Max, my heart thumping wildly in my chest, I peer up at him through the fringe of my lashes. "He probably wanted to protect me."

"Yeah. That would make sense. I mean, an Offering

being used as leverage against the Order"—*What?*—"I'd hate to see that happen to you."

Yeah. Me, too.

"I appreciate that, but back to Haven. What… what exactly happened to her?"

"Oh." Max looks a little nervous. "Um. Maybe it's better if I don't say anything—"

He stops talking. I swallow my annoyance, ready to lay my fingers on his hand, anything to convince him to keep talking.

And that's when I hear Adrian.

"What do you think you're doing, Avalon?"

Ooh. Full name. I've really pissed him off, haven't I?

Good.

NINETEEN
THE COURT

ADRIAN

This could have been an email.

As the meeting drones on, something about the new hospital, the upcoming mayoral election, and God knows what else... all I keep thinking is that there's no reason for me to be here instead of at home with my wife.

I mean, seriously. This can't go on much longer. Every time I think it's done, Jack stands up, mentions another order of business, then sits down with a smirk as one of his yes-men starts droning on and on about more bullshit.

Not even caring that I'm making it obvious, I check my phone for the time.

Fuck me. It's already quarter after nine. I still have to get Loni's cake. I'd be a shit husband if I didn't even have a cake for her birthday, or a present to go along with it.

Then there's dinner. The restaurant is just waiting for my call. The order was placed last week, but I want it hot and fresh. Thankfully, they don't close until eleven, but it's already getting so late.

Dinner might have to wait until tomorrow.

Maybe that's for the best. I've already told my clients that I'm taking a half day on Friday due to the appointment I have scheduled in the afternoon. We can consider today a wash, and though I know her birthday is today, we're adults. As long as we celebrate it, it shouldn't matter if it's today or tomorrow.

Right?

If this meeting doesn't end soon, I'll have no choice.

I'll make it up to her. I'd give her the fucking world if she asked it of me. Since the only thing she seems to desire right now is my head beneath a guillotine so that she can be free as a widow, I'm not that eager to comply. However, I'm hoping that the long black box I'd picked up at lunch might at least begin to show her that being Mrs. Adrian Heller isn't all that bad...

I'm just about to set my phone down again when, suddenly, it buzzes. I expect the text to be from Loni. Sure, none of the other messages I've received so far have been from my wife, but she has to be wondering where I am.

Only it's not my wife.

It's Sebastien.

BAS 🏍️

Hey, bro.

I know you're in that stupid meeting with Dallas and the King's men, but I'm at the Court.

So is your wife.

Did you know that?

It takes me a moment to understand what Bas is asking me.

Did I know that Loni was down at the King's Court?

No. No, I did not.

I don't even think. In the middle of Oliver blathering on about God knows what, I stand up.

"Adrian?" Jack purses his lips. "We're not done here. Sit down."

Bullshit.

"Family emergency," I grit out. "I've got to go."

Jack's smarmy expression does nothing for my blood pressure right now. He gestures at himself and Dallas. "Your family is right here. Unless you mean something happened to my sister?"

I shake my head. Let him think it's my idiot father in trouble, but no way in hell am I going to admit that my wife is down at the Court *without* me when I know—I *know*—that Jack's just waiting for any cracks in my relationship with Loni to show.

"I've got to go," I repeat, snatching up my suit jacket. My phone goes in my pocket. I nod at the men sitting at the conference table. "And next time? Shit like this really could've been an email."

I owe Bas big time.

Without letting Loni know that he's watching her, he's given me play-by-play reports of what she's up to. I'm glad she's avoided going anywhere near the backroom where the Used spend their time—I don't know what I would do if anyone mistook my wife as an available mistress—though I hate the idea of her sitting at the bar alone, nursing a gin and tonic.

At least she's alone, though... until I'm pulling up at the club, and Bas's latest message comes through my phone.

BAS

> Hurry up. You won't like this, but Max Roberts has been talking Loni's ear off the last couple of minutes.

Fuck, no.

Max Roberts. He barely got inducted into the Order a year after we graduated. His legacy was questionable, and when he *did* get in, he wasn't of a rank to get his own Offering.

Hell if I'll let him get anywhere near mine.

I swear, it's like everything from our high school days just keeps coming back around. Max was on the football team, plowing cheerleaders left and right because they were just regular townie girls, but I caught him eyeballing Loni once or twice. She never seemed to notice. I didn't care. I couldn't have him doing that anyway.

Not when Loni was *mine*.

So I spiked his sports drink with vodka, sent an anonymous message to the principal that a couple of players were drinking before big games, and he got booted.

Nowadays, he works down at the Harmony Heights car dealership. He married one of the cheerleaders, but even though she wasn't an Offering, just being a member of the Order means he can have his fun with his Used.

Is that why he's trolling the Court instead of being home with his wife? Because he's hitting on mine?

When I think of Max Roberts, I inevitably think of vodka. It might be fitting to grab a bottle of the high-end shit from behind the bar and smash him over the head with it...

Stalking into the club, ignoring the neon lights and the loud music on this side of the Court, I scan the crowd. I see Bas first, and he waves, then points at the bar. I nod and, seeing my beautiful bride leaning forward, listening to something Max is saying to her, I zero in on her like a great white shark going after its prey.

It doesn't help my possessive jealousy that Loni... my wife is the most beautiful creature in the world. Whether she's naked or lounging on the couch, wearing a t-shirt and sweatpants, I'm constantly fiending for her... but to see her wearing a little black dress with a low-cut top and fuck-me black pumps?

Max just might be a dead man, but right now, I could fuck through a wall to get to Loni's heat.

Palming my growing erection, I keep moving.

To hide the insane gleam in my eyes, I force a smile to

my lips right as I reach them. Then, when they don't sense my presence, I raise my voice. "What do you think you're doing, Avalon?"

Her head whips around. I see surprise, followed by guilt, and finally an anger that says that, whatever I interrupted, she's not happy about it.

Too bad.

I give the other man a pointed look. "Max."

"Adrian." His gaze immediately slides to the side. "Oh. Wow. Benny is waving at me. I, uh, think he needs me for something." He raises his voice, holding up a single finger. "One second, Ben!" An apologetic shrug follows. "Sorry, Adrian. It's so good to see you. You, too, Loni. But... yeah. Gotta go."

Smart Owed. Like the rest of Harmony Heights, he knows that I'm Loni's husband. What I did to Claim her and make her mine. Since he clearly doesn't want to suffer the same fate as Desmond, he makes an excuse and bolts, leaving Loni alone with me.

Very smart Owed.

Getting up from her stool, my wife crosses her arms over her chest, concealing that delicious cleavage, glaring daggers up at me when she notices my eyes had dropped to her tits. "Was that necessary?"

Yes. "If you weren't here, chatting with him, that wouldn't have happened."

Her back goes stiff. "I'm celebrating my birthday. Even if *you* didn't remember it, that doesn't mean *I* shouldn't have some fun on my own. A girl doesn't turn twenty-eight every day, you know."

Hang on. "You think I forgot your birthday?"

She unfolds her arms, waving her hand, dismissing it. Dismissing *me*. "It doesn't matter. If I hadn't come down to the Court, I never would've heard that something is up with Haven. That's what I was talking about with Max. She was my best friend. She got hurt, Adrian? Why didn't you tell me?"

Fuck.

I knew this would come back to bite me in the ass.

I couldn't, though. I *can't*.

Luckily, I don't have to. "Later, princess. I want to go back to the topic of your birthday. I didn't forget it."

She snorts, her obvious annoyance with me enough to get her to drop the subject of Haven… for now. It won't last, and I'll have to give her as many details about Haven's ordeal that are widely known so she understands how she'll only hurt her old friend if she continues to dig, but I can't stand the idea of Loni believing that I wouldn't celebrate the day she was born.

"Honest. Look." I reach into my suit jacket pocket. Tucked in there with my useless cigarette case, I pull out the long, skinny black box. "Here. I bought this for you. Happy birthday, Loni."

With a hint of suspicions lingering around her, she accepts the box. Flipping it open, her face falls. "Oh. A gold bracelet. How… thoughtful."

I blink. "You don't like it?"

"It's… fine. Jewelry. That's what a husband buys his wife, right?"

That's what I thought. It seemed a safe bet. For every

occasion in my mother and father's marriage, he bought her jewelry. The fact that her collection was bigger and more expensive than that of any of Dad's Used is one of the only reasons Mom still sticks it out instead of moving into her own place.

I realize my mistake almost instantly. A simple gold bracelet... for a woman whose only piece of jewelry is the ring I haven't been able to replace yet... and a reminder that, like the ring, she's just another stock-standard piece, doing what the Order expects of her.

Fuck, fuck, fuck.

What was I thinking? Sure, this is only one part of her gift—due to a slight miscalculation I uncharacteristically made, I have to wait until tomorrow for the rest—but, first, she believes I forgot her birthday. Now, I followed her to the Court, and instead of begging her for her forgiveness, I made it worse with a half-assed present.

I have to fix this, and it starts by getting her to like the bracelet.

I hold out my palm. "Here. Give me. Let me put it on you."

She snaps the box closed on the bracelet. "I'm fine."

I want her to wear it. "Come here."

When she doesn't make a move toward me, I go to take her hand and, oh, she doesn't like that.

"Loni?"

"Don't touch me," she hisses, and my heart sinks. She hasn't said that to me in weeks, and right when I thought that she was beginning to trust me, I fucked it all up again.

Goddamn it!

Loni takes a purposeful step around me as I curse myself to hell and back. "This is what I get for giving in so easily." Her pretty hazel eyes flash on that last word. "Now you think you own me. No one owns me."

"I don't want to own you, Loni."

She snorts, already starting to cross the floor of the Court. "Yeah, right."

If I can't convince her… "I mean it."

"Whatever."

No. She's not going to dismiss me—dismiss *us*—again that easily. "Listen to me. You're my wife, and—"

Loni pauses, whirling around, pointing a finger at me. "It's a piece of paper. It's a promise in front of poor Father Francis that you stole from me while I was in shock. Because, I don't know if you remember… I don't know if you've got any clue what it's like to have blood splattered all over you, your high school boyfriend dead on the floor, your fucking *bully* the one who put him there?"

I narrow my gaze on her. "He wasn't your boyfriend. Not really. We both know that."

A hollow laugh. "Of course that's what you get out of all of that. Jesus Christ, Adrian. How broken are you?"

Without Loni Heller? *Shattered.*

"I'd blame the Order, but you were even worse when we were kids. Or, hell, maybe that still means it's the Order's fault. Grow up with a silver spoon in your mouth, an entire damn town laid at your feet… no wonder you're all called the Owed. You think you deserve it, don't you? That you deserve me? You *don't*."

Oh, princess… don't you think I already know that?

I don't deserve this woman, but that's not going to stop me from keeping her.

I lash out my hand, reaching for her wrist, hoping to tether her to me.

Loni jerks her hand back before I can, tottering on her high heels. "I told you not to touch me."

I need to, and not only because it's nearly impossible to resist the urge to grab her, steady her, keep her from falling to the floor...

Through gritted teeth, I remind her: "You are *my wife*."

"Trust me, I know. But you know what else I know? The Order's rules when it comes to girls like me. You can't make me love you. You can't make me sleep with you. I did because I thought... *fuck*." She fists her hands, visibly hot and angry, but when her eyes are glossy with a sheen of unshed tears, I go cold. "It doesn't matter. Because you're right. I'm your wife. The rules say that I have to spend that one night with you. And I'd say that there's no way in hell I'm letting you touch me again, but we both know I'm full of shit."

"I won't." My answer is guttural. "Look. We start over." We have to start over. "I make tonight up to you, and you can put a hold on our Mondays for the next two weeks." That gives me time. The Claiming ceremony is in four weeks. That gives me two additional weeks to seduce her into choosing me in front of the whole damn Order.

If sex with Loni is the only way to get her to choose me, I'll use it. And, in the meantime, I'll work harder. She's upset that I stayed late for the Order's meeting? Next time, I'll tell Jack to stuff it. And, sure, I made a calculated error by dismissing her birthday because I wanted to surprise her with the bracelet—another mistake—dinner—that would be worthless now—and the gift that I can't pick up until tomorrow... but there has to be a way to fix this—

"You're lying."

Shit.

My jaw tightens. I feel like I'm going to hurl. "I don't lie to you, Loni."

"Yeah. I believed that once, too. But maybe that was another lie." She shakes her head, lifting her hands to knock her hair out of her face. "Your head is spinning, baby." *Baby.* I live to hear her call me that, but the way she spits it out right now is so derisive, I stutter-step back as though the pair of syllables are two fucking bullets to the chest. "Always plotting. Always planning. Look at you! I know you're already trying to figure out a way to manipulate me into being your good little wife forever."

Since I can't tell her that she's one hundred percent correct, I try to end this conversation before it gets worse.

I surge toward my wife. "Don't do this—"

Loni steps away. "I'm going home. Yes, Adrian," she adds, guessing from the look on my face my biggest worry, "*your* home."

No. *Our* home.

"I'll drive you."

She juts out her chin, pure defiance. "No. I found my way to the Court. I'll find my way back."

Another jealous wave crashes into me. "Not with Max, you won't."

"Are you serious? Oh my God. *No.* Why do... I talked

to him for, like, five minutes, and half of them were him telling me that my childhood best friend is a wreck. Which, I'll point out again, *you* never did."

"It wasn't my story to tell—"

"Whatever." I grit my teeth. Not *whatever* again. "I don't need a ride from an old friend." She pulls her phone out of the tiny black clutch she left on the bar top. "I'll order one. For me. Don't try to stop me."

It hurts me to do this, but I nod. "I won't."

"And another thing? I'm pissed, Adrian. I'll get over it." Shit, there's another hollow laugh. "I always do. You know that better than anyone... but I need time. So I'm telling you... don't try to use sex against me. The next time we fuck? It'll be because I initiate it, you understand? You don't touch me. *I* touch *you*. Got it?"

On one hand, I hate seeing Loni so upset. On the other, it's so fucking hot to witness her take charge like this. Watching her be meek and submissive is fun, but when she tells me she hates me while surrendering to me... I thought that was my favorite facet of Loni's fascinating personality.

I've changed my mind. Seeing her take complete control? Fuck, I shouldn't be getting even harder right now, especially since I'll have no choice but to follow her lead on this if I ever want her to Claim me. Jack... he's not bluffing. If he senses any weakness between us, he'll snatch Loni away from me, and short of shooting him dead in the chest, I won't be able to stop the King.

Long live the fucking King.

I swallow, trying to keep my composure. "Got it, princess."

A shadow of barely concealed fury dances across her face at the nickname. "I'm leaving. Don't. Follow. Me."

Schooling my own features into a look of contrition—don't smirk, Adrian, and don't let her figure out that you're sporting one hell of an erection right now—I promise, "I won't."

I need her to trust me. Trust is the basis of the foundation in any strong relationship. It's not something I can snap my fingers and command of her, either. I need to show her I'm worthy of her believing in me.

So when she leaves, I keep my shoes planted on the bar's floor until she's gone. Then, because every nerve in my body is twanging to go after her, I stalk off. Not toward the exit, though. I take a detour, heading right into the private bathroom designated for the higher-ranked Owed.

It's an honor system in the Court. Don't go where you don't belong, don't pick one of the Used who belongs to your brother, and don't interfere if a higher-ranked Owed tells you to get lost. I reluctantly admit that Max backed off the second he saw I was there. There's no rule about an Owed talking to an Offering—or a wife—even if I wished there was so I could challenge his standing in the Order.

But that's just my vindictive side showing. And as I shut the door behind me, stalking toward the mirror, I see it making my features taut, my eyes dark and wild.

Fuck.

I don't know what comes over me. Just like I'm in my gym, getting my aggression out on the punching bag, I rear back my hand and swing.

The mirror splinters, cracking, *breaking*.

Blood smears on the reflective glass. A hundred crazed Adrians stare back at me.

Every single fucking one of them belongs to a woman who would slit my throat with a jagged shard if I gave her the chance.

Gripping the sink basin, breathing heavily, I tell myself that I can't even blame her. What the fuck have I done to make it so that she'd ever want to Claim me back? Every time I think that I'm making headway at reminding Loni why she might've loved me once, I fuck it up.

Every goddamn time.

But this?

I can't fix the way I treated the whole Haven situation. Even if I could, I wouldn't. Connor deserves that much from me. Besides, now that Loni is back in Harmony Heights, there's time. Haven's made such progress over the last year. Give it another one and maybe my wife and Connor's can reconcile.

Too bad it's not just Haven Smith coming between us again, just like she did back when Loni and me were kids. I made a colossal mistake. Because I hate my birthday— each one passing a reminder that I'd spent another year without Loni—I treated Loni like it wasn't a big deal for her, either.

I had plans. I always have plans.

This one? It didn't work out.

Cradling my bleeding fist, I glare at the broken mirror again.

Broken... that's what she called me. I wish I could say

she was wrong, but I *am* broken. It's too much to expect any woman—especially *that* woman—to fix me. Too bad she's the only one who can.

I need Loni.

I'm not giving her up, no matter what it takes.

Thank fucking God the animal shelter is open tomorrow.

TWENTY
PEACHES

LONI

aven doesn't want to speak to me.

That's just the icing on the cake of what turned out to be an awful birthday. First, Adrian put the Order before acknowledging my birthday—even though he admitted he knew exactly when it was *and* that he bought me a bracelet that, spitefully, I tossed in a drawer to rot.

Jewelry? Could that gift have been any less personal? And though I'm not so unappreciative that I told Adrian that to his face, the fact that I didn't put it on was all he needed to know after he gave it to me.

Something happened at the Court after I left. Adrian's right hand was swollen and cut when he marched into my room and held out his hand, asking for the bracelet's box when he saw I still wasn't wearing it. I refused, but immediately asked him point-blank if he went after Max and punched him in the face

He looked me dead in the eye and said softly, "No," and that was the end of it; both the bracelet, and what happened after I left. I kicked him out of the room, and swallowing roughly, he went.

Lying in bed alone, I thought about it. I thought about *everything*. When it comes to that one thing, I believed him. He didn't punch Max out of some misplaced jealously.

No, but he sure as hell punched *something*.

He obviously didn't want to talk about the injuries to his hand. Fair enough. I decided I didn't want to talk about Haven with him, though he did tell me over break-fast the next morning that he reached out to Connor—who seems to have become her guardian or something since her 'incident'—and Connor apologetically told Adrian that Haven is aware that I'm in town, and that she'll speak to me when she's ready.

Only she's not ready yet, and that's just another blow to my self esteem that I so didn't need.

Did I think that I was lonely before? Knowing that the only good friend I ever had is happy to keep her distance from me cuts like a knife. And that's not fair. I know it isn't. Something happened to Haven, and from what I can infer, it wasn't good. She needs time. She needs space.

And I?

I don't know what the hell *I* need.

A husband who cared would be nice. Who spent time getting to know me instead of thinking of me as the girl he once knew, not the woman I've become. That's not asking much, right? I mean, when I think about how far he went to make me his wife in the first place... I don't know. Maybe I have been asking for a lot. So many Offerings end up in loveless marriages. At least Adrian seems to care for me in his own way. And I'm pretty sure that I don't have to worry about him going to one of the Used... for now.

The whole rest of the day after my birthday, I tried to convince myself that I should be satisfied with what I have. It could always be worse, and it could also be that my expectations were way too high for my birthday this year. After all, I've only been back in Adrian's life for a month. Most of the time, we're doing our own thing. It isn't fair of me to expect more when I've spent the last month trying my best to keep him out.

If he doesn't know the twenty-eight-year-old Loni that I am now, is that really his fault? Or is it mine, too?

It's fine. It's *fine*. I tell myself that repeatedly because, even if it isn't, there's nothing I can do to change it now.

And I've just about convinced myself of that fact when Adrian comes stalking into the living room where I'm mindlessly watching television.

I called out today. I didn't have to. Working remotely... as long as I hit my quota every week, performing my audits on time, my supervisor doesn't really care when precisely I'm on the clock. I had the entire day yesterday to myself because Maxwell and Dimmity's gives a personal day for your birthday. Since I'm still sulking today, I put in for another one.

Adrian had frowned when I told him that during breakfast. If he'd known, he would've rearranged his own schedule, but it looked like he couldn't. He had an impor-tant meeting in the morning, another with Jack and Dallas Collins for lunch, and then something planned in the afternoon he just couldn't miss.

Translation: sorry, Loni, but the Order still comes first.

I expected that to mean he wouldn't be home until well after dinnertime. I made myself a quick PB&J for lunch, planning to order in for dinner in case Adrian didn't show until late. Then, curled up on the couch in the living room, I zoned out.

When Adrian walks into the living room, the first thing I notice is that he already removed his tie. To me, that's a sure sign that his work day is over but, as I grab my phone and glance at it, I see it's only three o'clock.

Huh. That's early.

I open my mouth to ask him about that when I notice a *second* thing about him.

His hands are in front of his middle, cupped around something that is squirmy and orange and fluffy and mewing and holy fucking shit—

"Is that a kitten?"

My fingers fly up, covering my mouth in surprise.

Because it is. I see the reflective greenish-yellow eyes. The triangle-shaped ears. The tiny head peeking out from the hole he made in his hands.

Why in God's name does Adrian have a *kitten*?

With a slow smirk crossing his face, he moves into the room. Dropping down at my side, he opens his hands, placing the kitten in my lap.

"She doesn't have a name yet," he murmurs. "I thought I would leave that up to you."

"Did you... is she..." I pause, gathering my excited thoughts together. "Did you get me a kitten?"

Reaching out, Adrian rubs his pointer finger underneath the kitten's chin. She immediately starts purring like a motorboat, and I fall instantly in love with her.

"I went back and forth on this. For the last week, I've been deciding whether I should bring you to the shelter or if I should surprise you with one for your birthday. In the end, I went and rescued one myself because... to be honest, Loni... if you went, we would've come home with the whole litter."

"You know," I say, suddenly feeling more light-hearted than I have in days, "studies say that kittens do better when there are two of them."

"I'll keep that in mind. When you see how much stuff I had to pick up in order for the shelter to let me adopt her... you might just be satisfied with one."

Somehow, I highly doubt that.

For now, though, I'm just so excited to have even this one. I mean, does he think he can buy my affection with a kitten?

Shit.

He's not wrong.

I've always wanted a cat. It just never was the time. Once I didn't have a roommate with allergies anymore, I lived completely alone, and while I didn't have to go into the office daily back then, I was still away enough that it wouldn't have been fair to a companion animal like a cat.

But I don't go in to the office anymore. I'm home every day, and if I have a kitten of my own... maybe I won't be as lonely as I have been.

Maybe—

Wait.

What was it Adrian said?

For the last week...

"Are you saying that you were always planning on getting me a kitten?"

"You've always wanted one." He pets the baby cat, then strokes my jaw. "I didn't bring her home yesterday because the shelter was closed and I thought... fuck it, Loni. No excuses. I don't know what I thought. I should've gone on the 23rd, but I didn't. I made the appointment for the 25th instead because I'm a fucking idiot when it comes to you. I thought... I thought one day wouldn't matter."

Normally, it wouldn't.

But, normally, I'm not in a forced marriage with a husband who is trying to do everything he can to prove himself while I do everything I can to push back against it.

His brows draw together, a hint of vulnerability on a man who is so rarely vulnerable. "Do you like her? They told me that it's not so usual for an orange cat to be a girl. I liked her, though. The orange fur reminded me of your strawberry-blonde hair. You kinda match."

I glance at the kitten, then up at Adrian. "She has your eyes, too."

He chuckles. 'Yeah. I guess she does."

So maybe we aren't having kids just yet. But it looks

like we're the proud parents of a tiny kitten just waiting for us to name her.

Because Adrian adopted her for me.

Because he knew I wanted a kitten.

Because he knows me better than I thought.

Yeah. I'm in big, big trouble, aren't I?

TWENTY-ONE
JEALOUSY

LONI

Turns out, an adorable orange kitten wasn't the only way Adrian decided to make up for totally screwing up my birthday.

I love her to death already. It's only been about two weeks since Adrian placed the fluffball into my palms, but if anything happened to her, I don't know what I would do. And maybe I went a little overboard. When Adrian adopted her from the Harmony Heights shelter, he came home with everything the man at the shelter told him a first-time cat adopter would need: litter, a litter box, a breakaway collar with a little, jingling bell, wet food, dry food, and food bowls.

Since then, I've added a cat bed, a cat tower with a scratching post, toys for fun, toys for her enrichment, and a small carrier so that, if we need to leave with her, it'll be easier than holding her in our arms. The shelter did give the kitten to Adrian in a cardboard box, but she'd shredded a small hole in it during the car ride home, which is why he had to hold her in his palms. I guess I should just be lucky the little diva didn't jump from the car before he was able to snare her again.

She's so soft and fuzzy, I decide to name her Peaches. I don't let her free roam. When she's bigger, I will, but for now, I keep her in whatever room I'm in as long as the door can close. That means she spends most of her time in my upstairs office and my private bedroom, and since I spend my time off of work—when I'm not with Adrian— playing with her, some of my loneliness has finally subsided.

It's the best birthday present he could've given me, though his second idea? Yeah... that one's not so much fun.

For me, at least. For Adrian, I understand why he did it.

It's the damn gossip mills in Harmony Heights. By now, everyone knows I'm back. Just like how everyone knows that Adrian married me after getting rid of his so-called rival. Because I've refused to mingle with the other women in the Order—either other Offerings or the Used —rumors are spreading that Adrian is keeping me locked up.

His genius idea to get the rumors to stop? He throws me a birthday party the first weekend in August.

August is a busy time for the Order of the Owed. The Claiming ceremony is usually scheduled either mid-month or closer to the end. It's always in August, though, and so many members spend the second half of summer preparing for it.

I hoped that meant that only a handful of really curious lookie-loos would show up. Unfortunately, after I got Peaches settled down for the evening and joined Adrian on the first floor, I discovered that I was way off on that.

There were at least fifty guests milling around. Despite throwing the party together at the last minute, Adrian arranged for a full spread of food and drinks laid out on his massive dining room table. The more informal living room had a folding table with trays of elaborate snacks on them. Music blasted from a set of speakers that a local DJ set up in nearly every room.

And no matter where I went? Everyone stared at me.

Adrian told me it would be an informal affair. I took him at his word, choosing to wear a comfortable pair of leggings, one of my favorite soft yellow sweaters since the heatwave crashed and the AC is back to being at arctic levels, plus a pair of plain white sneakers. Adrian's wearing a suit, as usual, but while most of our guests have dressed more casually, there are a handful of bombshell women roaming the house that leave me feeling frumpy and underdressed whenever I run into them.

It might not have been so bad if Adrian stayed at my side. For the first hour of the party, he did, and while it got a little irksome, hearing the smug way he kept introducing me to every guest as his wife, when it became obvious that I didn't recognize most of these people, I was glad to be able to cling to him.

We always ran in different circles when we were kids. Mainly because his bullying me made me the town outcast so, despite my lineage, I never really meshed with those who had ties to the Order. I didn't really mesh with anyone except Haven, actually, and if I'm a little disappointed to hear that she was invited to the party but couldn't come, I try my best not to let it sting.

So it's not really a surprise that, ten years later, the higher-ranked members of the Order are all strangers to me. Adrian, of course, knows them all. I guess that's why I admit that it was inevitable that, at some point, he'd go off to speak to one in private while I floated around the house—*my* house—like I didn't belong.

I went and checked on Peaches. I refreshed my makeup and fluffed my hair. I didn't change because that would be obvious, but I did go out of my way to avoid the most dolled-up women so that I didn't look washed-out in comparison.

Then, when I narrowly avoided getting caught in a conversation with two Offering who wanted to know how I snagged one of the most eligible bachelors in all of Harmony Heights, I decided to do the unthinkable: I went looking for my husband.

And when I find him talking to a tall, striking brunette with big tits, big hair, and legs that go on for days, my heart just about stops.

I recognize her. Funny that, of all the people here, she's the only one I do. That's Sophie Vale, a girl I knew back when I was in school. She was a grade ahead of us, so she's quickly approaching thirty, and my stomach twists when I notice that she doesn't have a ring on that all-important finger.

What the—

Jealousy.

A loaded word, and an emotion that I long thought buried deep inside of me.

Why would I be jealous over a man I hated? Who bullied me, who betrayed me, and who thinks that I've forgotten—that I've *forgiven*—all because I was forced to stand there as he made Father Francis bond us together as husband and wife?

Adrian can make me his wife. He can't make me love him. In this battle of wills between us, I've made my stance clear.

So why do I want to march over to where Sophie is laying her arm possessively over his shoulder and rip it off before beating the pretty brunette over the head with it?

I don't. I can't. It would give too much of me away, and that's not anything Adrian deserves yet. He hasn't noticed me watching him, too involved in his conversation with Sophie, and before he takes his eyes off of her and sees me standing here, I bolt.

I wish I could say that I disappeared to the furthest reaches of Adrian's huge house. That it was easy to shake off the sudden jealousy. That I found something else at the party to distract me with and that, when Adrian eventually tracked me down, I laughed and said something like, "I barely knew you were gone."

That's not what happened, though. I only went to the other side of the room, dashing out the door before turning around and watching from a position where I hoped Adrian can't see me. I got some odd looks from other partygoers, but I ignored them.

Oh, no. My eyes were for Sophie and Adrian only.

The conversation wasn't a long one. To be fair, he almost immediately shook off her hand, his expression turning slightly bored long before he took leave of Sophie. He still lingered longer than my irrationally jealous mind liked. Irrational... that's the only way to describe what I do next.

Moments after Adrian drifts off to another room, I march right over to the brunette. Then, hoping like hell my acting has improved since my drama club days, I feign surprise at walking right at her.

I throw up my hands. "Sophie? Sophie Vale? Is that really you?"

Her lips split in an overly ecstatic greeting. "Loni! Oh my goodness, look at you! I mean, I knew you were here. This is your party, after all, but it's so good to see you."

I wish I could say the same thing.

No. *No.* That's not fair of me. It's not Sophie's fault that I saw her cozying up to Adrian and now I want to rip her hair out. So she clearly knows that I'm here. That it's my birthday party. Unless she's been living under a rock this last month, all of Harmony Heights knows that Adrian is my husband... so while I'm aggravated that I saw him flirting with her, shouldn't she have also known better?

"You, too," I lie. And then, because I can't help myself... "I thought I saw you with Adrian before."

"What? Oh, yeah. Me and your hubby go way back."

A punch to my gut. Damn. I don't know how I don't buckle over at that.

I don't know why I care.

Forcing a smile to my face, I ask, "Really? How do you know him?"

She blinks. "From school, Loni. Remember? We all went to Harmony Heights High together. You know that."

Right. Of course.

Yeah.

I open my mouth, hoping that whatever comes out doesn't reveal the sudden jealousy that still has a hold on me, when Sophie gives a careless toss of her thick hair over her shoulder and I get a front-row seat to the large oval brand on the side of her neck.

The same brand that covers Adrian's palm.

The mark of the Order—and Sophie wears it proudly on a very visible place on her body.

"Something wrong, Loni?" she teases. "'Cause you're gawking, sweetie."

"You're one of the Used," I point out needlessly.

A frisson of relief flutters through me.

Adrian doesn't touch the Used. He's made that perfectly clear. And while we've both tiptoed around the subject of any previous lovers we both may or may not have had over the last decade, it's almost like he wanted me to understand that—to him, at least—the Order's personal sex workers are off-limits.

So maybe they are just old friends that he stopped to say 'hello' to. That makes sense to me now.

But one of the town girls who iced me out because she was hoping to get an in—any in—with the Order...

Yeah. that makes sense, too.

"I am," she confirms easily before she lets out a throaty laugh. "I don't know why you're so surprised. I was never going to be an Offering, and thank God for that."

I've never heard any of the women seem glad to be one of the Used before. I'm sorry, but raised as an Offering...

I lower my voice. "You don't have to do that, right? I mean... you could leave the Order, couldn't you?"

My gaze flickers to the brand standing out on her neck. Maybe not. Even if she tried to leave, the scar on her neck would tell anyone who knows what that symbol means exactly how she was affiliated with the Order of the Owed.

As an Offering, there's no escape for me. Even when I tried, deep down, I knew I was only buying a little time. Now, did I think they'd use my dad against me to get me to behave? Naively or not, I never expected that Jack Collins would stoop that low. After all, he's the King... right?

I know better now. And if they would do that to someone they considered 'valuable', what would they do to a glorified prostitute?

"I could help you get out," I murmur, keeping my voice as low as possible while still allowing Sophie to hear me over the pumping music. I'm feeling a little magnanimous now that I know that she isn't after Adrian. "If that's what you want."

"Thanks, Loni, but no thanks. I'm happy where I am. Honest."

I never wanted to be one of the Used. That doesn't mean that there aren't those who choose it. Those who enjoy the attention, the gifts, the safety when they find one of the Owed who will give her whatever she wants as long as she'll fuck him in return. I shouldn't judge Sophie because her path doesn't look like mine. For all I know, she pities me for being forced into a marriage that, from the outside, I could never want.

Do I want it?

I... it's getting harder and harder to say no.

So, instead, I just nod. "Got it."

She gives me a cryptic smile. "After all, there are worse things than being Used."

Sophie's right.

Adrian and I have come to an impasse about Haven. I know from Max that something terrible happened to her, but while he was determined to make up my fail of a birthday to me, that was one line he wouldn't cross. When the time comes that I finally learn Haven's story, it would have to be from Haven herself.

Between the two guys, I know that she was hurt—and she was hurt because she was an Offering.

So what's worse than being one of the Used?

How about being given away, turned into property, into the perfect trophy wife as though my thoughts, my ambitions, my *dreams* mean nothing compared to a member of the Order's.

So what does Adrian want?

Me.

At least, that's what he tells me. But is he only telling me what he wants me to hear? I'm not sure, but—

An all-too-familiar clearing of a throat has my conversation with Sophie dying a quick death seconds before a voice I hear in my dreams says, "I'm sorry, but if it's okay with you, I'd like to borrow my wife."

Turning, I find that Adrian has joined us. When? How much did he hear? We were only really talking about the Used, but did he overhear me earlier when I attempted to grill Sophie about any relationship she might have—or had—with him?

The heat in his gaze tells me that *yes, yes he did.*

Oh, shit.

Realizing that he has my attention, his lip curls slightly. "My wife," he echoes, the words meant for me and me alone.

Ignoring Sophie... ignoring the rest of the party... Adrian steps behind me, scalding me with his heat, his voice a dark whisper at my ear. "You like being mine, Loni. You always have."

Yes.

I close my eyes, letting my head fall back on my neck.

He brushes his mouth over the side of my throat.

I swallow. "Adrian... people can see us."

"I know, princess. I know."

I remember what he told me once before. How, back when we used to sneak around, he *wanted* someone to see us.

That's not me, though. In the moments when I have Adrian Heller, I want him to be just mine. I don't want to share him, and in a soft whisper, I tell him that.

And that's how, before I even realize what's going on, he has my hand in his as he starts to pull me out of the living room and toward the stairs.

TWENTY-TWO
THE STUDY

ADRIAN

"Where are we going?"

I don't answer Loni. No point. If I tell her, she'll insist that we have to stay with our party guests. Fuck 'em. I wanted to make up for missing most of my wife's birthday, and I did. I gave her Peaches. I hosted a get-together for whoever wanted to gawk at the woman that Desmond St. James lost his life for. I gave her the space she needed to reacclimate to the world of the Order.

Now?

The visible jealousy did me in. She wants me; no denying that. So she won't tell it to me straight. I know her. I know her thoughts *and* her needs.

She needs me, and there isn't anything I won't give my wife when she requires it.

That's why I grip Loni's hand, leading her up two flights of stairs until we're on the third floor. For a moment, I see her confusion. She must think that I'm bringing her to her office space, but when I lead her toward the farthest closed door, she suddenly understands.

"Your study? You told me that you didn't want me in here."

True. My whole enterprise is stored in this room. There are things that I can't let even Loni see... but I locked everything up in their drawers before the party started earlier tonight. No one would ever dare search for me in this room—my fiercely guarded study has a reputation of its own—which makes it the perfect spot to have a little quiet time with my wife.

"Without me," I remind her. "But we're together, aren't we?"

"I... yes. But *why*?"

Oh, Loni. If you don't know the answer to that, I've done a piss-poor job as your husband...

Once we're in the darkened room, I don't bother with a light switch. Instead, parking Loni by my oversized (and suspiciously empty) mahogany desk, I head over to the fireplace on the opposite side of the room. There's a button on the wall beside it, next to the timer that sets how long the fire will burn. I figure we have a good twenty minutes before our guests notice that we're missing, and since I couldn't care less if they do or not, I set the timer for half an hour.

That's the minimum amount of time I need to enjoy my wife—or to let her enjoy me.

Turning on her, a lascivious and starving smile tugging on my lips, I prowl toward her. Suddenly, I'm the big, bad wolf bearing down on a wee, innocent lamb. Everything about my body language to my purposeful stalk sells the image of a hunter tracking his prey, especially when she takes a few uneasy steps behind the desk.

Perfect.

Before she knows it, I'm right behind her. A careful kick to my chair—careful so I don't break my toe or the chair's leg—has it skidding out of reach. She yips, and I grin.

Her back is to me. I grab the edge of the desk, pinning her between me and it. There's no fucking way she can miss my erection grinding against her ass in this position. Her leggings are delightfully thin. I could fuck her right through them if I wanted to, but that's not exactly what I do want right now.

Loni doesn't try to escape. Her breaths quicken, her pulse jumping, but as though we've done this a hundred times before—and we certainly have had experience in this position, only not since I forced her to marry me— she arches her back, presenting her ass to me so I can take her from behind.

But first—

Using my body to keep her in place, I grip the waistband of her leggings. One quick push, and I have them down by her feet. Normally, I would just grab her soaked panties, move them over her mound, and not waste time getting them off. But tonight... let's show some restraint, Adrian.

So, with a little more finesse, I work her panties down, and then I wait for her next move.

Loni wiggles her ass, letting out a sound of pure

impatience. "What's wrong? Why aren't you doing anything?"

Well... if she insists.

I drop down behind her, squatting so that my face is on the level of her ass cheeks. I palm one, squeezing it, loving the way she throws back her head and mutters my name as if she wants more.

I have a plan. After all, I usually do. But before I can enact it, I need to make sure that she's ready for me. And while I could use a finger, dragging it along her slit, testing to see how wet she is, she gave me permission when she asked why I wasn't doing anything yet.

The old Adrian would skip foreplay for a frantic fuck because he was too desperate to be part of Loni before she came to her senses and pushed him away. Now? I won't stop worshipping my wife until she finally under-stands that, while I call her 'princess', she's nothing less than a queen to me.

So I stick my tongue into her pussy from behind. She's so fucking wet, I get a solid mouthful of her juices. Musky and sweet, I lap at her, swallowing it straight from the source.

"Yes," she groans. "I... we shouldn't be doing this, but, God, *yes.*"

Shouldn't be doing this? No. We're married, and nothing will ever separate us again. I'll make sure of it, and if part of reminding her of that fact is fucking her until she forgets she ever hated me, that's what I'm going to do.

Only tonight? I'm going to do one better.

Rising up again, I fist her hair, turning her head so that I can make her taste herself on my lips as I kiss her.

Loni whimpers, but she doesn't pull away. She kisses me in return, and I find a little relief, thrusting slightly against the cleft of her ass.

I swipe my tongue along her bottom lip, then bite down on it with my two front teeth. Not hard, never hard, but it's hard enough that she jerks in place, backing up fully against my groin so that not even I can move away from her promising heat.

I'm still dressed. Her leggings are down at her ankles, her panties twisted among the fabric. I have my hands under her shirt, squeezing her tits as I bury my face into her hair.

It would be so easy to unzip my pants, pull out my cock, and slip it right inside of her. That's definitely what she expects.

Tonight? I want to do the last thing she would.

Swallowing my intense arousal, keeping my voice as royal and commanding as I can, I tell her, "Unbutton your husband, princess."

For a second, I think she's going to refuse. That I took a calculated risk and failed. That she's going to push me away or maybe even slap me for the seductive command. After all, she made it clear last time that she won't fall prey to my charms again anytime soon. If she wanted to fuck me, she would initiate sex on her own. Until then, I was at her mercy.

But the way she was glaring daggers at Sophie Vale, the overt jealousy my sweet bride couldn't hide... to me, she *did*. Maybe not with words, but if Loni ever thought that I'd choose another woman over her, I'm ready to show her that she's the only one for me.

I won't fuck her, though. That goes against the spirit of trying to make her fall for me by being the husband she deserves. She wanted to be the one to initiate? Fine. Then everything that happens from this point on will be because she did it.

And that begins with Loni undressing me.

Her fingers twitch. I hold my breath, steady for a slap, hoping that she'll lower her hand, snapping the button on my pants. She doesn't; at least, not right away. With a determined look on her gorgeous face, she turns in my hold and reaches for the top button on my shirt.

The first one snags a little, but once she figures out that my buttons are on the opposite side than she's used to, she makes quick work of the rest of them until my shirt is flapping open.

"Good girl," I purr. "Now take off my jacket."

"Your hands broken, Adrian? Because you seemed to have no problem getting my pants off as quick as you did."

I smile. "And then I remembered that you said you wanted to be in control next time."

She raises her eyebrows. "I said I wanted to be the one to decide when we would be intimate again."

"So make a decision. If you want to fuck your husband... if you want to see who this cock belongs to... why you never have to be jealous of another woman because you're the only one who has me so desperate, I'll bend you over and fuck your brains out with a houseful of people two floors below… then all you have to do is take off my jacket, Loni."

She could say 'no'. I'll hate it, but I'll respect it. This isn't about me doing whatever I can to convince her to Claim me in August like Jack expects. This is about seeing that uncertain expression flickering across her face because she caught Sophie talking to me.

I could tell her that the Used just wanted to ask about Haven. I could remind her that there isn't a single one of the Order's sex workers that I've been with, let alone one who we went to school with together.

I could do that, but I don't. Instead, I'll show her.

Or, better yet, I'll let her show *me* that as much as she belongs to me, Adrian Heller is *hers*.

"I'll take off the jacket," she concedes. "But leave the shirt on."

Interesting. "If that's what you want. Tonight, princess, you call the shots."

I might live to regret that, but when she swallows roughly before stepping into me, I decide that I don't care. Regret comes later.

Giving my wife what she needs… that comes *now*.

Loni shoves at my right shoulder, pushing my jacket off of it. "Then this is what I want," she promises, doing the same for the other shoulder. Reaching around me, keeping her body positioned between me and the desk, she grabs the back of my jacket and shimmies it off of me before tossing it to the floor.

Just like she said, she leaves my shirt where it is. Her eyes drawn to my chest, she slides her hand from my navel up to my left pec, slipping it under the open shirt flap, flicking my nipple with her thumbnail.

I shudder, leaning forward, bracing both of my hands on the desk behind her, trapping Loni in my arms.

"Fuck, that felt amazing," I grit out. "Do it again."

She's bending a little herself, our bodies flush as I nuzzle her throat, rumbling under my breath as her hands rover over my chest. She doesn't pay specific attention to my nipple again, but the gentle caress feels almost as good that I let her do whatever the fuck she wants to me.

Slowly, slowly, she moves her hand until she reaches the button I'd hoped she'd go for in the first place. She fiddles with it for a moment—I hold my breath—before she has it open, her fingers tugging urgently on the zipper.

"That's a very good girl," I tell her, my voice raw and throaty. With her taste on my lips and my cock aching to get inside of her, this slow pace is fucking *killing* me. "Now grab me."

Loni hesitates, but then she does.

"Oh, yes. Now turn around, bend over, and put it in."

I should've known that I was pushing my luck. Her hand is still holding onto my erection, her back arched so that she's in the perfect position to do just that after she listens to me and bends, but she doesn't make any move to fuck me.

Damn it.

Maybe she needs a little more guidance. "You want your husband's cock? I know you do. So take it. Put it in."

This time, she freezes. "Are you going to make me

beg? Is that it? With all your friends here, you need to remember who's the one really in control?"

Bending over her, cursing myself for pushing her too hard, too fast, I nibble her earlobe, ignoring it when she lets go of me and reaches up to swat at my face. "No, princess. You have that all wrong."

Loni lowers her hand. She doesn't grab my cock again, but she's not pushing me away, either. "I do?"

"Mm." I kiss the skin behind her ear. Every part of her tastes fucking amazing. "This isn't about me showing you that I'm in control. This is about you taking it for yourself. You want to fuck me? Do it. I'm your willing slave tonight. If you don't want my cock, that's fine, too. I have fingers..." I reach around her, tweaking her nipple through her bra. "My tongue." I lick the edge of her jaw. "But if you want my cock, it's yours," I promise her, pushing the head of my weeping erection against her bare ass. I stay away from any holes so she doesn't get mixed signals, but she needs to know I'm ready—and that I'm serious. "*Only* yours."

If my wife wants to fuck, I won't unless she initiates it. I'm not being petty, either. I want this woman with an intensity that, sometimes, I doubt I'll survive.

But right now? I need her trust even more than that.

She keeps her eyes trained on the desk for a moment. And then... "You mean it?"

I have just one response:

"Would I lie to you?"

TWENTY-THREE
CONTROL

ADRIAN

'm not being fair because, truth is, I *have*. I wish I could say that I didn't; that I *don't*. There are so many things that I've kept from her... but this amazing woman honestly believes that I always tell her the truth. I like to think that I do when it counts. My lies are all meant to protect her, to keep her safe, so maybe that's why they don't matter to Loni like they should.

Either way, my wife's foolish trust in her villainous husband works in my favor because she whispers the word, "No," a second before I feel her soft fingers taking a firm and possessive hold on the base of my erection.

Yes.

"That's my girl," I grit out as she lodges the head of my cock at her entrance. "Now take me, fuck me, and show me that I'm *yours*."

That's all I want. To be Loni's... that's all I've ever fucking wanted. And maybe I'm using that fleeting jealousy I caught earlier to manipulate her into being the one to fuck me, but hell if it isn't working.

I nearly nut, knowing that my impulsive plan is paying off.

Loni grips the edge of my desk. She moves slowly, taking my full length into her body at a pace that has me breaking into a sweat, barely resisting the urge to fill her completely myself. And when she finally has taken all of me, pausing to see if I'm going to break my word and start pounding into her, I clench my jaw and hiss through my teeth, "Do it, princess. Fuck your husband."

I trail a hand down her back as she begins to move.

Thank fucking God.

"That's it. You know exactly how to take your pleasure from your husband. Because that's what I am, Loni. I'm yours. I've always been yours."

Claim me, damn it. Give me some sign that, in less than a month, you'll spit in Jack's face and tell him that you choose to be mine.

Loni doesn't. She does exactly what I said instead, focusing on fucking me to the point that, before I even know it, I'm sensing the familiar tingles of an approaching climax at the base of my spine.

"Holy shit... oh, *yes*. You did it, princess. Look at you, taking what belongs to you. And I 'm so fucking happy to let you have it." I grunt, eyes rolling back in my head as she shoves her ass back up against it. "That's it... hold tight, Loni, 'cause I'm about to come harder than I ever have before."

Because she's *mine*, but I'm hers, too, and the way she's fucking me like this... she knows it.

Only I should've known better. Loni Heller is nowhere as meek and submissive as Loni Dougherty once was. So... yeah. Announcing my impending orgasm like that? Big mistake.

My wife immediately stops what she's doing. "No."

What?

"Excuse me?"

"You heard me. I said *no*."

"Avalon—"

She laughs under her breath. Fuck if I know why since, the way my balls ache, my body ready to come, I don't see anything funny about her deciding to stop fucking me right before I could. "Do you know something? Whenever you get pissed at me, you go right for the full name. Avalon."

"I'll call you whatever the hell you want if you just keep fucking me."

"But that's my point. You said I was in control."

"You are."

She gives me a pity bounce. I meet the thrust, slamming home into her, only realizing after she starts *tsk*-ing that I failed some kind of test.

Right. Because I told her to fuck me. That if she wanted pleasure, she had to take it from her husband.

If *she* wanted pleasure...

I dig my fingers into her hips. "Loni. *Loni*. My wife. My beautiful, beautiful wife... you're not going to get off and leave me like this, are you? Because you can't. I need you." An open-mouthed kiss to the side of her throat. "I need this. I'll give you whatever the fuck you want. A friend for Peaches? A night out at the Court together? The deed to my house"—that I had the Order's lawyer add her name to the same day that I filed our wedding license—"or my car. You want my car, princess? Let me have all of you... let me Claim you again and again... but just... Claim *me*."

That's all I want. All I'll ever need. For the Offering I've been obsessed with since I was a lonely little boy to realize that, no matter how I teased and poked and terrorized her, I did it all out of a twisted sort of love and affection. To give me the love I hungered for in return, accepting that my addiction to her was as inevitable as the sun rising the next morning.

Surrounded by fire, lit up by flames, the heat of Loni's body sears me to the soul more effectively than what's flickering beyond the grate of the fireplace. And when she reaches behind her, finding my bare ass cheek, digging her fingernails into it as she lets out a soft laugh... I would burn happily for her.

"Loni..." I groan.

"I swear to God. No one would've believed me if I told them I could make Adrian Heller beg on his knees."

Is that what she wants? "I'll go on my knees right now, but only if you keep that pussy right where it is. I'd love it if you rode me like that."

"Ah, baby, I'm sure you would."

The rare pet name is almost enough to have me coming without any other stimulation but the warmth of her cunt snuggling my cock. Baby... she would always apologize whenever it slipped out, as though worried that my public persona would switch on in private, and I'd tease her for it.

I never did. Not then, and not now. But I won't deny

that, in public, I did things—said things—to Loni that I'm not proud of. If I spend the rest of our lives together working to make it up to her, even that won't be enough, but fuck if I'm not willing to try.

I'll do anything for her.

Even suffer the worst case of blue balls I've ever had if it gave her a little bit of power over me to reclaim…

"So what do you say? Should we move this to the floor?"

She pretends to think it over for a second. "No."

"*Loni.*"

My wife giggles. "You wanted me to fuck you. That means we go at my speed. So you just stand there and let me use you like a dildo, and when I'm ready to go off, I'll let you know. Maybe then I'll give you permission to do the same."

"Do you know how degrading it is to be compared to a piece of mindless silicone?"

"It's you or my vibrator, Adrian. I'll get off either way."

Holy hell, I love this side of Loni. Especially since she's bluffing. "When I had my guys move your stuff here, I specifically looked for anything like that. You want dick, real or fake? You come to me."

"Sorry, but they did a shit job, baby. I have a lipstick vibe that I keep in my makeup bag. It's kept me company six days out of every week."

Right, because Mondays, she's *mine.*

I suck on her neck. "Shouldn't have told me that, princess. The second I can get my hands on it, it's going right in the garbage disposal. Your pleasure is mine. Your orgasms are mine—"

"Yeah." She starts rocking against me again. "Prove it."

Gladly.

Together, we develop a rhythm where I'm not doing any of the work, but fuck me, I'm enjoying the complete loss of control. I'm always so wound up, making plots, making plans, getting the job done... it's a relief, if only for a few stolen moments, to let Loni take the lead.

And that's when, right as she starts panting, her orgasm imminent, I hear a knock at the door, followed by the sound of it easing inward.

No!

"Adrian? You in there?"

I don't have to turn around to know that it's Dallas at the door. And because it *is* Dallas, I don't pull out and kill him for walking in on me and my wife.

Though, for a second there, the temptation to go searching for my Tomcat is *real*.

Dallas... My cousin and I used to have baths together when we were boys, and long before I first convinced Loni to let me fuck her, our circle jerks were legendary. There was nothing like the two of us hanging out in my room, watching porn on our phones, and seeing who could last longer before we nutted into our come rags. There wasn't anything sexual about it, either. It was two thirteen-year-old, horny bastards who discovered tugging on their cocks felt good, and watching women with huge tits get railed online was better than doing our home-work. It was our hobby that summer until I mentioned that, when I wasn't watching free porn online, I jerked it to one of the girls in school.

He knew who I meant. I should've realized then that

my obsession with Loni was the biggest open secret in Harmony Heights, but I brushed it off that Dallas knew because he knows me.

Whatever it was, it was fine. He never spilled. Dallas had his own secrets even then, and just like I'll always keep his, he'll forever keep mine.

Right now? It's not like he's going to go downstairs and tell the whole party that their host has the guest of honor bent over a desk, begging her to let him come. I'm no sub, but when it comes to Loni... I'll do whatever she wants, and if there's anyone who understands that, it's Dallas.

Besides, there was that time one New Years, before I gave up casual sex, when we were twenty and we shared a girl. No swords crossed that day, the townie we picked up more than willing to focus on us separately before offering up two distinct holes for us to fuck, so he's seen me in the act before. God knows he's more than aware of what my ass looks like.

It's Loni I shield from his gaze. Pushing my chest to her back, making sure that all he can see is my dick in her pussy, and my ass sticking out as I crush her down, I cover her with my body.

She lets out a soft *oof* that becomes a squeal when she realizes we have company.

"Adrian? Shit. Get off. Get off! Is someone there? Who's there?"

I free a hand, stroking Loni's brow, dragging my fingers through her hair in a soothing gesture.

Then, calling out to Dallas, I say, "Whatever you need, it can wait. I'm fucking my wife right now, and that comes first. So if you value your eyeballs at all, get out." I pause. "Know what? Go to the end of the hall. Watch the door. I don't want any other interruptions."

Normally, Dallas would give me crap for bossing him around like my hired help instead of calling in a favor from my bro. Sure, I've always been the leader of our group—even when everyone knows he'll eventually take over for his father as the new King—but as close as we are, we both accept that he'll be the face of the Order, I'll be the brains, and we'll fix all the shit that my uncle got wrong.

But this is my wife, and not even Dallas is safe from *my* jealousy.

He's a smart guy. Without a word, he leaves, and I have no doubt in my mind that he's doing exactly what I said.

I wait for the door to click closed before I return my attention to Loni. I want nothing more than to continue what we were doing, but just in case, I ask, "Do you really want me to get off of you?"

Her response is to arch her back again, pushing her ass against me, taking my cock all the way inside of her. She's panting softly as she murmurs, "Depends. I heard the door close. Is he gone?"

I huff, not sure if I'm amused or annoyed at what she's implying. "You don't think I'd let someone stay and watch me fuck you? Hell no, princess. Those pretty little whimpers are mine and mine alone. Fuck. If it was anyone but Dallas, I wouldn't have threatened their eyes. I would've grabbed the fire poker, plucked them right out, and come back to you before you even knew I'd left the warmth of your sweet body."

The ruthless vow is out before I can think better of how she might receive it. I almost regret the brutal honesty—even if it's one of only a few things my wife actually appreciates about her husband—but then she shudders, and I don't know what to think about that.

"What's the matter, Loni? Afraid of your husband?"

She shakes her head, a muffled groan tearing out of her throat.

No?

I think of the groan. Of how, when I promised to pluck out my cousin's eyes, her pussy fluttered, then squeezed me. Afraid... no. Loni wasn't afraid.

She was turned all the way the fuck on.

I have to make sure I'm right. "You don't... you like it when I get violent over you?"

She bobs her head, and it's my turn to squeeze *hard* to keep from nutting without her permission. I haven't gotten it yet, and I'm the one who is terrified that she'll put an end to this moment if I take over after promising that she can be in control.

I have to do something, though. So I bow my head, biting through her sweater. I don't find skin—or, if I do, it's not enough to hurt her—but I can't resist the urge to pin her down any way I can and fuck her until she admits that she cares for me.

Maybe she won't love me. Maybe I've done too much damage to ever expect that from her. But there isn't anyone I won't threaten or shoot or *destroy* for this woman. Hearing that she *likes* it? I spent so long, terrified that my dark side would be the breaking point for Loni. The bullying wasn't; even when I treated her like shit in school, she would seek me out and fuck me after it. Forcing her to marry me... she went along with it.

Seeing Desmond St. James dead at her feet? I thought... I thought I would have to keep her my unwilling bride, my forever captive, locking her with me if I had to, using every fucking bylaw in the Order's charter to keep her as mine.

But she *liked* it.

Because I was right. Because I knew it.

Because this woman was always meant to belong to Adrian Heller, and not even a casual threat of maiming, dismemberment, and death will kill her attraction for me.

It's a start. If that's all I can have, I'll take it.

I'll take it all—and like I vowed to her on our wedding night, I will never, ever let her go.

TWENTY-FOUR

WHAT'S THIS

LONI

"Peaches?" I ps-ps-ps, calling for the kitten. "Peaches? Where are you, sweetie?"

Did I honestly believe that a four-month-old kitten would wave her paw and say 'here'? Of course not. But considering I spent fifteen minutes tearing my room apart, another ten searching Adrian's, and it's now been an hour of pure anxiety because I've gone through nearly every room in this mansion and there's still no sign of Peaches... it would be kinda nice if she did.

I blame the party from a couple of nights ago. I made sure to keep her food bowl filled, her water fresh, and her litter box clean before I went downstairs to join it. My door was closed so that she couldn't escape into the rest of the house and disappear with all the unfamiliar people everywhere.

At least, that was the idea. At some point, an amorous couple found their way to my room and borrowed my freshly made bed. Peaches got a front-row seat to what had to be some wild sex, based on the state of the room when I eventually left Adrian's and went back to mine late the next morning.

I was super annoyed that someone got it on in my bed. Worse, it made me think of how I fucked Adrian in one of the Reynolds's spare guest rooms during our high school graduation party. We weren't the only ones going at it, either, even if I was the only one whose virginity got called into question when the party was over, and it seems like—ten years later—the old crew hasn't changed at all.

I'll never know who snitched on us back then. I still think that it had to be Desmond. That he guessed something was going on between me and Adrian, and he went running to Jack Collins, never realizing that it was a full-blown affair that we were having—or that, in my naïveté, I would admit to having sex with someone before being Claimed during the Claiming ceremony.

I'll never know, I guess. If it *was* Desmond, then he took that to the grave with him. If it wasn't? Does it really matter anymore? I have Adrian now... it's just the question of whether I want to keep him or not.

Jealousy... seeing him with Sophie made me realize that I've been fooling myself. I honestly believed I could get out of this arrangement before I was in too deep, and definitely before I got my heart broken again. Then we had that stolen moment in his study and... yeah.

I'm fucked, and not just because of what we did up there the other night.

Whatever happened in *my* room, though, left its

marks on my poor kitten. She's been more than a little skittish ever since, and though Mrs. Gammond cleaned up the room and laundered the bedding for me, there are moments when Peaches finds a new place to hide, and I spend the time until I can find her panicking that she somehow got lost.

I can usually get her to peek her head out by shaking the bag of treats she seems to like. Today, I'm shaking these things like a pair of maracas. There's still no sign of her, and my worry is only growing as I climb the stairs to the third floor.

Today is Mrs. Gammond's day off. I had breakfast with Adrian before he headed out to do some errands, and he promised to bring home food from my favorite diner in Harmony Heights when he finished up at his office. I gave him my order for both lunch and dinner, depending on when his workday was over, and planned on getting some of my own done.

But then I couldn't find Peaches, and my anxiety decided that I couldn't sit down to work until I knew where my kitten was.

Adrian gave her to me. She was my birthday gift. What kind of shit kitty mom am I if I lost her within two weeks of owning her? No. She has to be here somewhere. She was in my room before breakfast, and I know I closed the door behind me.

I did.

Right?

I thought I did. And it's not like Mrs. Gammond was by and accidentally let her out. As for Adrian... he wouldn't. In his own way, everything he's been doing lately, he's trying to make amends for our youth. I might've been hesitant to give him a second chance in the beginning, but the more time I spend with him, the more I remember why I fell for him in the first place, even after all those years he picked on me.

It's simple. When Adrian Heller's attention is on you, it's like the sun shines on your face without a trace of clouds in the sky. I'm a sunflower, turning toward him, eager for his warmth because I know what it's like to be in his shadow.

For the first time in our lives, he doesn't have to hide his attraction to me. Whatever affection he feels toward me. Just like how, by becoming his wife, I'm not his dirty little secret anymore. He Claimed me in the eyes of God and the Order, and it's been longer than I want to admit since I even thought about breaking free of him.

Oh, no. I want to stay, and that's a very dangerous thing to admit, even to myself.

He's still holding back. Secretive as ever, I don't think I'll ever know every part of Adrian. Sometimes I tell myself I'll just have to be satisfied with what I can have. But is that enough? It's too soon to tell.

For now, I'm only worried about a tiny orange kitten lost in a house this big. When I work in the upstairs office that Adrian arranged for me, Peaches joins me. She curls up on the windowsill, basking in the sunlight, while the silly human she looks out for has to tap-tap-tap on a box with keys. I wouldn't be surprised to find her in there, though I'm disappointed—and frustrated—when I don't.

That leaves Adrian's study.

Anxiety is a bitch. I know we turned the fireplace off

after we were done in his study the other day, trading the desk for his bed, ignoring the fact that my birthday party was still going. I'm not sure he's been back in there since, and if he has, there's no reason to assume he turned the fireplace on.

And, yet, I can't stop imagining the small fluffball somehow making her way behind the grate, sizzling away as she mews painfully, dead because I didn't bother checking *every* room in the house.

So far, the only two I haven't are the basement gym and Adrian's study. The gym is locked—for my safety, supposedly, though I wonder if he only did it because he was afraid I'd grab one of his weights and bean him in the head those rough early days of our marriage—so I'm not worried that Peaches pulled a Houdini and got down there.

But the study?

The door turns easily under my hand. It's not locked, so I figure I can take a quick peek around to make sure that Peaches didn't follow Adrian in earlier and get stuck.

It takes five minutes for me to admit that Peaches isn't in here, either. The fireplace was off—the first place I checked—and considering the study is made up of a row of locked filing cabinets, a large desk, stacked bookshelves, and nothing else, she wouldn't be able to get lost in this room.

I should leave. There's no reason for me to stay. I should leave...

I don't.

I guess I'm just too nosy. During my search, I noticed that Adrian left two folders out on top of the desk, plus a large black book with a red ribbon serving as a book-mark. I disregarded them at first, but curiosity gets the better of me.

He's a financial manager. That's what he told me. Like me, his work is all numbers, and I can't help myself. I want to see what exactly he's working with.

The top folder makes my stomach drop. I flip through countless sheets, hoping that I'm reading them wrong. I mean, I *have* to be. These aren't the sort of papers that a legitimate financial manager would have in their portfolio.

Closing the top folder, I switch it with the other.

Along the edge, two words are written in Adrian's blocky print: **AVALON DOUGHERTY.**

What the fuck?

I flip that open with so much force, I nearly spill the contents onto the desktop. The first sheet is a copy of my lease; I recognize my signature—my fake signature since the lease is for Marie Howard—at the bottom and know it's legit. Beneath it, printouts of my bank statements, both my hidden Loni account, and Marie's where I received my paycheck.

What the...

I don't look any deeper. I don't want to know what else he researched about me and my old life. So, instead, I place the two folders onto the edge of the desk, reaching for the big, black book.

Flipping it open to the page marked with the ribbon, I read it upside down from my position in front of the desk, my jaw dropping at what's written on *that* page.

"Loni? What are you doing in here?"

I jump, slamming the black book shut.

Fuck. I never even heard him come in or close the door behind him. He has. Adrian—dressed in the same suit as he was this morning, the familiar unlit cigarette tucked behind his ear—is standing in front of the door, an unreadable expression on his handsome face.

Now, I know I'm not supposed to be in here. He told me from the beginning that the study was off-limits unless he was with me... but I guess I thought he got rid of that rule after we christened this very desk the other night.

The tendons standing out on his neck tell me otherwise.

I gulp. "I was looking for Peaches."

"I thought you wanted to keep her in your room. That it would be the safest spot for her until she was older."

"Yes—"

"If that's the case, she wouldn't be in my study."

"She isn't. I... I still haven't been able to find her."

"That's okay." He gestures for me to leave the desk, to go to him. "Come with me, Loni. I'll help you search."

Oh. It hits me suddenly. *Oh.* He's not mad at me for coming in here. I read that way wrong. Adrian... he's shitting bricks that I might've seen something I wasn't supposed to.

And I did, didn't I?

"It can wait," I tell him. "I'd like to ask you about this first."

"About what?"

I hold up the pair of folders. The one with my name on it is understandable. With his legacy and his wealth,

I'd think him an idiot if he didn't run a background check on me. But the sheaf of papers in the other one? It doesn't make sense.

"I saw these on your desk. You want to explain them?"

A muscle tics in his jaw. "Not particularly."

I figured as much.

"Okay." I tuck the folders under my arm. Adrian's fingers flex, eager to snatch them from me... which is all the more reason why I keep them close. "How about this black book, huh?" I turn to the page marked with the ribbon. "Maxwell and Dimmity's. Why is information on my firm in your book?"

Names. I recognize all of these names. My bosses. Some of my co-workers; recent ones, and those who have moved on. There's Bradley Figueroa, a sweet guy I dated for six months under my supervisor's nose before some puritanical 'co-workers can't date' clause ended with Bradley in the UK, and our relationship over.

His name is crossed out so fiercely, the page is ripped.

What the hell is that about?

I show Adrian what I'm looking at, waiting for an answer.

He purses his lips. His fingers tap against his upper thigh, and I'd bet all the money in his account that, if I plucked the unlit cigarette from behind his ear and offered to light it, he'd agree.

I wait.

He sighs, resigned. "I have a stake in that firm."

"Monetary?"

"A little. But more like I have a vested interest in their staff."

He *what*? "What do you mean by that?"

I thought one thing already based on the files I was looking at before he walked into the study. But this... I don't understand it.

Or maybe I don't *want* to...

Reading my mind, Adrian asks, "Do you really want to know?"

No. "Yes."

"Then it's pretty simple. My mentor insisted that they hire you." He pauses a moment. "It was a favor to me."

I blink, unable to say anything in response to that bombshell.

And then, as if it's the most obvious thing in the world, he tells me: "If I knew where you were, I could keep tabs on you without ever having to leave Harmony Heights. Your promotions, your moves... I had a hand in all of it."

There it is. Confirmation I never knew I needed.

"You..." My mouth works, but nothing comes out. I give my head a clearing shake. "All this time, I thought I got my promotions through my hard work." A scoff as my heart fucking *shatters*. "Figures. I haven't earned anything my entire life."

"Yes. You have."

"No. No, I haven't."

And, like everything that's ever gone wrong in my life, this man is to blame.

Pushing away from the door, Adrian sidles past me. I expected him to grab me, to hold me close, to explain... but he doesn't do any of that.

My heart leaps into my throat when he jabs the

button to the fireplace, the flames starting small before growing steadily. I checked the grate. I checked the whole damn study. Peaches isn't in there, but there's still that moment when the fire comes to life when I brace myself for a yowl.

It doesn't come. Instead, Adrian watches the fire for a few moments before turning around. He heads for the desk, moving to stand behind it rather than meeting me at the front.

He lays his hand on the back of his desk chair. "You've earned my heart, Loni. As black as you think it is, it's yours."

What if I can't accept it?

A man who would interfere in my life even after I thought he was no longer a part of it?

A man who forced me into marrying him, and now I'll never be free of him?

I thought...

I thought—

The fire crackles in Adrian's study, but it does shit to warm me up. I'm cold all the way down to my bones, and this time, it has nothing to do with the powerful central air conditioner pumping into every room of this house. Oh, no. It's the realization—cemented by that first folder—that Adrian is more indispensable to the Order than I ever thought.

He isn't just a member. He works for them. He got rich off of them.

There will never be a moment when I'm more important than the society, even with this proof that he meddled in my life long before now. They own his loyalty, and me… I'm just the woman he got as a prize for a job well done.

I grab the folders again, snatching them out from under my arm. I didn't want the pages to mean what I *thought* they meant, but if he could control my life from a distance all these years, there's no end to the criminality he could be involved with.

Honestly? Why am I so fucking surprised? He's a *murderer*, a fact that I conveniently keep forgetting, if only because I wanted to see Desmond dead.

But this?

I shake the folders at him. "You're laundering money for them, aren't you?"

"For Maxwell and Dimmity?"

I swallow. "For them, sure. But mainly, I meant the Order."

"It's yes either way."

He doesn't say it like it's a confession. No. It's simply a fact, and one that I took too long to notice.

I set the folders in my hand down harder than I mean to. Papers spill out onto the desk. I recognize them; having gone through this folder already, I know what they are. Ledgers. Bank statements, the ones on top clearly coded. Investment portfolios that funnel money through six or seven different shell companies so that they come out clean on the other side.

"All these accounts," I tell him, jaw tight, voice shaky, "tied to hospitals, construction sites, campaign funds to the sheriff's election last year—"

"The Order owns Harmony Heights," Adrian cuts in. "Someone has to keep it running. Keep Jack and the others from destroying it from the inside. I do what I have to."

My heart pounds, hoping that I was wrong. That, like I once accused him of being, he isn't the villain of this tale. That Adrian Heller can be my *hero*... "You do this to help the town? You go against the Order?"

His loyalty isn't to the Owed? It's to—

"No," he says, and our eyes finally meet. I don't even realize that he was avoiding looking at me directly until I see the steely flint in his light green eyes. "I do this so that they can't fuck with me. That they *owe* me. I'm an Owed, right? I want every fucking person in this town to owe me, and when they do? I'll know that I'm untouchable." Fire flashes in the depths of his pupils. "And that makes *you* untouchable."

I shake my head. "You're profiting off of it."

"Of course I am." He grips the top of the chair tightly. I can tell he wants to touch me, but he knows better than to do that when I'm trembling angrily on the other side of his desk. "Because I needed the power to Claim you. I needed leverage. If I just followed you out of Harmony Heights without any... if I was just one of the basic Owed... do you think you'd be my wife right now? Or would you be in the back rooms of the Court, fucking any Owed that climbed into your bed?"

"You took Desmond's place because Jack Collins is your uncle—"

"I took Desmond's place because you've always belonged to me. You're fucking *mine*, Avalon. You always have been. Even when you thought I hated you, I was protecting you. Because, damn it, I *love* you."

I wish I could believe that. I want to, but like always with Adrian, there are so many goddamn secrets. Financial manager, huh? God, I was such an idiot. The way he smirked when I asked him about his job... financial manager, he told me. I guess when you're cooking the books for an entire town, that's the easiest way to describe what you do.

He's a crook, and he's a liar.

He lies.

And I'm the silly little girl who spent way too long convincing herself she was special. That he would be honest even if it hurt, but nothing hurts more than discovering everything I thought I knew... it wasn't true.

He loves me?

That might be the biggest lie of all.

TWENTY-FIVE
CONFESSION

LONI

have to get out of here. That's all I'm thinking.

I make it halfway to the door when Adrian is suddenly right there.

He grabs my elbow. It's not a rough snatch, though he uses his strength to whirl me around.

"Don't walk away from me." It's not an order. It's a *plea*. "Not after I told you I loved you."

My chest feels tight. "You used to tell me that so you could fuck me," I shoot back. "If you meant it then, I wouldn't have had to leave Harmony Heights."

"That's where you're wrong. If it came out then, my uncle would've been the one shipping you out of town. And that's if you survived."

"What?"

"He wanted me to Claim Haven, remember? I wasn't allowed to choose. My Claiming would've been a joke. Just like he decided Dallas would pair up with Morgan

Peyton, I was supposed to end up with Haven. The only way around it was refusing to Claim anyone until I could Claim you... but you were gone before I could explain."

"You knew where I was." He's never come out and admitted it before now, but after the last few weeks as his wife... the things he's let slip, how he knows me almost as well as I know myself... he found me long ago. I suspected it. His interfering with my job just proves it. "You could've explained then."

"I could've. If I thought it would save you from the Order, I would've."

I shake my head, jerking on my arm at the same time. He releases me, but he doesn't back away.

Not yet.

"Do you know about my Aunt Reese?"

I'm not expecting him to change the subject so quickly—though I have to admit that I know a little about her.

Therese Collins. While Jack was very rarely referred to as his uncle, he always called her 'Aunt Reese'. They weren't blood; Jack is Adrian's mother's brother. It didn't matter. She was a sweet-faced blonde woman who was the Offering given to the man who would be King.

And then, about five years ago, she died. Oh, my dad said it was an accident. It was during our Father's Day phone call, and though I didn't want to hear anything about the Order, even I was interested in learning about Reese Collins's tragic death. She was alone on the balcony of her family's penthouse apartment at the Fortress one moment. The next? She was flying without wings, landing on the asphalt out back.

Everyone says she jumped. Of course they do.

Because no one would ever blame the King—except for his rogue nephew.

"Offerings... wives... you're supposed to be protected. But think about this: if my uncle looked the other way when I desecrated St. Catherine's and killed the only son of a powerful family in town because I could and he allowed it from a Collins, do you think he would let it slide when his wife had an affair with a man who *wasn't* part of the Order?"

Holy shit. "Is that what happened?"

"The men have their fun. The women... they play their part. He wouldn't give up his mistress, but he wouldn't give my aunt the freedom to live her own life when he no longer wanted her as part of his. So, instead of continuing in a marriage of convenience, he took the cheap way out. And now my aunt is dead, and Jack can fuck anyone he wants."

I want to ask if he's sure. I want to know how that affected him. And Dallas... poor Dallas. It was common knowledge as kids that he hated his dad and worshipped his mom. Five years ago... Dallas would've been twenty-three when she died.

I was sixteen when I lost my mom, and I miss her every fucking day. But she was sick, not murdered, and suddenly I see why it wasn't a big deal to Jack when Adrian gunned down Desmond...

Adrian Claimed me. I was his Offering, and now I'm his wife. I'll be the first to admit I haven't made it easy, and he doesn't deserve for me to.

But... "Would you do that to me?"

I don't have to elaborate. Adrian knows exactly what I mean.

He takes my chin in his hands. "No."

I close my eyes, letting his warmth and his denial wash over me.

His voice becomes more determined. "I'm not fucking lying, Loni. You are the only person in this fucked-up world that is safe from me."

I blink, looking up at him, taken aback by the sincerity in his words. I almost believe him... but, hell, I can't forget the past. He told me I had to... to forget the past, focus on the future... but I *can't*. "It didn't used to be like that."

"Because I was a fucking idiot. Simple as that. I did what I thought I had to, and if I pushed you away, at least you were safe. But I finally have you where you belong. You're here, with me, and there isn't anyone I won't sacrifice to be your husband."

It's always been that I'm his wife. Having Adrian refer to himself as *my* husband?

"Adrian—"

"It was always going to be you and me. The king-maker and his princess. But I knew better than to try and Claim you before I had all the cards. The deck's stacked now, though. Those books... they're my safety net. But it's not my safety I'm worried about. It's yours."

Fuck. This time, I kind of *do* believe him.

No. I shake my head, loosening his hold on me. Recognizing that I need space, Adrian lets go of me. I dart around him, heading closer to the fireplace, flames licking at the grate, the warmth a sensation I need desperately.

He grabs the back of the desk chair again, forcing himself to stay there instead of coming after me.

"I was a stupid kid who thought I could make it up to you. That, being an Offering yourself, you'd eventually understand the games we're forced to play in the Order. But you left, and I stayed behind so that none of us could hurt you again." A shadow falls over his face. "Especially me."

I look away, taking in the spilled papers, the folder with my name on it, the book open to the page dedicated to the firm I work for...

My stare returns to him, my chest breathing hard and trying to hide it. "You're acting like this is some noble mission. That you're a hero. You made deals with monsters, Adrian."

A whisper of his usual smirk. "If only, Loni. I *became* one. For you."

My stomach tightens now. "I didn't ask you to."

"No," he agrees softly. "But you *needed* me to."

"Control," I breathe out. That's what this is about. What it's *always* been about. He let me have it just the once, then snatched it right back... but in reality? He never handed over any of it. "You've done everything you can to control me. I still don't see how love is involved at all."

With those as my final words, I start to leave again. This time, Adrian doesn't stop me.

As I pass the desk, something metal tinkles as it hits the top of it.

My head turns, and I see there's a small ring of keys there that wasn't there before.

I shake my head and keep walking.

"Take the keys. Unlock the drawers." His voice follows after me like cigarette smoke. "Go through the books, Loni. Read every fucking line. See who I've helped, who I've protected. Who I paid off, and who I cut out. Then do me a favor. Ask yourself if a man who doesn't worship the damn ground you walk on... would he threaten an entire *empire* to make sure that I'm the only one you could ever be Owed to? Because I've done it, and I'll do it again. For you."

Is that it? Is that what he wants me to believe? That this is all because of his need to *own me*?

I hover in the doorway, fingernails biting into the ornate wood. "That doesn't change my point about control."

"No," he echoes, firmer this time. "It doesn't."

***

PEACHES IS CURLED UP ON MY LAP, SNUFFLING SOFTLY. I run my fingers through her downy fur, finding a moment of peace as I try to forget what happened barely an hour ago.

It's impossible, and it only grows even more so when the phone tossed next to me on the bed buzzes.

Trying not to disturb the kitten, I pick it up and only just resist the urge to throw it as far away from me as I can.

ADRIAN

Come back to the study.

Please.

I almost ignore the summons. If he hadn't added 'please' to the end of it, I would've. But as Peaches purrs softly and my heart thumps wildly, I think about Adrian still upstairs, all alone, wanting to speak to me.

Something restless stirs beneath my skin. I was so discombobulated after I fled down the stairs, looking for as much of an escape as I could get knowing that Adrian will only come after me... trying not to let it sting that it took ten years for him to do just that... that I locked myself in my room.

Moments later, Peaches popped her head out from underneath the bed, completely unaware of the shit she stirred by hiding as effectively as she had. I forgave her, though, because her tiny meow was just so stinking cute, and when I dropped down on the bed, she clambered up the comforter and curled up in my lap.

I hate to leave her now, but I stroke her head, then settle her next to me. She blinks sleepily at me, and I smile. Good kitty.

Bad pussy.

I should know better than to go back up there. We parted at odds, and I'm still not sure what I think about everything he told me. Even so, I pull myself up and out of my bed, powerless to ignore Adrian when he needs me.

When I let myself back into the study, Adrian is standing in front of the fireplace. His jacket is gone, his shirtsleeves rolled up to his elbows, his toned forearms on display. His tie is missing, too, and the three top buttons on his shirt are undone.

His hair is a rumpled, tousled mess. Like he's been up here, thinking, running his fingers through his curls. The flames flicker off of his golden earrings, the way they gleam in the firelight drawing my attention to the shell of his empty ear.

I focus on that.

"Your cigarette is missing," I point out. "What happened, Adrian? Your conscience get the better of you and you finally smoked it?"

"You want to kiss me and find out?"

This last month, he insisted on claiming his kiss in exchange for continuing to go cold turkey when it comes to his smoking. I liked kissing him, just like it made me feel a slight sense of accomplishment that all it took was me disapproving of his smoking for him to quit just like that. I used the excuse to get close to him, telling myself I had no choice, that it was something I *had* to do...

"Not right now."

His disappointment is palpable, though he doesn't do anything other than shrug.

Damn it. The casual motion has my eyes dipping to the tanned skin peeking through his dress shirt.

I gesture at him. "You look like you've just rolled out of bed."

Another half-hearted comment: "You like it?"

I do, but I'm not about to admit that at this moment. Instead, I can't help but once again remember what happened between us the first time we came up to his study together. Add that to the come-hither look in his eyes and the way he's already half-dressed…

I ball my hands into fists. "If you had me come up here because you want sex like the night of the party, screw you. Or not. Because *no*. Just no. No kisses. No fucking. In case you can't tell, I'm still spiraling from everything I learned before."

"So am I."

"Those were your secrets, Adrian."

A second nod. "They were. But you left before you found out the biggest one."

Oh? "And what's that?"

"You found one of my ledgers, but you didn't find this."

Before I can ask what he's talking about, Adrian stalks quietly over to the desk, pausing only to trail his finger along the back of my shoulders. I shiver as he pulls open one of the drawers on the left side of his desk. Reaching inside, he grabs a small cedar chest about eight inches long, five inches wide.

Setting it on the top of his desk, he flicks the clasp, knocking the lid back.

The first thing I see on top is a lock of hair in a tiny baggie. It's a little bit reddish, a little bit blonde, and every bit of the hair that grows out of my head.

"Where did you get that?" I breathe it.

"I cut it and you never noticed," he says shamelessly. "Years ago. I had a pocket knife on me the first time we slept together. Remember?"

Actually, yeah. "I remember thinking you were such a bad boy for a rich kid. You took out that knife and cut my underwear off of me after pushing me down on your bed. I thought you'd nick me, but you didn't." I pause, thinking back. "I never saw those panties again."

"Of course not. I have them, too."

I glance in the wooden box.

He huffs, a sound that might be a laugh if I didn't know how serious he was being. "That's my prized possession, princess. You think I'd let it take on the scent of cedar? No. It's in a sealed bag, as delicious as the day I cut them off of you."

I blink. I don't even know how to react to that.

"Does that scare you? That I've kept a lock of hair as a memento all these years? That, when I missed you the most, I rubbed a pair of your ten-year-old panties against my cheek?"

Does that scare me? Not even a little.

But it does scare me how much that turns me on...

Dipping his fingers into the box, he pinches something else. It's a used cigarette with the faint remnants of a pale pink lipstick around the filter.

"The one and only time you shared a smoke with me. After I put it out, I stole the butt because your mouth had been on it."

Again into the box, this time pulling out a candid shot of me in a cap and gown.

"When you graduated college. I couldn't be there, but Connor did me a solid. He snuck in and got a picture of you getting ready backstage."

He did?

"Adrian."

"There's more. If you want to see it, I can show you.

But understand this: when I tell you that I love you, Avalon Heller, believe me. When I tell you that I'm obsessed… know that I'm telling the truth." His eyes darken to a deeper shade of green. "Odds are I'm under-selling just how fucking addicted to you I am. Your smell. Your taste. Your laugh." Adrian moves toward me. He lifts his hand, pointer finger ghosting over my cheek. "Those freckles. All of you. Do you know what my first real memory is?"

I shake my head.

"You. In overalls and pigtails, a smudge of chocolate on your nose after you broke your cookie in half and gave me the bigger size back in kindergarten. Do you understand what I'm saying? What I mean? You, Loni. It's always been you.

"Look. I'm not good. I'm not nice. If I ever talked to a shrink, they'd probably fill a notepad with everything that's wrong with me. But my love for you? It's the one thing that makes me remember I'm human."

Oh, Adrian. "You are, baby. You say that like there's something wrong with you."

But there's not. To see this vulnerable side of him… how can there be?

And then he makes another confession: "You're my greatest love, but that makes you my greatest weakness."

Oof. "Wow."

"I… shit. I said that wrong. That's not what I meant, Loni."

"It's fine," I lie.

"No. It's not. It never was, and that's on me. I didn't know how to protect you then. Putting a wall up between us... doing what I could to make all of Harmony Heights believe that you were meaningless to me when it couldn't be further from the truth..." He reached toward the desk, closing the lid on the box as though he can't look at his collection any longer. "I tell myself I was saving you from the Order. From my uncle. But the truth of it is that I've been protecting you from myself most of all."

"I was never afraid of you," I admit.

"Not even now that you know I've been stalking you for the last ten years? From a distance, yes, but there's no denying that I haven't followed your life every step of the way."

"Even then," I tell him, my words coming out like a quiet promise.

"I watched over you," he says, matching my volume. "Not because I expected you to come back. I knew you wouldn't unless I went and dragged you here—"

"Or Dallas did."

A tiny, begrudging chuckle. "Or Dallas did. But either way... you were such an important part of who I was. I held onto it even when I didn't have any right to."

He steps closer again, just not that close. One purposeful step before our eyes lock and I understand. Like the other night, if I want him, I have to take him.

So I do.

Without giving my body the orders to do it, I'm right there, wrapping my arms around him.

He finishes the embrace, holding me tight. "I've spent ten years regretting what I did and what I didn't do. What I let happen. You... you think this is all about control.

That I wanted you back in Harmony Heights so that I could force you into something you don't want."

"Isn't it?" I whisper.

"No," he says flatly. "This is about finishing what I started all those years ago. I Claimed you when I was a boy." His voice drops notably. "Now I'm a man. And I'm still yours. Even if you never Claim me back."

My throat seems to close in on itself.

Adrian rests his chin on the top of my head, tucking me under him. "You don't have to forgive me. For everything I've done... I can't see how you could. But I need you to know this: I never stopped choosing you."

In my husband's arms, I don't know what to say, so I don't say anything at all.

More importantly, I don't leave, either.

Not yet.

And, after tonight, probably not ever.

TWENTY-SIX

MARTINO'S

ADRIAN

Do you know how good it feels to have it all?

I'm sitting in my office at the Fortress, shoes kicked up on my desk, arms folded behind my head as I smile like the lovesick fool that I am.

I thought the night of Loni's birthday party was enough to erase the worst of her memories of that last one we attended together—and then there was yesterday...

This is it. My second chance. Bas's graduation party all those years ago is the moment I pinpoint as when my life as I planned it went right off the rails, and I'm so fucking glad to have finally righted it. For an entire year, Loni was my secret. At the Claiming ceremony, when I chose her instead of Haven in front of the newly inducted Order and the old guard, no one could've stopped me from Claiming her.

No one, except for Loni herself.

Now it's ten years later, another Claiming ceremony on the horizon, and it's like déjà vu. Only, this time, the whole fucking world knows that Loni belongs to Adrian Heller, and when I bring her to the Fortress to stand before the fire, she will Claim me back.

I know she will. If she can forgive me for interfering with her life, for stalking her, for hiding the depths of the obsession I've felt for her since I was a kid... there isn't anything that will keep us apart.

And I can't fucking wait to see the look on Jack's face when he realizes that.

In a far better mood than I have been for days, I take the unlit cigarette from behind my ear, letting it nestle on the edge of my bottom lip for the moment.

It's another marker of how quickly everything changed in only a few hours. I was so close to lighting up yesterday after weeks of going without that I ripped it from its new usual spot and tossed it in the fireplace before I gave in to the temptation.

Loni noticed. I didn't want her to think that I had relapsed, that nicotine was more important to me than she was, so even though she didn't accept my offer of a kiss at first, I made sure she did later. When she pointed out that I didn't taste like cigarette, I told her the truth.

That at my lowest, when I honestly believed that there wouldn't be any coming back from her walking away from me so easily, I thought about lighting up—but I didn't. Because I told her I wouldn't, that I would quit, and if she ever decided to kiss me again, I didn't want her to taste ashtray on my breath.

Did I expect that she would let me so soon? I'd *hoped*,

but my pragmatic side told me that I was delusional. I guess I underestimated just what a turn-on it could be for Loni when I was both vulnerable and honest with her. For one of the only times ever, she actually believed me readily when I was telling her the God's honest truth, and I got to ssee a totally different side to my wife.

I liked it. I liked it a lot.

Fuck me, I'm on cloud fucking nine. Nothing can bring me down now—

My timer goes off. Removing my shoes from the top of my desk, I reach for my phone. At the same time, a notification from my calendar app pops up on the screen:

LUNCH WITH BAS: 1:15 @ Martino's

Of course.

That's right.

Lunch.

It takes ten minutes to drive downtown to Bas's favorite café. It's one o'clock now. Jack scheduled a meeting at two-thirty between me, Stephen, and two local business owners to talk about the Order taking them over as another front for our money laundering operation. Stephen represents the old guard, I explain the benefits of selling to Jack, and if they hesitate, we call up for one of the enforcers. Luke or Dallas or even Marcus... someone will stand behind the powerpoint presentation, glaring menacingly while I do my sales pitch.

When Bas called me last night, shortly after Loni curled up next to me in bed again despite the fact that it definitely *wasn't* Monday, I almost didn't answer. Only the fact that Bas, Dallas, and Connor are the only ones other than Loni that I actually care to talk to had me waiting for Bas to call back—a second consecutive call being our boyhood sign that it was urgent, but that we didn't want to leave a text trail or a voicemail—and when he did, I answered with a muttered whisper so that I didn't disturb my sleeping beauty.

She snored delightfully through my entire call, and by the end of it, I'd agreed to meet Bas for lunch the next day.

Eventually, my old friend will start cashing in the favors I owe him. Between showing up at the church for my wedding and, now, using his tight friendship with Connor to help me, I'm definitely in his debt.

I'll pay him back. I always do.

I itch when any relationship is one-sided. My ledgers have to be balanced, but when it comes to my wife... there isn't anything I won't do.

Sebastien's bike is parked along the curb when I show up at Martino's. He got lucky. The rest of the side-street parking is full, and unless I want to drive around, looking for one, I'm shit out of luck.

So I double park. If anyone has an issue with it, they can come to me. Either they're a townie who will be easily bought with a couple of hundreds and a charming smile, or they'll be one of the Owed who'll know better than to fuck with Adrian Heller.

Grabbing my phone and my keys, I climb out of the car, glowering at the driver zooming past me. They swerve, I scoff as I lock my Mustang, and then I'm heading toward the front of the café.

"Adrian. Hey, Adrian! Over here."

My head snaps, body detouring toward the back of the crowded outdoor seating area. Harmony Heights is in the middle of a slight cool snap—it's mid-seventies, with a forecast for thunderstorms later today according to my weather app—so I'm not surprised that Bas chose to sit outside.

He has this thing with confined spaces. Sometimes, I think that's why he prefers to hop on his bike and just drive. He craves freedom, him and the open road, and if I know it's because he's outrunning his family's legacy, I keep my mouth shut. Why judge? Especially when my uncle will never let me forget who I am.

Bas is wearing his road jacket, a sleeveless white tank underneath the open leather coat. His eyes are covered in a pair of expensive shades, his motorcycle helmet an odd decoration in the middle of the delicate table setup. When he saw me, he flagged me down, and he kicks out the seat opposite him as I wind my way through the filled tables.

"Thought you'd be late, Adrian. Didn't want to think my oldest friend stood my sorry ass up."

I roll my eyes. "It's 1:13. I'm technically early."

"Yeah, yeah. I've been here since one. You know what they say. Timeliness is next to godliness."

I lower myself into the seat he picked for me. "Isn't that supposed to be cleanliness?"

Bas shrugs. "Who the fuck knows? When Maman is pissed at my old man, she speaks in French. You know she likes to use those kinds of phrases, but they never translate right. That or my French is still shit after all these years."

Ambre Reynolds is a unique case in the Order. She came to Harmony Heights about thirty years ago as an exchange student. Guy Reynolds fell for her at first sight, and when she was supposed to leave at the end of the summer, he seduced her, then Claimed her that August. He was twenty-three, she was eighteen, and if the name Heller or Collins means something in this town, that's nothing compared to the legacy of the Reynolds family.

It didn't matter that Ambre wasn't an Offering. His father was the King at the time, and whatever Guy wanted, Guy got. He married Ambre, trapping her in Harmony Heights, and when she realized how he'd manipulated her, he trashed her passport so she couldn't leave. Then she was pregnant with Alexandre, with Bas coming fourteen short months later, and she gave up on leaving Guy.

She never petitioned the Order for an escape, either. However, the old guard turned on the King. Led by my uncle, they decided that because Guy married out of the Order, he wouldn't be allowed to succeed his father as King. They gave him the choice to abandon Ambre, he refused, and that's how Jack wormed his way into being Mitch Reynolds's heir.

Then Mitch... died, Jack took over the Order, and it's understood that Guy Reynolds did it all for love.

For obsession.

For a woman that he'd sacrifice anything for…

And Jack has hated the Reynolds family ever since, if he didn't already.

"How are your parents?" I ask Bas.

"Worried that Alexandre is still going to fuck up the Claiming ceremony deadline. Yours?"

"Vacationing in Hawaii." I laugh a little under my breath. "They still don't know I'm married."

"That'll be fun when they find out."

That's what Bas thinks. "I figure they won't need to know until Loni has our first kid. They're so oblivious to anything I do, I doubt they'll even notice if I shove a crying baby under their noses."

"Wow, Adrian. I mean, I know you were fucking, but you knocked her up already? Before the Claiming? I guess that's one way to make sure she has to accept you, but—"

"Nope," I cut. "Not pregnant. Not yet."

"What's the matter? You shooting blanks? Or is she insisting on a condom? Some of my girls won't let me fuck 'em without one. And, sure, they may be Used, but if they ask, you gotta wrap it up."

Only Bas would casually talk about his hook-ups at a place like Martino's. And since he is…

"No. She knows better than to think I'll let anything get between us. Not even a piece of rubber. But she's got an IUD. For the next two years, I can nut in her whenever I want without worrying about being a daddy before I'm ready."

"Good shit, buddy. Congratulations."

I shrug, then gesture over his shoulder with my chin.

"You ready to order? Looks like they finally realized I sat myself down."

"Yeah. I told Walt that I was waiting for a guest. I probably should've had you go up front, but that's fine. I'm not in any rush."

If I didn't have that meeting today, I wouldn't be, either. "Do you know what you want?"

Bas looks over his shoulder at the curvy blonde approaching with her order pad. He winks at her. "Hey, Polly. Do me a favor, would you? Put me down for the usual."

She flushes even as she smiles shyly at Bas. Normally, he won't use his good looks in his favor, but when he's comfortable around someone, he can be even more charming than I am.

"You got it, Mr. Reynolds. And for your friend?"

I never even bothered picking up the menu. "I'm not picky. Whatever Bas ordered, that's fine with me."

"Two Waldorf salads, dressing on the side. Sparkling water, twist of lime. I'll put your order right in."

I look over at Bas.

He gives me an impish grin.

I resist the urge to roll my eyes. Instead, I nod at the waitress. "Sounds great."

Polly flashes a smile my way, far less genuine than the one she gave Bas, and then she's gone.

"Hey. I got us a table outside on purpose." He nods at my ear. "You can smoke out here if you want."

Reaching up, I rub my finger along the filter of my cigarette. "Can't. I quit."

"Really? You've been smoking for, like, fifteen years, bro."

"I know, but Loni asked me to."

"She did?"

"Well, she told me she stopped thinking that kissing an ashtray was sexy when she was seventeen so... yeah. Maybe she didn't *ask* me, but I sure as hell stopped cold turkey for her."

Bas slaps the top of his helmet, laughing. "God, you're whipped."

I am, and I won't apologize for it.

I do, however, change the subject. Because I know that a salad won't take long to serve, I BS with my buddy, talking random shit so that we're not in the middle of an important conversation when our waitress comes back.

I'm right. Barely five minutes after we placed our order, she's back with a large tray.

"Here you go." Polly places one of the serving plates in front of Bas, the next in front of me. She follows it with a glass of bubbly water each, then says, "Anything else I can get for you?"

"How about another pretty smile, Polly?"

She giggles. "I can do that," she says, and then she smiles.

Bas nods lazily. "That's all for now, sweetheart. Thanks."

As she bobs away with her empty tray, much happier now than she was when she first approached the table, I give him a wry look.

"I tip fifty bucks every time I come here," is his explanation.

Right. And his pretty face, biker helmet, and the sexy way he's lounging in the wicker chair doesn't have anything to do with it, huh?

Bas digs into his salad, spearing a hunk of walnut, chewing it in a way that no one would describe as attractive—which is on purpose, I bet. Me? I set mine to the side, ready to get down to the reason we're meeting.

"So..."

He swallows. "Right. So, I spent a couple of days hanging out with Connor and Haven, like you asked."

Guilt slithers down my spine. "How is she? Doing better? What about Loni? Is she ready to talk to her?"

Bas shakes his head. "Sorry, Adrian. I tried. Connor was really pissed that I mentioned Loni was back in town because, turns out, he didn't tell her at all. Only said he did, but backed down when I brought Loni up because Haven shut down. If you ask me, he coddles her too much."

I raise my eyebrows. "Wouldn't you?"

He thinks about it for a second as he savors a bite of fresh apple. "Yeah. You're right. It's just... after what she went through, therapy might help, but Connor won't let her out of his sight. It's not healthy." He nods at me. "At least you're not up Loni's ass every second of the day."

With a small smirk, I tell him, "If you'd ever had her ass, you'd know that there's no better place to be. Actually, no. Don't think about Loni's ass."

"Jesus fucking Christ, bro. You're so possessive of that woman, you're trying to police the fantasies that *you* just put in my head?"

Huh. I guess I am.

"She's not just 'that woman', Bas. She's my wife."

And the reason why I tried to get Sebastien to talk to Connor on my behalf. I thought... I don't know. I guess I thought that, if Haven heard from someone other than Connor that Loni was in town, maybe they could reconcile. I know that Loni would love to talk to her friend again, and I was hoping that seeing a familiar face—one that had nothing to do with Johnny Winter or the Owed—would be good for her.

Obviously not.

It was a plan. A good one. Bas has a place of his own, but he's always had a tendency to couchsurf; one of the rooms in my house is solely dedicated to him for when he wants to stay over. Sending him to visit Connor and Haven when he's the only one that Connor will let past their front door, it was a good plan.

Next time, I'll have a better one.

Bas reaches out, giving me an apologetic clap on the shoulder. "I tried, but you know Connor... he's as protective as you are, and with him freaking out about the auctions... he just won't let Haven out of his sight because he's terrified that Jack will order his wife down to the basement."

I blink. "The basement?" Of the Fortress? "What the hell for? Offerings don't go in the basement."

Bas sits back in his seat. "I know. And that's why Connor's freaked. After what happened to Haven—"

"It wasn't her fault."

"Tell the King that. She would be sent right down to

be part of the auctions if he could figure out how to get her away from Connor."

Hang on—

"The auctions?" He mentioned it before, but I blew past it. But again? "They don't exist anymore."

"I used to think they were bullshit myself... like a myth or something... but it looks like the King brought them back. I saw Luke and Kev at the Court a couple of months ago. They confirmed it. Said that Jack started up monthly auctions about..." Bas's forehead scrunches. "You know what? It was shortly after his wife's accident."

Accident.

We both know it wasn't an accident, but in Harmony Heights, you also never know who's listening.

Still, I don't understand. Or maybe I do. When Aunt Reese died... that was around the time that I stopped paying attention to any other woman in town: Order or not. I get why Jack didn't tell me about the auctions, either. Dallas and I were against them, and as kids, we let Jack know.

According to my uncle, some women are too damaged to be Offerings, too valuable to be Used—and, during the auctions, they become Bought. He sells women to the highest bidder, usually men who come from out of town and leave Harmony Heights with their new 'wife' in tow.

But that doesn't make sense. If Jack brought back the auctions, there'd be a huge influx of cash. I'm in charge of the Order's books, the legit ledgers, and the cooked ones. If we had sex trafficking money, it would come through me.

Unless it wasn't for the Order.

Unless Jack is embezzling from the society he rules…

This is something I should know. I can't blame Bas for not mentioning it before. He avoids everything Order-related in town, and if he accidentally gets information, he makes himself forget it as though it's meaningless to him.

But now that I *do* know, this leverage… I can definitely use it.

It's probably the worst possible time, but I smile.

Yes. Fuck Jack Collins. If he's embezzling from the Order, I can use that against him. He wants to come between me and Loni? Good luck when the old guard votes to get rid of him because he betrayed the society.

I smile—and it lasts just as long as it takes my phone to buzz four times, so quickly, it rattles against the glass tabletop.

I pick it up, and my heart stops.

DALLAS 🔥

Emergency!!

Get your ass back to the Fortress

Jack has Loni in your office

NOW!!

No.

No.

I have two weeks. Two whole fucking *weeks* until the Claiming ceremony. There's no reason Jack would send someone to get Loni, or for her to go to him without telling me…

Unless my uncle did it. He figured it out. He knew that I refused to tell Loni that she *has* to Claim me at the end of August or else he'll have our marriage annulled—and he's using that against me.

And it's true that I never did. I *couldn't*. If she knew she had an out, the Loni I first married would've taken it in a heartbeat.

Is she taking it now?

No...

"Adrian? Adrian... what's wrong? What did Dal say?"

I shake my head, trembling fingers pulling up Loni's number. I've had it in my phone for the last two years, ever since I convinced Todd Dimmity that I needed it for my records. If he thought that it was weird that someone in Harmony Heights requested she be hired only to then ask for her number, he was paid enough to not ask questions, and he didn't.

Sometimes, when I couldn't help myself, I would use a burner number to call Loni for the two seconds she would say 'hello... hello?' before she'd inevitably hang up. I made a display of getting her to give it to me after our bloody wedding—relief flooding through me when the numbers she spat out were the same as the ones I already had—but the truth is that I've had it long memorized.

I can't dial. I'm too busy losing my shit to punch in nine numbers. I select her contact instead, stomach dropping when I see the candid photo I snapped of my wife sleeping in our bed, and wait for her to pick up.

When she doesn't, I call again.

And again.

"She's not answering." My mind goes blank, my voice icy cold. "Loni… she's not answering."

And my fucking uncle has her.

LONI

When the blond-haired brute walked into my house, telling me that Adrian needed me at his office downtown, that my husband sent him to retrieve me, I panicked.

Worse, I *believed* him.

I only had enough time to gather Peaches up in my arms and return her to my private bedroom—since we haven't had the chance to move her to a room closer to Adrian's and mine just yet—and grab a pair of sneakers before he was snapping his fingers at me, telling me that it's urgent, that we have to go.

I was frazzled. I admit it. Since I returned to Harmony Heights, doing everything the Order expected of me, I forgot about the danger a secret society like ours can pose. Not everyone is honest, and while I figured my dad was safe as long as I played my part, I never thought the Order would come after me.

So, yes, I believed this man when he said that Adrian needed me. After all, he knew where my husband lived, and he even flashed the Order's brand on his palm. I had no reason to distrust him—which was my mistake because, in the rush of everything, I left my phone behind.

He put me in a car similar to the matte black coupe that Dallas Collins drove in Bridgewater. I asked his name, he grunted out 'Luke', and that was all he said despite me asking what was going on.

What happened to Adrian?

No wonder he didn't answer me. Because now that I'm sitting in a heavy leather chair, swallowing my nerves as I face off against Jack Collins himself, I finally understand.

It wasn't Adrian who wanted me to come to the downtown office.

It was the King.

The last time I was ever in the same room with this man, I was seventeen, he was with my dad, and the two of them were grilling me about that graduation party. As the King, Jack was the only one I could prove my innocence to. He had the ability to keep me as an Offering or make me one of the Used.

I wasn't innocent. I couldn't lie, either, and in front of my father and the leader of the Order of the Owed, I admitted that I had been seeing someone. I didn't think it mattered. Really, the Order's laws and rules were so ridiculously outdated, I secretly hoped that I wouldn't get in trouble for sleeping with Adrian.

But I did. And if I'd admitted that Adrian was the one in the room that night, so would he.

I confessed to my own sins, but even when I felt betrayed... even when I hated him... I refused to throw him under the bus. He had a bright future ahead of him, the kingmaker who would rule Harmony Heights when the crown was on Dallas's head, and I...

I would be one of the Used. That's what Jack decided the last time I heard from him. And, yet, sometime over the last ten years, he changed his mind. He gave me to Desmond. I became an Offering again, and I can hardly believe what he's telling me now...

"What do you mean, I'm not really married to Adrian? We... we had a ceremony in the church."

"After he murdered the St. James boy, yes. I know."

I ignore that sly jab. "We filed a marriage certificate. I have an appointment at the DMV to change the last name on my driver's license. I'm sorry, Mr. Collins, but I think we *are* married."

"Perhaps," Jack says, steepling his fingers on his desk. "And maybe I put that wrong before. You *did* marry my nephew, but Ms. Dougherty—"

I swallow the nervous lump in my throat. "It's Heller. Mrs. Heller."

His lips twitch, but that's no real smile. "Yes. But that's why I called you down to my office... Mrs. Heller." He makes a face like saying my married name is the same as sucking on a sour lemon. His lips twitch again, his eyes dull yet angry. "In the Order, an Offering is given to her Owed, but only if she accepts his Claim. It's come to my attention that you were never given the chance to accept *Adrian*'s Claim, were you?"

Technically, no. He just walked into St. Catherine's with a gun, and after Desmond was dead, he married me. I guess my saying 'I do' to the wedding vows I repeated counts as my acceptance, but the way Jack's watching me right now... I don't think he agrees.

I fold my hands in my lap, trying to hide how shaky they are. Something... something's not right. "I married him," I repeat. "I am his wife. I'm sorry... is Adrian okay? That man... Luke... he said something was wrong. That I needed to talk to Adrian. But I've asked before and no one will tell me where my husband is."

Jack glances at the large clock on his wall. It's one-thirty. "I assume he's out to lunch. If not, he'll be in his office. There's a very important meeting he's attending at two-thirty, and if I know my sister's boy, he'll be preparing for it." He laughs softly, but there's no humor in it. "But that brings me back to my point. What if he wasn't?"

"In his office, preparing for this meeting?"

"No, dear girl. Your *husband*."

What? "I... I don't understand."

"Oh, I think you do. That fancy education you got outside of Harmony Heights... I think you know exactly what I'm asking."

The way he mentions leaving Harmony Heights feels dangerous somehow. The lilt to his voice makes it worse.

"No. Sorry."

He exhales roughly. Great. I've annoyed the King. "Then let me make it clearer. I can annul your marriage." He snaps his fingers. "Just like that. I say the word, make a few phone calls, and you go back to being Loni Dougherty. You can leave Harmony Heights, return to your life as... ah, yes. Marie Howard. How would you like that, Marie?"

Jack knows. I shouldn't be surprised that he does—like Adrian, it makes sense that he would know everything about his Order, including those who managed to escape it for a time—but I really, really wish he didn't throw the fake name I uselessly adopted all those years ago in my face like that.

He leans back in his seat, his gaze roving over my expression, looking for some sign that I'm going to crack.

I refuse.

And then he says, "You look so confused. I wouldn't have thought that any of this would be news to you. Especially since I warned Adrian right after that wedding of yours that he had to let you know that, if you don't accept his Claim, there is no marriage. But looking at you now... why do I get the feeling that my secretive, plotting nephew decided to keep that little tidbit from his wife, hmm?"

Shit. "No. He didn't. I knew..."

His face calls me a liar, and I am. "And you chose to stay? It's okay, my dear. It's just you and Uncle Jack. If I told you that your father could live out his retirement in the Order... hell, I'll even promote him a rank... and all you'd have to do is refuse Adrian's Claim, what would you say?"

Holy crap. He's really pushing this. For some reason, and I have no idea what that is, Jack doesn't want me to be Adrian's wife.

Well, tough shit.

If he'd come to me six weeks ago and made that same offer, I would've jumped at it. I know better now. Why didn't Adrian tell me that our marriage would only truly be finalized in the eyes of the Order—in the eyes of Harmony Heights—if I did some kind of bullshit 'acceptance' of his Claim? Because, to him, I *am* his wife. Jack doesn't come out and say it plainly, but considering it's coming up, I assume he wants us both to take part in the Claiming ceremony.

No. That goes against the rules of the charter. I married Adrian. That's it. Whether I wanted to or not is a moot point. We got married, and no one has a Claiming ceremony *after* that. A delayed wedding reception, sure, but attending the Claiming ceremony with my husband is like him proposing after we've already gotten hitched.

No wonder Adrian didn't mention any of this to me like Jack told him to. It was pointless—and that's not all. My husband swore he would never let me go. If he thought that Jack would use his position as King to separate us, he would've done everything he could to put a stop to it.

It's not lying, right? More like an omission of truth, and I get it. I do. This is the man who spent ten years stalking me. Even longer telling all of Harmony Heights —in words and in twisted actions—that I belonged to him. He *killed* for me. And maybe I'm as broken as I once accused him of being, but to me, those are signs that when he says that he loves me, he is one hundred percent telling the truth.

I blame it on growing up in the Order. As a future

Offering, I was warned that love might look different between the Owed I was given to and me. There might not even be love at all, but there would at least be an agreement. An arrangement.

So Adrian is a murderer. So he's obsessed. He also adopted Peaches for us, likes to watch TV with me, and cooks like a damn pro. His touch has me melting no matter what, and I finally believe him when he says that he worships me.

He loves me.

And you know what?

I love him. I think I always have. That's why it hurt so bad when we were kids and he didn't stand up for me in front of all of Harmony Heights. He *let* me go, but now he's promised that he never will again.

I'm going to hold him to it.

I give him an impish shrug. "No, thanks."

"Excuse me?"

"I'm okay. I don't want an annulment. If the Order says I have to let him Claim me or whatever, I'll do it. We can have a redo wedding where no one dies... but Adrian is my husband. I'm keeping him."

Jack's faux friendliness slips right off of his face. He sighs. "I should've known when he tried to Claim you after graduation that you would be a problem."

Wait... he did?

Ignoring my sudden surprise, Jack continues, "I let you get away. I told your father to encourage you to stay away. I wanted Adrian to marry the Offering I chose. Not some silly little girl who couldn't even wait until marriage. But no... you still cared for him after all these years. I thought it was fear that had you running. Then I used fear to get you to return... but you weren't supposed to end up with my nephew."

I can't help myself. "Why not?"

"Because Adrian loves you."

It's a gut punch, hearing it from a man who looks like he's never loved anyone a day in his life, but I refuse to let Jack see. "I'd hope so. I am his wife."

Jack ignores my cheeky response. "In the Order, love is a liability. Marriages work out when two people of good breeding form a partnership. That's what we need for the Order to thrive. Not love."

He sounds so cold. So heartless. And maybe I'm being reckless, trying to get some emotion out of this man, but I remind him, "You were married once. You must have loved her."

"I *was* married," Jack agrees. His eyes dart to the window. A slow, sardonic grin pulls on his lips. "Mistakes happen. So do accidents."

I suck in a breath. Crap. Adrian was right. I mean, I didn't doubt him exactly, but I never thought that Jack Collins would make it obvious to a mere Offering that he was responsible for his wife's death. Accident? All of Harmony Heights believes Reese Collins jumped to her death... except for those who actually *know* this man.

I don't. I've met him once, but it doesn't matter. Because he has some fixation on his own nephew, he's hated me the same way I thought Adrian once did.

I can see it. In the derisive way he looks down his perfect nose at me, and the sneer he can't quite restrain when he says shit like 'dear girl'. He hates me, and I have a sinking feeling that I'm not going home to Adrian and Peaches anytime soon.

Mistakes happen. So do accidents…

Another annoyed sigh passes his lips. "This wasn't supposed to be an issue. When the St. James boy decided he'd take you off my hands… for a very hefty fee, I'll add… I thought Adrian would get over his silly crush and do what he was told." Jack huffs, yanking open his desk drawer. He pulls out an aged piece of paper with something rust-colored spilled in the center. He slaps it with the flat of his hand. "Who thought that he'd remember this?"

The slap makes it obvious what I'm looking at. It's a bloody handprint. A really old bloody handprint.

Beneath it? Adrian's familiar scrawl and a hand-written date.

July—*ten years ago.*

I suddenly understand. Why Adrian showed up at the wedding and, instead of trying to stop it with words, he put an end to it by shooting Desmond. Why he disregarded the act as murder because, and I quote, he 'had the right to do it'. A blood oath… if he spilled his blood while telling the King that he Claimed me, then he *did.*

That date… it's right after I told him I never wanted to see him again. I meant it, too. After Jack Collins said to me over the phone that Adrian got disgusted at the idea he was the boy I got caught fucking, that I would end up one of the Used, I blocked Adrian everywhere, then I never saw him again…

Jack.

Jack told me.

Oh, no. Can I believe him? Can I believe anything he said back then when he's revealing that he never planned on letting me marry into his family? The blood oath... if Adrian swore this in front of Jack—and I see the King's seal in the corner, so he must have—then his uncle knew that he intended on Claiming me at the ceremony, 'disgust' or not.

So that's why it was so easy to disappear. That's what this asshole *wanted* me to do.

But Adrian... he never stopped wanting *me*. I can't say for sure that what he felt for me was love over the years, but he chose me once before, then he chose me again. So long as he always chooses me, I'll choose him right back.

And I'm just about to tell Jack that when he grabs the blood oath and rips it in half.

I gasp. "What are you doing?"

"I'm done playing these games, little girl. I paid Desmond St. James more than your worth so that you were out of Adrian's reach. I can't let you distract him, not when he's the one keeping the Order running behind the scenes. So that leaves only one alternative."

It hits me then why Adrian is so important to his uncle. It's not this sense of loyalty to his family, or even this grand idea of pairing up the proper Offering to a high-ranked Owed like his nephew. He tried to give Haven to Adrian precisely because he didn't want her. Without any feelings for his Owed except a sense of duty, he'd be free to do whatever Jack required of him.

The books. It all comes down to the books. The laundering scheme that keeps the Order in charge, and the money coming in. Then there are the copies of ledgers he showed me, all written in Adrian's hand, lists of secrets and blackmail material he's gathered since he was a teen to make himself untouchable.

No, I think, remember what he said.

To make *me* untouchable...

I rise up from the seat. "I don't think so, Mr. Collins. In fact, I think I'm going to head down to the twentieth floor and go see my husband."

Jack clicks his tongue. "No. I don't think that will be possible." Raising his voice, he calls out, "Luke?"

The blond bully who dragged me up here after tricking me into leaving my home must have been waiting just outside for Jack's signal because he shoves in the door, stepping into the office almost immediately.

"Take Ms. Dougherty down to the basement. We have an auction starting at three." The speculative look he gives me, coupled with the ominous word *auction*, has shivers coursing down my spine. "I lost enough on her already. Might as well get some of my money back."

What?

IN LESS THAN TWENTY MINUTES, I'VE BEEN CORRALLED INTO an elevator, taken to the lowest floor of this skyscraper, and nearly shoved down a flight of stairs when I got the nerve to finally fight back a little.

It was useless. Luke was too strong, and I was too scared. The word 'auction' kept running on repeat in my panicked brain, and when he grips my bicep, marching me through a tight, dim, smoky basement dwelling, I realize it's exactly what it means. Especially when Luke leaves me with a bigger enforcer who tells me to strip down to my underwear so that, when I go on the makeshift stage, the men will know what I have to offer.

Because it's an auction, all right. Where women who won't be missed get sold to men with no ties to the Order or Harmony Heights.

There are worse things than being Used...

Sophie was right.

It's being *Bought.*

That's exactly what Jack plans on happening to me, and Adrian has no idea.

My husband will never let me go? When I'm bought and sold and trafficked... he might not have a choice.

TWENTY-EIGHT
THE BASEMENT

ADRIAN

Dallas is waiting for us on the sidewalk outside of the Fortress.

Order members have priority parking along the street. I let Bas pull his bike into the spot closest to Dallas, then double park again to save time. I already wasted precious minutes trying to talk him out of coming with me. Bas ended the argument by throwing a hundred-dollar bill on the table, grabbing his helmet, and running for his bike.

I owe him too much to get him involved with Jack's bullshit when we all know my uncle's been gunning for the Reynolds family for years. If he's decided to target Loni, my blood oath allows me some protection. Not like that matters. I killed once for my wife, and I'd go after Jack in a heartbeat if I had to. But Bas...

As we jog over to Dallas, I try one more time. "You don't have to do this."

"The fuck I don't. Dallas said they moved Loni to the basement. If Jack knows you're here, he'll never let you down there. But if I go up and distract him…"

I know. I *know*. "He'll salivate at finding a reason to boot you from the Other at last," I finish.

"Exactly. And I wouldn't care. I mean, unless he decides whatever made-up offense I did is worth losing my head or something, it doesn't matter. It'll be a bitch to burn off the Order's mark on my palm because, fuck, did that fire *hurt*… but I'd be free. And you? You'll be happy with your wife."

I had my own reasons for never Claiming an Offering. Since we were eighteen and newly inducted, Bas made it clear that he wasn't bothering because, technically, he didn't have to. In a founding family like his, it's the first-born son who needs to carry on the line, choosing a wife before they're thirty. That's why Alexandre is feeling the pressure, and Bas is ducking his brother. If Alex doesn't take a wife, then Bas *will* have to.

And I know the truth. I know the real reason why he sticks with the Used instead of requesting his own Offering. But like how I shield Connor and Haven, and I keep Dallas's secrets, I sure as hell will keep Sebastien's.

"It's easy," he continues. "I'll go up and see if he's in his office—"

Dallas joins us, cutting in with a quick, "I'm pretty sure he was before I came down here. Jack doesn't realize that I showed up at the Fortress early for that meet with the vitamin company, or that I saw Loni be hustled inside —or to the basement."

Jack. Even Dallas can't call his father by anything other than his name.

I ball my hands into fists. "Hustled? Who had their paws on my wife?"

"Luke. I saw him yank her out of his car, dragging her into the building. I followed behind and watched them go into the elevator. It went to the top floors. To Jack's office. No one can go in there when he's busy in the penthouse so that has to be where they went." Dallas glances at his phone. "I called the vitamin guys. Told them to postpone the meet. Stephen took a late lunch at the Court so his drunk ass wasn't coming anyway. As far as Jack knows, though, Adrian and me are doing Order business on the twentieth floor."

"He won't expect us to check out the basement."

Bas nods. "That's my point. I'll go to his office, see if Loni's still there. If she isn't, I'll call you. Once, okay? It'll ring a couple of times and you'll know Jack's distracted."

Dallas scoffs. "Knowing my old man? Even if he isn't in the office, he'll be distracted. He has Kiersten come over to the penthouse every other day about this time. If not Kiersten, then Abigail. Sick fuck needs his twenty-year-old pussy daily or he thinks his dick will shrivel up and fall off. Charlotte comes at night. Every night." His green eyes gleam in disgust. "Poor girl thinks she'll be the one to take my mom's place. As if Jack will ever marry one of the Used."

I rub Dallas's shoulder. "Your father is fucking awful. You know that. I know that. But are you prepared to go against him? 'Cause I'll tell you the same thing I told Bas,

Dallas. You don't have to come with me. I'll go to the basement alone."

If she's down there, it won't be easy to rescue her. You need a code and a fingerprint belonging to one of the old guard—or any other enforcer besides Dallas since Jack obviously knows better than to involve his boy in whatever the fuck he's doing on the bottommost floor of the Fortress—but I'll deal with it when I have to.

For now, I just need a direction to go before I plan.

Bas has his part; I'm not persuading him to quit. If Dallas wants to continue with his quiet rebellion, I understand. I love Loni, and there isn't anything I won't do for her, but I'm not going to ask my brothers—because one's my friend, one's my cousin, but they're my brothers —to risk themselves.

Then Dallas gives me a quelling look. "I'm not afraid of Jack."

"I know."

"You need backup, Adrian. Fuck being the King. I'm an enforcer. Let me do my job."

I don't remind Dallas that he's only an enforcer because his father likes to see him squirm. One day, Dallas might be the King, but until then... Jack will make his life hell. That's what we do in our family, I guess. Hurt the ones we're supposed to love...

Loni.

I nod. "Go, Bas. If we don't get that call from you in five minutes, I'm going in anyway."

No one is keeping me from my wife.

Taking his helmet off, shoving it at Dallas, Bas says,

"Hold this. Jack loves bitching at me if he thinks I'm riding around without a helmet."

And Bas loves spoiling for a fight whenever he can…

Dallas knows that, but instead of trying to talk sense into Bas like I did, he simply accepts the helmet. "I'll drop it off inside."

"Got it. Five minutes." He pulls his phone out of his jacket. I do the same. "If the elevator's on the ground floor, expect it to ring in three."

And, with that, Bas jogs toward the Fortress.

Dallas gives me a look, warning me from saying anything else about challenging his father way before we expected we would have to. In a way, I always thought this day would come, but like me marrying Loni, I figured I'd have to wait until I was thirty—to be considered part of the next guard, not the young guard—before we went after him.

But then he interfered with me and my wife, and that's just inexcusable.

I keep my focus on my phone, watching the minutes tick by excruciatingly slow. At three minutes, I hold my breath, waiting for it to ring. At four, I start stalking toward the front of the building, Dallas right behind me.

Right before it hits five minutes, my phone buzzes. It's Bas. Out of habit, I answer it, lifting it to my ear.

Through the open line, I hear Bas mutter something about a slow elevator before the call disconnects.

I glance back at Dallas. "Let's go."

Together, we walk into the Fortress as though we have every right to be in there—and we do, don't we? Dallas is the Heir to the Order, and with the leverage I have on nearly every high-ranking member of the society, no one will dare stop me.

It takes too damn long for the elevator to reach the lobby again. Once the door opens, we step in, jabbing the **B** button.

Basement.

I've never been down here before. I know that there's an outer room, kind of like a break room, with the locked door that leads to the actual basement. I'm kicking myself in the ass that I've ignored it, but that changes today.

I asked Dallas on the ride over what to expect. Because his father was careful not to involve him with the goings-on down in the basement, the most he can confirm is what I know: that it won't be easy to get down there.

There are certain enforcers who get sent down. Dallas long thought it was a gag, that basement duty meant taking a nap or sneaking a Used over when you don't have a free office in the Fortress to fuck them in. He's just as pissed that he didn't know, and when this is all done, the three of us—Bas, Dallas, and me... and maybe Connor, too—will sit down and make sure we're all on the same page.

Especially if, one day—and fucking soon—the four of us will rule Harmony Heights.

For once, luck is on my side.

Dallas and I stride together out of the elevator, taking the outer room in as quickly as possible. There's a bright light, a single table, a solitary figure sitting at it, and a solid vault of a door on the opposite wall.

I recognize the figure hunched over the table, counting a huge stack of money. Luke. The same prick who likes to stand outside of Jack's door, acting big and bad even though he'll never be more than a basic enforcer.

Maybe I was wrong. If Jack lets this idiot anywhere that much money, it's because he's in on it. He has to know that that's blood money. Sex money. The men who traded fat stacks to buy a woman at auction...

Fuck. If he's counting money now, and Loni was picked up specifically today... how much do I want to bet that she's down there at this very moment, ready to be someone's Bought?

No fucking way.

"Where is she?"

Luke's head whips around. His mouth falls open, and for a moment, he looks frightened. He recovers quickly, sneering at me. Sneering at *Dallas*. He takes a few threatening steps toward us before planting his feet against the floor. "I'm not telling."

He didn't ask who 'she' was. Either he doesn't care— or he knows exactly who I'm looking for.

"Wrong answer, asshole," I snap. "My wife. She's down here. I know she is. I want her back."

I'm bluffing. The only way I'll know for sure that she's in the basement is by laying eyes on her myself. But Luke doesn't know that, and the way his beady eyes flicker toward the locked door tells me that my bluffing worked.

He shakes his head. "Sorry, Heller. Once a girl goes

down, the only way she comes back up is on the arm of the rich bastard who Buys her."

"I have a blood oath—"

"And that's Order biz. This? This is all the King's doing. You ask Jack Collins, okay?" Another hate-filled look sent Dallas's way. "Talk to your old man. It ain't worth my head to get mixed up with you two. If that bitch got sent to the basement, too bad. Nothing's saving her from that."

Wanna bet?

I glance at Dallas. He nods.

Good.

I reach into my front pocket. As a boy, I carried my pocket knife with me everywhere I went. When I traded it for the Tomcat, I put it in my dresser drawer and left it there. And then I showed Loni my box of treasures last night and... maybe I was feeling nostalgic, because I dug out my old pocket knife this morning and shoved it in the front pocket of my suit pants.

I have my Tomcat, too; if it's not on my waistband, it's in my car, and I grabbed it before heading for the Fortress. I can't risk damaging the pad of his finger by accidentally blowing the whole fucking thing off, but my pocket knife should do pretty nicely.

I flip it open.

"Hold him."

Dallas kicks Luke in the knee. He puts all of his strength into the strike, and I don't know what's louder: the *crunch* or the howl of agony that tears out of Luke's throat when Dallas's boot breaks something. I could give a shit. Luke goes down, Dallas putting all of his weight against him, keeping him in place. He uses one hand to hold down Luke's shoulder, the other to drag him back to the table and slam his cheek down on it.

Once he's immobilized, I grab Luke's hand. As though he knows exactly what's going to happen, he struggles, but another slam of his head against the wood dazes him enough that I have his arm outstretched, right hand flat in front of me.

Eenie-meenie-miney-

That one.

The knife slices through his finger a lot easier than I expected. The bone gives a little resistance, but I'm determined enough to hack that fucker right off.

Luke howls again. Dallas slaps his hand over his mouth, muffling the scream.

I bend down so that Luke's wide eyes can't miss me. Then, showing him his severed pointer finger, I ask, "What's the code?"

He mumbles.

"Dallas? If you would?"

Dallas removes his hand.

Luke lifts his head up enough to glare at me with pain-filled, unfocused eyes. "Fuck you."

Thud.

"Motherfucker!"

"My mom's in a grave," Dallas retorts darkly, prepared to slam Luke's head down again if the prick gives him a reason to, "and I ain't into banging dead chicks. Keep giving us shit, though, and we'll see if there's some sick fuck who won't mind shoving their cock up your ass after we leave you rotting somewhere."

I smile. "One more time, Luke. What is the code?"

He thrashes against Dallas.

Come on. "Okay. Look. I only need one finger. However, what if I drop it? What if it doesn't work? What if it's the wrong one? Maybe I need *another*—"

"No! *No*. Shit. Three-six-oh-four. It's three-six-oh-four. Leave my fucking fingers alone!"

"See? Wasn't that easy?" I poke him in the ear with his own fingertip. "Keep 'em here, Dal. Let's see if he's telling the truth."

Dallas nods, increasing the force of his push against Luke's head.

I race over to the door, too panicked to care if it shows. I see the keypad. Above it, there's a sensor that's gotta be for the fingerprint. I maneuver the bloody finger into place, muttering 'yes' when the light turns green. Using *my* finger now, I enter 3-6-0-4 into the keypad.

Something *clicks*. I grab the door handle and yank on it. It opens.

Yes!

I throw Luke's finger at him. "If you hurry, you might be able to save that. Dallas? Get your gun out."

With another kick, Dallas sends Luke falling to the floor onto his back. Just as I said, he pulls out his gun— and then, without any remorse at all, he shoots Luke between the eyes.

I watch the dead body jerk, then go still. "Oh. I guess there's no point in saving the finger after all."

"He shouldn't have made that crack about my mom," Dallas says as I fold my pocket knife, shoving it in my pocket before grabbing my gun from its place at my waist.

I don't point out that I use the term 'motherfucker' all the time. Luke was a piece of shit. If Dallas took the curse a little too personally, that's fine. A trash enforcer on the take is dead, Dallas feels a little better, and there's no one to warn Jack that we're heading downstairs.

Huh. That's even better than if I planned it myself.

After that, it's almost too easy. We race down the stairs, guns leading the way. Another enforcer—Jeremy—is down there, with one of the old guard, Trevor, serving as an auctioneer for the crowd of about fifteen men hanging back in the shadows of the musty basement. Dallas handles them easily with his gun since, like us, they'll be armed.

Me? I'm looking for my wife.

I see at least four women lined up on a makeshift stage, each stripped down to their bras and panties. Our arrival, followed by Dallas killing two men in front of them, has the women screaming, huddling together, but when I lift my gun up, firing a third shot—a warning shot into the ceiling—every single fucking person down here goes silent.

"I. Want. My. Wife."

That's all I have to say. From behind a curtain I didn't notice at first, Loni comes stumbling out. She's also been stripped down, and if my magazine had enough bullets in it to kill every other man in this cramped room (save Dallas, of course), I would have.

Instead, I throw open my arms. The sob she lets out as she runs right toward me despite the weapon in my hand will stay with me for the rest of my damn life. Same as the way she squeezes me tight before gasping out,

"Adrian, it's you. It's you. You came for me. Oh... you *came*."

I close my arms around her, still keeping my gun in my grasp. Anyone who makes a move toward my wife will get shot, I swear to fucking God—and they *know* it. If not me, Dallas has at least three more rounds in his gun, and these rich fuckers down here... I don't think there's a single weapon between them.

With my free hand, I rub Loni's back. My hand shakes as I do. "Of course I did, princess. I made that mistake once. I will never fucking do it again. You hear me? I will *always* come for you."

She dissolves into tears that scald me through my dress shirt. She's only been down here for an hour at most—nothing like the two months where Haven was missing—but even one *second* was too long. I suddenly have a moment of clarity when it comes to Connor and the way he guards his Haven so fiercely.

I'll do the same for Loni.

No. I'll do *worse*.

As Dallas uses the threat of his gun to get the men to gather on one side, the terrified women on the other, I can't bring myself to release Loni. So I don't. However, I do slip my hand inside of my suit jacket, pulling out my cigarette case.

She shivers. I make a soothing sound in the back of my throat. "It's okay. I still got you."

She nods. "I know. Baby... I *know*."

I kiss the top of her hair. Then, palming the cigarette case, I remove my jacket as efficiently as I can until I have no choice but to release her for a few seconds. She gasps, and I hurriedly help her climb into my suit jacket to give her something to cover up with.

I'll find her clothes. Her shoes. That's at the top of my to-do list so that Loni isn't half-naked and vulnerable a moment longer.

But first…

Pulling her back into my embrace, I pop open the cigarette case. Nicholas Reed's card is right on top.

I smile.

As soon as I take care of my wife, I'm making a phone call.

TWENTY-NINE
LONG LIVE THE KING

LONI

I t takes a week before Jack Collins calls Adrian and tells him that he'd like to see him at his office. Not so surprising. My husband had refused to go back to the Fortress after he whisked me out of it, wearing nothing more than my bra, my panties, and his suit jacket.

Adrian was about to search the hidden backroom for my clothes, but the shock that set in after I was forced at gunpoint to remove my clothes before being assaulted made it so that I clung to him like I was fucking velcro. I couldn't let go of him. It was like I had this terrible feeling that, if he released me, I'd be up on that stage, sold like a piece of cattle, and sent home with some stranger to do whatever the fuck they wanted to me.

I didn't tell Adrian why I was behind the curtain. As the most recent addition to the afternoon's monthly auction, they separated me from the other girls so that any man who might be interested could visit me in the back and get an idea of my worth before I went on the stage.

One faceless man—because masks, damn it, they wore thin *masks* with their business suits—squeezed my tits. Another slid his hand inside of my underwear, palming my ass. Two came in, murmuring about a shared deal, then shook hands. Another pinched my pussy through my underwear. The last one grabbed my hair, only murmuring his appreciation when he yanked and I squealed.

He wanted a squealer, he told me, then tugged one last time for good measure before slipping back out into the shadows.

My clothes were thrown in a pile so high, it made my stomach crawl to think about how many other women were put through this same degradation. I didn't care if I ever saw that shirt or those jeans again. My shoes? I could buy a hundred pairs of shoes. I just wanted to leave.

He ordered Dallas to stay behind, and he did. I think it stunned the enforcer to see what his father was capable of; Adrian confirmed that neither he nor Dallas had any idea that Jack was selling 'undesirables' in a basement auction to very wealthy businessmen all over the country. Dallas even killed two... no, *three* enforcers since Adrian had to lead me out past Luke's dead body... Adrian's cousin killed the men who saw nothing wrong with what was going on in the shadows.

When I stopped trembling so much, I decided that I might forgive Dallas for being the one to track me down in Bridgewater.

Maybe...

Jack knew there was trouble. He knew he was caught. He had five traumatized girls on his hands, three dead enforcers, and who knows how many corrupt businessmen to deal with after Adrian and Dallas rescued me. Though I should add that Dallas made a call to get the girls out, then made another so that the sheriff could round up as many of the men as possible. They all bought their way out of trouble almost immediately, but at least someone tried.

Sebastien Reynolds was there, too. As Adrian hurried me out, Sebastien was waiting by his motorcycle as if he knew what was going down inside of the Fortress. Adrian passed him his gun, said two words—'basement' and 'Dallas'—and then the most rebellious of the Heirs went stalking inside of the building.

I haven't heard anything about him since. Dallas decided to take a week's vacation out of town, and I'm pretty sure Sebastien went with him. As for my husband, he spent the last week at home, cuddling up with me and Peaches, promising that everything was going to be okay.

We talked about what happened. How Luke lied to me and I fell for it, how I left my phone behind on accident, and how Jack Collins tried to do everything he could to convince me to leave Adrian. He stayed silent at that part, though he got quietly furious when I admitted that I knew about the blood oath—and that Jack destroyed it.

"It doesn't matter," he said at last, holding me tight. "We're married and nothing can change that."

He seemed so certain that I refused to question it.

And when he had to leave the room to take a few curious phone calls, I refused to let the old suspicions come to life again. Adrian has finally proven that I can trust him, and if he says he's got everything under control, for once I'm more than happy to let him take it, no complaints.

I wondered if one of them was from his uncle. No. That call didn't come until late last night when a slightly slurring Jack contacted Adrian, telling him that there was some sort of miscommunication between them, and that he would like to see him at twelve sharp the next afternoon.

With the sexy smirk that I've never been able to ignore, Adrian admitted once the call had ended—and he agreed that he and his wife would *both* show up at Jack's office in the Fortress at noon so long as his 'mentor' Stephen sobered up long enough to also make an appearance... and hopefully Uncle Jack would do the same—that his uncle had decided to simply ignore what happened. That his enforcers were dead, his sex trafficking auction was revealed, and he'd tried to sell his nephew's wife to the highest bidder.

Adrian didn't like that. So, using his financial management skills, he sent the Order's portfolio straight into the toilet. By the time Jack got drunk enough to contact his sister's son, they were two point two million in the red, with the numbers falling every few hours.

He told me he could easily correct it. But since money was the only thing Jack cared about, he used money to force his uncle's hand.

I didn't know what that meant. Just like I didn't understand why my husband would insist that I join the meeting with him. But I've decided that, if we're going to make this marriage work... and we *are*... that I do need to trust him.

I always thought he would put the Order before me. I know better now. If his loyalty was to the King and the old guard, he would've accepted his uncle's command. His obsession might live on, but if the Order was more important, he would've left me in the basement because that's what a devoted Owed would do.

Instead, he showed his vicious side again. He cut off a *finger* to get to me. If that doesn't say 'you're the most important thing in the world to me', I don't know what does.

And that's why, at twelve noon sharp, we walk together into Jack Collins's office, hand-in-hand.

His lips purse when he sees me. I don't think that he expected I would have the balls to show up after what he tried.

But I did. Because I have Adrian Heller at my side, and as long as he Claims me, I'll Claim him right back.

There are four seats today instead of the single one that I sat in little more than a week ago. A man in his early fifties, with salt-and-pepper hair, rheumy eyes, and a sickly sweet scent clinging to his suit, sits in the one farthest on my left.

Adrian guides me to the one all the way on the right. Once I'm seated, he takes the one next to me.

Jack sits behind the desk. His attention is solely on Adrian, and if he was a weaker man, he might've quailed under the weight of Jack's stare.

But he's not a weaker man so, instead, he lounges

lazily in the seat, legs spread, expression daring. He takes the cigarette from behind his ear, tucks it in the corner of his mouth. He doesn't light it, though. He hasn't had a cigarette in nearly two months, but hell if he doesn't look goddamn sexy with it hanging off of his lip like that.

Once he's perfectly posed, Adrian holds out his hand to me. I clutch it.

He looks at his uncle. "Well. You wanted to talk to us?"

Jack opens his mouth, but before he can say a word, someone else enters the door Adrian purposely left open.

"Pardon." The King bares his perfect white teeth at the intruder in an obvious warning. I bet he'd say it was a welcoming smile… nope. I know what I saw. "We're in the middle of a meeting. What are you doing?"

I look over at the man. He's about thirty or so. Good-looking. He has these sculpted features that look like they belong on the cover of a magazine, with dark hair carefully tousled. His deep blue eyes are striking against his complexion, and despite Jack's less-than-welcome welcome, he shows off the bottle of whiskey in his hands.

Jack waits.

The man shuffles his way in, presenting the bottle in front of him as though that's his ticket into Jack's office.

To be fair, it works.

"Sorry. Sorry. My name is Hunter. Hunter Reed? I think I sent you a message last week about applying to be a member of the Order? I got a response that, so long as my donation went through, I'm in? Well, thank you, Mr. Collins. The notification from my bank came back this morning. One of your secretaries told me I can be inducted at the end of the month, but I was so excited, I wanted to drop by and give a little something to show my appreciation."

Huh. I'm not even a little surprised that Jack is selling memberships into the Order. As far as I knew, it was either by legacy or by manner of being a significant citizen in Harmony Heights. But if Jack sold women, why wouldn't he sell the Order's brand and all the perks that come with it if he can?

The man is nice to look at, but I wouldn't think of him as Order material. Between being dressed all in black, a skull patch on the side of his jeans, and an almost amused look in his deep blue eyes despite the obvious fawning act... I guess I shouldn't judge. In a way, he reminds me of Sebastien Reynolds, only there's something about him that's not quite right.

He's dangerous. That's the vibe he gives off. Despite his words, everything about his body language says this is not a man to fuck with.

Can Jack tell? I'm not sure, but he does accept the bottle. "Thank you. Reed, was it?"

He nods. "Hunter, yes."

"Good man, Reed. I look forward to seeing you at the bonfire."

It's a dismissal, and an obvious one at that. Hunter bows his head before turning away from the desk, heading out the way he came. Before he leaves, though, he glances up just enough to shoot a look over at Adrian and me.

And he winks.

What the—

Jack rises up from his seat. He heads to a cabinet I never noticed before on the other side of the room, grabbing three glasses. He peers at his guests, nods at Adrian, then puts one back.

I know why. Every single Owed in Harmony Heights has a vice. Some gamble. Some drink. Some do a variety of different drugs. Some lose themselves in the Used. Adrian doesn't drink. His vice used to be cigarettes.

Now?

It's *me.*

He squeezes my fingers as Jack comes back, carrying two glasses. He makes quick work of opening the bottle, pouring two fingers of whiskey into each of the glasses. He keeps one, then gives the other to Adrian's mentor.

He takes it gladly, but pauses when Adrian releases my hand so that he can point at him.

"Stephen. Don't you think you've had enough already today?"

The older man blinks. No wonder his eyes look like that, and he smells the way he does. It's only noon, but when you're an alcoholic, you can start drinking anytime.

He sets his glass down.

Jack scoffs. "Come the hell on, Steve. Don't tell me you're going to let one of the boys tell you what to do."

Adrian's tone turns steely. "I just thought we should go into this conversation with a clear head, Uncle Jack."

Jack picks up his glass, swirling the alcohol. "Absolutely not. To get through this... I think we'll all need a drink." Before he takes a swig, he says, "So, how are you going to blackmail me, boy?"

"Who said anything about blackmail?"

"You did. When you tanked the Order's portfolio on purpose." Jack bares his teeth at his nephew, another not-quite-smile. "Don't be coy. Stephen's head's either in a bottle of rum or in between a pair of tits down at the Court, but if I pull him out long enough, he still knows how to do the job I gave you, Adrian. I know what you did. I had to put in an extra half a mil alone today to replace the funds before the rest of my men found out what you've done."

"Selling women seems to be very lucrative. I bet you barely notice it's gone."

Jack sets down the glass, untouched. "I knew it. Is that what this is about? The girl?"

Adrian lays his hand over mine again as though he needs the connection before he gets up and slaps his uncle across the face like he really wants to. "That 'girl' is my wife."

"This again? Alright. You win. I'll let you keep the Dougherty girl, you go back to work and fix this mess you made. How about that? As long as you don't fuck up the books anymore, you can keep her. Deal?"

That's what Adrian wants. I think that's what he's wanted all along.

But instead of accepting the offer, he stays quiet and waits.

Jack huffs, rolling his eyes. "Children," he mutters under his breath. Grabbing his glass, he downs the shot he poured in one gulp.

Adrian leans forward in his seat, eyes gleaming in anticipation.

I look at him curiously. He shakes his head, puts a finger to his lips, and gestures for me to watch the desk.

So I do.

Jack's face turns red almost immediately. He coughs a few times, then sets down his empty glass. He rubs his throat. He clears it.

He gags.

"Jack?" Stephen blinks, staring at the other man in confusion. "Jack? Stop fooling. You said this meeting would only last ten minutes. Come on."

With all of us as witness—and none of us able or willing to help—Jack struggles. He grabs his throat, squeezing it, gasping, choking, until a dribble of red wells up in one corner of his mouth. He stands up, stumbling a few steps away, before he lands on the carpet, face-down.

"Jack? You trip or something? Jesus, Mary, and Joseph. Alright. I'm comin'."

Stephen gets up from his chair, crouching down at the other man's side. I don't think he realized what was happening at first, but suddenly he curses under his breath, then grabs for Jack's neck. It takes him a few seconds to check for a pulse. When he does, but can't find one, he yelps. Babbling nonsense, running from the room, he's gone long before Jack Collins will get cold.

The whole thing took about two minutes tops.

"Poison," Adrian announces with a satisfied grin. I stare at my husband, shocked, and he shrugs. "When I called Nicholas and told him he owed me a dead body, he gave me the options, but he really pushed for poison for some reason. Something about showing up the Hummingbird." He shrugs. "It was on short notice, and he promised to pull through. If Nicholas Reed wanted to use poison, that's fine with me."

"Nicholas?" I'm so fucking confused. Kinda grateful that King Collins is dead, but... what the fuck just happened? I latch on to the one thing I'm sure of. "He said his name was Hunter. Was it a fake name? Like I used to use?"

"Nope. Guys like these get off on killing the bad guys right under our noses. They don't use pseudonyms. But that Reed? That was his identical twin. Seems like Nicholas is the manager. Hunter is the muscle. Trust me. If you saw them both together, they look the same, but they're very different."

I get it. "Like you and Dallas."

Ah, shit.

Dallas...

Adrian nods. "Right. And Stephen did exactly what I needed. Poor drunk was the witness that proves the poison came from that bottle, and that bottle came from a future Owed who doesn't actually exist. That donation? It never happened, but Jack was so damn money hungry, he never even checked."

That makes so much sense. And no wonder Adrian firmly told his mentor not to take a sip. Otherwise, we'd have *two* bodies on our hands.

Should I be freaking out more that I've just watched another man die? I guess, after your groom is assassinated on your wedding day, you kind of get sort of blasé about things like this... especially when everyone in Harmony Heights knows that, in the Order, murder is just another hobby.

Still—

"Won't you get in trouble? Killing Desmond is one thing… I saw the blood oath… but the King? Adrian, you might've gone too far."

Leaning over his seat, he strokes the side of my jaw. "When it comes to you, there's no such thing."

"What about Dallas?"

"He knows. Don't worry, princess. He signed off on it. His first official act as the new King of the Order."

The King is dead.

Long live the King.

Adrian gets to his feet. Holding out his hand, he waits for me to place mine in his again. Once I have, he helps me up. "I figure we have maybe two minutes until Stephen comes running back in here with whatever Order members he can find. Once it gets out that Jack was stealing from the Order, he'll be lucky if they don't just chuck him in an unmarked grave. Selling girls? I've done some fucked-up shit, but even that's too low for me."

Hooking my arm in his, the two of us walk casually out of Jack's office, leaving his corpse behind. There's no secretary waiting out here, or any enforcers, either. More of Adrian's handiwork?

I'd put every cent I have down on it.

Whistling softly, he leads me into the elevator. I lean into him. He presses floor **20**, and away we go.

This is the first time I've been in his office, and if Jack hadn't told me it was on the twentieth floor, I don't know if I would've found it… and I believe that until I walk in and something about the room just screams 'Adrian Heller' to me.

The color.

The scent.

The blown-up picture of me in my bloody wedding dress...

I have no idea where he got that from. I don't remember any pictures being taken throughout our fateful ceremony, but there I am, a look of horror and resignation on my face as though I was just about to sign a deal with the devil.

Did I? Maybe it's too soon to tell, but as Adrian shuts the door behind us before backing me up against the first wall he can find, kissing my neck, hands grabbing at my clothes to get them off as fast as possible... I wouldn't have it any other way.

He's panting in my ear. "I need you. Loni, I need you now."

"You can have me. Whenever you want me, baby, I'm *yours*. You saved me. You killed for me—"

"I'd die for you," he vows darkly.

I grab his cock through his suit pants. A bubble of laughter rises up my throat, amusement at just how goddamn right we are together. "Really? Right when I was beginning to think I might like you?"

He nips my earlobe. "Don't fool yourself, princess. You *love* me."

"Yes."

A moment's hesitation, as though he can't believe my easy agreement, before his hands are making quick work of my clothes—and his. "Tell me again," he demands.

"And not because I won't let you come if you don't. Tell me 'cause you mean it."

Sure. After all, he deserves it. He's certainly earned it. "I love you, my husband. My Adrian. I love you, I love you, *I love you*."

That spurs him to get inside of me even faster. "Do you know how long I've waited to hear you say that, Loni Heller?"

I do. "Four years?"

He has my pants and my underwear both down past my ass. I hear his zipper, the rustle of his boxer briefs as he yanks his cock out through the opening. "No."

It's hard to think as he's filling me up with the hard, hot length of him, but... "Ten?"

"Not quite."

I groan as he slams home. I lay one hand flat against the wall. The other reaches for any part of him I can grab as he fucks me so passionately, it's like I'm seventeen again and I'll die if I can't have all of him.

"I... I don't know," I finally gasp out. "How long?"

The force of his thrusts has me going up on my tiptoes. I throw back my head, careful not to bash it in the wall, even more distracted as he sucks on my neck, grazing my skin with his teeth, touching me everywhere and anywhere while Jack Collins's body lies abandoned ten stories above us.

Shit will hit the fan. I know that. But, if only for this moment in time, it's just me. It's just Adrian—

"I told you. I decided when I was in fucking kindergarten that you were meant to be mine. Sure, I didn't get the idea in my head that I could have you under me until

I was a teen, but... tell me, Loni, my love... my wife... is there anywhere you'd rather be?"

I shake my head. "No, Adrian. *No*..."

"Good, because I told you once, and I'll tell you again... I will *never* let you go."

Can't have all of him?

Of course I can.

I always *have*.

EPILOGUE

LONI

Adrian is propped up on the bed—*our* bed—with his hands folded behind his head, curls falling forward into his heavy-lidded eyes, fingers trailing lazily along my bare shoulder. He's wearing nothing but his familiar smirk, plus the cigarette that he keeps tucked behind his ear as a signal to me that he'll choose me before anything else.

Over his nicotine addiction.

Over his own obsessive need to manipulate any given situation, pulling strings behind the scenes to end with the outcome he wants.

And, more importantly, over the Order...

His heart is racing, though his caress is slow. Soothing. Gentle. His eyes are closed, savoring the moment.

I snuggle against his chest, draping my arm over it. My palm covers his heart; like he said when I collapsed over him after sex, I own it… why shouldn't I lay my hand over it possessively?

Such pretty words. Adrian's always had a way with them, but a week past our two-month anniversary—and after the old guard confirmed that Jack's death was an accident… as in, he accidentally drank poison, and whoops, he shouldn't have done that—I think I might… I might finally start believing them.

He Claimed me. While I'm sure taunting me with the decade-old piece of parchment of cardstock or whatever that was with Adrian's bloody palm print on it was just another way for Jack Collins to twist the knife and remind me that he thought I was no good for his nephew, all it did was show me that the boy I loved as a girl really *did* love me back. If he didn't, he was at least willing to make me his, just like he once told me.

And if I could accept that he was telling the truth about that, it became a lot easier to start believing other things he said.

Like how it's always been me. Like how he's loved me since he was five, but didn't know the words… since he was eleven, and couldn't understand his feelings… since he was sixteen, and already coming up with a plan to tie me to him, including seducing me after he blackmailed our twelfth-grade history teacher into pairing us up as part of a group project together…

It'll take time. I won't pretend like it won't. I've forgiven most of the bullying from our youth, but the betrayal I felt before I left Harmony Heights… that one cut deep.

The way he killed Desmond to have me helps. That

he arranged for the assassination of his uncle—and the *King*—to avenge what Jack pulled, both a decade ago and now... that was a big one. He swore he'd leave the Order if I asked him to, but with Dallas preparing to take over for his father, I knew he couldn't do that. It needs him more than ever, and with Dallas wearing the figurative crown, Adrian will be the kingmaker I always thought he was.

Maybe he can change facets of the Order in the modern day. He already convinced the old guard that sex trafficking is out. The auctions that had me about to go up on the block? Done. Adrian, Dallas, Sebastien, and a few hand-picked men oversaw the dismantling of the hidden basement rooms themselves.

And that's only the beginning...

I need to get up. Not because I want to shower him off of me, but because I really should go pee. But I'm cozy, and a sweat-slicked Adrian smells so musty and delicious and *mine* that I just start to close my eyes a little, too—

Crash.

My eyes fly open, my body jumping at the loud crashing sound. A second later, one set of claws scrabble against the wooden floor, then another, two bundles of fur racing for the open bedroom door.

My heart is beating just as fast as Adrian's now from the quick fright. I start to adjust myself, settling down on him again, when I notice that he's also opened his eyes.

"What was that?" he murmurs, voice sleep-roughened though, despite us being together in bed for the last three hours, we haven't quite slept yet.

"Peaches is playing with Cream. I think they knocked your deodorant off your dresser."

He rolls his eyes, but it's obvious that Adrian thinks the kittens' antics are more charming than annoying. Good thing, too, because I don't think I could ever really love a man who isn't a cat person. "Better that than my cologne," he says, running his fingers through my hair. "Remind me later that I need to put it somewhere different. Those little furballs scale shit like it's Mt. Everest in here."

I grin up at him. "I know. Isn't it adorable?"

He shrugs, but I know he means 'yes'. After all, why else would he have gone back to the shelter and retrieved the last remaining kitten from Peaches's litter? A fluffy, fuzzy, white-furred kitten with striking green eyes, Adrian brought him home just last week, christening the kitten 'Cream' for obvious reasons.

When I asked him why he did, he reminded me how I mentioned that kittens do better when there are at least two of them. He did his research. Then he saw that there was one kitten left, and something about Cream being left behind tugged on his heartstrings.

It didn't hurt that it was our two-month wedding anniversary—or that, since Jack's death, we've both been a lot more open and honest and vulnerable with each other.

Like the other day, when, in a moment of remorse, I mentioned that we wasted ten years, and Adrian, in his heavy-handed way, told me that we didn't.

"How do you figure it?" I asked.

"It's simple. We were apart, yes, but you got to live life without the Order breathing down your neck. You got to experience it outside of Harmony Heights. And me? I worked toward the moment we would be together." He got a little cocky as he added, "I had no doubt in my fucking mind that we would."

"Yeah?" I had smiled because I couldn't help myself, then pointed out, "What if I had found someone?"

His returning smile had a wicked edge to it. "Like Bradley?"

I narrowed my eyes, remembering the torn page with the scribble through Bradley's name. "How do you know about Bradley Figueroa?"

He was probably my longest, most serious relationship I had outside of my fling with Adrian. We made it six months before Bradley was relocated, and I'd started to have questions about that when I saw his name crossed out so violently in my husband's book... questions that were quickly answered when Adrian smirked.

"Someone had to arrange for him to get out of the country and far, far away from you." The twist of his grin reminded me of the cat that got the canary. "And then there was Justin."

We made it three months before he ghosted me. I didn't ask Adrian how he knew about Justin because, well, I now know he was following my life even from Harmony Heights, but... "What did you do to Justin?"

"Not me, princess. That was Dallas. He paid the dentist a visit for me. Bas had fun, pretending to be your scary biker boyfriend to scare off Theo. Hell, even Connor got into it when we first found you at school."

No wonder I hadn't had anyone interested in me the entire time I was at college...

"You know something, baby? You'd make an excellent King. You were always meant to rule."

"Nah. That's Dallas."

I pointed at him. "But who tells Dallas what to do?"

Adrian nodded, conceding my point. "Yes, but once he accepts it's time and fully takes over, he'll be a good King."

"Yeah," I agreed, almost begrudgingly. "With you there to give him a hand, at least."

"He already ended the auctions," Adrian said, and he was right—the basement stage was dismantled almost immediately after they discovered it existed. "And then there's the Used."

I stopped him there. I had been doing a lot of thinking about the way women are treated in the Order —and there can be a *lot* of improvements—but when it comes to the Used... "The Offering/Used system works, for now. As long as we agree with our designations... I mean, I never wanted to be one of the Used, but then there's Sophie... and she did. She has the choice—"

"You didn't."

He was wrong about that. "I did. Don't forget... an Offering has to accept their Oweds' Claim. And me? I always have. You're mine, Adrian," I told him, and considering I pushed him back until he was sitting in the nearest seat, pulling out his cock and climbing on top of him to prove my point... I guess it's safe to say I came out on top for *that* conversation.

Things are changing. One of the biggies? This year, Jack's former inner circle—the old guard—decided to forgo the Claiming ceremony. With Jack's funeral being considered a big affair, regardless of how he would've been excommunicated for embezzling Order funds and trafficking women on Order property, it was agreed to hold off on inducting new members and giving away Offerings. After all, Jack was the King and, technically, the entire Order of the Owed is still in mourning.

The Claimings will resume next August, giving anyone who turned thirty this year one more chance to either find a wife or accept their lot as a lower-ranked member.

Who knows, I think, snuggling against Adrian as our kittens run amok somewhere else in this huge-ass house... maybe there might not even *be* a Claiming ceremony next year...

But that's next year's problem. For now, I'm with my husband, whom I do love, who worships the ground that I walk on, and whose chest is moving so slowly, I'm beginning to think he's fallen asleep.

Yeah. That sounds like a *great* idea—

A buzz sounds somewhere on the other side of Adrian, breaking up our content quiet.

I don't make a move for it, though I do say out loud, "I think that was your phone, baby."

A soft rumbling sound beneath my cheek replaces the buzzing noise. Adrian loves it when I call him 'baby', just like how I've grown to adore that way that the kingmaker thinks it's fitting to refer to me as his 'princess'. He's happy, but if someone messaged Adrian's phone, it might be important.

I poke his pec. "Aren't you going to see who it is? Considering how late it is, it might be Order business."

"Fuck the Order," he grates, twirling a lock of my wild, well-fucked hair around his finger.

That's music to my ears.

I know how important the society is to him. Like me, it's colored his entire life for the last twenty-eight years. It's not going to be easy for us to withdraw from it completely, and I don't really want him to. As long as he remembers that I come first, I get a kick out of watching him work.

Plus, the Heirs... they *are* his family. His brothers. Sure, Desmond didn't count, but Adrian made sure I knew that he considered Des out of the group the second that the slimy prick knew how much Adrian was fixated on me in high school and *still* asked me out. Then, ten years later, he decided to try to Claim me in order to get revenge on a high school fling gone wrong, only to end up in a grave because of it.

I poke him again. "It might be Dallas."

That does the trick. Especially since Dallas is refusing to admit that he's struggling with the death of his remaining parent, Adrian won't leave him hanging.

I felt guilty when Adrian mentioned that over dinner, but not so much when he hurriedly confirmed that Dallas's issue? It isn't that his terrible father is dead. It's that he waited this long to see the man go, all because he's not so keen on the idea of leading the Order.

Still holding me close, Adrian stretches until he can grab his phone off of the nightstand. He enters his passcode with his thumb—my birthday, and proof that he does know when it is—and goes through his notifications with a practiced scroll.

"Nope. No messages on my phone." He shakes his head, placing it back down. Then, grabbing mine from its place beside his, he hands it to me. "Here you go, princess."

He's come a long way in a short time. The old Adrian would've figured out my passcode, typed it in, and gone through my phone whenever he wanted. Even now, when the message is on the front screen of my phone, he doesn't read it.

So I do.

I glance at my phone—and I smile.

"It's Haven," I tell him. "She says 'hi'."

'til death do they part
lori and adrian

AUTHOR'S NOTE

Thank you for reading *Bloody Wedding*!

I hope you enjoyed this foray into the world of the Order of the Owed. While Loni and Adrian have their HEA, I have three more stories planned, with Sebastien's coming up next! Keep scrolling/reading/clicking to see the cover of his book, plus the blurb that introduces his heroine!

Also, in case you're wondering what the deal with Haven is, the answer to that is in *Dance with the Devil*, the fourth book in the **Deal with the Devil** series. Haven doesn't appear in that book, though she's mentioned, and her ordeal is discussed. However, Connor and Haven will have their own side story separate of **The Order of the Owed** series—including her reunion with Loni—in early 2026!

Don't forget, if you purchase a physical copy of this book—paperback, discreet paperback, or hardcover— please send me your name and mailing address via email (carin@carinhart.com) and I'll mail you a free bookmark and a signed bookplate :)

Until then...

xoxo,
Carin

He wasn't supposed to have an Offering... until her. Now he'll accept nothing else—even if she's convinced it's all fake.

ANNALIESE

In Harmony Heights, there's no such thing as a choice. At least, not when your family has ties to the Order of the Owed.

I always knew that there was a fine line between being one of the Offering and one of the Used. When the time came for the society to decide where I'd land, one tiny mistake means that I'll never be more than a mistress... unless I find a husband first.

I'm desperate. To save my family's position in the city —to save my sister—I need to belong to one of the Owed. I'll do anything, even sell myself to the highest bidder. All he has to do is sign on the dotted line and I'll be the best fake wife he could ever imagine, with all the perks and none of the commitment.

Sebastien Reynolds is the perfect man for the job. With a devil-may-care attitude and a disdain for being descended from one of the founding families of the Order, if all I have to do is share a house—and a bed— with him, I'll do it.

I'll do anything. Anything, but fall in love again…

SEBASTIEN

I had an out. As the second-born son of a founding family, only my brother needed to take an Offering, have a kid, and try to continue the Reynolds name.

As Harmony Height's biggest screw-up, I always knew that the best I could hope for was settling down with someone outside of the Order, having my fun with the Used, or accept that it'll just be me, my bike, and a long drive out of the oppressive city that thinks it can tame me.

I sure as hell wasn't going to marry one of the pristine, untouched women given only to the men who deserve them… but when Annaliese Crawford walked into an Order bar, her head held high, her eyes desperate, I would've killed every single guy in there to be the one she chose as her fake husband.

She asked for a year.

I already know I won't settle for less than forever.

I had an out… but I don't want it anymore.

I want Annaliese—and nothing will stop me from keeping her.

* *Inconvenient Marriage* is a dual-POV dark romance that continues **The Order of the Owed** series.

This will be a night to die for, sweetheart...

CASSIDY

I needed to start over.

My job was a dead end. My ex got too clingy, too fast. My rent was outrageous, and I went no contact with my parents a long, long time ago.

Shadowvale promised a new start. A new life. A town that has its own superstitions when it comes to Halloween, I was looking forward to the holiday... until things began to get weird.

I feel like I'm being followed. No one knows I'm here, but I can't shake the sensation that someone is out there. Watching me. Like I'm being haunted or something.

It's weird, but I chalk it up to the spooky season. Plus, there's something about the diner where I'm working... it draws all types.

It drew *him*.

Johnny Gray. He showed up at breakfast, asked me out for lunch, and by dinner... *I* was his dinner. It's a Halloween to remember, and if he seems both obsessed with and blasé over 'tomorrow', I decide to just live in the moment.

Too bad Johnny can't.

Because my supposed one-night-stand?

He died in 1953.

JOHNNY

When I died, I lost two things: the race, and my girl.

They say ghosts stick around because they have unfinished business. I guess I'm proof of that because I'm still here, still haunting Shadowvale, decades after I bit it.

Because of her. Because of my Cassie.

Only Cassie... she died the same night I did, after she made me promise to wait for her. But she didn't do the same for me. She moved on.

I didn't.

And then *Cassidy* walked right into my diner and I knew she was what I've been waiting for. She's my Cassie returned to me, and I won't let this one get away.

Death can't stop me. And Halloween? In Shadowvale, where the veil between worlds is flimsy as hell, I can become a living myself for one day only.

This year, I plan to spend it with Cassidy. And when the night is over, I'll have one question for her:

Will you still love me tomorrow?

* *Tonight You're Mine* is a twisted Halloween romance where there's definitely a HEA because Johnny? He's playing for that *ever*.

KEEP IN TOUCH

Stay tuned for what's coming up next! Follow me at any of these places—or sign up for my newsletter—for news, promotions, upcoming releases, and more:

CarinHart.com
Carin's Newsletter
Carin's Signed Book Store

facebook.com/carinhartbooks
amazon.com/author/carinhart
instagram.com/carinhartbooks

ALSO BY CARIN HART

Deal with the Devil series

No One Has To Know *standalone

Silhouette *standalone

He Sees You *standalone

The Devil's Bargain

The Devil's Bride *newsletter exclusive

The Devil's Playground

Dragonfly

Dance with the Devil

Ride with the Devil

Reed Twins

Close to Midnight

Really Should Stay

The Order of the Owed

Oubliette

Bloody Wedding

Inconvenient Marriage

Husband Who

Standalone

My Wife

Tonight You're Mine

www.ingramcontent.com/pod-product-compliance
Lightning Source LLC
Chambersburg PA
CBHW020653010826
48969CB00012B/863